I0582769

THE GOLDEN MOUNTAIN

J.D. RHOADES

BLOODHOUND BOOKS

Copyright © 2025 J.D. Rhoades

The right of J.D. Rhoades to be identified as the Author of the Work has been asserted by him in accordance with the Copyright, Designs and Patents Act 1988.

Published in 2025 by Bloodhound Books.

Apart from any use permitted under UK copyright law, this publication may only be reproduced, stored, or transmitted, in any form, or by any means, with prior permission in writing of the publisher or, in the case of reprographic production, in accordance with the terms of licences issued by the Copyright Licensing Agency.
All characters in this publication are fictitious and any resemblance to real persons, living or dead, is purely coincidental.

www.bloodhoundbooks.com

Print ISBN: 978-1-917705-26-4

CHAPTER ONE

T he spirit of her mother, six months dead, hung in the air over the table where Isobel sat, transfixed. The ghost's white dress billowed out around her as if blown by a gentle yet steady wind, the blurred face above the archaic lace collar of the dress shining a sickly greenish white.

"Ma...mama?" she whispered. "Is it really you?"

"If you are really Adelaide Howard," the woman who sat opposite Isobel at the large round table intoned, "give us a sign."

The moment the woman stopped speaking, the room was filled with a series of sharp reports, as loud as gunshots. They started on the wall behind Isobel and spread quickly through the dark-paneled walls of the room, beating an insistent rhythm until the entire space resounded like the inside of an African drum. Isobel squealed with terror and shoved her chair backward. Suddenly, the drumming sounds stopped, leaving behind a ponderous silence.

"Fear not," the medium said. "Your mother is here with us now."

"We need more," another voice spoke up from halfway around the table. It came from a woman dressed entirely in black. Her widow's veil was pushed back away from her face. "We need a better sign."

The medium frowned, but the unveiled woman interjected before she could speak. "Something beyond banging on walls. Isobel," she turned to the woman quailing in her wicker chair, "ask the apparition something only your mother would know."

"Sister Marjorie," the medium's voice was tinged with impatience, "it's not wise to test the spirits."

The woman in the pushed-back veil smiled. "I believe the spirits are up to the test."

The medium's frown deepened, but her response was cut off by Isobel's eager interjection. "Yes. My mother will know." She addressed the floating but still silent figure shimmering over the center of the table. "Mama. What was my favorite doll's name when I was little?"

The room was silent now, frozen in anticipation for the answer. Even the woman in the pushed-back veil leaned forward, her eyes eager, yearning for evidence of real contact with the afterlife.

The waiting silence was broken by a shriek of agony. The ethereal figure hovering over the table collapsed, the empty dress crumpling into a heap on the round table. The medium's back arched, her hands reaching backward to claw at something behind her, then she pitched forward onto the table, her perfectly coiffed hair coming loose and spreading across the white tablecloth.

Isobel's blue eyes were wide, and she leaped up from her seat as if to flee. Marjorie, on the other hand, sprung forward, moving toward the medium slumped over the table. She was the first one who saw the long blade thrust through the back of the medium's high-backed chair, slick and dripping with her blood.

"Call a doctor," Marjorie snapped at Isobel, who responded to the order by fainting dead away. Marjorie muttered a curse under her breath and looked around at the curtain-draped enclosure that the medium had ponderously described as her sacred space. She thought she saw one of the curtains move slightly, but she couldn't be sure. The door to the séance room opened. A young black woman was standing there, dressed in a modest gray skirt and white blouse. Her eyes widened with shock at the sight of the lady of the house sprawled across the table, a red stain spreading across her back.

"Don't just stand there, Eleanor," Marjorie snapped. "Miss Givens has been attacked. Help me get her into bed, and then send someone for a doctor."

The young woman took a deep breath, then rushed to her employer's side. The spirit medium was stirring now, moaning in pain.

"Who would do such a thing?" Eleanor whispered as she and Marjorie helped get Givens up off the table, bracing her between them.

"I don't know," Marjorie said, her mouth set in a grim line, "but I know who can help us find out."

CHAPTER TWO

L.D. Cade was seated with his booted feet up on the polished wood of the desk in his storefront office, a copy of the *Daily Alta California* open in front of him. It was a slow news day in the Bay Area; a substantial portion of the front page was taken up with a story about the raising of a substantial flagpole in Oakland and another about incursions of the Cheyenne and Comanche along the route of the recently completed Union Pacific railroad. The latter was a story so common recently it hardly counted as news at all. Cade sighed and folded the newspaper. He looked over at his partner, Samuel Clayborne, who was bent over his own desk on the other side of the room, scribbling furiously in a notebook.

"What are ya workin' on over there, partner?" Cade said.

Clayborne's reaction startled Cade. The black man looked up from his writing as if caught in some shameful act, slamming the notebook shut and laying the pen down. "Nothing."

If Cade hadn't already been so bored, he wouldn't have pursued the subject. But he was in need of amusement, so he raised a sardonic eyebrow. "Love letter, maybe? Some poetry for your sweetie?"

Clayborne scowled. "I said nothing. Leave it."

Cade raised his hands. "Okay, okay. Sorry." *Jesus*, he thought, *sometimes I forget what a moody cuss he is.*

Clayborne sighed. "Sorry. Didn't mean to snap at you."

"No problem. Your private business is your own. I was just makin' conversation."

"I know." Clayborne looked down at the notebook. "If you really want to know..."

They were interrupted by the jangling of the bell they'd installed over the front door to announce the entry of prospective clients. So far, the bell had not tolled for those.

Cade stood up, smoothed his shirtfront and vest down, and ran a hand through his thick brown hair. He addressed the man who stood in the doorway. "Good day to you, sir. How may we be of service?"

The man in the doorway didn't answer at first, merely regarded Cade gravely, as if sizing him up. Cade was doing the same. What he saw didn't fill him with confidence that this was going to be a paying client.

The man wore a threadbare blue Army uniform topped with an absurd-looking beaver hat with a peacock feather stuck in it. He held a cane in one hand. His beard was streaked with gray and looked as if it had last been trimmed with a pair of hedge clippers. When he spoke, however, it was with an air of ponderous dignity.

"Do we have the pleasure of addressing the owner of this establishment?"

Cade groaned inwardly. This was clearly another one of the lunatics that seemed to be everywhere in this city. "I'm one of them. But we don't have—"

Clayborne interrupted him. "Your Majesty!" He stepped from behind his own desk and gave a deep bow.

Cade stared as if his partner had lost his mind.

The old man bowed his head gravely. "And you are?"

"Samuel Clayborne, Your Majesty. Partner in this firm. We're honored by your presence."

"Yes. You are." The man looked around. "We are intrigued by the sign outside. What exactly is meant by *Investigations* and *Personal Protection*?"

"Well, Your Majesty," Clayborne said, "we are sometimes hired to make discreet inquiries about certain matters. Personal protection, we hope, would be self-explanatory."

"Like the Pinkertons?" The old man's lip curled a bit.

Cade bristled, but Clayborne silenced him with a look and a subtly raised hand. "Same line of work, sir. But we strive to avoid that firm's more notorious excesses."

The uniformed man nodded in satisfaction as if they'd passed some sort of test. "Good. It's a profession that has long needed honorable men." He leaned his head back slightly and squinted at Cade. "Unless I miss my guess, sir, you are a military veteran."

"Yes," Cade glanced at Clayborne and added, "Your Majesty."

"Cavalry. Yes." He raised his cane and pointed it at Cade. "You have the bandy legs of a cavalryman."

Cade looked down at his legs. They looked normal to him, but he'd learned it was a useless exercise to argue with a madman. Besides, he'd guessed correctly somehow. "Yessir. First Michigan."

The man lowered his cane and stamped it on the floor as if applauding. "Capital. You gentlemen are just the sort this city needs." He gave them both a beatific smile. "Henceforth, you may advertise your business as Operating by Royal Commission of Norton the First, Emperor of America and Protector of Mexico."

Clayborne bowed again. "Thank you, Your Majesty. We appreciate the honor beyond our ability to express."

Cade, still baffled, inclined his head. "Much obliged."

The man nodded, turned, and left. The bells on the door jangled in the silence he left behind him.

Cade turned to his partner. "You mind tellin' me what the hell just happened?"

Clayborne was wiping his eyes with his handkerchief and laughing. "Mr. Cade, we have just had a rare honor. We have just received the blessing of The Emperor Norton himself."

"The who what?"

Clayborne put his handkerchief away, still laughing. "He's a local legend. Came to the city a few years ago. Born rich. Lost his fortune, then seems to have lost his mind."

Cade grunted. "Not an uncommon affliction in this vicinity."

"True. Anyway, a few years ago, he declared the Congress of the United States ineffectual—largely, I suspect, due to its inability to preserve the Union—and said that he was taking over. After another few months, he declared himself Protector of Mexico as well."

"Huh. Nice work if you can get it."

"Indeed. Most of the city has more or less adopted him as one would a dotty relation. It's said he eats free in every restaurant and lays his head in the finest hotels."

Cade snorted. "Maybe we picked the wrong business."

"Could be. But don't discount the impact of his blessing. Some businesses have had their fortunes made from it. It's like a good luck charm."

Cade shook his head. "Mr. Clayborne, I've said it before and I'll say it again. Some days I have trouble deciding if this is a city or a lunatic asylum."

"Allow for the possibility, Mr. Cade, that it may be both." Clayborne nodded toward the door. "However, for the moment, we have another visitor."

CHAPTER THREE

It wasn't a client who entered, although it was someone who made Cade happy he'd spruced up a bit. The lady who entered was dressed in a widow's black dress and veil, but the face he could see behind the veil was a familiar one, and well-loved.

"Mrs. Hamrick," Cade said softly.

She inclined her head slightly. "Mr. Cade." She was still officially in mourning, and the formalities had to be observed, at least in public.

"Ma'am," Clayborne said. He was standing as well. The notebook had disappeared into the drawer of his desk.

Marjorie Hamrick turned to him with a smile of genuine pleasure. "Samuel. You're certainly looking prosperous. Or I suppose I should refer to you as Mr. Clayborne now?"

Her former servant smiled back at her. "Either one will do, Mrs.—I mean, ma'am."

She nodded. "Was that His Majesty the Emperor I just saw leaving?"

Cade shook his head. "Am I the only one who doesn't know that old—that old fellow?"

She laughed, the husky musical laugh that had a tendency to scramble his brains. "You may be." Her face turned serious. "And how is business, Mr. Cade?"

He cleared his throat and looked away. "Well. Ma'am. It's early days. As of yet, I mean." He didn't want to tell her that the business she'd invested a considerable sum into had yet to be employed by a single client. The Pinkertons had cornered the market in San Francisco when it came to private investigation and personal protection. He'd had a few not-so-subtle hints delivered indicating that they intended to keep it that way.

She didn't seem dismayed by the tacit confession. "Well, then. You should have no conflicts in taking on the business of a dear friend of mine. A Miss Athena Givens."

Cade frowned. "The name sounds familiar, but I can't place it."

Marjorie nodded. "Sister Athena, as she's commonly known, is one of the country's most prominent Spiritualist mediums. She's established a residence in San Francisco for a month now, and has begun giving her readings. As she calls them."

A sound from Clayborne made her turn toward him. "You have something to add, Mr. Clayborne?"

He looked down. "No, ma'am."

"Please," she urged, then paused before speaking again, more quietly. "During your former employment with my household, Mr. Clayborne, I came to rely on your judgment. A great deal, in fact."

"You did?"

She nodded. "I did. It was one of the reasons I decided to fund this enterprise with Mr. Cade."

"It was?" Cade said.

"Yes." Her voice became more peremptory, the voice of a

lady used to being obeyed. "Now. Mr. Clayborne. Your thoughts."

Clayborne took a deep breath. "I have to say I don't have much faith in these table-tappers and wall-bangers, taking people's money to connect them with the spirits of their dead relatives." He looked at her, unsure of whether to go on, then went ahead. "I've seen folks like that among my own people. Selling charms and magic dusts, telling people what they want to hear from their dear departed." His face twisted in disgust. "For the right sums of money, of course."

"Hmm. So, you're a skeptic." Marjorie turned to Cade. "And your opinion, Mr. Cade?"

"About the same. Meaning no offense to your friend, but I've seen a lot of grifters who say they can talk to the dead." He grimaced. "Can't see why anyone would think that was a good thing. In my estimation, it's best to let the dead stay dead."

She put a hand on his for a moment, then drew it back. "Thank you both for your honesty. It assures me that you are the perfect men for the task at hand."

Cade blinked in surprise. "Ma'am?"

"Someone tried to murder my friend Athena. I need someone to find out who it was."

There was a brief silence. Finally, Cade spoke up. "Does your friend have any idea who it was that might have tried to kill her?"

"Yes," Marjorie said. "She's convinced it has to do with her other work."

"Other work?" Cade said.

"It's a bit complicated."

Cade and Clayborne looked at one another. Clayborne spoke first. "Guess I'll put a fresh pot of coffee on."

———

CHAPTER FOUR

They sat around Cade's desk, sipping their coffee from the mismatched mugs scrounged from the cupboard. Marjorie paused to take a long sniff over the cup. Her face broke into a wide smile. "Samuel," she said, "I have truly missed your coffee."

He inclined his head, his expression pleased. "Thank you, ma'am."

Cade took a sip from his cracked mug. The thick brew was strong enough to strip paint, but that was just the way Cade liked it. Marjorie, who'd been introduced to coffee through beans brought from the East by her merchant-captain father, shared his taste.

"So," Cade said. "Tell us about this attack on Miss Givens. Where and when, and who was there?"

Marjorie shook her head. "It occurred at a séance she was hosting. The only people in attendance were the people around the table, all of whom were in plain sight of one another."

"Servants?" Clayborne spoke up. "Anyone in the household have a grudge?"

Marjorie shook her head. "Athena says not. And they were all downstairs, in any event."

"They all confirm that?"

Marjorie nodded. "All nine of them. Together in the kitchen. That's what every one of them told the police. They all vouched for one another."

"If it was one of the servants, they'd all have to be in on it."

"Unlikely," Clayborne said. Cade and Marjorie turned to him. "Remember, I've lived downstairs," he said. "The odds of nine servants getting together on anything are damned—are mighty slim." He looked down. "Sorry for the language, ma'am."

"No." She'd taken off her hat and veil, and she stroked the brim of the hat absentmindedly as she pondered. "I suspect you're right. So, it had to be someone who'd gotten into the séance room. I thought I saw one of the curtains move after she was stabbed, but I was too busy tending to Athena to go after anyone."

"What do the police say?" Cade asked.

"Let me guess." Clayborne's expression was bitter. "They're concentrating on the servants. Looking for one to hang it on."

Cade and Marjorie looked at one another, startled by his vehemence. "Actually," Marjorie said after a moment, "they haven't taken much interest at all. In fact, the officer I spoke to seemed to almost regret that the attacker hadn't been more successful."

Cade frowned. "You sure about that?"

Marjorie's expression grew chilly. "And why would I not be sure, Mr. Cade?"

"I mean, a lady gets stabbed in the back, the way you describe, in a nice house in one of the town's rich neighborhoods, and the coppers say, 'Good'? Beggin' your pardon, Mrs. Hamrick, but that doesn't add up."

Marjorie looked away. "Miss Givens is not, shall we say,

popular with some elements in the echelons of power in this city." She sighed. "Athena Givens is not just one of the country's leading Spiritualist mediums. She's also one of the leaders in the national suffragist movement."

"Ah," Cade said.

"Hmm," Clayborne agreed.

Marjorie's eyes narrowed and her voice grew chilly. "And what exactly are these muttered interjections supposed to mean?"

"It does tend to increase the pool of people with motive," Clayborne said.

Cade nodded. "Votes for women ain't exactly a popular cause."

Clayborne's mouth twisted as if he'd bitten into a lemon rind. "Why, next thing you know, they'll be letting the Negro vote."

"May I remind you, Mr. Clayborne," Marjorie's voice grew frosty again, "that, thanks to the recent amendment to the Constitution, the Negro has the franchise in more places than women at the moment."

Clayborne's face went blank. "Yes, ma'am." His jaw tightened and he spoke a little louder. "So long as he doesn't try to exercise it. Ma'am."

Her bland politeness was a match for Clayborne's. "What do you mean by that?"

"I mean, ma'am, that I recently went down to the clerk's office to register myself to vote, pursuant to the Fifteenth Amendment, and was told that until that clerk had an original signed and sealed copy of the proclamation from the hand of President Grant himself, he was going to abide by the Constitution of the Great State of California, which only allows White males to register. Seeing as how this state never actually ratified the amendment."

Cade didn't see any point in letting the two of them get into a fracas over the issue. "Well, whatever Miss Givens's political leanings, that don't give anyone just cause to try to kill her. Especially by stabbing her in the back." He frowned. "Don't have much use for backstabbers. And if the local law don't want to take an interest, I suppose this firm can."

Marjorie composed herself. "Yes. Thank you. I will arrange a meeting with Miss Givens as soon as possible." She stood, followed by Cade and Clayborne. "Thank you for your time, gentlemen." She restored the hat to her head, pulled the veil back over her face, and started for the door. Before she got there, she turned. "Mr. Cade. There are some other business matters I wish to discuss with you. Would you be available this evening? Say, around seven? My suite at the Royal Hotel? I'll be glad to provide supper."

Cade nodded, his mouth suddenly dry. "Yes, ma'am. I'll meet you there."

She nodded and swept out.

CHAPTER FIVE

"So," Clayborne said in a wry voice, "I suppose I can lock the doors and douse the lanterns early this evening?"

"You can go to bed as early or late as you like," Cade said gruffly.

The two men had decided to save money in the early days of their business by sharing quarters above their office, a pair of tiny bedrooms converted from a storeroom at the top of the stairs. Cade saw the utility in the arrangement, but it did give his friend and partner a bit more access than he cared for into the particulars of his personal life.

Clayborne shook his head and let the matter drop. "When should we pay a call on this suffragist spiritualist? Or spiritualist suffragist? Whichever."

"I suppose that's one of the things we'll be discussing over dinner," Cade said.

"Of course. While you're at it, Mr. Cade, you might want to get a little more into the particulars of who's actually going to be paying us for this work we've signed up for." He smiled sardonically. "You may be able to live on love, Mr. Cade, but we common folk require a bit more sustenance."

"Mr. Clayborne?" Cade said through gritted teeth.

"Yes, Mr. Cade?"

"Would you do me the favor of shuttin' the fuck up?"

Clayborne stood and gave a slight ironic bow. "My apologies."

Cade glared at him a moment, then he chuckled, looking down and rubbing at his temples. "I'm bein' a damn fool, aren't I?"

Clayborne sat back down. "I'd say you both are." He sighed. "It's clear to everyone with a working pair of eyes that you're in love with her. And I think I know Mrs. Hamrick well enough, given that I spent a few years in her family's service, to judge that she feels the same way about you. So, frankly, Levi, all of these machinations are beginning to seem less like drama and more like farce."

Cade shook his head. "It's not so simple. She's a lady, one of means now that she's got control of her money again. I'm..." He trailed off, looking around the sparsely furnished office.

"I know," Clayborne said. "A broken down saddle tramp." He rolled his eyes. "Lord knows I've heard that enough from you." He stood up and walked over to Cade's desk, leaning over it with his clenched fists against the rough wood. "But this is the West, Mr. Cade. This is where men come to change their station in life. If not you, who?"

Cade looked away. "There's...the other thing."

"Ah." Clayborne straightened up. "The other thing."

"Well, I did shoot her husband."

"Who was trying to kill her, and who would have killed you, if you hadn't shot first." Clayborne grimaced. "I worked for the man for years. I know what he was. He was a monster, and you slew him. Doesn't slaying the monster mean you win the fair lady?"

"Does it?" Cade looked out the window at the bustling street. "This ain't a fairy tale, Sam."

"Don't I know it," Clayborne said softly. His eyes went far away for a moment, then he shook his head as if to clear it. "I suppose we start by talking with this Miss Givens." He smiled. "Don't forget to get the particulars at, ah, dinner."

"Sam," Cade said.

"Shuttin' up, suh," Clayborne drawled.

He rolled off her, gasping for breath, and collapsed onto the bed. When he'd caught his breath, he closed his eyes. "Goddamn," he whispered.

Marjorie chuckled and brushed a sweat-soaked auburn curl away from her face. "I'd say that sums it up."

He gathered her into his arms and she snuggled against him with a contented little sound. "That was wonderful," she murmured.

"For me, too." He stroked her face gently, tracing the curve of her jaw, then running his fingers along her cheek until she grabbed his hand, kissed his fingertips, and guided his hand to her shoulder. He pulled her closer and she responded by kissing his chest. She looked up, her hazel eyes probing his. "Are you happy, Levi?"

He looked back, smiling. "If I was having a better time, I think it'd be illegal."

She laughed. "Not in San Francisco, it wouldn't." Her face grew serious again. "But are you *happy*?"

He didn't answer right away, just lay back and looked at the ceiling. The smile was gone.

She sighed. "I know it's hard. Keeping our distance in public. I want you to know it's hard for me, too."

He didn't look at her. "Is it?"

She propped herself up on one elbow, took his chin in her free hand, and turned his face to hers. "It is. It's torture. But I hope you understand why it has to be this way. For just a little while longer."

"I guess." He grimaced. "I don't want to be any kind of disgrace to you."

She sat up, scowling. "Do you think that's what it is? You think I'm ashamed of you?"

He didn't answer.

She shook her head in exasperation. "That's not it at all, Levi." She broke the embrace, sat up, and pulled her knees up to her chest, pulling the silk sheet up to cover her. "When my husband died," she began.

"When I shot him."

"Yes, yes," she said impatiently. "And if I haven't thanked you for that enough, thank you. The son of a bitch tried to have me locked in a madhouse, then tried to poison me. I shed my last tear for him at his funeral, and that one was false." She looked over to the bottle he'd left on the bedside table. "May I have a drink of that whiskey?"

"Sure." He poured a jigger into the shot glass beside the bottle. She motioned "more" with her hand and he filled it to the rim.

She nodded her thanks, tossed the shot back, and took a deep breath before going on. "I didn't know until later the disaster he'd made of our finances. He'd taken my inheritance, the shipping line my father built, and mortgaged it nearly into ruin to provide for his own ventures. Some of which you know about."

Cade nodded. In his previous employment as John Hamrick's bodyguard, he'd witnessed firsthand some of the man's seamier investments down in the notorious Barbary Coast. "Seemed like they were making some money."

"They were. None of it, though, was going to pay our legitimate debts. It was all turned into flash living and ostentation. My late husband," she almost spat the last two words, "had built a house of cards, and now I'm trying to turn that back into a house that will stand." She put a hand on his arm. "But to do that, I need credit. I need to be taken seriously. And, Levi, you have no idea how hard it is, even in San Francisco, for a woman to be taken seriously by the so-called legitimate banks." She looked away from him. "Will you pour me another drink?"

Without speaking, he poured her another, to the brim.

She tossed it back quickly. "Levi," she said quietly. "I've gotten an offer of financing from the Chinese. Your friend Mr. Kwan."

Cade blinked in surprise. "Not sure I'd call him my friend." Lee Kwan, the head of Chinatown's shadowy Green Dragon Tong, had had Cade kidnapped, then set him to finding out who was behind a scheme to blame the Chinese for an attack on the Hamrick household. The man he'd exposed as the manipulator behind the attacks had disappeared as if into thin air, and Cade didn't want to think too much about what had happened to him. He strongly suspected it was the work of Kwan's merciless female assassin, known in Chinatown as The White Orchid.

"You don't want to be in with them," Cade said.

"I don't, Levi," Marjorie said. "But if there's a whiff of scandal, the major banks won't go near me. I won't have any choice if I want to save my father's legacy. Kwan's representative has been very persistent. I'm getting the feeling they don't want to take no for an answer. And once they get hold of a shipping line, God knows what they'll use it for. Opium. Guns." Her face twisted. "Slaves. I'll burn every one of my father's remaining ships to the waterline with my own hands before I'll see them carrying girls into slavery."

The passion in her voice made Cade reach out and put his arms around Marjorie's shoulders. "That's not going to happen, honey lamb. I won't let it."

She put her hand on his. "Thank you. I love that you feel that way. That you want to protect me." She sighed. "But in the end, Levi, it's up to me."

He clasped the hand back. "Maybe. Or maybe I can talk to Kwan."

She was silent for a moment. "And do what? Try to back him down?" She shook her head. "You know what he's capable of. Not to mention...her."

He knew who she meant. They'd both seen The White Orchid, with a blade in each hand, tear through a mob of armed hoodlums like a wolf through a henhouse. Cade had been grateful for the help, since that mob had been trying to burn one of Marjorie's ships with her household—and Cade—aboard. Gratitude didn't stop him, however, from wanting to give the Green Dragon as wide a berth as possible. As dangerous as they were as enemies, he couldn't help but think they'd be almost as dangerous as friends. "You mentioned Kwan's representative. Chinese?"

She shook her head. "A lawyer named Jenkins."

Cade sighed. "Of course."

"You know him?"

"Yeah. Kwan hired him for me when I was locked up. He's slicker than owl shit."

She smiled. "That's a pretty apt description."

"I'll talk to Jenkins. Let him tell Kwan your business isn't for sale."

She frowned. "Won't that be dangerous?"

"If he's using a lawyer, things haven't come to a face-off." He smiled. "We'll be real civilized."

"Thank you." She kissed him. "But first, will you help out my friend Athena?"

"Yeah. Sure. But, ah..." He stopped and looked away.

She frowned. "What's wrong?"

"Well," he began, "it's just that...well, Samuel wanted to know about...ah..."

Realization dawned on her face. "You want to know how you're going to get paid."

"Um. Yeah." He pulled away slightly. "Except this ain't exactly the venue to discuss business in."

She laughed. "You'd be surprised." At his quizzical look, she quickly went on. "Never mind. Don't worry. Athena Givens has more than adequate funds to pay for your services."

He couldn't keep the relief out of his voice. "Good."

"What, did you think you were going to have to ask me for more money?"

He shrugged. "I didn't know."

She cocked an eyebrow at him. "That would bother you."

"Yeah. A little."

"Ah. Let me make sure I understand. If you were beholden to me for money, that might interfere with our lovemaking."

He laughed softly. "Yeah. It might."

Her face grew serious. "Then, Mr. Leviticus Deuteronomy Cade, I will make you a solemn promise." She crossed her heart. "You will never see another red cent from me." Her solemn expression broke, and she laughed. "Now come here. You've got me all randy again."

Cade was not a man to question good fortune.

"Sometimes, brother," Kwan Fang said, "I think you aspire to *be* one of the white devils."

Kwan Lee, head of the Green Dragon Tong, regarded his brother stonily. "And sometimes, Younger Brother," he said, putting particular emphasis on the diminutive, "you forget who the head of this family is."

Fang bowed. "My sincerest apologies if I've offended," he said with offensive insincerity. "But my duty as your second in command is to counsel you when I believe you are taking the wrong path. And this attempt to ingratiate yourself with the white devils is the worst possible path for this family."

"I don't care about that," Kwan said. "But there is money to be made in doing business with the whites."

"Business, yes. Take their money for our opium. Take it from them gambling. But *give* them money? This is madness."

"Investment in legal business for a good return? How is this madness?"

Fang sighed. "Do you think the white devils will ever deal fairly with you in their own businesses? They will cheat you with their lawyers and their corrupt politicians. Mark my words.

We need to continue to make our money from their weaknesses. Those we can always depend on." He shook his head and his voice softened. "You want to be respectable in the eyes of the white devils. I tell you, Older Brother, they will never respect you. You will always be an animal in their eyes." He looked over to the woman who sat silently in one corner of the room, watching the conversation with no expression. "Even *she* will not be able to change that." With that, he turned and walked out of the room, not waiting to be dismissed.

Kwan sat silently for a moment, then rubbed his temples wearily.

After a long pause, the woman in the corner spoke. "Do you want me to deal with him, Great One?" Her voice was soft, musical, but there was a coldness underneath that still chilled Kwan Lee to the bone.

"No," he said. "He is my brother."

"I understand, Great One. But sooner or later, it will need to be done. Sooner rather than later, I think. He means to displace you."

Kwan grimaced. "Leave me be, woman."

The White Orchid's voice was implacable. "You know it to be true. And it isn't just loyalty to you that motivates me. I know what will happen to me if he takes your place."

"He doesn't trust you," Kwan said.

"He shouldn't. He hates me. He also desires me."

And why shouldn't he, Kwan thought. The White Orchid was one of the most beautiful women he'd ever seen. When he'd first taken her into his employment, he'd thought to bed her himself, until he'd tested the skills he'd heard about by sending her to deal with a pair of soldiers, known as *boo how doy*, from a rival tong who'd tried to take over one of his gambling halls. Before the day was out, she was standing before his desk, having somehow slipped past his own guards. Without preamble, she'd dropped a burlap sack onto his desk that landed with a sickening thump. He'd regarded the sack for a moment, then leaned forward and opened it. The heads of the two *boo how doy* leered up at him. What had been done to the faces was... unspeakable. It still troubled him to think that they may not have been dead yet when the mutilations were done.

"With your permission, Great One," she'd said in that soft, mellifluous voice, "I will deliver these personally to their boss, Ah Ming."

It had taken every ounce of self-control Kwan Lee possessed to remain calm. "You'll never get past his guards."

She smiled. "I got past yours. And yours are quite good."

Kwan nodded. "Ah Ming is not to be harmed. I want to send a message, not start a war."

She inclined her head. "As you wish, Great One."

Ah Ming's incursions on his territory had ceased immediately, as had any desire Kwan Lee had felt to take The White Orchid into his bed. He'd as soon copulate with a serpent.

She interrupted the memory. "Your brother wants me for a plaything. That will not happen."

"I understand. But you are to leave him alone. For the moment."

She stared at him with those beautiful cold eyes, then nodded. "Yes, Great One. For the moment."

He let that last part go.

CHAPTER SEVEN

It was going on six in the morning when Cade returned to the office. He let himself in with his key, whistling softly. He was pleasantly exhausted and looking to grab a few hours shut-eye before he paid a call on Athena Givens. He'd just closed the door behind him and reached the foot of the stairs which led to the upstairs apartment he shared with Clayborne when he heard the scream.

It was a horrific, soul-tearing scream, a terrible sound of agony and despair. Cade didn't take time to think. He reached beneath his coat and drew the Colt Navy Revolver he'd carried since the war, pulling the hammer back with his thumb as he bounded up the stairs. He paused at the top. The screaming had stopped. Cade raised the revolver, one hand on the doorknob, and listened. There was nothing but silence on the other side of the door. He eased the stairwell door open.

It opened into a short, narrow hallway with a ceiling barely high enough for Cade to stand upright. Doors on either side of the hallway led to the two tiny bedrooms. "Sam?" he called out softly.

There was silence for a moment, then a voice came weakly from behind Clayborne's door. "I'm here, Cade."

Cade advanced slowly, the gun held in front of him. "You okay?"

The voice was a little stronger now. "I'm fine. Go to sleep."

Cade didn't know what to believe. He knew how prickly Clayborne was about his privacy, which didn't make living in these tight quarters any easier. But he didn't know if his partner was in danger, with someone compelling him to say everything was all right.

He turned the knob and slammed the door open, advancing quickly into the room, the gun tracking back and forth.

Clayborne was sitting up in the bed, wearing a worn striped nightshirt. He flinched back against the wall as he spotted Cade's gun. He was alone. He was also soaked with sweat. It poured from his face and turned the linen of the nightshirt dark.

"Jesus, man." Cade lowered the gun. "What the hell is going on?"

Clayborne scowled, but Cade could see he was trembling. "Nothing, Cade. Just a bad dream."

Cade lowered the pistol and let the hammer down. "I'll say it was. Jesus. Sounded like you was bein' killed."

Clayborne looked away, embarrassed. "Sorry."

"No problem, partner," Cade said. "Hang on just a second." He walked out of the bedroom, across the hallway, and into his own equally tiny chamber. He opened the battered bedside table and replaced the bottle of whiskey in the top drawer with the Navy revolver. He carried the whiskey back to Clayborne's room, uncorking it as he entered. Clayborne was lying back on the bed, staring at the ceiling.

"Here," Cade said, holding out the bottle. "This'll settle your nerves."

Clayborne sat up, still frowning. He looked at the bottle for a moment as if it were a poisonous reptile, then took it and took a deep swig. He pulled the bottle away from his lips and handed it back to Cade. "Thanks," he murmured.

"No problem. But if you don't mind my askin', is this likely to be a regular occurrence? 'Cause I might need to invest in some cotton wool to plug my ears."

Clayborne's jaw clenched. "This isn't a joking matter for me."

"Sorry."

"Don't you ever have bad dreams, Cade? From the war?"

Cade nodded. "Once in a while, yeah. But I don't get the screamin' fantods from them."

"You're lucky, then."

Cade took a drink and passed the bottle back to Clayborne. "You want to talk about it?"

Clayborne took the bottle, looked at it, then handed it back to Cade. "No." It was as definite as a slammed door.

"Okay." Cade put the cork back in the bottle and carried it to the door. "You going to be all right?"

Clayborne nodded, not looking at him. "Fine."

"Sleep well, then." Cade closed the door behind him. He stood outside Clayborne's door for a moment, then shook his head and went back to his own room.

CHAPTER EIGHT

The fish, crabs, eels, and other sea creatures glistened on their shining beds, but all the ice in the world wouldn't have kept Mei cool at the moment. She paused for a moment in her constant motion among the outdoor bins to wipe her brow with a white silk cloth, then got back to work. The fish market was filled with customers, jostling and looking at the offered wares with critical eyes. Mei wasn't worried about the scrutiny; she'd made sure that her grandparents' business offered only the freshest and best quality seafood to be had in Chinatown. The patronage of the Green Dragon Tong made it possible for them to afford the ice, brought by ships from the far north, that helped make that possible. Once, they'd been struggling to stay afloat; now, Mei's only worry was keeping up with the constant demands made by the pushing throng. She answered the customers' questions, fought off the more aggressive hagglers, and made sale after sale. From time to time, she glanced over at her grandfather, dozing in his chair by the front door to the building that served as the indoor part of the shop, its office, and their home. She sighed. Another pair of hands and eyes was sorely needed to keep up with the crowd, but Mei's strong sense of filial piety wouldn't allow her to go shake the old man awake. She turned back to the crowd in time to catch sight of a boy of about fourteen years looking conspicuously sly as he attempted to slide a filleted albacore off its ice bed.

"Hey," she raised her voice, but another person had already stepped up and seized the boy's wrist. The boy looked up in terror as he saw who'd stopped him.

It was a woman, tall and slender and dressed in flowing white silk pants and a quilted jacket. She was as conspicuous as a flower on a dung heap in this mass of sweaty, shoving men. The white authorities had forbidden the importation of women by legitimate immigration, so the only women normally seen in Chinatown were prostitutes, and they rarely left the brothels and squalid cribs where they earned a living for their owners until they were worn out, discarded, and left to die. But the beautiful woman looking down at the would-be thief was no prostitute; she was a fable, a bogeyman, a spirit whose name was invoked to frighten misbehaving children as far away as Canton. "Be good," the saying went, "or The White Orchid will come for you."

The White Orchid looked down at the would-be thief, who was now visibly shaking with terror. She said something to him that Mei couldn't catch, and the boy quickly put the fish back on the ice. She said something else to him, her face showing nothing but sorrow and disappointment. The boy fell to his knees, weeping and kowtowing before her. The crowd had grown silent, staring at the spectacle of the boy on his knees, wondering with horror when the legendary assassin's blade would fall. Then she did a most extraordinary thing. With a sigh, she bent down and took the boy's hand, raising him to his feet. She looked over at Mei and gave a slight bow. "Good day, Younger Sister," she said.

Mei bowed back, a little more deeply. "Good day to you, Elder Sister." While not related by blood, the two women's friendship made the honorifics appropriate.

The White Orchid grasped the boy by the shoulder. "This ruffian meant to steal from you, although," she looked around the crowd as her voice grew chilly, "he knew, or should have known, that this shop is under the protection of the Green Dragon Tong." She grabbed the boy by the ear. "Isn't that right, little thief?"

"Yes, mistress," the boy whimpered. "Please. Please. My uncle was injured working on the Iron Road. He can't work. We're starving."

The White Orchid nodded. "So you say. And so, the Green Dragon will be merciful." She turned to Mei. "I will buy this boy and his family dinner. Once." She reached into a purse at her waist and pulled out a gold coin. "Younger Sister?"

Mei packaged the albacore in white butcher paper and handed it to the boy, taking the gold coin from the hand of The White Orchid.

"Keep the change," the older woman said. She turned to the crowd and her voice rose. "You came to this country because you were told it was the Golden Mountain, where no one goes hungry and no one suffers." She smiled sadly. "But now we know differently, do we not? The white devils will not take care of you when you are sick. When you are hurt pushing their Iron Road through the mountains. When you are starving. But the Green Dragon, my friends...the Green Dragon is here for you. The Dragon is the one who guards the true Golden Mountain." Her face became stern, and a couple of men closest to her stepped back involuntarily. "But do not abuse its generosity. Do not presume upon the Dragon's patience." She looked at Mei. "And do not trifle with those who live under the wing of the Dragon." She bent and whispered something into the boy's ear.

His eyes grew wide and he nodded. She straightened up. "Now," she said brightly. "Who wants to buy some fish?" She stepped behind the bins and stood by Mei, still smiling, and clapped her hands peremptorily. "Come on, then, everyone needs to eat."

For the next hour, Mei and The White Orchid worked side by side, selling the shop's rapidly dwindling stock. The White Orchid proved to be a surprisingly good saleswoman, shrewdly figuring the customer's needs and ability to pay, laughing, cajoling, even flirting on occasion to get a hesitant male customer to part with his hard-earned coins. It didn't hurt that people seemed eager to court the favor of the Green Dragon by their patronage of a favored business. Finally, the rapidly melting ice bins were almost bare, a few trash fish left that would most likely end up as bait or food for the feral cats in the alleyway behind the store.

Mei wiped her hands on a rag, knowing that she'd need a more thorough scrubbing to get the fish smell off. "That was kind," she told The White Orchid, who was likewise scrubbing her hands in the ice. "What you did for that boy."

The White Orchid gave her a thin smile. "What I did for that boy was business, Younger Sister. A reminder that the Green Dragon is here for the Chinese when no one else is. We are the true guardians of the Golden Mountain. And if he knows what's good for him, when I send for him, he will be ready to repay the favor I did him and his family."

Mei shook her head. Lin, The White Orchid, was the only true friend she had in the world, but she remained an enigma. And sometimes, Mei had to admit to herself, she was frightening. "Will you come in for a cup of tea?" she asked.

The White Orchid was looking at Mei's grandfather, still snoring lightly in his chair. An amused smile played across her lips. "It seems he can sleep through anything."

Mei looked at him and sighed. "He's worked hard all his life. He deserves his rest."

The White Orchid turned to her, and the expression of sorrow and loss on her face brought quick tears to Mei's eyes. "How does a girl as good as you exist in this terrible world?"

Mei put her hand on her friend's arm. "I'm not so good as you think, Elder Sister."

Lin put her own hand on Mei's for a moment and squeezed. The stricken expression vanished, replaced by the familiar serene and beautiful smile. "Let's get him inside," she said, "then I'll treat you to a bowl of noodles at Mr. Chang's."

CHAPTER NINE

"Hordes of mongrels have been placed in the front ranks," the newspaperman read, "paving the way for the Chinaman." He folded the paper he'd been reading from and pushed his spectacles back up his nose. "By God, gentlemen, I may have to try to hire that scribe away from the rag he's working for. He writes a cracking good story."

"And now," the banker said sourly, swirling his expensive whiskey around in his glass, "we have some crazy bitch in town trying to stir up women to vote."

"We are losing everything," the doctor said glumly. "Everything we've labored so long and hard to produce in this world."

"Nonsense," the railroad man said. All eyes turned to him. The railroad man looked out the window of the club's upstairs meeting room, drawing contemplatively on one of his fat cigars, shipped all the way from Spanish Cuba. No one spoke, as if awaiting the word of the Lord. Capital was holy in this quiet, dark-wood-paneled room, above the bustle and squalor of the streets below. Capital was holy, and the railroad man had more of it than anyone. Finally, he spoke. "We are losing nothing.

That's defeatist talk, and I despise a defeatist." He looked around at the other men in the room. Most looked away from his intense gaze, eyes hooded like those of a hawk, but twice as merciless. "This is a time of change, gentlemen. The dawn of a new age." He regarded his cigar contemplatively. "Have you read any of Mr. Charles Darwin's work, gentlemen?"

At that, the minister, who'd been nodding over his cups in the corner, raised his head. "Blasphemy!" he croaked.

The railroad man smiled. "Perhaps, Reverend," he said. "But perhaps Mr. Darwin's central idea, that the strong and best-adapted displace the weak," he took another pull on the cigar for dramatic effect, knowing that the men in the room were hanging on his every word, "perhaps that reveals the ways of God to man. Does God provide for the strong to survive, the way the farmer breeds the best to the best, thus improving the species, while the weaker branches of the breed fade and die off?"

He looked over at the minister, looking for an argument, but the minister had nodded off again. The railroad man shrugged off his disappointment and turned to the rest of the room. The other men were clearly shocked, some no doubt in sympathy with the comatose churchman, but no one spoke up. The railroad man sighed. It wasn't nearly as enjoyable when they proved his point for him. "We are losing nothing, gentlemen," he blared in a voice like an Israelite's ram horn shaking the foundations of Jericho. "We are engaged in an epic struggle. The strong against the weak. The white race who has conquered this continent against the savage Indian, the degraded Negro, and the degenerate Chinese, not to mention these hermaphroditic creatures, born female, but with a pathetic desire to attain the power of the male." His lip curled. "The best humanity has to offer against the worst. Is there anyone here who doubts the outcome?"

There was only one possible answer to that. The men around the room in their padded chairs and on their comfortable sofas shook their heads and murmured their assent: "No." "Of course not."

"Well, then," the railroad man said. "Let us hear no more about how we are losing. Let us turn instead to determine how we will win."

He nodded to the steward hovering silently by the door. The man, a slender black man dressed in the club's ornate livery, bowed slightly and opened the door. A man entered, dressed in the long gray coat and silver star of a police officer. He looked around the room, nodding coolly.

"Captain Smith," said the railroad man. "Tell us how we may be of assistance to each other."

CHAPTER TEN

Fang had gathered his most trusted lieutenants in the back room of one of the restaurants protected, but not owned outright, by the Green Dragon Tong. They'd been well fed and sated with plum wine, and they were mellow and ready for Fang's message. A servant girl was refilling the wine cups, and Fang observed Fat Chung's eyes on her, lingering on her backside. He resolved to have the girl visit him later and offer him whatever pleasure he desired. Money, power, sex...the man who could parcel those out could bend other men to his will, and Fang had become master of that bending, learning at the feet of his older brother. Now, however, it was time for the student to be the master.

"Did you enjoy the meal, brothers?" he asked.

Skinny Chung, so called to distinguish him from his bigger compatriot, belched politely. "Excellent, sir."

One-Eyed Vang spoke up. "Certainly better that what we've had lately from Old Kwan."

Fang eyed him sternly. He'd primed Vang, the only one of the *boo how doy* he totally trusted to help him in his grab for power, to feel the others out, but the script had to play out. "Be careful, brother," he said. "My elder brother, for all his faults," he cast his eyes about the room, silently inviting agreement, "is still the head of the Green Dragon Tong."

"Is he, though?" Skinny Chung spoke up.

Fang was surprised. Of all the tong's foot soldiers he'd cut out and groomed for this rebellion, he'd expected it to be Fat Chung, not his slimmer namesake, to be the first one to consider revolt. "If you mean The White Orchid..." He trailed off.

"I mean exactly that. Her." Skinny Chung belched. Fang saw that the slender killer was drunker than he'd realized, and thus more likely to express and feed the dissatisfaction he was cultivating. "Are we, the strongest of all the tongs in Chinatown, to be ruled by a whore from the Pearl River?"

Fang sighed. "I confess," he said with a mock sadness that fooled no one in the room, "I'm vexed by the hold this woman has on my brother."

"Her and the fishmonger's daughter," Fat Chung agreed.

"And the white devil Cade," Vang added.

They all nodded at that.

"Cade," Skinny Chung said. He shook his head. "Why would the Green Dragon wish to risk so much for a *gwai loh*?"

It was time to spring the trap. Fang sighed, for all appearances the long-suffering younger brother. "My brother says he wishes to make an...accommodation with the white devils." He shook his head. "Sometimes I wonder if he doesn't want to *be* one of them."

The look on the men's faces let Kwan Fang know the trap had been sprung. They were his now. *So sorry, Elder Brother*, he thought, *but your time is over. Change is the way of things.*

They sat on wooden stools at the counter of Mr. Chang's noodle shop, which was little more than a stand set back in a niche between two wooden buildings. The noodles were excellent, the tea only palatable. The White Orchid slurped her noodles noisily, not looking around. Mei couldn't help but cast her own eyes about, even though the few male patrons of the shop studiously avoided noticing them. The ban on female immigrants had left eligible females in short supply, so any time Mei went out, she'd found herself the object of oppressive amounts of male attention. Now, however, the presence of the Green Dragon's enforcer seemed to repel any unwanted advances.

"What are you looking about for, Younger Sister?" Lin said. She straightened up from her bowl and burped, her hand covering her mouth.

Mei smiled and turned back to her noodles. "Nothing."

Lin grunted, took a sip of tea, and made a face. "Bat urine," she said. She banged her cup on the counter. "Hey!" she called out. "Old Chang! What is this swill you serve us?"

Mr. Chang, the noodle shop's owner, scurried out from behind the curtain separating the shop from the living quarters in the back. He bowed deeply. "Apologies, Noble Lady," he said, voice quivering with fear. "Are the noodles not to your liking?"

"The noodles are acceptable," Lin said. "But this tea is garbage. It smells and tastes like backwash. Bring us the fresh stuff."

Chang bowed again. "At once, Noble Lady." He disappeared behind the curtain.

"The tea is not that bad," Mei observed. "Perhaps something else is weighing on your mind?"

Lin grimaced. "Nothing you should worry about, Younger Sister." She sighed. "Nothing you can do anything about."

"Whether I can do anything about it, you are my friend," Mei said firmly. "I am glad to listen and offer what advice I can."

Lin reached over and squeezed Mei's hand.

Mei placed her own hand over Lin's. "Now tell me."

Lin did. She spoke of her fears that Fang would make some power play that would leave Kwan Lee dead and her vulnerable. She spoke of her frustration that the elder Kwan either could not see the danger facing him or that he was so blinded by family loyalty that he chose to ignore it. By the time she was done, Chang had put fresh cups of tea before them and scuttled away.

Mei took a sip of her tea and smiled. "This is better," she told her friend. "Thank you." Her expression became serious. "So, you see Mr. Kwan's brother Fang as a danger." She shook her head. "I'm sorry to hear it. Fang was kind to me when I first came to Kwan's."

Lin nodded. "He can be very charming. When he wants something."

"Hmm." Mei looked down into the cup, swirling the tea around contemplatively. "And you fear that if you kill his brother, Kwan Lee will cast you out. Or worse."

Lin nodded. "He will not order me to do it. And if I do it on my own, the man to whom I owe my very survival will hate me forever. And, lest we forget, he has an army on his side. Not just me."

"But," Mei drained the cup, set it down, and looked Lin in the eye, "what would happen if someone else were to kill Fang?"

Lin's brow furrowed. "Someone...else?"

"There is the man Cade," Mei said.

CHAPTER ELEVEN

Cade awoke to the sound of knocking on his door.

"Cade?" It was Clayborne.

He sat up and rubbed his eyes. "Come on in."

Clayborne entered, dressed in his starched shirt, waistcoat, and trousers pressed with a crease so sharp Cade thought he could shave with it.

"Well," Cade said, "you look gussied right up."

"And I suggest you do the same," Clayborne said. "While you were lazing about in bed, I've been tending to the firm's business. I've received a messenger. Our new client is sending her driver for us in an hour."

Cade picked up his watch on the bedside table and checked the time. "Damn. I've slept the day away."

"Yes. So, you should be bright-eyed and bushy-tailed. Now get dressed. We need to make an impression."

Cade grinned. "Don't think I can compete with you in the arena of sartorial elegance, Mr. Clayborne."

Clayborne smiled thinly. "Nor should you try, Mr. Cade. Let's just try not to embarrass the firm, shall we?" He ducked behind the door to avoid the boot that Cade chucked at him.

An hour later, Cade was dressed, hair combed, and wide awake thanks to the half-pot of coffee he'd downed.

The carriage sent by Athena Givens arrived just as the clock struck five. It was an elegant black brougham, with a plump, whiskered white driver seated on his perch in front. The man didn't speak or dismount to open the passenger compartment for them, just stared stolidly straight ahead as if the two men weren't there.

They looked at each other, then Clayborne shrugged, walked over, and opened the door. Cade mounted the step and took his seat in the narrow, luxuriously padded compartment. Clayborne joined him and shut the door. The interior of the carriage matched the flat black of the exterior, the ebony leather soft and comfortable.

They rode in uncomfortable silence for a few minutes, then Cade spoke up. "Not sure where we're headed, but if I start smellin' brimstone, I'm divin' out of this thing."

Clayborne laughed. "It is a mite spooky, I'll admit. Good thing I'm not a superstitious man."

They eventually arrived in front of an opulent house on Nob Hill. Cade resisted the urge to whistle at the richness of the exterior as they pulled through an open iron gate a short distance down a gravel drive, and beneath a marble-columned porte cochere at one side of the house.

As they pulled to a stop, Cade glanced out the window and blinked in surprise at what he saw. "What the hell...?"

The man who stood in the doorway was a giant, nearly seven feet tall and as broad across the shoulders as a wagon yoke. His height was only accentuated by the elaborate green turban he wore. He had a high-cheekboned, aristocratic face, with dark eyes that regarded them coolly beneath thick black brows. He was dressed in loose flowing white pants and a billowy linen shirt. His skin was the color of a copper penny. Without changing expression, he advanced on the brougham and yanked the door open, as if catching the two in some transgression.

"How do?" Cade said.

The turbaned man looked at them for a moment, as if sizing them up. When he spoke, his voice was deep and impressive. "I am Akbar. Madam is waiting for you. Follow me." Without waiting for a response, he turned and walked to the door set back behind the columns of the porte cochere.

"Akbar?" Clayborne said. "Miss Givens has an Arab servant?"

"Arab, my hind leg," Cade said in a low voice. "If that big bastard isn't pure-blooded Lakota, I'll eat my damn hat."

Clayborne frowned. "Hmm."

The man who called himself Akbar was looking at them impatiently, one hand on the door.

"Well," Cade said, "guess we best go on in."

The interior of the house was as luxurious and ornate as the outside. Akbar led them down corridors jammed with side tables that were themselves crowded with figurines and artwork. They ended up in a sitting room with a large bay window overlooking a garden with a fountain. Bookshelves lined the walls. Akbar motioned them to a pair of velvet upholstered chairs near the window. They took their seats and the man disappeared. They both looked around in silence at the stuffy room before Clayborne stood up and walked to the bookshelves. He studied some of the titles: *The Principles of Nature, Her Divine Revelations and a Voice to Mankind. Philosophy of Spiritual Intercourse. Spirit Messengers.*

He shook his head. "She's sure enough done her homework."

"And why should I not, Mr. Clayborne?" a woman's voice came from the door.

They both turned to look, then stood as the woman entered the room.

Athena Givens was a thin, narrow-faced woman dressed in a severe black dress with a button-up collar. In face and figure, she looked to be in her early thirties, but her dark hair had a few pronounced gray streaks and she walked hesitantly, bent over a cane. The servant Akbar walked behind her, eyes fixed on her hobbling steps as if he was prepared to swoop down and pick her up if she stumbled. She made her way to a chair across the room and slowly lowered herself into it, wincing in obvious discomfort.

"Forgive me, gentlemen," she said with an exhausted rasp in her voice, "I am still recovering from my wound." She motioned with a limp hand. "Please. Sit."

They sat. "Miss Givens," Cade began. "Sorry to hear you're still sufferin'. Do you have any idea who might have—?"

She interrupted him. "Mr. Cade. I agree to see you at the behest of my dear friend Marjorie." She smiled. "She seems to think you and your associate," she inclined her head toward Clayborne, who nodded back, "might be able to protect me." She leaned forward over her cane and fixed Cade's eyes with her pale blue ones. "However, I am not afraid. I believe in what I'm doing. I can deal with earthly powers. I do not believe there is anything that will be allowed to harm me."

"Do you think the spirits are going to protect you?" The skepticism was apparent in Clayborne's voice.

She looked at him, then stood up and walked over to where he sat, her eyes fixed on his. He looked up at her, sudden apprehension on his face. But when she spoke, her voice was gentle. "You are not a believer."

He swallowed nervously, visibly unsettled by her nearness. "Ma'am, it's not what I believe. It's—"

"Give me your hand."

Clayborne frowned. "Ma'am?"

"Please," she said in a low, insistent voice. "Give me your hand."

Hesitantly, as if he was extending a hand to an angry dog, he raised his hand. She clasped it gently in her long-fingered, bony one and bowed her head as if in prayer. Clayborne looked at Cade, who was frowning. Before he could say anything, Athena Givens spoke. "Fire. Fire and rope."

Clayborne's eyes widened. "What did you say?"

Her voice seemed to come from far away. "Your parents. And your..." She looked up at him, her eyes narrowed and intense. "Your sister."

Clayborne's voice sounded to Cade as if he was being choked. "What about my sister? And my parents?"

"They want you to know they are all right. They see you, and they love—"

Clayborne leaped up from the chair, pulling his hand away. His voice was a low, furious growl. "You shut up about my family."

"Sam!" Cade leaped up, aghast.

Givens's eyes never wavered from Clayborne's. "They felt the rope. But they have passed beyond the fire, and they are at—"

"SHUT UP!" Clayborne was shouting now. "SHUT UP!" He bolted for the door where the massive Akbar was standing. Cade wondered for a moment if there was going to be a fight, but Akbar merely moved out of the way and let Clayborne run from the room.

Cade picked up his hat. "Ma'am, I apologize for the behavior of my partner."

She only smiled. "The first realization of a world beyond the Veil can be unsettling. Unnerving, even. I completely understand. Go see to your friend. I will wait."

"Thank you, ma'am." Cade exited the room under the impassive gaze of Akbar.

CHAPTER TWELVE

"Cade," The White Orchid said, looking down into her teacup and swirling the dregs around. She pursed her lips in thought. "He owes a debt to Kwan." She smiled coldly. "He owes me." She put the cup down. "But he was very clear when speaking to him. He said he would not kill for him. Would not be an assassin."

Mei sighed. "Yes. That's true. It was a silly idea."

"However," Lin went on, "he is only a man. A *gwai loh* at that. Men are easily manipulated. *Gwai loh* even more so."

Mei didn't answer. She didn't like this side of her friend, the cold, calculating side. The killer. She knew Lin had used her beauty to bend men to her will, and more often to lure them to their deaths. She tried very hard not to think about it. Lin had been kind to her when she was alone and afraid, and she wanted to believe the friend she called Elder Sister was good at heart, despite what circumstance had made of her.

Lin went on. "Cade's woman, the red-haired one he took from her husband, has been seeking finance. Mr. Kwan has been making overtures, but she's resisted." Lin grimaced. "She doesn't want to be in debt to the tong."

One can hardly blame her, Mei thought, but remained silent. She herself was uncomfortable with being financed by the Green Dragon. The money Kwan had provided had helped her make improvements to the fish shop, opened her door to other suppliers, and set the place on the way to greater success than she'd ever dreamed, but somewhere in the back of her mind, she wondered what would happen if the tong demanded something of her other than the monthly repayments of principal and interest.

Lin shrugged and gave voice to the thought that Mei had kept to herself. "She wonders if the Green Dragon will demand some service of her and her ships that she can't live with."

Mei hesitated.

Lin caught the look on her face and inclined her head quizzically. "Perhaps you wonder the same thing, in regard to your own family's debt."

Mei looked away. "I know you would never ask me to do something that would hurt me or my family," she murmured.

"Good," Lin said. She reached out and took Mei's chin gently in one hand, turning her back to look into her eyes. "I promised you on my life no harm would come to you. And I still do."

Mei blinked back tears. "Thank you. But I still don't understand why."

Lin released her. "Because, Younger Sister, I say again. In this world of shit and garbage, you are the best person I have ever met."

Mei looked down, embarrassed. "Thank you," she said again.

"Besides," Lin said, "Mr. Kwan has a plan."

Mei could hardly believe the sardonic inflection in her friend's voice, as if she was mocking the head of the Green Dragons. "What plan?" she asked.

Lin sighed. "He thinks that by investing in the white devil's businesses, he can stop doing the things the foolish white devils have made illegal. He thinks he can make himself respectable."

Mei was shocked at the now unmistakable contempt. "You don't believe it."

Lin shook her head. "We are Chinese, Younger Sister. The white devils will never treat us like human beings. To them, we are cheap labor, only fit to be worked to death on the Iron Roads. Or as a source of the opium they dull their senses with. Or," her face twisted, "as whores to satisfy their lust on."

"You agree with Fang, then."

Lin chuckled bitterly. "A pretty situation, isn't it? I agree with Fang about the white devils, but, like them, he would make me his whore. Or worse."

"What about Cade?" Mei said. "Or his friend. The black man. They've been kind."

The White Orchid pondered for a moment. "The black white devil may have some potential," she said. "His people have been under the heel of the other white devils, so he may understand. But Cade? I don't know about him."

"Perhaps if we approached him as a friend," Mei ventured, "instead of as someone to be used, he might be willing to help."

"Help what?" The White Orchid scoffed. "Kill Fang?" She shook her head. "No. If Cade will not be intimidated into killing Fang, I know he will not do it for friendship." She looked thoughtful. "But if he thought Fang was trying to kill him...or his woman..." She smiled, pushed the bowl away from her, and stood up. "Thank you, Younger Sister," she said. She reached into a hidden pocket of her jacket and pulled out a couple of gold coins. "As always, your excellent counsel has helped to focus my thinking. Now I know what I need to do." She tossed the coins on the table.

Mei blinked in surprise. "What?"

The White Orchid took Mei's hands in her own and squeezed. "Until next time?"

"Yes," Mei said, "of course. But what are you...?" But Lin was gone.

Mei stared at the coins on the table, wondering what decision her friend believed she'd helped her to, and dreading the answer.

CHAPTER THIRTEEN

He found Clayborne down one of the hallways, leaning against a wall. He had his head down and was breathing hard. "Jesus, partner. Are you okay?"

Clayborne looked up. "I'm sorry, Levi. I think I just cost us this job."

"Not yet." Cade looked back in the direction of the sitting room. "I don't think our Miss Givens was all that unhappy about the reaction she got." He turned back to Clayborne. "Which was, if you don't mind my sayin', a bit startling. What the blue blazes did that woman say to get under your skin like that?"

Clayborne straightened up, smoothing the front of his coat. He'd ceased his panting, but Cade could see his hands were still trembling. "Nothing. She...it was one of her Spiritualist tricks."

"Well, from where I was sitting, it looked like her trick worked. I don't think I'm gonna be playing poker with that one any time soon."

Clayborne's laugh was shaky, but it was a laugh. "No. Best not."

Cade looked back down the hallway again. "Our

prospective employer seems to take a certain amount of pleasure in toying with our minds."

"Mine, at least."

Cade nodded. "Which means I'll most likely be next." He shook his head. "Truth be told, Sam, I'm inclined to just tell this crazy woman thanks but no thanks, make tracks out of here, and go find a place where the two of us can get drunk."

Clayborne took a deep breath. "Thanks, Levi. I appreciate that more than you know. But we really can't afford to turn down work right now."

Cade smiled. "I been broke before."

"So have I. But we do have an investor now. And she wants us to help her friend."

Cade grimaced. "Yeah. Let's do it. But we need to watch our step."

"And each other's backs," Clayborne said. He held out a hand.

Cade smiled and gripped the proffered hand. "You got that right."

As they reentered the room, Athena Givens was seated by the window, looking out at the garden and its fountain. The servant Akbar was nowhere to be seen. She looked over at them. "So," she said, then smiled. "You came back."

"Miss Givens," Clayborne said, "I want to apologize for my behavior. I was rude. Inexcusably so. I hope you will forgive me."

She inclined her head. "There is absolutely nothing to apologize for, Mr. Clayborne. You've had a shock."

"Yes, ma'am," he said with the lack of expression that Cade had come to know meant his friend was repressing a deep and seething anger.

He redirected the conversation. "You said that you're not

afraid of whoever attacked you, that it's an earthly power you can deal with. Does that mean you know who it is?"

Givens had been staring fixedly at Clayborne, but now she swiveled in her chair to regard Cade with the same unblinking stare. "Do *you* believe in the world beyond this one, Mr. Cade?"

Cade took a deep breath. "Ma'am, beggin' your pardon, this ain't about me. Or about Mr. Clayborne. So, if you don't mind, it would be a help to our work if you'd answer my question."

She held his stare, then looked away. "There are people who do not wish me well," she said in a small voice.

Cade saw an opening and pressed the point. "People in this world? Not in the...what did you call it...the world beyond."

She continued to look out of the window. "Mrs. Hamrick told you about my other work?"

Now we're getting somewhere, Cade thought. "Yes, ma'am."

She turned back to him. "And what do you think about the idea of votes for women, Mr. Cade?"

He felt the conversation slipping away again. Trying to get a straight answer out of this woman was like trying to lasso smoke. "Ma'am," he said, trying to keep the annoyance out of his voice, "I am completely without opinion on the subject of suffragism. Now can we—?"

"I very seriously doubt that," she broke in.

At that moment, Akbar walked back into the room. He'd changed into a white caftan, ornately embroidered with gold filigree, and a matching turban. He nodded at Givens.

She painfully got to her feet, leaning on her cane. "I regret, gentlemen, that I have an engagement to attend." She smiled grimly at them. "A suffragist rally, as it turns out. Would the two of you like to attend with me?"

Cade looked at Clayborne, who cleared his throat uncomfortably. "Well, ma'am. Um. We haven't exactly been..."

"Hired yet?" She waved a hand dismissively. "Consider

yourselves retained as my personal bodyguards. If Marjorie Hamrick vouches for you, it's good enough for me. Just send me the bill. Now, we have to get ready to leave." She stumped out of the room on her cane.

"Well," Cade said. "Guess that's settled."

Clayborne shook his head. "I guess."

Cade pulled the Navy revolver out of the shoulder holster rig he'd had made and double checked that it was loaded. "You ready, Mr. Clayborne?"

Clayborne took his Smith and Wesson revolver out of his own holster and made his own check. "I am, Mr. Cade."

"Well, then. Let's go to work."

CHAPTER FOURTEEN

T he driver was the same surly fellow as before, but this coach was larger, more luxurious, with room for four in the covered passenger compartment behind the open driver's seat. Miss Givens and her silent "Arab" sat in the forward-facing seats.

Cade studied the layout, then gestured to Clayborne. "You ride inside. I'll take lookout next to the driver." Clayborne nodded and stepped up into the compartment with a startled Miss Givens. Cade swung himself up to the driver's seat. "Shove over, friend. I'll keep you company."

The driver looked at him sourly. He didn't move. "Don't need no company."

"Well, you got it." He lowered his voice. "We're joining the household, fella. Like it or not. So, I might as well know your name."

The older man looked at him sourly. "Clinton. Silas Clinton."

Cade smiled as insincerely as he knew how. "A pleasure, Mr. Clinton. Glad we can reach an understanding here."

Cade noticed the driver wasn't looking at his face. He was

looking at the butt of the pistol showing beneath Cade's opened coat. Clinton swallowed nervously and squirmed his ample behind over a little to give Cade space.

"There ya go," Cade said in as friendly a voice as he could muster for a man he'd quickly come to dislike.

The driver snapped the reins and the two-horse team started off at a walk.

"Where are we headed?" Cade kept his gaze moving, looking for threats on each side and ahead of the carriage.

"Randall Hall." The driver said it as if it hurt his mouth to form the words.

"Don't know the place. But I notice you don't sound happy about it."

Clinton grimaced. "You'll see."

As they drew closer, Cade did. A crowd had gathered before the doors of their destination. The hall had seen better days; the paint was chipped on the tall Corinthian columns across the front, and the brass on the large double doors that led to the lobby was green and tarnished. The group of men gathered on the cobbled street before the hall was raggedy and frayed-looking as well, a slovenly collection of about twenty idlers and layabouts, red-faced with anger and drink. Cade saw a few bottles held in grimy hands and sticking out of patched pockets. The crowd gave off a low, foreboding sound, the voices of outraged men blending into an ominous buzz. Some of them were hefting stones and loose cobbles in their hands. They were eying the banner stretched across the building's front: VOTES FOR WOMEN. As Cade watched, one of them reared back and let fly with a fist-sized stone. It impacted on the linen of the banner and fell to earth without effect.

Cade glanced across the street. A trio of mustachioed bruisers in the uniform of the San Francisco Police lounged against the front of a tobacconist's shop, their ever-present billy clubs safely stowed. As one of them noticed the carriage approaching, he spat into the gutter. There'd be no help from that direction. Cade noticed another figure, dressed in a long blue coat, standing nearby, arms crossed across his broad chest. Cade could swear he'd seen him before, but the cop's attention had drawn the attention of a couple of men at the edges of the crowd.

"Hey!" One pointed at the carriage. "Here comes one of them now!"

"Ah shit," Cade muttered, forgetting the man in the blue coat. He turned to the driver. "We need to get the hell out of here."

"Nothin' would make me happier, friend," the man said through gritted teeth, "but *she* wouldn't permit it."

"Cade?" Clayborne's voice came from behind him. Cade turned. Clayborne was leaning out the window, eyes narrowed, staring at the crowd.

"They got a coon with 'em!" someone in the crowd called out.

The buzz rose into a low, threatening rumble. All eyes turned to the carriage and the group began to move.

Cade quickly weighed his options. If he and Clayborne started firing, the milling herd could quickly turn into a pack, a mob baying for blood, and he didn't think the two of them could hold the whole mass of them off in that case. He spotted a man at the front of the group begin to pull his arm back to toss another fist-sized cobblestone, this one aimed at the carriage. Cade's Navy revolver was out of its shoulder holster in one smooth motion, the hammer pulled back before Cade realized he'd done it. The sight stopped the mob in its tracks, but the angry muttering kept on. Cade pointed the gun at the man who stood with his arm half-cocked for a throw, his eyes wide with shock.

"Put that goddamn thing down," Cade growled.

The cobblestone was out of the man's hand and thudding to the ground before the man realized he'd let it go. The crowd grew silent, but their furious stares were still locked on the carriage. The air felt electric, like the tang of ozone in the air before the storm breaks.

A voice from the crowd, made braver by anonymity, spoke up. "You can't shoot all of us."

"No," Cade said. "But I got six bullets for the first six sons of bitches who decide to get frisky. My partner can add another six to the game while I reload, then it's raise, call, or fold. So, who's ready to ante up, boys?"

The men looked at each other, then at the carriage. Cade could see them working themselves up, steeling themselves to make the move. He felt his stomach knotting as he saw his bluff about to get called.

At that moment, the three policemen he'd seen loafing against the building appeared at the edge of the crowd, clubs out and at the ready. "All right," the biggest one prodded a skinny unshaven lout, "break it up. Break it up. Move along. Come on now, show's over."

The shock of the unexpected intervention broke the spell. The nascent mob's attention wasn't enough for two targets. A few complained halfheartedly, but the expression on most faces was unmistakably relief. In moments, the group was shuffling off in various directions, leaving a clutter of rocks, cobbles, and brickbats behind.

One of the cops pointed his billy club at Cade, still standing up in the driver's seat. "You. Put that away."

Cade slid the gun back into its holster, touching the brim of his hat. "Thanks, Constable," he said in a dry voice. "You got here just in the nick of time."

The copper's eyes narrowed and he looked as if he was

about to say something, but Clinton had the horses moving again. The policemen moved aside, glowering. Cade looked around for the man in the blue coat, but he was nowhere to be seen.

Clinton steered the carriage around the edge of the building, into an alley between the hall and the building next to it, until they stopped at a tall wooden gate. At a word from Miss Givens, Clayborne got out and opened the gate.

CHAPTER FIFTEEN

They entered a shallow courtyard surrounded by a wooden fence as tall as the gate. There were a couple of other carriages pulled into the space, horses munching contentedly on feed bags as the drivers, one black and one white, leaned against the fence on opposite sides of the courtyard, neither one speaking to the other. A platform ran along the back of the building, accessed by a short flight of steps.

Cade swung down from the driver's seat and opened the door, holding out his hand. "Ma'am."

Miss Givens took the proffered hand and let him help her down, wincing a little, as if the wound in her back still pained her. She looked at Cade severely, as if she'd caught him in some indiscretion. "Mr. Cade. I heard you dealing with those men in the crowd. Would you truly have opened fire on that man? Just because he was ready to throw a rock?"

"No, ma'am. I would have plugged the man standing behind him and to the right."

She frowned. "And why him?"

"Because, ma'am, that was the one with the pistol stuck

down the front of his pants. Once the ball opened, he was going to be the first one to draw."

"And you'd have had no problem killing him."

Cade shrugged. "Wouldn't have been my preference, ma'am. But if they'd have made a move, we wouldn't have had much choice."

"You could have run."

"I suppose. But that's not my way."

She stared at him for a moment, then turned to Clayborne. "And you, Mr. Clayborne?"

He looked back at her without expression. "What about me, ma'am?"

She arched an eyebrow at him. "Is it your way? To run?"

He didn't answer at first. He looked away, then back. "No, ma'am. I took on this job, and I mean to see it through."

She held his gaze with her own. "That hasn't always been the way, though. Has it?"

"Ma'am," Cade began, but he was interrupted by a voice from the platform.

"Athena?"

Cade looked around. A large woman in a black dress was standing at the edge of the platform, gesturing to them. "Come on," she said. "We're late. The place is full. Your audience is waiting."

Miss Givens smiled at Cade, then gave Clayborne a nod that was a little too knowing for Cade's taste. "We'll talk more." She mounted the steps to where the woman who'd spoken to them was holding a door open. Light spilled from inside, and Cade could hear the low rumble of what sounded like a large crowd. The fake Arab dismounted the carriage, gave the two of them a disdainful look, then followed.

Cade looked at his partner. Clayborne looked as if he'd been stunned by a blow to the head. "Sam?" Cade whispered. Then, more sharply, "Sam!"

Clayborne shook his head sharply like a man awakening from a bad dream. "Yeah," he murmured. He took a deep breath. "Yeah." He focused on Cade. "I'm okay."

"You sure? You look like you've just seen a ghost."

"I'm fine," Clayborne said, but he didn't look it.

Cade shook his head. "Sam, I don't know why this crazy woman is tryin' to rattle you, but I need you sharp. I get a feelin' we ain't seen the last of trouble tonight. You sharp?"

Clayborne nodded. "Yeah. I'm fine, Cade." He smiled thinly. "I'm sharp."

Cade didn't know if that was true, but the circumstances gave no help. "Okay, then." They followed her up the stairs.

The hall was packed, every seat filled, the excess spread across the back and spilling down the aisles. Cade noticed that, without exception, everyone in the place was female. The atmosphere was so hot and close and emotionally charged, however, he didn't feel a bit relaxed.

He bent close and murmured into Clayborne's ear. "Take the right side of the stage. Keep an eye out." He was glad to see that his partner had shaken off whatever spell their employer had tried to cast on him; Clayborne just nodded and moved across the back of the stage to take his station.

When Athena Givens took the podium, the crowd erupted. It reminded Cade of some revival meetings he'd dropped in on, that magic moment when the preacher everyone had been waiting for made his appearance. Athena stood at the podium, hands spread to grip each side, head down as if she was gathering her thoughts and her strength. Her hesitation only seemed to raise the crowd before her to a higher pitch of excitement. Just when it seemed as if the place was about to devolve into utter chaos, she raised her gaze and her arms, holding her hands up, palms turned to the front. The gathering quickly subsided; the whole place focused on the silent figure before them. *Damn, she's good*, Cade thought.

When Givens spoke, it was in a clear, strong voice that blared through the hall like a bugle sounding the charge. "Women of San Francisco," she began, then stopped. She bowed her head again, then raised it to fix the audience with her gaze. "No. Women of America." She looked down again, shaking her head back and forth furiously in further negation before looking up again, this time at the ceiling of the hall, as if appealing to the heavens. "Women of the WORLD!"

The place went wild again, the cheers and handclaps augmented by the stomping of a hundred or more booted feet. Cade wondered if they meant to shake the place down. After a few moments, the ruckus subsided and Givens spoke again.

"Our time has come." Another round of cheers began, but quickly diminished as it became clear that she was done waiting for applause lines. "For too long, the role of women in this society has been denigrated. Diminished. Despised. Even as we, half the population, have propped up this country. Sustained it. Bound its wounds. Well, ladies, I tell you, no more. No. More." As the applause grew again, Givens raised her voice to shout over it. "It is time that women had the most basic say in the running of the country they nurture. The country they helped bring into being. The country they now try to heal. It is time for women to have the vote!" The applause and shouts of approbation had been loud before; now they became deafening.

The speech went on for at least another forty-five minutes. Athena Givens reasoned. She cajoled. She threatened both divine and secular retribution if the country failed to follow the clear moral imperative she set out. Cade had to repeatedly tear his attention away from the speech in order to keep his eyes moving across the crowd, looking for threats. Eventually, he learned to blur the words from his consciousness, just following the rise and fall of the crowd's emotions as the speech went on. From time to time, he glanced over to the other side of the stage and was glad to see that Clayborne's gaze was likewise roaming over the hall, seeking out potential problems and finding none. Then Givens said something that reacquired Cade's attention.

"Let us not fool ourselves. This fight will not be without losses. There are those who will stop at nothing to keep the women of the world in what they see as their rightful place." She paused, the words hanging in the charged air. "I myself have been subject to a vicious attack, in my own home."

The crowd rumbled with shock and anger. "No!" a voice called out. "Shame!" another cried. "Infamy!" called a third. The crowd looked ready to boil out of the hall and start smashing things.

Cade lightly rested his hand on the butt of the Navy revolver in its shoulder holster, sensing that this was the last and worst chance for anything bad to happen.

"But fear not," Givens said. "No pain, no threat, no assassin's blade will deter us. We will not be stopped. We will not fear. And we. Will. Triumph!" The speech ended, Givens stepped back from the podium and bowed slightly to acknowledge the thunderous applause, then she was at the back of the stage, looking expectantly at Cade. Clayborne joined them, nodding to Cade as he took up a position on her other side. Without speaking, they escorted their charge out the back of the theater to the courtyard.

The carriages that were there when they'd arrived were gone; theirs was the only one left. The huge "Arab" Akbar was waiting by the door of the carriage. He took Givens's extended hand and drew her up into the interior.

"Where ya been, stranger?" Cade asked, an edge in his voice beneath the jocular tone.

Akbar just stared at him without speaking, then swung himself into the carriage.

Clayborne looked to Cade, one eyebrow arched quizzically.

"Go on in," Cade muttered. "Keep an eye and an ear cocked. But if things go sideways, don't expect any help from that big son of a bitch."

Clayborne looked into the darkness of the carriage. The corner of his mouth quirked. "Don't worry. I don't."

Cade shook his head. "His ancestors must be rolling in their graves." He climbed up onto the side of the carriage, hanging off by one hand. As he looked up at the coachman, he caught the sweet smell of whiskey coming off the man like a fog. "Jesus, Clinton," he whispered, "you fit to drive this thing?"

The driver leaned back and squinted, as if to bring Cade into better focus. "Sonny," he said, with a distinct slur on the S, "I could get this goddamned thing home in my sleep."

"Let's hope you're right," Cade muttered. He jumped down, went to the gate and swung it open, peering down the alleyway as he did so. He didn't see any obvious threat, but the narrow alley was a prime spot for ambush, so he proceeded down the narrow space, hand on his pistol beneath his coat, motioning for the carriage to follow. He heard the slow clop of the horses' hooves following as he crept down the alley. When he reached the street, he held up a hand to stop the carriage while he took stock. There was a crowd of women gathered on the steps of the hall, laughing and chatting, talking over the spectacle they'd just observed. Other than that, all he could see was the usual chaos of a San Francisco street in the middle of the evening. As he assessed the situation, the carriage rolled out past him, apparently oblivious to his signal to pause.

Cade swore under his breath and grabbed the side, swinging himself up nimbly to perch by the driver, who was swaying a bit and crooning to the horses as he proceeded. "Goddamn it," Cade snapped. "Didn't you see me signal you to stop?"

Clinton blinked. "What?"

Cade sighed. "Never mind. Just get us home." Cade had time to wonder why in God's name Athena Givens would employ such an incompetent drunkard to shepherd her through the streets of San Francisco. That was something he was going to have to look into.

CHAPTER SIXTEEN

As a captain in the San Francisco Police Department, Harcourt Smith had gotten used to a certain amount of deference. Lower ranking officers called him sir and even the higher ranking ones, up to the lofty level of commissioner, addressed him by his rank. As for the wretched scum he was required to police...well, it was gratifying to see how humble a lowlife suspect could turn when in front of a man who held a billy club, a pistol, and a badge that granted him unlimited power to wield both without consequence. Not that he got to indulge himself in those enjoyable pastimes anymore. The burdens of command took up most of his time now. Sometimes, those burdens brought him to luxuriously appointed rooms like this one, their very design intended to remind him that there were powers above him, powers he served, powers to which even he had to bow and scrape. So, he sat silently in a leather upholstered chair that managed to be both beautifully crafted and tortuously uncomfortable at the same time while the banker ignored him in favor of examining some incomprehensible documents.

That was another thing that rankled Smith. When he'd first

been recruited into this group, he'd assumed he'd be dealing directly with its head, the railroad magnate whose charismatic presence had obviously brought the group together. But now he realized he was an underling, dealing with other underlings. He knew, or at least hoped, that this would eventually bring him to greater power, but that didn't seem to be what was happening now.

Eventually, the banker sighed and put the papers he'd been studying down. "Tell me what happened at the hall. Why wasn't the meeting broken up?"

Smith kept his voice as level as he could. "We had people in place. But we weren't told that Givens would be bringing armed bodyguards."

The banker frowned. "What difference would that make?"

Smith shook his head as if he couldn't quite comprehend the question. "We'd paid these men to break up a women's meeting. Not to get shot. Sir."

The banker inclined his head quizzically. "And you believed that these unexpected bodyguards would actually fire on the crowd?"

Smith nodded. "One of them, at least. Lieutenant Webster was on the scene and recognized him. A man named Cade. I've..." he hesitated, "...dealt with him before."

"Yes. He was, I believe, a suspect in the death of John C. Hamrick."

"Yes, sir," Smith said, more than a little concerned by how much the banker and his cronies already knew. "But there was nothing we could prove." He took a deep breath. "We believe he's backed by certain Chinese interests. To round it all off, he's recently gone into business with a Negro partner."

The banker regarded Smith with a look that said, as clearly as fiery letters written on the wall, *You have been weighed, and measured, and found wanting.* Finally, he spoke. "So, this man

Cade is allied with not only the suffragists, but the Negroes and the Chinese?"

Smith swallowed nervously. "Yes, sir."

"Well," the banker said, "this is exactly the sort of degeneracy we've been fighting." He looked at Smith impatiently. "We believed, Captain Smith, that you were our ally in this fight. Why haven't you dealt with him?"

"Dealt with him, sir?"

"For God's sake, man, you know what I mean. You should have gotten rid of him. And his black associate. Don't worry about the Chinese. They have no concept of loyalty, and they certainly aren't going to intervene on behalf of what they call a white devil."

"Well, sir," Smith said, "this Cade has a certain facility with the gun."

The banker rolled his eyes. "Men like that are prone to random and violent deaths, are they not? Especially in this city. Do I have to think of everything for you? Are you feeble-minded?" He stopped, as if to regain his composure. " Since you have so far failed to deal with Cade, I will do so."

Smith frowned. "Beggin' your pardon, but how, sir?"

The banker paused, looked away for a moment, as if considering whether to answer. Smith found himself leaning forward, hanging on the possibility that he'd get a response. He recognized that he was being played like a fish on a line, but he didn't care. When the banker smiled, it sent a rush of pleasure through him, and his next words, delivered in a low, confiding voice, brought him, or so he thought, into some inner circle he'd always known existed and had always wanted to be a part of. "The secret to controlling men like Cade, Captain Smith, is finding what they want most in the world, then offering it to them. For a price. Actually, I believe I already know what that price is. When I have confirmed my suspicions, I will offer it to him, and he will be my creature from that moment on." Before Smith could inquire further, the banker leaned back, the intimate tone gone. "As for this suffragist harpy Athena Givens, I understand that she has recently reported an attack on her person. An attempted murder."

Smith nodded. "Yes, sir. We didn't give it much credence. Supposedly happened at one of her séances. We figured it was just so much of her usual hoodoo. Expected her to claim it was ghosts or some such."

"Well, then," the banker said, "we shall make the spirit flesh." At Smith's baffled expression, the banker sighed. "The Arab, you fool. Arrest the Arab. Or whatever he is. He is her closest companion and her supposed spirit guide. Arrest him, and the scandal will destroy not only her Spiritualist flimflammery, but it will take her suffragist nonsense down with it." He picked another sheaf of papers from his desk and began studying it. The dismissal was unmistakable.

Smith rose from his chair, hat in hand. He had his orders. Shoot at least one man, maybe two, in the back, and frame a man he wasn't sure was guilty. He believed in order, and there was no question in his mind that these people threatened that order. What he was doing was in the service of a greater good, he knew. But he didn't have to like the way it was being done.

CHAPTER SEVENTEEN

They made the ride home without incident, but by the time they reached the Givens mansion, Cade's neck was getting sore from constantly scanning the shadows and alleyways for threats. It didn't help that he had to keep nudging the driver awake. Clinton had said he could get the carriage home in his sleep, but Cade wasn't inclined to test the idea on a night when there were threats about. Finally, they pulled up to the gates of the house and he clambered down from the driver's platform to swing them open. He gave one last glance at the street as the carriage trundled slowly past. His eyes narrowed as he caught sight of a figure slouching in the shadows, just outside the globe of light cast by a gas street lamp. He considered crossing the street to find out who or what the figure was and what it was up to, but he decided to close and fasten the gates instead. He had to trot to catch up with the carriage. By the time he got there, the passengers were debarking, the silent Akbar standing by with arms crossed across his chest as Clayborne helped Miss Givens down from the passenger compartment.

"Mr. Cade," she said as she reached the steps, "a word, if you please. In the sitting room."

"Yes, ma'am," Cade said. He turned to Clayborne. "See if you can get the layout of the property. Roam around a bit. See if you can spot weak points where people might get in." He leaned closer and spoke in a whisper. "And look sharp. I think I saw someone skulking across the street."

Clayborne nodded. "Got it." He touched the brim of his bowler hat and bowed slightly to Akbar. "Thanks for the conversation," he said. As he moved off, the big man looked as if he was going to move to stop him, then he glanced at Givens, who was waiting impatiently at the top of the steps. For the first time since Cade had met him, he looked uncertain. Cade drew on his limited knowledge of Lakota. "*Hau Kola, Takuwe ni lel he?*" ("What are you doing here, honored friend?")

The uncertainty left the big man's face. His eyes narrowed and he snarled something under his breath that Cade couldn't translate word for word, but he could pick up on the fact that it definitely wasn't friendly.

Miss Givens spoke again. "Mr. Cade."

"Coming, ma'am." He followed her as she turned and walked into the house, leaning on her cane. Cade heard Akbar's heavy tread as he fell in behind Cade. He felt a shiver between his shoulder blades, but he calmed his nerves with the thought that the manservant probably wouldn't plunge a blade into the back of someone his mistress clearly wished to speak with. Probably.

They reached the room where they'd talked earlier. There was darkness outside the windows, but Cade could still hear the soft trickle of the fountain. A fire burned low in a grate on one wall. As Akbar busied himself lighting the gas lamps, Givens sank into a chair near the bay window, grunting a little with the pain as she did so. Cade took a chair across from her. He removed his hat and looked round for a place to set it. All the tables were crammed with knickknacks, so he set the hat on his knee.

"Akbar," Givens said. "I'd like some tea. See if Eleanor can scare some up. Mr. Cade?"

"No tea, ma'am. Thank you."

"Something stronger, then?" Before Cade could answer, she told Akbar, "A dram of whiskey for Mr. Cade. Neat."

Akbar didn't look at Cade, just nodded and departed the room.

"Thank you, ma'am," Cade said.

Givens looked out the window before she spoke. "So, Mr. Cade. What did you think of tonight?"

Cade didn't know quite how to answer. "Well," he began, "I think we need to start planning a little farther ahead when it comes to your security."

She rapped her cane on the floor impatiently. "Bother my security! The speech! What did you think of the speech?"

"Um." Cade cleared his throat and considered. "It was... quite powerful, ma'am."

She inclined her head slightly. "Thank you. Did you find it persuasive?"

"Persuasive, ma'am?"

"Did it move you toward acceptance of women's right to vote?"

Cade fidgeted with his hat in his lap. "Is that important, ma'am?"

She frowned. "What do you mean?"

He cleared his throat. "I mean to say, ma'am, are you looking for a bodyguard or a disciple?"

She drew back slightly, her eyebrows raised, a slight smile on her face. "Why, can't I have both?"

"Well, ma'am—" he began.

She cut him off. "Since we are going to be living cheek by jowl for the foreseeable future, I think we can reduce the ma'ams to one an hour, Mr. Cade. Please do speak your mind."

He squared his shoulders, then turned to face her head-on. "Okay, then. Here it is. There's going to be times when, to keep you safe, I'm going to have to tell you what you're doing is damn foolery and you need to not do it. A bodyguard can do that. A disciple can't."

She looked back out the window, then nodded. "An excellent distinction." She turned to him and smiled. "During the course of your employment, you may feel free at any time to tell me I'm engaged in...how did you put it? Damn foolery. You have my word that there will be no penalty for the honest expression of your opinion."

He nodded. "That's all I ask for."

"However," she went on, "There are things I must do, regardless of whether you think they are safe." She sighed. "If I wanted to be completely safe, I would not have undertaken this work in the first place. I promise I will give your advice all consideration, but the final decision on what is to be done will be mine. Is that understood?"

"Yes, ma'am."

"With that established, I can ask you again. What is your opinion on votes for women?"

He laughed. "You've flanked me on that one." He thought for a moment. "I confess it's not something I've given a whole lot of thought to. But I reckon when it comes right down to it, women can't make any more of a hash of things than men have. So why the hell not?"

She threw back her head then and laughed. It was a good laugh, hearty and rich, and it was the first reaction Cade had seen from her that he felt sure was genuine. When she wound down a bit, she wiped her eyes. "Indeed, Mr. Cade. Why the hell not?"

At that moment, Akbar returned, bearing a silver tray containing a decanter of brown whiskey and two glasses. Clayborne followed behind him, and was followed in his turn by a young black girl dressed in a plain dark blue skirt and white blouse. She was carrying a tray of her own, this one with a teapot and a single cup. Akbar set his tray down on a nearby side table and backed away, leaning against a far wall with his arms crossed over his massive chest, his eyes staring at nothing.

"Please feel free to pour, Mr. Cade," Givens said. "Akbar, as a devout Mohammedan, cannot, of course, serve alcohol."

"Uh-huh." Cade got up and moved to the side table, uncorking the decanter and pouring two fingers of the rich-smelling brown whiskey into one of the exquisitely cut crystal glasses. He raised the other empty glass to Clayborne. "A drink, Mr. Clayborne?"

Clayborne shook his head. "I'll pass for the moment, Mr. Cade." He took a seat in one of the overstuffed armchairs.

Cade resumed his seat and took a sip of the whiskey. It was excellent. He leaned his head back and closed his eyes, savoring the taste for a moment. When he opened them again, he saw that the female servant had bent to her task of serving tea to Miss Givens. Cade couldn't help but notice that she was young and pretty, nor did it escape his notice that Clayborne's eyes followed her every move. He cleared his throat. "What did you see, Mr. Clayborne?"

Clayborne tore his eyes away from the slender young girl who was straightening up, teapot in her hand. He cleared his throat. "There's a high wall around the property. It could be breached, but it would be difficult." He frowned. "But there's an awful lot of it to watch."

Cade nodded and took another sip of the fine whiskey.

"Penny for your thoughts, Mr. Cade," Athena Givens spoke up.

He sighed. "You may not like them. Ma'am."

She took a sip of her tea. "I'll have them just the same."

"First," he stood up, "I'll need to see the house. All of it."

She frowned. "Now?"

"Yes, ma'am. The job starts now."

"Very well." Givens stood up, using the cane to help her get to her feet, wincing as if her wound were paining her. "Eleanor, would you do the honors?"

"Yes, ma'am." The young woman stood up. "Where would you like to begin, sirs?"

"Front door's as good a place to start as any."

Eleanor looked over at Givens, who gave her a slight nod. "This way." She took an unlit candle from a holder on a nearby table and lit it from one of the gas lamps.

CHAPTER EIGHTEEN

The front hall was spacious, the ceiling going up two stories, with a second-floor mezzanine overlooking it. Stairs on either side swept up to the mezzanine. It was a room designed to impress, and despite himself, Cade was impressed. Beneath the mezzanine was a double doorway leading to a large square space which Cade supposed was meant to be a ballroom. Tonight, however, the great glass chandelier in the middle of the room was darkened, the room cavernous and still. Eleanor led them through, the flickering candle held high and providing the only illumination. Behind the ballroom was a large, shallower room dominated by a long dining table. Portraits of severe-looking men and women in Georgian-era finery glowered down from the walls.

Cade gestured to the portraits. "These the Givens family?"

Eleanor shook her head. "They were here when we moved into the place."

As Cade and Clayborne looked at each other, Eleanor led the way out the back door of the dining room. Cade thought he heard a conversation behind the next door, but it fell silent as they entered.

The kitchen behind the dining room was better lit, but crammed with enough stoves, tables, and other kitchen gear to prepare three hot meals a day for a cavalry troop. Cade drew up short at the sight of a trio grouped around a table in the middle of the room. The two men and a young girl were dressed in servant's clothing, and none of them looked happy to see Cade. There was a whiskey bottle in the center of the table.

Cade nodded. "Evening, folks. Don't let me interrupt the party." They just stared at him. He pasted a smile onto his face. "And who might I have the pleasure of addressing?"

The three looked at Eleanor, then back at Cade. Still, none of them spoke. It was Eleanor who broke the silence. "Mr. Cade, Mr. Clayborne," she said, "this is Lucius, the footman." One of the men, a tall, dark-haired young man whose gaunt cheeks and pale complexion gave him the look of someone recovering from consumption, nodded with ill grace. Eleanor pointed at the other man, a stout, ruddy-faced man with thinning black hair. "Fabrice, the head chef." The chef gave a slight bow, looking no more pleased than the footman. "And Carine, the cook's assistant." The girl, a blue-eyed blonde who looked barely out of her teens, looked down and giggled. The cook hissed something at her in a language Cade didn't know. The girl gave him a venomous look that was shocking on such a baby face, then turned to them sullenly and gave a shallow curtsy.

Cade nodded back. He kept his voice easy despite the obvious tension in the room. "Pleasure to make your acquaintance. I'll be wanting to talk to you all later. About the attack on Miss Givens."

Lucius spoke up in a distinct Missouri drawl. "We didn't have nothin' to do with that."

Cade smiled, still pleasant. "Glad to hear it."

"We already speak to the police," the chef protested in a thick accent. "We tell them everything."

"I'm sure." Cade turned to the girl. "How about you, young miss?"

"She won't be much help," Lucius said. "She doesn't speak English. Only French."

"We'll deal with that as it comes." He turned to Eleanor. "Miss Givens said there were nine people on staff. Where are the rest?"

"You've met Clinton. He's the driver. He's..." She stopped, unsure of what to say.

"Probably sleeping off his drunk," Cade said.

She ignored it and went on. "The stablemaster and the groom—George and Jephthah—have their rooms above the stable."

"Of course," Clayborne muttered.

"And the gardeners, well, they don't stay here. They come in the morning, early. And go back home at sundown."

"And their names are?" Cade asked.

Eleanor looked embarrassed. "I'm sorry. I don't know."

It was Lucius, the footman, who spoke again. "Kam and Liang." His lip curled. "Chinamen."

Cade sighed. Even among the servants, everyone seemed to need someone to look down on. He thought of telling Lucius that he'd learned that the Chinese found that term offensive, but he doubted he'd care. He highly doubted that anyone in the house spoke Chinese. He put the thought aside for the moment as he crossed the kitchen to a wooden door on the back wall. "What's this?"

"Door to the servant's quarters," Eleanor said. "Downstairs."

"Show me." Cade said.

"Here now," Lucius objected.

"Don't worry, sonny," Cade said. "I'm not gonna be rifling through your things. I just want to see the ways in and out."

Lucius jerked his chin toward Samuel. "Is *he* gonna be comin' with you?"

Cade turned to Clayborne and arched an eyebrow. "What say you, Mr. Clayborne?"

Clayborne smiled. "Right behind you, Mr. Cade."

Cade chuckled. "Well, then." He looked to Eleanor. "Lead on, miss." He turned to the silently fuming Lucius. "We'll try not to be too long."

The stairs down to the servant's quarters were narrow, and the stairwell hadn't been painted, Cade thought, since the place was built. The stairs ended along a narrow corridor, so cramped it reminded Cade of his one and only visit to a coal mine. The walls were of flimsy wood, with doors set along the hallway every few feet. The doorways were so close together that the rooms they opened into must have been little larger than monk's cells.

Suddenly, a sound like a sawmill blade biting into an oak log split the air. Cade's hand went to the grip of the Navy revolver, then relaxed as the buzz-saw whine trailed off to a wet snuffling. "That would be Mr. Clinton snoring, I presume," Cade said to Eleanor. She nodded, a sour expression on her face. The coachman wasn't apparently popular with anyone. Cade filed that away for future reference.

Cade looked to the end of the corridor and saw only a blank wall. "Is there any other way in or out of the servant's area?"

Eleanor shook her head. "No."

"Be a bad place to be if the house ever caught fire," Samuel said.

"Yeah." Cade turned to Eleanor. "Come on, miss. Let's check out the upper floors."

They passed through the kitchen, past the hostile stares of the footman, the chef, and his assistant. "So," Cade asked, "do you stay downstairs with the rest of the crew?"

Eleanor shook her head as they mounted another set of hidden steps off the kitchen, a narrow servant's stairway leading to the second floor. "I have a bedroom upstairs. Near Miss Givens. I attend to her."

"And what about Mr. Akbar?" Clayborne asked. "Does he attend to her, too?"

Her voice turned frosty. "I'm sure I don't know what you mean, Mr. Clayborne."

"Leave it," Cade said.

The upstairs was naturally more opulent than downstairs, the corridor wider and paneled in rich dark walnut. Eleanor paused before one door. "This is Miss Givens's suite." She bit her lip nervously.

"We don't need to get in there just yet, miss," Cade said, "But we do need to get the lay of the land, so to speak. Where, exactly, does Mr. Akbar reside?"

She hesitated, then sighed. "Next door."

"With a connecting door?" Cade asked. She didn't answer. "Come on, girl," he said impatiently, "we haven't got time to play games. If you care about Miss Givens, and I suspect you do, then you need to tell me what I need to know to keep her safe."

"Yes," the girl said sullenly, looking at the floor. "They have adjoining rooms."

"Okay, then." Cade looked down the hallway. "And where is your room?"

Eleanor continued to look down, like a sulky child. "On the other side of Akbar's."

"Fine." Cade paused. "Now we'll need to have a look at where Miss Givens does her, whatever you call them. Readings."

"Séances," Eleanor said. "And I'm sorry, but that won't be possible."

Cade was expecting this, but he inclined his head as if curious. "Beg pardon?"

Eleanor's careful composure was beginning to unravel. "Miss Givens's séance room is...well, she calls it a sacred space. She's very particular about who enters."

"Uh-huh," Cade said. "I guess I'll need to take it up with her, then. Can you take us back to the drawing room?"

Eleanor still looked apprehensive, but she just nodded and led them down the corridor, which, Cade had figured, made a circuit around the second floor.

As they turned a corner, Cade stopped at a door. "Wait a second. What's in here? Another bedroom?" He reached out to test the knob.

Eleanor's reaction startled him. "Stop!" she said, almost shouting.

He paused, his hand above the knob, and looked at her. "Something wrong, miss?"

She looked flustered. "That room is...off limits as well. It's locked."

Cade nodded. Then he put his hand on the doorknob and tried to turn it. "Yep. Locked. And why is that?"

"I honestly don't know, Mr. Cade."

"She doesn't have a squad of dead husbands hanging up in there, does she?" He was startled to see that she didn't take the suggestion as a joke.

Her voice was close to tears as she replied, "I told you, I don't know."

Clayborne spoke up. "So, this isn't the séance room, then?"

Eleanor shook her head. "No. That's on the first floor. Behind the library where you just were."

"And," Clayborne said, "directly below this mysterious locked room. Another," he paused, "sacred space."

Eleanor looked at him sullenly. "I suppose."

"Okay," Cade said. "Take us back downstairs."

They made the trip back to the library in silence so complete Cade could hear the fluttering of the candle flame. When they re-entered the library, Athena Givens was seated in the same chair as when they'd left. Akbar was standing, looking out the window, his arms crossed over his chest.

"So," Givens said, "did you find what you needed to know?"

"No, ma'am," Cade replied. "Not half of it. And if we're going to continue on this job, there's something you need to do."

She smiled indulgently. "And what is that, Mr. Cade?"

"You need to fire your staff," he said. "All of them. Tonight. Send them packing." He pointed at Akbar. "Starting with him."

CHAPTER NINETEEN

Givens looked as if he'd slapped her across the face. "What?"

Cade heard Akbar growl something from across the room that he didn't understand, but the tone made his hand move toward his pistol. He stopped himself and let the hand drop to his side. He kept his eyes on Givens. "Someone tried to kill you. In this house. They tried to stab you in the back. All of your guests at the time were in front of you. You say none of the servants will admit to seeing or hearing anything untoward. Only explanation is that one or more of them is lying, and in the time we'd take puzzling out which one, they could try again. The next time, they may not miss. It's going to be hard enough guarding this house from outside threats with two men. If the threat could be from inside, it turns impossible. So, the only logical thing to do is cut 'em all loose." He nodded toward Akbar. "Startin' with that one."

Akbar snarled something and started toward Cade. Cade stood and reached for his pistol, but before he could draw, Clayborne was on his feet, his own weapon drawn and pointed at the center of the big man's chest. His voice when he spoke was calm, but steely. "You need to take a seat, sir."

Akbar stopped, eyes narrowing. For the first time, he spoke in perfect English. "I will take that gun and shove it up your—"

"GENTLEMEN!" Athena Givens was on her feet, cane thumping against the floorboards. "Stop this foolishness! Akbar, step back. Mr. Clayborne, Mr. Cade. Sit down." Her voice softened. "Please."

There was a long moment of tension, but finally, Akbar stepped back and folded his arms across his chest again, still staring at Clayborne, his eyes as hard as flint. Clayborne took his seat, but he didn't put his pistol back in the holster.

Only Cade and Athena Givens remained standing. Cade's own gun didn't waver. "I'm telling you, ma'am, that this man is not what, or who, he pretends to be."

"You think I don't know that?"

Cade was so startled, he took his eyes off Akbar. "Pardon?"

"I know Akbar is not from Arabia, Mr. Cade. I'm not foolish."

He lowered the pistol. "You do?"

She nodded. "Please, gentlemen, put your guns away. And sit down. Let me explain to you how things are, and how I know Tatanka would never mean me any harm."

Reluctantly, Cade sat back down, holstering his pistol as he did so. "Tatanka?"

She sat as well. "His full name is Tatanka Ptecila." She smiled at him fondly. There was no mistaking the look.

"So," Cade said, "are you two...?" He trailed off.

"We are business partners," Givens replied firmly. "Nothing more."

Cade shook his head. "Sorry, ma'am, but I'm all abroad here."

"Tatanka, like many of his people, has a better connection to the Other Side than most whites, caught up as we are in," her face twisted in distaste, "modern society." She sighed. "But some foolish people would not be guided by an Indian. They would hate and fear him."

Having seen some of the handiwork of the Lakota when they were well and truly pissed off, Cade couldn't really blame them. But when he looked over at Tatanka, the big man looked away. Cade was actually beginning to feel sorry for the poor bastard, cooped up in this madhouse and trotted out like a dancing bear. "And how does Mr. Tatanka feel about all this?"

She picked up her teacup. "Why don't you ask him?"

"I think I am. Ma'am." He hoped the last honorific would distract her from the insolence in his tone.

Tatanka looked back at him, his face still expressionless. He said nothing.

Athena Givens stood up again, using the cane to lever herself upright. Cade and Clayborne stood as well.

"I will leave it to the two of you to discuss arrangements for my security. But for now, I am fatigued and will retire. Tatanka, will you assist me to my quarters?" Her face as she turned to Cade was drawn with pain. "He will rejoin you in a moment, gentlemen." She slowly made her way out of the room, followed by Tatanka, who didn't look back.

Cade sat down again and poured himself another two fingers of the whiskey. "Sure you won't join me, Mr. Clayborne?"

"Actually, I think I will." Clayborne nodded his thanks as he took the glass from Cade and sat back down. "Do you think Mr. Tatanka, or Mr. Akbar, or whoever, will be back, or will he be carrying out his, ah, other duties?"

Cade took a sip and looked at the ceiling. "I don't know, partner." He sighed. "When you were outside, did you see someone skulking around the edges of the property?"

"No. I didn't *exactly* see anyone."

Cade raised an eyebrow. "But?"

Clayborne shook his head. "Could have been the wind. Could have been stray cats. But I think I saw something stir the hedges."

Cade nodded. "Okay."

They drank in silence for a few moments until Clayborne spoke up. "What do you make of our employer's implication that her, ah, business associate will be participating in her security?"

Cade shook his head. "I don't trust the bastard."

"Hmm." Clayborne finished his glass. "I don't blame you at all. Still..." He trailed off.

Cade frowned. "What are you thinking, Sam?"

Clayborne held out his glass again. Cade poured another finger, then another for himself. Clayborne leaned back in his chair and thought for a moment before taking a sip. Then he leaned forward and set his glass on the table. He held up a single finger. "One. In defending a big house like this, more men are better, right? You said so yourself."

Cade nodded, not completely happily. He had said so when he and Clayborne were working out a defense for Marjorie Hamrick's house, shortly after they'd met.

Clayborne raised another finger. "Tatanka, or Akbar, or whatever he calls himself, has a vested interest in Miss Givens's safety. Lover, business partner, whatever, he needs to keep her alive."

Cade pondered that a moment, stroking his chin. "Maybe. Unless he wants to take over..." He stopped. "No. That's foolish."

"Exactly." Clayborne nodded. "He can't run the show himself, because he's supposed to be looming impressively in the background. I'm thinking he can't go back to his people.

He'd be—" Clayborne stopped suddenly as Tatanka re-entered the room.

No one spoke as he strode over and took his seat in the chair where Athena Givens had just been sitting. He crossed his arms across his chest and glared first at Cade, then at Clayborne. He didn't speak.

Cade was the one who finally broke the silence by clearing his throat. "Yeah. Well. Sorry about the misunderstanding there, hoss. But it looks like we're goin' to be workin' together, so—"

Tatanka interrupted. "Are you going to offer me any of that whiskey?" His lip curled. "Or are you afraid of the heap bad Injun getting drunk?"

Cade looked around. "We seem to be short a glass, but if you could scare up another..."

"I think I can manage that," 'Eleanor said. She was holding two short glasses, one in each hand. "And I'd like to join, if I may. Sir."

Cade nodded. "Sure, why not?"

CHAPTER TWENTY

They all took their seats, with the black maid pouring whiskey in each of their glasses before pouring one for herself and taking a seat. *Well*, Cade thought, *damned if this one ain't bold.* She took a sip and looked at him over the rim of the glass before lowering it.

"How long have you been working for Miss Givens?" Cade said.

Her mouth twisted in an ugly grimace. "So, this is where the inquisition begins. Did you bring your thumbscrews and rubber hoses?"

"Easy, Eleanor," Clayborne said in a soothing voice. "We're not going to be beating confessions out of anyone here."

She turned her gaze to him. "Are you sure, Mr. Samuel Clayborne?" She nodded at Cade. "You trust the white man that much?"

Clayborne spoke before Cade could interject. "I trust this one."

"Thanks," Cade murmured. "Back to the question. How long have you been part of this household?"

She drank the rest of her drink and looked away for a

moment before she spoke. "Two years. She found me in St. Louis. I didn't have a penny to my name. I was..." She paused. "I was about to have to shame myself just to put food in my stomach."

There was a brief embarrassed pause, broken when Clayborne spoke up. "Miss Givens rescued you." He turned to Tatanka. "And you, sir? What's your story?"

The Lakota didn't answer, just turned his face away. Only the twitching of the muscle in his jaw betrayed his tension.

Clayborne nodded thoughtfully. "She found all of you at the lowest ebb of your fortunes, and brought you into the fold. I suspect that all of the other servants will have similar tales."

Eleanor nodded. "We would each of us be in our own particular Hell without Miss Givens."

"And therefore," Clayborne said, "totally loyal to her."

Cade downed the rest of his drink. "And yet, someone in this house either tried to kill Miss Givens or let in the person who tried to do it." He slammed the glass down on the table. "Sorry. I'm not buying this." He stood up. "It's late. If I can't toss you out, then everyone needs to get to bed." He looked pointedly at Tatanka. "Including you."

The Lakota stood as well, his eyes defiant. "I don't take orders from you, white man."

Cade nodded. "And that's a problem we're either going to settle tomorrow with Miss Givens, or we won't. Maybe you'll be rid of me, and maybe you won't. But for tonight, we're here, we're looking after the place, and you two are retiring for the evening."

Tatanka continued to glare at him, the tension gathering in the silence like the air before a thunderstorm, until Eleanor stood.

"Yes, sir." She gestured to Tatanka. "Come on." The two of

them left together, Tatanka giving Cade one last murderous look over his shoulder as they exited.

"Well." Clayborne poured himself another two fingers of whiskey and took his seat again. "That went well."

Cade topped off his own drink and sat down as well. "I'm telling you again, partner, my gut is telling me to walk out of this madhouse and never look back."

Clayborne smiled and looked down into his drink.

"What?" Cade demanded.

"Nothing." Clayborne took another sip.

Cade was getting annoyed. "You got something amusing to share, Sam, let's have it."

Clayborne set his drink down, still with that slight smile that was beginning to nettle Cade. "I just couldn't help but be amused at the look on your face when Miss Eleanor spoke to you. You're not used to a black girl speaking to you like that."

Cade frowned. "I'm used to bein' spoken to in a lot of ways. Her color don't signify."

"I'm sure."

Cade felt the blood rushing to his face. "What the hell's that supposed to mean?"

The smile left Clayborne's face. He sighed and looked away for a moment before speaking. "Levi." He paused, then looked at Cade. "In our short acquaintance, we've been through a lot together. Fought alongside one another. Saved one another's lives. I tell you in all sincerity, Leviticus Cade, I trust you more that I have ever trusted any white man."

Cade blinked in surprise, his rising anger shunted aside. He picked up his glass and drained it. "Thanks. Again."

Clayborne went on as if he hadn't spoken. "But I also tell you in all sincerity, Levi, that there are things about living in this skin that you will never understand."

Cade shook his head, perplexed. "Well? I'm listenin'."

"I know. Still." Clayborne looked around the room. "You find this house strange, enigmatic, frustrating. I do, too. But I kind of like it. It intrigues me. It seems...different. More free."

Cade grunted sourly. "I think you also have a liking for Miss Eleanor."

Clayborne chuckled. "I won't deny she is part of the appeal. But I also seem to recall you sticking with the job as bodyguard for the Hamrick household because you were intrigued by the lady of the house."

That made Cade laugh. "You got me there." He sighed. "Okay. We'll stick. But I'm not working with that big Indian bastard."

Clayborne looked amused. "Oh? And why is that, Mr. Cade?"

Cade looked at him in amazement. "Because he's a prickly, arrogant son of a bitch."

"Hmm." Clayborne looked thoughtful. "I seem to remember a time when you held the same opinion of me."

Cade shook his head again and laughed. "Mr. Clayborne, I concede. You have outplayed me at every turn. You win." He looked at the last couple of inches of whiskey in the decanter and decided against another drink. "I reckon we need to make a plan for guarding this place for the rest of the evening." He smiled at Clayborne. "One of us should patrol inside, until we make sure of the servants. One should stay outside, to make sure no one comes over that wall. Maybe you'd like to take the interior patrol. In case Miss Eleanor wants to, ah, discuss the household situation."

Clayborne shook his head. "Thank you, Mr. Cade, but no. I think I should take the outside patrol and you the inside."

Cade's brow furrowed. "Really? And why is that?"

Clayborne tossed back the last of his own drink and regarded Cade with a sardonic grin. "Because if Eleanor were to approach me, it would most likely be out of sincere attraction for my manly charms. If she were to come to you offering her favors, we will know for sure that it was part of some devious scheme."

Cade started to nod, then caught himself. "Hey, wait a minute."

Clayborne laughed at the expression on Cade's face. "You know I'm right."

Cade grimaced. "Yeah. Probably." Then he laughed as well. "I'll also note that it is you who has the devious and a twisted mind."

The smile fell from Clayborne's face. "That's called careful planning, Levi. And that is also what it takes to live in this skin."

CHAPTER TWENTY-ONE

Cade had thought that his years of long nights and sentry duty would have him accustomed to walking guard late at night. But, he had to confess to himself, in those days, he hadn't had several shots of whiskey before taking his post. Most of the time.

After Clayborne had gone out to patrol the grounds, Cade decided the only way to keep awake was to keep moving. He prowled the hallways of the big house, walking as quietly as a big man in boots could manage. The house was as silent as a tomb, save for the creak of his footsteps. He walked down the hallway past the library, testing doors until he found one locked. That had to be the séance room he'd been barred from. He looked up at the ceiling. Unless he missed his guess, the room above was the second-floor room that Eleanor seemed so nervous about.

Cade looked around at the dark wood and expensive carpets and wondered, not for the first time, where the money for this mansion had come from. There seemed to be no Mr. Givens in the picture. Had to be more money in this talking to the spirits thing than he thought. Or maybe it was the suffragists who were financing her. Some of the women he'd seen in the crowd seemed well off, but by no means all. And, he recalled, the elegantly dressed and those in shabbier clothing seemed to mix and mingle without difficulty. *This place seems different,* Clayborne had said. *More free.*

Cade was beginning to see the attraction. But, he reflected, it took money to live freely. Clayborne had said that the West was where a man could come to raise his station in life. But as near as Cade could figure, that took money. And lots of it.

He thought back to the reason he'd left Michigan after coming home from the war. He thought about the girl with golden hair who he'd thought about every day of the long brutal slog, through battle after battle, long nights in camp, and cold, wet, seemingly endless marches on horseback. He'd thought that maybe coming home a hero of the war to preserve the Union might make him good enough in her well-off family's eyes, to wipe out his hardscrabble upbringing. The sting of her father's horsewhip across his back and the sound of her voice pleading, *Just leave, Levi, just go,* had disabused him of that notion. He'd ridden West that night and never looked back. After a few years of wandering, he'd fetched up here, in a place where a man—or a woman—might become respectable. But he saw more clearly than ever now, that took gold.

He found Clayborne in the garden, pacing slowly along the gravel paths, his gaze constantly moving. He nodded his approval. The man walked sentry better than most of the recruits he'd had to deal with. He stood well back and called out softly. "Sam."

Clayborne stopped dead, his right hand going to the pistol inside his coat. He turned slowly, drawing with deliberation. "Cade?"

"Yeah." He chuckled. "Guess we should have worked out passwords."

"Maybe." Clayborne holstered his pistol. "That may be a shade more military than I'd like to get. At least for the moment."

"Well, anyway. Now that it's just you and me, maybe we can talk plain."

Clayborne shook his head, then gave a short laugh. "Maybe."

"Seems to me our Miss Givens has a particular skill for keeping you rattled."

Clayborne nodded. "But it seemed as if...Cade, it seemed as if she knew things. About my past."

"Fire and rope?" Cade said. "You probably know this better than I do, partner, and you know me enough, I hope, to know I mean no disrespect, but talkin' to a man of your complexion about fire and rope is more than likely to strike a chord."

"Yes. I know that, Levi." He looked up, longing in his eyes. "But she knew about my sister."

Cade sighed and shook his head. "She threw that out there. Maybe you had a brother, maybe you had a sister, she had an even chance that she'd sink the hook."

Clayborne grimaced. "I know this," he said in a tight voice. "I know all of it. You do me no favor by reminding me."

Cade's voice grew gentle. "I know you're pinin' to see or hear from your kin again. Most people are."

Clayborne looked at him curiously. "But not you."

Cade shrugged. "That's another story."

"Indeed. And I've never truly told you mine."

"Some other time, maybe. Right now, we need to figure out how we deal with an employer who won't play straight with us."

"Other than just packing up and leaving."

Cade nodded. "Whatever Miss Givens's faults, they don't support knifin' her in the back. We took this job, and I intend to see it through."

"How?"

"I don't know," Cade confessed. "I'm figuring this out minute to minute. Like always."

"Hmm," Clayborne said. "And how's that working?"

Cade smiled and spread his arms out. "Still standing, ain't I?"

Clayborne shook his head. "Why does this not fill me with confidence?"

Cade laughed. "Go on back in. I'll take outside duty for a while." He looked back at the darkened house. "Looks like everyone's bedded down. Go ahead and grab some sleep if you like. I'll cover the grounds."

"Are you sure?"

"Yeah. Get your head down. You can spell me in a couple of hours."

"Okay."

Clayborne headed back to the house. Once inside, he made his way back to the sitting room. All of the cups and glassware had been cleared away, the gas lamps lit. The last embers of the fire glowed red at the side of the room. The moon was rising outside, and a few cold white beams provided Clayborne with enough illumination to navigate in the dimness. He set his hat on a chair, took off his coat, and settled himself on the couch. It wasn't quite long enough for him to stretch out fully, but he could curl up a bit and be reasonably comfortable. He removed his pistol and shoulder holster, set them on the floor beneath the couch, and laid down gingerly. A second thought made him sit back up and remove his boots. He wasn't sure how Miss Givens would react to him napping on her fancy couch, but he was pretty sure she'd make strong objections to his boots on the fine fabric. In a few moments, he was asleep.

He wasn't sure exactly what it was that awakened him. It may have been the noise, or perhaps the cold draft that washed over him and raised goose bumps on his skin. All he knew at first as he opened his eyes was that the room was suddenly brighter, and there was a chill breeze coming from somewhere. He blinked the sleep from his eyes and sat up, instinctively groping for the gun he'd stowed beneath the couch. "Miss Givens?" he croaked, his voice rusty from sleep. "Eleanor?"

The figure that stood before him was unmistakably female, dressed in a long, flowing white dress. No, not white, he realized. It was glowing, as if lit from within. He couldn't see the woman's face. It was shining even brighter, the lambent radiance obscuring any features. Clayborne had fumbled his pistol out of the holster on the floor, but now he let it drop to his side. *One of the woman's tricks*, he told himself, trying to stop his legs from trembling. *Just a trick.*

Then the figure spoke to him. "Samuel," it said. "Samuel."

The voice was thick and breaking with sorrow, but it was one he knew as well as his own, one he heard now only in his dreams. "Mama?"

CHAPTER TWENTY-TWO

"Samuel," the voice said again, and now the tone grew sharper, accusatory. "Why'd you leave us, Samuel? Why'd you run away?"

Clayborne felt a jolt go through him, a feeling like being struck by freezing lightning. "Mama!" This time he was shouting. "Mama, no! I din't." The years he'd spent cultivating his speech fell away and he spoke in the accent of his childhood. "I din't, Mama!"

"Liar," the voice hissed. "We needed you. You *left*! You *ran*!"

"MAMA!" He collapsed backward onto the couch, tears streaming down his face. He kept trying to tell himself it was all a trick, a carnival show. But that voice. It was her voice. And she was speaking truth, ripping away the facade he'd built so carefully over the years. He was a coward. He'd run. He'd left them. He felt the heft of the pistol in his hand. *I don't deserve to be here*, he thought. *Not when they're dead*. He stared at the gun, working up the courage to raise it to his own head.

"SAM!" A voice cut through the terror and self-loathing. Not his mother's voice this time. It was Cade.

He stood there in the doorway of the sitting room, his own gun drawn, his eyes darting, searching for enemies. The white figure was gone, as if it had never been there. Cade locked eyes with Clayborne. "Sam," he said, softer now as he saw his friend's distress. "Another bad dream?"

Clayborne took a deep, shuddering breath and shook his head. "No. Not this time. She was here, Levi. As real as you or me."

Cade looked puzzled. "Who?"

"My mother." He raised a hand at Cade's skeptical look. "I know what you think. But she knew things, Cade. And it was her voice, I swear it."

A figure was approaching from the hallway, preceded by the soft glow of a candle. "What's happening?" Athena Givens demanded. "What's all the shouting I heard?"

Cade stood aside as she entered the room. His face grew cold. "Miss Givens," he said stiffly. "I don't know if what just happened to my partner here was intended as some sort of joke, or if you're trying to throw some kind of hoodoo on us. But I tell you, I'm not going to have it."

She shook her head. "I have no idea what you mean." She looked at Clayborne on the sofa and her eyes widened. "Have you had a visitation, Mr. Clayborne?"

Clayborne nodded weakly.

She clapped her hands together. "But this is wonderful, Mr. Clayborne! You must tell me all about it!"

Clayborne looked away. "I saw my mother."

"You saw some kind of magical trick," Cade said. "Come on, Mr. Clayborne. We don't need to put up with this bullshit."

Once again, Givens spoke as if Cade wasn't there, as if he himself were a ghost. "And did she tell you all was well?"

Clayborne shook his head. "She was angry. At me."

"Oh dear." Givens's brows drew together. "That's not

good." She crossed over and sat next to him, putting a reassuring hand on his forearm. "An angry spirit can create all manner of trouble. We need to find out what's troubling your mother, and do what we can to make sure she finds rest. Why was she angry at you?"

Clayborne looked at the floor. "I can't say."

She leaned forward, her voice soft but insistent. "You must."

"No." Cade crossed the room to stand over them. "He doesn't have to talk about it if he doesn't want to." He held out a hand. "Come on, partner. We're leaving."

Givens looked up at him, arching a brow curiously. "And how do you propose getting back home, Mr. Cade? It was my carriage that brought you here."

That stopped Cade for a moment. He clenched his jaw. "We'll walk if we have to."

"Levi." Clayborne spoke up, but he didn't raise his eyes. "It's okay. I'm okay."

"We're done with this place," Cade insisted.

Clayborne looked up at him. "No."

Cade stepped back. "What do you mean, no?"

Athena Givens stood up. "I will leave you two gentlemen alone to discuss how you intend to proceed." She had a smile on her face that Cade didn't like a bit, as if she'd already won the contest. She seemed to glide out of the room, not looking back.

Cade took a deep breath. "Okay," he said.

Before he could go on, Clayborne broke in, his voice low and bitter. "I suppose you think I'm just another superstitious darkie, afraid of the haints."

"I think there's something here you want to believe. Real bad. So bad it overtook your reason." He sat down in the chair across from Claiborne. "Somethin' happened with your mother. Givens is trying to use that to hornswoggle you. Why, I don't know. Maybe to get you on her side." He leaned forward. "You once told me I wasn't ready for the story of what happened to your family. Well, am I ready now? Or can you afford to wait until I am?"

Clayborne smiled ruefully. "It wasn't that you weren't ready, Levi. It's that I wasn't ready to trust any white man. Not even you." He grimaced. "Maybe especially you." He raised a hand at Cade's expression. "Not because of who you are. Because of who you used to be."

"A soldier."

"A Union soldier."

Cade started to say something, then thought better of it. "I am, as usual, completely confuzzled."

Clayborne sighed. "I know. Deep down inside, Levi, you, and other white men, feel like we Negroes should be grateful to you. For setting us free."

"I never said—"

"I know. But tell me you've never thought it."

Cade didn't answer.

Clayborne smiled sadly. "Thanks for not trying to deny it."

"Okay," Cade said. "So, tell me your story."

CHAPTER TWENTY-THREE

"My family lived in Georgia," Clayborne began. "On one of the plantations. Not so big as some, but the people who owned it were well-off enough to own at least one family. It was me, my father and mother, and my little sister."

"Were you...?" Cade began, then he stopped as Clayborne looked at him with dead eyes.

He shook his head. "You want to know what they all want to know. Were we beaten? Whipped? Were members of my family sold off?" His face twisted. "Were my mother and sister used by the white master?" He shook his head. "No. But we knew that could happen. Any time. Any time we gave them an excuse. Or for no reason at all. That's what it means to be a slave, Mr. Cade. To always live in fear."

"But that ended."

"Oh, it ended. It surely did." He was silent for a moment, then spoke again. "Soldiers in blue came to the farm. Outriders from Sherman's army. The master and his wife fled. We whooped and sang and danced. We praised God and Mr. Lincoln. The day of Jubilee had come."

Cade felt a chill crawling up his back from the look on Clayborne's face. He almost didn't want to ask. But he did. "What happened then?"

"They took everything that wasn't nailed down, then they took whatever they could pry up. All the corn. Everything from the cellars. They tore the paneling from the walls to make sure there was no silver or gold hidden inside. They slaughtered the cows and butchered them in the yard. The pigs, too. They used the wood they'd taken from the house for fires to smoke the meat. Then they burned what was left of the house to the ground. But we still were happy. We knew, when they moved on, we'd go with them."

Cade shook his head. "They wouldn't. Not cavalry. We... they...had to keep moving."

"As we found out. When they started to ride off, my father begged them. We had no food, no place to go. He held on to the leader's reins and begged. With tears in his eyes, he begged." The anger had crept back into Samuel's voice. He stopped, took a deep breath, then began again in that same dead voice. "When they'd left, we started to look around. To find what morsels of food might be left. There was nothing. We walked down the road, looking to see if there was anything. Everything was burned. Ruined. There was nothing left. By the third day, we were eating grass. Like animals." He paused. "Then a group of Confederates found us."

"Ah, hell," Cade whispered.

For the first time in his recitation, Clayborne looked him in the eye. "Hell doesn't begin to describe it. They were deserters. The worst scum you can imagine. They accused us of collaborating with the enemy. They tied my mother and sister and me up and made us watch while they hanged my father. Not quickly. They hauled him up slowly and let him dangle till he was almost dead. Then they'd cut him down and start over.

When that wasn't enough for him, they built a fire. Underneath him. They roasted him alive."

"But you got away."

"Yes. Yes, I did, Mr. Cade. While those animals were torturing my father to death, over what felt like years, I found a jagged rock embedded in the ground. I worked my bonds against that rough edge until they broke. Then I ran."

"You..." Cade stopped again.

"Yes, Mr. Cade. I left my mother and sister behind."

Cade let that go. "How did you live?"

Clayborne's voice was flat, without emotion. "Like an animal, Mr. Cade. I hid out in the woods. I stole food. Sometimes, kind families tried to help me." He grimaced. "All of those families were black, of course. But none of them could afford to feed me for long. So, I kept running. Until I came to New Orleans." He paused. "I fetched up half dead on the steps of a convent. The Catholic Sisters took me in." He grimaced. "They taught me to cook and clean and take care of a household, so I could have a trade. They also taught me to read. I think they had a notion that I could be their missionary to my race." He looked bleakly at Cade. "But any idea I ever had that a benevolent God existed died in me the day I heard my father screaming. When I smelled his flesh burning."

"How old were you?"

Clayborne shook his head. "I have no firm idea. I don't even really know how old I am now. We were slaves, Levi. Any records of our birth were in the property records of the house that had just burned down. But I was old enough to have at least tried to save my family."

"No," Cade said firmly. "They were just waitin' to do you the same way. Probably worse. You had no choice."

"Of course I had a choice. But all of them were bad." He wiped at his eyes with the back of his hand. "Sometimes...often, really...I think about what must have happened to my mother and sister. In my most hopeful fantasies, they were killed quickly. But I don't have any real faith that that's what happened." He sighed. "So now you know. I'm a coward."

"Bullshit." Cade's voice was so vehement that Clayborne looked up, startled. "I've seen you fight, Sam. I saw you take on a crowd of those fucking hoodlums that were trying to burn us alive. You stood up then, Sam. You took a damn bullet fighting next to me. You ain't yellow, not by a long stretch. And for what it's worth, I'm sorry about what happened to you when you were just a kid."

Clayborne looked at him and shook his head in wonder. "I think you actually mean that."

"Of course I mean it. That's something that shouldn't have ever happened to anyone. And now I understand why you ain't exactly brimming over with gratitude toward the US Army. But damn it, that wasn't me. I didn't have a goddamn thing to do with that."

"Are you honestly saying that you would have treated us differently? That you would have helped my family? That you would have sheltered us from those...from those—?"

Cade looked away. "I was just a corporal. I wasn't in command. I like to think I would have spoken up. But in the end...I would have done what I was told. I won't lie."

Clayborne's face held a grim, joyless satisfaction. "At least you remain honest."

"Yeah. I can't say honesty has always been a help to me. At least now I know why you're so damn angry."

Clayborne chuckled. "Oh, Mr. Cade, when it comes to why I'm angry, that is only the beginning of the list." He sighed. "Sometimes, Levi, I'm going to take that anger out on you. It may not be fair, but it's the way things are."

Cade nodded. "I get it a little better now. But I hope you don't expect me to like it."

"No. I don't."

"Okay, then. Now that we understand each other better, how are we going to get this job done," he smiled, "partner?"

Clayborne looked up. The sky was beginning to lighten in the east."It's getting on toward morning. And if I recall correctly, you have an appointment with Mr. Kwan's lawyer early on."

Cade grimaced. "Not looking forward to that."

"No doubt. But..." Clayborne trailed off, looking thoughtful.

"Sam," Cade said, "what are you thinking?"

"The tongs, as we've seen, have certain resources."

"I know," Cade said. "That's what worries me."

"I know. But perhaps some mutually agreeable—"

"Damn it, Sam," Cade broke in, "the point here is to stay out of debt to the Chinese, not get further into it." He sighed. "While I'm at my meeting, there's something you need to do."

"Which is?"

"We need to find someone who can translate French for us. So we can talk to that little French girl, away from that chef. And we need someone who can get us into that locked room."

Clayborne frowned. "How am I supposed to find either of those...?" He stopped. "Ah."

Cade nodded. "Our old friend Mr. Simonson said he could find us more than just these fancy duds. I get the impression he can find a fellow just about anything he needs in this town. On one side of the law or the other."

"I suppose," Clayborne said. "I'll see if Mr. Simonson has what or who we need in his inventory. And good luck with your meeting."

Cade looked around. "Not sure how I'm supposed to get there, actually. I'm not sure I want to wake up the driver. He doesn't seem all that damn reliable even when he isn't sleeping off a drunk." He shook his head. "Frankly, I'm baffled as to why she keeps him on."

"Hmmm," Clayborne said. "Let's find the stable. Maybe we can find you a horse." He smiled at Cade. "Would being back in the saddle help improve your mood, Corporal Cade?"

CHAPTER TWENTY-FOUR

The stables were attached to the house, a long wing stretching away from one side. It was a two-story wooden building, with the only windows on the second floor. There were a few wide doors opening onto a packed-dirt yard in front of the building, and a regular-sized door at the far right.

Clayborne stood back for a moment, observing the building, then advanced and pounded on the door. "Open up!" he called out. "Hey! Open up!"

After a moment, a flickering light appeared in an upstairs window, then disappeared. Clayborne stood patiently before the door until it opened. A boy's face poked out from behind the partially opened door. He was black and looked no more than twelve. "Yeah?" he said. "Whatchoo want?" He looked past Clayborne to where Cade was standing. "Yes, suh?" he amended at the sight of a white man.

"My partner needs a horse," Clayborne said. "A good one."

The boy blinked at Cade. "Your...partner?"

"Do I stutter, young man?" Clayborne demanded. He

cocked his head. "Unless I miss my guess, you would be Jephthah."

The boy looked as if he was about to faint. "Yes, sir."

"So," Clayborne spoke with elaborate patience, "we know who you are. Do you know who we are?"

Jephthah nodded. "You're the ones Miss Givens brought in." He swallowed nervously. "To keep someone from doin' her in."

"Just so." Clayborne nodded. "And I assume she told you to do what it takes to aid us in our inquiries?"

The boy looked miserable. "She din't tell me nothin', sir. All her conversations were with Mr. George." He looked back at the second story of the stable building, clearly dreading what came next.

"Ah," Clayborne said. "Well, young man, perhaps you should fetch Mr. George."

The boy looked apprehensive. "Beggin' your pardon, suh, I believe Mr. George is sleepin'."

"Then wake him up," Clayborne said, his voice mild. He looked up at the sky. "Judging from the hour, I imagine he's almost ready to get up anyway."

The boy was still hesitant, and this time, Clayborne's voice snapped like a whip. "GO!"

With a squeak of alarm, the boy disappeared behind the door.

Cade looked at his partner and raised an eyebrow. "Is he coming back?"

"He'll be back," Clayborne said.

Sure enough, Jephthah returned, in the company of another black man. This one was much older, with a dark beard shot through with streaks of gray and red-rimmed eyes that glared harshly at Clayborne. His voice, when he spoke, was deep, gravelly, and thoroughly pissed off. "What the hell do you people want?" he growled.

Clayborne touched the brim of his hat respectfully. "Thank you for seeing us so early, sir." He inclined his head toward where Cade stood. "My partner here requires a mount."

Cade likewise touched the brim of his Stetson. He'd dealt with enough stable masters to know that they were a touchy breed, fiercely protective of their charges. "Good morning, sir. You would be Mr. George?"

"I am." He looked sour. "Suh."

Clayborne spoke up. "Mr. George, we've recently taken employment in the household. To try to figure out who might have assaulted Miss Givens."

The old man's face lost all expression. "I din't have nothin' to do with that." He jerked his chin back toward the stable. "Jephthah'll confirm. We was here the whole time."

"You're not a suspect," Cade said. *Not yet*, he added to himself. "But I need to get to an appointment."

"And Mr. Clinton appears to be...indisposed."

"Drunk, you mean," George snorted. He looked at Cade. "You want a horse, do you? That Akbar fellow approved this?"

"Actually," Clayborne said, "I think the loan of a horse might annoy Mr. Akbar."

Cade looked at him with amazement, but when he looked back at George, the old stablemaster's face was nearly glowing. "Well, hell, boy," he growled at Clayborne, "why didn't you say so?"

Chiang Kam and his father Liang had arrived at the Givens mansion at dawn, as usual, starting the long walk from

Chinatown well before the sunrise. It was an arduous commute, but the pay they made working for Athena Givens was better than anything they could have hoped for in Chinatown, and Kam enjoyed the work. Making things grow had always brought him pleasure, and he thought his father felt the same way, although the old man was so silent most of the time, it was hard to tell.

They went first to the garden shed at the back of the property, where the flats of asters they were to be planting today waited for them to be transplanted to their beds along the driveway. Kam had come up with the idea, his imagination stimulated by the idea of the riot of colors that would greet arriving guests.

"Please check the flowers, Father," he asked, putting the proper amount of respect into the request. "I'll make sure the beds are ready."

The old man grunted his assent and trudged into the shed.

Kam sighed. He knew his father hated the idea of taking orders from his son, no matter how respectfully phrased. Truth be told, Kam felt a bit uncomfortable with it himself. But Chiang Liang had been born and raised a fisherman, with no more sense of design than the fish he'd caught. It was Kam's designs that pleased the lady of the house, and pleasing that lady was what kept food on the table in the Chiang family's household. Kam headed through the immaculately tended gardens.

"Hey," a sharp voice greeted him. "Boy."

Kam stopped. The voice was Chinese, unmistakably female. It was odd enough to hear a woman's voice in this city speaking Chinese, at least one that wasn't trying to tempt men into an opium den or a brothel. But this voice didn't have any such wheedling quality. It was a strong, peremptory tone, and it got Kam's back up. He turned.

The woman was sitting cross-legged on one of the benches

along the garden path. The first thing that struck Kam was the exquisite beauty of her face. As she unfolded her legs from her seat and stood up, the second thing Kam noticed was the grace and power in her movements. She looked at him without expression. "Do you know who I am?"

Kam shook his head. "No. Should I? And what are you doing here?"

The woman inclined her head gravely, her eyes amused. "You have never heard of The White Orchid?"

He snorted. "The White Orchid is a myth. A folk tale. Something the Green Dragon uses to—" Before he could finish the sentence, he was on his back. The woman was straddling his chest, holding the point of a dagger directly beneath his chin. Kam's head was spinning. It was impossible for anyone to move so fast. She had closed the gap, swept his legs from beneath him, and pinned him down before he had time to even register what was happening.

"Welcome to the myth, handsome boy," the woman crooned to him.

"Please," Kam said, his voice a strangled croak. "I don't have any money."

"I'm not after money, handsome but insolent boy," the woman said. "What I want is—"

She was interrupted by a keening cry from the edge of the garden. "Aiiii...."

The woman turned her head, then the weight on Kam's chest was gone. He sat up, slowly.

His father was standing in the garden path, eyes wide with fear. The woman was standing a few feet away, the dagger held in one hand, her eyes moving back and forth between the two men. Liang dropped to his knees and knocked his forehead against the ground. "Please, Honored Lady," he whined. "Please don't hurt my son. He is just a boy."

The woman looked over at Kam. "He lacks manners."

"Please," Liang said. "He is all I have in this world."

Kam got to his knees, then slowly to his feet, his hands outstretched to show he was no threat. He hated seeing his father humble himself like this, to a woman, no less, but he was stunned to hear his normally cold and distant father express himself with such anguish. He stole a glance at the woman.

"Well," she said, "at least someone recognizes me." She started toward the old man.

"No," Kam said.

The woman stopped and turned to him. "No?"

"Leave him alone," Kam said.

She smiled coldly at him. "I'm not going to hurt him, handsome boy. I'm going to show you both the value of respect." But she didn't come any closer. Instead, she turned to Liang and bowed. "Please rise, Honored Sir."

The old man began to get to his feet, slowly and painfully.

"May I help him?" Kam said.

The woman nodded. "Of course."

Kam rushed to his father's side and helped him up. He turned to The White Orchid. "What are you here for?" He hesitated. "Honored Lady."

"Information," she answered. "Tell me about the white devil Cade. And the black white devil with him. Why are they here?"

CHAPTER TWENTY-FIVE

Clayborne had been right. Being back in the saddle had done wonders to settle Cade's mind. He steered the magnificent Arabian the stablemaster had lent him through the streets of San Francisco in the dawn. Clayborne's insinuation that the loan of a horse might irritate Akbar had been the key that unlocked the doors to the stable. Apparently, Miss Givens's favored companion wasn't popular among the other servants. In fact, the entire household seemed to be at war with itself.

The black mare, whose name was Midnight, had shied and pulled away when Cade had first attempted to saddle her, but when he firmly caressed her neck and murmured soothingly to her, she'd quieted. When he'd swung himself up into the saddle, she seemed to accept who was the boss. Soon, it was as if they'd been matched for life.

This early in the day, the thoroughfares were mostly deserted, but a few shopkeepers and tavern owners were out, cleaning the sidewalks and looking up to stare at the figure trotting through the streets. Cade had originally intended to head home before realizing he had no facilities at his shop to care for the black mare. There was only one other place he knew with stables on the grounds, and that was a place he'd been yearning to go anyway. He steered the horse toward the Hamrick mansion.

When he arrived at the gated walkway that led to the house, however, he hesitated. He had no invitation, he wasn't expected, and the stables were in the back, behind another set of gates. He dismounted and led the mare over to the low fence in front of the property. He looped the reins over the iron railing and tied them off as best he could.

"Stay here, girl," he murmured.

The mare dipped her head and peered with dark and rolling eyes up at the house on the hill. She pawed at the sidewalk, but stayed quiet.

Cade opened the gate and walked up the steps to the front door. He hesitated for a moment, then knocked. There was no response at first. He looked back down to where the black mare waited patiently. He heard the door open behind him and turned to see the diminutive figure of Marjorie's cook Bridget standing in the doorway. She regarded him with a sour expression on her pinched, narrow face. "So," she said, "ye finally show yer face around here."

Cade couldn't help but chuckle. "Thanks so much for the warm welcome, Miss Bridget."

"Hmph." Bridget turned away, then turned back. "Ye might as well come in. Breakfast will be on the table in a few minutes." She sighed, as if greatly put upon. "It's only oatmeal, so I suppose I can make it stretch." She looked over Cade's shoulder. "Will Mr. Clayborne be joining us?" She tried to keep the hope out of her voice and failed.

"Sorry, ma'am," Cade said. "He's on other business. But I'll convey your regards, if you wish."

Bridget stiffened. "What ye convey to Mr. Clayborne is yer own business."

"Yes, ma'am." Cade looked back down to the street. "I'd like to put my horse up in the stable. If I may."

Bridget craned her neck to look past Cade and down to the street. The black mare stood patiently, lashed to the fence. Bridget's eyes brightened and she gave a low whistle. "That's a beauty, that one."

"She is. And she's on loan, so I need to see that she's cared for."

Bridget nodded decisively, her usual prickliness gone. "Surely." She looked soberly at Cade and bit her lip before going on. "I hate to say it, Mr. Cade, but we are in what you might call reduced circumstances. We've got neither groom nor stableboy. But I can let you in the back, and you can feed and water that pretty girl with what we have left."

"That'd be fine, Bridget."

Cade had been in Hamrick's stables before, and was startled to find them empty of both horses and vehicles. There was some hay there that was not too old, a bucket and pump, and a brush. He poured the black mare some water, which she bent to drink as he brushed her down. After a few minutes, he looked up to see Bridget standing in the doorway. "Breakfast is on the table." She hesitated. "And Mrs. Hamrick is expecting you."

Cade looked at the black mare, serenely gnawing on the hay he'd put out for her. He continued brushing. "I'll be in in a bit."

Bridget stepped forward. "I'd be glad to look after her, if you like, Mr. Cade."

Cade was taken aback. "Truly?"

Bridget nodded. "I grew up around horses."

"In Ireland?" Cade ventured.

She nodded. "I miss it."

Cade handed her the brush. Everyone, it seemed, had a story to tell here. "I'll be inside. Her name is Midnight."

"Midnight," Bridget murmured, caressing the horse's neck.

The mare looked at her, then went back to eating.

Marjorie sat at one end of the high table in the kitchen, her daughter Violet seated on a stool next to her. Marjorie slid off the high-backed chair as Cade entered the kitchen through its side door. "Mr. Cade." He couldn't tell if she was pleased.

He doffed his hat. "Mrs. Hamrick." He nodded to Violet. "Hey there, Little Bit."

Violet regarded him with a regal hauteur. "Our name is Violet, not Little Bit."

Marjorie leaned over and whispered to Cade. "She's been reading about Queen Victoria. She's a bit fixated on nobility. She enjoys the royal we."

"Ah." Cade bowed more deeply to Violet. "Your pardon, Lady Violet."

The girl nodded condescendingly and returned to her breakfast.

"Please, Mr. Cade," Marjorie said. "Join us." She looked around. "I can't imagine where Bridget has gone."

"She's tending to my horse, ma'am. In the stable."

Marjorie looked away. "She has always been one to appreciate horses. She and Samuel used to…" She broke off. "I apologize for our lack of hospitality."

"No apologies necessary, ma'am," Cade said. He looked at the silver bowls. When last he'd eaten there, they'd been filled with scrambled eggs and fat, glistening sausages. Now, there was only a thick oatmeal. "With your permission, I'll serve myself."

"Of course."

"Mama." Violet slid down from her high stool as Cade secured a plate from the sideboard and spooned a last helping of oatmeal onto it. "We wish to review our troops. They are awaiting our inspection in the playroom."

"Then by all means," Marjorie said gravely, "you must go. Can't keep the troops waiting."

Violet nodded and swept out of the room like the noblewoman she played at being.

Marjorie watched her go, then turned her attention back to her plate.

They ate silently for a few moments, then Cade put his spoon down. "I'm sorry if I came at a bad time."

She looked up, eyes widening in surprise. "Oh, no," she said, brushing a stray ringlet of hair away from her face. "I'm glad you're here. Truly." She took a deep, shuddering breath, then smiled wanly. "Truth be told, seeing your face is something I didn't know I needed as badly as I do."

He got up and strode over to her. He put an arm around her shoulder. "I needed to see you, too."

She leaned her head against his chest. "I wish..." Her voice trailed off.

"What?"

She shook her head. "Nothing."

"Tell me."

She looked up at him. "I wish I'd met you first. Instead of John."

He smiled down at her. "You wouldn't have given me a second glance. An ex-soldier, no prospects, barely a dime to his name."

She leaned against him again. "You think so little of me?" she murmured.

"We were different people then, honey lamb. We found each other at the right time."

She wrapped her hand around his waist and squeezed. "Maybe you're right."

He went on. "And the right place." He looked around, but his thoughts were beyond the walls of the Hamrick mansion. "When I first got here, I thought this city was a madhouse. And it may be. But maybe that's a good thing. Here, people can be something different. Different than where they started." He chuckled. "I mean, look at Samuel. When I met him, he was driving a carriage for your husband. Now, he's a man of business."

"As are you."

"Yeah." He kissed the top of her head. "I met a fellow, a friend of your friend Athena. A Lakota brave, if ever there was one. But he's living with her and passing himself off as some kinda Arab mystic. If that don't tell you something about this place..."

She pulled away slightly and wiped her eyes with the back of her hand. He was surprised to see she'd been crying. "What it tells me is that nothing here is as it seems. That everyone is hidden behind walls of artifice. Even me." She laughed, low and bitter. "Maybe especially me." She looked at him, her eyes red-rimmed with tears. "I'm about to lose the house, Levi. I don't have the money coming in to pay for it." She looked away. "I may have to accept the offer from the Chinese."

Cade felt sick to his stomach. "You financed my business. Me and Sam. Is that why...?"

"No, no, Levi," she said. "That's not it at all."

"I can give you the money back." In truth, he wasn't sure how he was going to do that. He'd sunk a lot into the place already, and it had yet to turn a profit.

She smiled sadly. "I love you for saying that. But I know you don't have it. Not yet. But it's not your fault. And I have faith that you'll pay me back." She sighed. "When I helped you open the business, I was in good shape. Or thought I was. But the business is changing, Levi. The clippers, lovely as they are, can't compete with steamships. And the canal in Suez is changing everything. I need money to keep up with the changes, and no one will lend to me because I'm a woman." She laughed bitterly. "Except the Celestials."

He drew her back to him. "I'm on my way to talk to Kwan's lawyer. I won't let him get you into something you can't live with." He kissed her hair again.

She hugged him, then looked at him sadly. "My knight on horseback. But you can't fight or shoot your way out of this, Levi."

He was about to answer when Bridget re-entered the kitchen. Cade was startled to see that she was smiling as he'd never seen her smile before. "Your horse is fed and ready, Mr. Cade," she said. "Thank you for letting me care for her."

Cade nodded, barely able to contain his surprise. "You're welcome, Bridget."

She looked back over her shoulder at the stables. "Pure-blooded Arabian," she said. "Haven't seen one of those in...well, a long time." She shook herself out of her reverie and resumed her accustomed demeanor. "Is there anything ye need?"

Cade and Marjorie looked at each other. It was Marjorie who spoke. "No, Bridget. That will be all for the moment." The maid nodded and left the room.

"See?" Cade said. "You can even find something in this town to make Bridget smile. Anything is possible."

Marjorie had to laugh at that. "Go on with you, then. And good luck."

CHAPTER TWENTY-SIX

"So," The White Orchid said, "someone has tried to kill the lady of the house."

Kam nodded. "A few nights ago."

"And who would have a reason to try to do such a thing?"

This time it was the father, Liang, who spoke. "Some say it is because she tries to involve herself in the white people's politics." He shook his head uncomprehendingly. "Why would a woman want to do that?"

"Why indeed?" The White Orchid looked thoughtful for a moment, then stood up. "Keep your eyes and ears open. I may be back. I want to know what's going on."

Liang bowed his head, but when he raised it, his lined face was troubled.

"What is the problem, Uncle?" The White Orchid said, her voice gentle.

"We will do as you ask, Honored Lady," the old man said, "but you should know, we pay our protection money to the Hip Yee Tong."

She nodded. "It was wise of you to tell me, Uncle. I assure you, none of this business will bring us into conflict with the

Hip Yee. This is a separate affair." She produced a gold coin from the folds of her robe and held it out to Kam. "And it doesn't hurt for an industrious man such as yourself to have a little extra income, wouldn't you agree?"

Liang looked at the gold coin and licked his lips. "I suppose not." He reached out.

"Father," Kam said. "I don't know if we should..." He trailed off as he looked at The White Orchid.

She smiled coldly. "Your concern for your aged father speaks well of you. I will remember it."

Liang took the money from her hand and bowed his head. "Thank you."

The White Orchid nodded at the old man, then turned to the son. "Say nothing of this. But remember everything. You will see me again."

"Please," Kam said. He paused, then he squared his shoulders and faced her directly. "If you have anything more to say to us, deal with me. My father is old, and all he needs to concern himself with is his gardening."

She looked at him for a moment, her face as cold as a marble statue. Then she broke into a smile. "You are an insolent boy, but I will do as you ask." The smile broadened, lost some of its coldness. "And there is someone I think you should meet."

Clayborne stood outside the shop and looked up at the sign, the words outlined in fake-gilded letters. R. SIMONSON AND CO. MEN'S HABERDASHERY. Clayborne knew from previous experience that the shop offered much more than bespoke clothing. He was about to test exactly how much more. He entered the shop, a bell on the front door jingling as he closed it behind him. He looked around. Various elegantly tailored suits adorned mannequins around the shop. A polished wooden counter faced him. He approached and rang the silver bell that sat on the counter.

"A moment, sir," came a high-pitched voice from behind a curtain leading to the back of the store. In a moment, a man shuffled into view behind the counter.

The first thing that would strike a person on first meeting R. Simonson, Men's Haberdasher, was his size. He was tiny, no more than four feet tall. The second thing that would strike that person was the rigid dignity with which the man carried himself. He stopped as he spotted Clayborne. "Ah," he said, without enthusiasm. "Mr. Clayborne."

Clayborne smiled and removed his hat. "Mr. Simonson."

Simonson looked around and behind Clayborne. "And where is your employer?"

Clayborne's smile turned slightly frosty. "I am, at the moment, sir, self-employed. Or, more accurately, I come on the business of a firm I have formed with someone else with whom you might be acquainted. Mr. L.D. Cade."

Simonson's head bobbed. "So I have heard. And I remember Mr. Cade quite clearly." He looked confused. "Surely, he is the senior member? Perhaps I should be dealing..."

Clayborne sighed and bit his tongue to restrain himself before proceeding. "Mr. Simonson," he said, "I understand that you might have some discomfort in dealing with a man of my complexion. However, sir, I can assure you that I have full authority to speak for..." He stopped as he realized that his voice had tightened and risen with anger. After a moment, he began again, more softly. "Mr. Simonson. I would put to you the proposition that we are in some ways alike, in that we are both too often judged by others on account of physical attributes over which we have no control. I suggest that may be an impediment to doing business. If you like, we can wait and let you talk to Mr. Cade. But that will delay the business we hope to accomplish."

Simonson looked away. "Mr. Cade," he said in a low voice, "has made disparaging remarks about my size."

"For which he has apologized," Clayborne reminded him. "One thing that has struck me about Cade, Mr. Simonson, is his unusual capacity for learning. Have you noticed it as well?"

Simonson looked thoughtful, then he chuckled under his breath. "I have." He squared his shoulders. "So perhaps I can learn to put aside my preconceptions as well. What is it you desire, Mr. Clayborne? Some new formal wear? The latest silk cravats from Paris? They're quite—"

"No, thank you," Clayborne said. "You have admirably provided for us in that regard. But you had previously mentioned that there were certain other goods and services you could connect us with."

Simonson looked around the empty shop as if looking for spies lurking behind the mannequins. "That depends."

"On what?"

"On what you are asking me to provide."

"What we need," Clayborne said, "is someone who can translate the French language."

Simonson gave a contemptuous snort. "Child's play."

"And one," Clayborne went on, "who can pick locks."

Clayborne had expected the man to balk, to hem and haw, but he merely furrowed his brow. "Do the French speaker and the screwsman need to be the same person?"

Clayborne was so surprised, he had to laugh. "No. They don't". He paused. "Wait a minute. If I needed someone who could both speak French AND pick locks, you could supply that?"

Simonson nodded absently, still clearly lost in thought. "Of course. It might take a bit longer, but..." He snapped out of his reverie and smiled at Clayborne. "This is San Francisco, after all."

"Indeed." Clayborne put his hat back on. "I look forward to hearing from you soon."

As he turned to leave, Simonson said "Mr. Clayborne."

Clayborne turned. "Sir?"

"I have another item which might interest you. Something that might come in handy, considering what I have heard regarding your current line of work."

Clayborne raised an eyebrow. "Indeed? I'd be pleased to see it."

Simonson walked past him, turned the sign to CLOSED, and locked the door. "Follow me, if you please."

Simonson led Clayborne through the store, past a back room filled with suits on display, then another lined with shelves holding a variety of fabrics, to a heavy wooden door which he opened with a brass key.

"All very mysterious, Mr. Simonson," Clayborne observed.

Simonson nodded. "For a particular class of customer, Mr. Clayborne." He swung the door wide and entered. Clayborne followed him into what looked like a mechanic's workshop. Various tools hung on the walls and a heavy wooden workbench dominated the center of the room. Clayborne looked around, taking in the sight, then noticed Simonson was taking off his suit coat.

"I've just received a very interesting and cunning device," he said, "manufactured in Germany." He took a complicated-looking assemblage of metal and leather off the workbench and began strapping it around his left forearm. Clayborne could see the glint of a silver blade among the parts of the device. "It just occurred to me that it might be useful for a gentleman in your, ah, particular profession, who might need to be armed without appearing to be so." He took an identical machine from the workbench and began attaching it to his right forearm. When he turned back to Clayborne, he appeared to be wearing braces on each arm.

"I'm not sure I understand," Clayborne began.

Simonson interrupted him by calling out, "BEHOLD!" in the dramatic tone of a stage magician. He bent his arms, then snapped them to full extension. Suddenly, the blades he'd seen were in each of Simonson's hands. Before Clayborne quite knew what was happening, the little man bent his arms again and sent the pair of knives whizzing by Clayborne, one passing on either side, to bury themselves in the wall behind him.

Clayborne turned and saw that the far wall held a pair of man-shaped targets drawn on the wood. A silver blade was buried in the blank face of each one. He turned back, nodding in appreciation as he took his hand off the butt of his pistol. "A cunning machine indeed," he said. "Does it come in my size?"

Simonson frowned, as if unsure if he was being mocked. "I can adjust the devices as needed."

"Very slick," Clayborne said. "I'll talk to my partner and let you know."

"Best order fast. I expect this item to sell out quickly." He looked pensive. "I may even keep them for myself."

CHAPTER TWENTY-SEVEN

The law offices of Walter B. Jenkins, Esq. occupied an entire floor of a recently constructed building on Union Street. The place was so new, Cade could smell the sawdust. Cade stood before the exquisitely crafted oak desk of a dapper clerk who looked at him with a pleasant but slightly puzzled smile. "How may I help you, sir?"

"L.D. Cade. To see Mr. Jenkins." Cade was acutely aware that, even dressed in his fancy clothes, he looked ragged and unshaven. "I have an appointment."

The young clerk's face brightened. "Yes, sir. You are a bit early. Would you care for a refreshment while you wait? Tea? Coffee?"

Cade looked at the clock on the wall. He was all of forty-five minutes early for his nine o'clock appointment. He cursed himself silently. It wouldn't do to seem too eager. "Thanks," he said, trying to regain his equilibrium. "I'll have coffee. Black."

The clerk nodded, still smiling. "Right away, sir." He disappeared through a door off the outer office.

Cade looked around at the lushly upholstered leather furnishings and brass lamps of the outer office. He'd expected a bit more of a superior attitude in a fancy law office like this, and the welcome he'd gotten—if not warm, at least not condescending—unsettled him a little.

In a moment, the door opened again, but it wasn't the clerk who came out, it was Jenkins himself.

The last time Cade had seen the lawyer, it had been in a grubby police court attached to the jail where Cade was being held on suspicion of murder. Jenkins had managed, using a combination of his own charm, a bit of unspecified influence, and a healthy dose of utter balderdash to set Cade free on the streets of San Francisco. All on the behest of Lee Kwan, the head of the Green Dragon Tong.

Jenkins smiled widely. He was dressed in a silk shirt and trousers of excellent quality, but he wore neither waistcoat nor jacket. He was fastening his cuffs as he spoke. "Mr. Cade!" he said, as if encountering a long-lost friend for the first time in years. "Such a pleasure to see you again."

Cade stood. "Mr. Jenkins. Good to see you, sir. Never had the chance to thank you properly for what you did for me a few weeks ago."

Jenkins his head slightly. "It was my honor to assist you, sir." He stepped back and opened the door he'd just come through. "Will you join me in my office?" Without waiting for an answer, he stepped away. Cade followed.

Cade was surprised to see that the desk in the inner office was nowhere near as opulent as the one out front. It was a battered, splintered, worn-looking affair, piled high with papers and equally worn-looking leather bound volumes. Jenkins smiled as he took in the expression on Cade's face. "My original desk from St. Louis." He ran a hand lovingly over the few inches of desktop not already covered. "I keep it to remind me of where I'm from." He took a seat in a leather chair behind the old desk.

"If I want to cow someone with opulence, I have a number of conference rooms for that."

Cade's mouth quirked. "Glad you're not trying to impress me."

Jenkins leaned back and steepled his fingers, looking Cade over. "I do not believe, Mr. Cade, that you are one to be impressed by fancy leather and brass fittings. That's why I decided to meet you here, in my inner sanctum, as it were." He gestured to a single leather chair across from where he sat at the desk. "Please. Take a seat."

Cade could tell he was being courted. The ostentatious folksiness, the illusion of intimacy, all got his guard up. He took the offered seat anyway. "I'd also like to thank Mr. Kwan for engaging your services on my behalf."

Jenkins nodded. "Always glad to be of service for the friends of Mr. Kwan."

"Well, that's something we maybe need to talk about."

Jenkins looked blandly interested. "Indeed?"

"See, I appreciate Mr. Kwan helping me out. And I think I may have provided him with a reasonable recompense for that help."

Jenkins nodded. "I'd tend to agree. I don't believe I'm speaking out of turn when I say he was quite grateful for your efforts in exposing the plot to frame him."

"Right. But I'm a mite worried that Mr. Kwan may consider some debts kind of open-ended."

Jenkins leaned back in his chair, still smiling. "And now we get to the crux of the matter. Your friend Mrs. Hamrick."

Cade was taken aback. He hadn't expected Jenkins to be aware of the situation with Marjorie. "Well. Yeah."

The lawyer laughed, low and quiet. "She is concerned that accepting an investment of money from Mr. Kwan will put her in thrall to him. Cause her shipping lines to be used for," the smile vanished from his face, "nefarious purposes."

"That's about the size of it. Meanin' no offense to Mr. Kwan, of course."

For the first time since they'd met, Jenkins seemed at a loss for words. He looked down at the desktop, drumming his fingers absentmindedly. Finally, he spoke up. "Of all the clients I have met since coming to San Francisco, I would have to say that Lee Kwan is the most complex. It may astonish you to hear that he has never, not once, demanded nor even requested that I do anything illegal. Or even immoral." He looked up at Cade and smiled. "I may have gone to the edge of what law and ethics allow, but I have never, at least in my opinion, gone off that ledge. And Kwan has never asked me to."

Cade cleared his throat in embarrassment. "Right before you spoke up for me in court, you told me that the fix was in."

Jenkins shook his head. "No, sir, you said that. I merely allowed as how it would be a possibility. I don't personally know of any bribes paid or any influence exerted."

"Uh-huh," Cade said.

"You're skeptical. And one could hardly blame you. But you see, Mr. Cade," the lawyer went on, "I believe that part of the secret to Mr. Kwan's success is compartmentalization."

"Com...part...what?"

"He keeps one thing separate from another. The left hand truly does not know what the right hand is doing. Only Kwan knows. And he keeps certain of his business interests separate from the others. Everyone has their part to play in Kwan's organization. And mine is to carry out his legal interests in a way that is legal and aboveboard."

"And if anyone else in his organization—well, let's just call it what it is, Mr. Jenkins—in his tong takes another way?"

Jenkins shrugged. "If asked, I will advise Kwan as to what is legal and what is not. But he doesn't ask."

"Of course not." Cade rubbed his temples. This conversation was making his head hurt.

Jenkins smiled sympathetically. "If you want my opinion as to Lee Kwan's intentions in regard to your friend's shipping company, I can only say that he has recently asked me to explore investments in businesses that are completely legal. He is, in my opinion, either diversifying his interests, or attempting to move into businesses less risky than his usual endeavors."

Cade nodded. "Trying to go straight."

Jenkins's face took on a bland expression that was becoming all too familiar to Cade. "That would imply that Lee Kwan's businesses are not all legitimate. I am not, of course, suggesting—"

"Right, right," Cade interrupted. "I get it." He sighed. "How do I know which side of the line he intends for Marjorie—for my friend?"

The smile was back on the man's face and Cade didn't like it. "I suppose you could ask him."

Cade snorted. "The last time Mr. Kwan wanted to meet with me, I got etherized and hauled off to his house with a bag over my head."

The smile vanished from Jenkins's face. "I see. You've met...*her*, then."

Cade was surprised. "Have you?"

"Yes."

"And from the look on your face, I'm thinking you'd like to avoid that again."

Jenkins nodded.

Cade didn't press the matter. Even a brief encounter with The White Orchid could unsettle a man. A thought occurred to him. "He's had another young lady working for him from time to time. Maybe I could talk to her. You may even know her. I guess she lives in Chinatown. Family has a fish market. Mei, the name was. Maybe you could put me in touch with her."

Jenkins shook his head. "The name doesn't ring any bells. There are a lot of fish markets in Chinatown."

"Right. But I'll bet this one has Mr. Kwan's special attention. He seemed to think a lot of the young lady."

Jenkins nodded. "Will you find this girl an acceptable intermediary between yourself and Kwan?"

"What I need is a translator," Cade said. "An honest one. And yeah, I trust that girl."

The lawyer stood. "All right, then. I will attempt to arrange a meeting with the three of you." He smiled. "Without the need for ether or bags over the head."

"That'd be good," Cade said. "I'll be at Miss Givens's house." He thought of the Chinese gardeners Lucius, Athena Givens's footman, had mentioned. Kam and Liang, if he remembered correctly. "And if Miss Mei would like to pick up a spare dollar, I might have some work translating as well."

Jenkins had pasted that professional smile back on his face. "We'll be in touch."

It was the best Cade could hope for, at least for the time being.

CHAPTER TWENTY-EIGHT

ith nowhere else left to go, Cade rode the Arabian mare back to the Givens house, ignoring the stares of the pedestrians. In the saddle, he felt truly himself, a thousand miles away from the worries of the city. The mare seemed to share his detachment, tossing her head contemptuously at the horses shackled to cargo wagons and rich people's conveyances. They made their way through the busy streets, up the hills to the Givens mansion. He frowned as he approached the gates. A landau was parked in the street, by the curb. It didn't look out of place in the neighborhood, not exactly, but it didn't seem to have any particular reason for being there, and something about it made Cade uneasy.

He walked the horse up to the side of the coach, where a black driver looked down at him without expression. Cade touched the brim of his hat. "Morning, friend," he said. "Nice day for a drive."

The driver looked at him, then looked away without answering. Cade's frown turned to a scowl. He was getting ready to hail the coachman again when the low-set side window opened and a young man leaned his head out. "Pardon me, sir," he said with a toothy smile and a plummy New York accent, "do I have the pleasure of addressing Mr. L.D. Cade?"

Cade nodded. "I'm Cade. And you are?"

The young man chuckled. "Oh, my name is not important, sir."

"If you say so," Cade said, and picked up the reins. "Well, then. Have a good morning."

"I'm bringing a message," the young man said, still smiling. "An invitation, actually."

Cade relaxed his hands on the reins. "I seem to be quite in demand these days."

"Indeed, sir. Enjoy it while you can." The smile never wavered, but Cade's eyes narrowed at the words.

"Meaning what?"

The young man looked surprised at the tone in Cade's voice. His tone grew more soothing. "Why, nothing untoward, sir. It's just that in San Francisco, one's standing can rise and fall very quickly." He gave a little shrug and a rueful smile. "One day, everyone is clamoring to see you and the world is your oyster. The next," his mouth turned down in exaggerated sadness, "everyone is mysteriously out when you call."

Cade grunted. "I appreciate your concern for my welfare, fella. But maybe we can skip the folderol and you can deliver your invitation, or message, or whatever. Starting with who it is that's doing the inviting. I'm assuming it's not you."

"Indeed? Why not?"

"Because you have *errand boy* painted all over you. So come on, out with it. Who wants to see me, when, and why?"

The young messenger's smile had slipped a notch, but it was still hanging on gamely. "As to who, I'm afraid that information must, for the moment, remain confidential. As to why, well, my employer may be able to provide some aid to you and your friend, the Widow Hamrick."

"Uh-huh. And how come this aid is being offered out of the window of a coach on the street? Instead of, say, over a banker's desk with fountain pens and other oily so-and-so's like yourself standing around."

The smile was almost gone now, but the voice remained unctuously polite. "There are certain, ah, ramifications. Conditions, you might say. That would be best to discuss in private."

Cade said nothing, just stared at the young man.

After a moment, the last vestiges of the smile blew away, and the young man's gaze broke down and away from Cade's. "I can assure you," he said, "that the rewards will be substantial."

"When does your boss want to see me?"

"Now would actually be preferable. If you'd like to stable your mount there—beautiful animal, by the way—I'll be glad to transport you to—"

"No," Cade interrupted. "I'll follow you. I like having my own ride home."

The messenger blinked in surprise, then nodded curtly. He barked an address up to the driver, then withdrew. The driver flicked the reins and set off, not looking at Cade. Cade shrugged and fell in behind.

It was turning into a busy morning.

They made their way down the hills, back into the business district, following behind the landau. Midnight maintained a sprightly pace to keep up, but she showed no signs of tiring.

They wound through the streets until they came to the busy corner of California and Sansome Streets, where the great Bank of California loomed like an ancient stone temple over the intersection. Cade had figured that was their destination, but the carriage clopped along, bypassing the huge building, making a number of turns before coming to a stop before another massive ornate structure on Montgomery Street.

The place was a fantasia of cupolas, turrets, and arched windows that looked like a giant gingerbread house. The carriage pulled to a stop, and a pair of black valets in livery gaudy enough to match the building itself stepped forward. One took the reins of the coach as the driver swung down from his seat on the front, the other opened the door to let the young errand boy debark. Cade looked him over as he straightened up and adjusted his clothing. As Cade figured, he was a dude, his immaculately cut gray suit decorated with silver piping along the legs of the narrow trousers and the tight-cut morning coat. A silver-headed cane completed his costume. He said something to the man helping him from the carriage, pointing to where Cade still sat astride Midnight and bending down to whisper something in the black man's ear. The valet looked at him dubiously, then started forward as Cade dismounted. Suddenly the driver of the coach was there, standing beside him. Cade was so startled he nearly went for his gun.

"With your permission, sir," the coachman said, "I'll look after your horse."

He was a tall, lanky black man, his features sharp and bony. Cade squinted at him. "And why would that be?"

The driver looked at the liveried valet who had stopped, scowling at the interloper. "Because I do not believe these... gentlemen...will treat this fine horse with the respect she deserves."

Cade looked the coachman over. The man looked back at him serenely.

"Okay," Cade said. He looked at the messenger, standing at the curb, an impatient look on his face. "I don't reckon I'll be long."

"And you may need to make a quick exit," the coachman said.

Cade frowned. "You know something I don't?"

The coachman shook his head. "Just simple prudence, sir."

"Thanks." The messenger was looking at him, tapping his cane impatiently on the curb. Cade took a deep breath. "See you soon."

CHAPTER TWENTY-NINE

ade had thought he'd be used to the opulent lobbies of hotels by now, but the Grand was a cut above even the Royal, where he'd been used to meeting Marjorie. One thing that was consistent, however, was the side room the dudeified messenger boy guided him to. Cade was getting used to how much of the business of this town was done in elegantly paneled rooms, secluded from the public view. The messenger, smiling with a poisonous courtesy, swung the door open.

The man Cade had come to meet was seated at a round table in just such a room. A plate of oysters in their shells sat before him, and he was digging one out with a tiny fork as Cade entered. Another man loomed behind him, his massive arms folded across his chest. As Cade stepped through the door, the big man behind the banker moved toward him. The messenger stepped aside, getting out of the way of the big man.

Cade fixed the approaching guard with a hard stare. "You best back off, son."

The big man stopped. He looked uncertainly at the man behind the table, who was applying himself diligently to the consumption of his oyster brunch. With no guidance from that quarter, the guard looked at Cade. "I got to search you. For weapons."

Cade pulled his coat aside. "There you go. Colt 1851 Navy revolver, modified for cartridges." He let the coat fall back. "And a dagger in my left boot. Made in Italy, or so the man who sold it to me claimed. Now you know what I'm wearing. Happy?"

The guard scowled. "I got to take those from you. "

"No."

The bodyguard looked stunned. He clearly wasn't used to being denied.

"Sonny," Cade said, "I'm here because your boss wants to parley. If I wanted to kill you, I'd have come in blasting, and you'd be laid out on the floor bleeding." He looked over to where the banker was spooning a raw oyster into his mouth, his eyes fixed on Cade with a bright look of interest, not terror or even concern. "Look," Cade said, "even he knows this is bullshit. So, let's quit trying to measure who has the biggest pecker and let's get down to goddamn business."

At that, the man at the dinner table burst out laughing. The outburst was so startling, Cade put his hand on the butt of his gun, but when the banker at the table stood and wiped his hand on a linen napkin, then extended his hand to Cade, he relaxed his grip. "By God, sir," the banker said, "I am truly pleased to make your acquaintance."

That set Cade back on his heels. The only thing he could do was extend his own hand and shake the offered one. "Likewise," he mumbled.

The banker sat down as his bruiser withdrew into a corner of the room, glowering in a way that made Cade a little nervous about having the big bastard in his rear.

"May I offer you some oysters, Mr. Cade?" the banker said. "I assure you they are the best San Francisco has to offer."

"No, thank you, sir," Cade responded. "I've already eaten."

The banker looked disgruntled at that for a moment, then he smiled. "You know, some men would accept a gift of prime oysters on a full stomach just to avoid offending my hospitality."

"I can't speak for any other man, sir. And I assure you, I mean no offense. I'm just not hungry." Cade returned the smile with equal insincerity. "What I am, sir, is a man who's had a taxing couple of days. So, I hope you can see your way clear to getting to the goddamn..." He stopped and took a deep breath. "Sorry for the rudeness, sir. To the reason for which you've summoned me."

The banker put down his oyster fork and leaned back in his chair, his hands folded across the belly that strained against his waistcoat. "Mr. Cade," he said mildly, "I can't tell if you are deliberately trying to provoke me or if you are just an ill-mannered lout."

"Let's just proceed on the assumption that both are true. Whatever I am, you brought me here, I assume, to make me a proposition. So, let's have it," Cade said.

The banker nodded. "I was told you were a man who valued directness, Mr. Cade, and my information seems, as always, to be accurate. So, let us be direct."

"That, sir, would purely overjoy me."

The banker looked around the room as if seeing it for the first time. "Do you like the surroundings, Mr. Cade? Are you pleased by the appointments of this hotel?"

Cade was nonplussed. "It's a nice place."

The banker leaned forward, his eyes bright. "What would you say, Mr. Cade, if I was to tell you I was building a hotel across the street that would dwarf this one? That would rival the great resorts of Europe and make San Francisco a city to be reckoned with on the international stage?"

"I guess I'd wish you good luck."

"And would you, Mr. Cade, not want to be part of that bright future?"

"That would be something a fellow might be interested in," he said carefully.

"I imagine it would," the banker said. "And the man responsible for the security of that place would be handsomely paid."

Here it comes, Cade thought. *The bait's being dangled. Just need to watch for the hook.* "So, this is a job offer? To provide security for this new hotel?"

"Yes," the banker said. "The investors I've spoken to are very enthusiastic about employing you." The banker smiled. "You are, after all, a veteran of the late war, and everyone thanks you for your service to the Union."

"Much obliged," Cade muttered. Six months ago, he'd have leapt at a chance like this, but the time he'd spent in San Francisco had made him wary of apparent good fortune. "Of course, I'll have to talk it over with my partner."

"Ah. Yes. That," the banker said. "You would, of course, have to sever relations with..." he cleared his throat, "...that person."

"I assume you are talking about Mr. Samuel Clayborne."

"Yes." The banker nodded. "And, of course, any, um, Chinese interests." The banker folded his hands on the table. "You wish things to be clear, Mr. Cade? Then let us be clear. My bank is willing to completely finance you and your," he smirked in a way that made Cade want to punch him, "special friend Marjorie Hamrick on the most favorable of terms. In return, you will sever all ties with the suffragist Athena Givens, the Chinese tongs, and, as noted, the Negro Samuel Clayborne."

And there it is, Cade thought. *There's the hook.* If he stuck by his friend Samuel, Marjorie would suffer. If he stuck with the job he'd taken on at Marjorie's behest, Marjorie would suffer. Lee Kwan and the Green Dragon Tong had saved his life, but if he continued to stick with them, Marjorie would suffer. And Marjorie was the woman he loved. The love he felt for her was like an ache in his chest that could only be relieved by her smile and her presence.

The banker went on. "San Francisco is a promised land, Mr. Cade. A place of unlimited opportunity, unlike the hidebound cities of the East, locked as they are in their obsessions over old money and desperate grasping over heredity. This is a place where men can make something new of themselves. And," he smiled condescendingly, "women. Under proper guidance."

Cade's father had been a preacher at times, and he'd taught his sons to resist the Devil and his temptations. Those temptations had included gold and the pleasures of the flesh. But his father's teachings had never taught him to resist the Devil when he came offering not only those things, but the salvation of those he loved. He looked at the banker, and hated the man for the indulgent and confident smile on his face. Cade knew the rich bastard thought he had him right where he wanted him.

The worst part was that he might be right.

"Take some time to think about it, Mr. Cade," the banker said. "But not too long. I'm sure you'll make a wise decision." He scooped another oyster from the shell and slurped it into his mouth. When he'd swallowed, he wiped the corners of his mouth. "Are you sure you won't indulge? These oysters are first-rate."

Cade shook his head. He felt nauseous. "Not right now. Thank you kindly."

"Well," the banker smiled, "there will always be more."

The messenger was suddenly back at his elbow. "This way, Mr. Cade."

Cade let himself be led, back out through the lobby and to the front of the great hotel, to where the coachman who'd led him there stood holding Midnight, gazing serenely at the uniformed valets who glared at him from the steps.

Cade took the reins. "Thank you."

The coachman looked at him, still not smiling, and nodded. "My pleasure, sir. She's a beautiful animal."

Cade nodded back. "I'll pass that along to her owner." He looked at the horse, who tossed her head and whinnied. "I suspect this lady already knows it."

"I reckon." The coachman touched the brim of his hat. Cade couldn't tell if the gesture of respect was to him or the horse, and he thought it best not to ask.

"Thanks," Cade said as he swung into the saddle.

CHAPTER THIRTY

Normally, time on horseback helped Cade settle his mind and clarified his thinking. Today, it didn't work. His mind was still in turmoil by the time he'd made his way back to the Givens house.

Nothing seemed to be stirring in the front or in the gardens, so he made his way to the stables. The stableman was outside, brushing down a huge bay stallion. He regarded Cade sourly as he rode up and dismounted.

"Where you been at with my girl?" he rasped.

"Don't worry," Cade said, "she's been well taken care of." He grimaced. "Hell, in most of the places I've been today, people have been happier to see her than to see me."

"Hmmph. Most likely 'cause she a damn sight prettier."

"Can't argue with you there, sir."

Mr. George—Cade still didn't know if it was his first or last name—called back over his shoulder. "Jephthah! Come look after this one!"

The young man Cade had seen earlier scurried out of the stable and took the brush from George's hand. The older man didn't look back at his young assistant, but walked up and down, surveying the mare with a critical eye. Cade stood patiently holding the reins, until the old stablemaster was satisfied he hadn't damaged his prize. Finally, Mr. George grunted. Cade couldn't tell if it was satisfaction that the mare hadn't been ill-used or irritation at not being able to berate anyone for insufficient care, until he took the reins from Cade's hand and nodded to him with grudging respect.

Cade decided to seize the moment. He still hadn't made his decision over the offer made to him, but while he mulled it over, there was still a job to be done, and Cade was not one to leave work unattended to. "I know you gentlemen are busy. But if you can spare a moment, I'd like to talk to you about what happened the other night. When Miss Givens was attacked."

George and Jephthah looked at one another. Cade had no way of reading that look. George turned to Cade. "Tack room, five minutes."

The tack room of Givens's stables felt familiar to Cade. A blanket hung in the doorway separated the small space from the rest of the stable. Rough wood paneling covered the walls. Harnesses, leads, and other gear hung from wooden pegs. A pair of rough-hewn wooden chairs faced a battered table. An iron stove, unlit at present, stood in the corner. Cade took one of the chairs and waited. After a few minutes, Mr. George entered, brushing aside the blanket, then turning to smooth it down. He took a seat in the chair opposite Cade. He didn't speak, just glared at Cade, as if daring him to open the conversation.

"Okay," Cade said, then cleared his throat. "Thanks for taking the time to talk to me. I appreciate you talking to me alone. Without your assistant."

"That boy's got nothing' to do with nothin'," George said, his expression and tone unexpectedly fierce. "You leave him be."

Cade nodded. "I understand. Would you feel easier if my partner talked to him?"

George's eyes narrowed. "Your partner?"

"Yeah. The young fellow I came here with."

George shook his head. "You're saying that high toned Zip Coon's your partner?"

"I think Mr. Clayborne might take offense at that characterization, but yeah," Cade said.

George snorted. "And what do you care about what a black man takes offense at?"

"Well, Mr. George," Cade said mildly, "I guess I feel the obligation to look out for my partner, just as you look out for yours."

The old man regarded Cade expressionlessly for a moment, then settled back in his chair. "Okay. Ask your questions."

***

Clayborne looked up from his notebook as the front door bell of their office jingled. He stood as he saw Simonson enter, followed by a man in a suit which had clearly seen better days. Simonson walked up to the desk. "I believe I have found the gentleman with the skills you were seeking," he said stiffly.

Clayborne eyed the scrawny apparition who stood behind Simonson, holding a battered plug hat in his hand. He looked as if he hadn't eaten in a week or shaved in several days. "Is this the translator or the lock picker?"

Simonson looked pained. "I will be providing the translation services you require. As for Mr. Lamarche's service...he prefers the term screwsman."

"Indeed." Clayborne held out his hand to the ragged man. "Pleased to make your acquaintance, Mr. Lamarche."

Lamarche looked at the offered hand as if Clayborne had held out a live rattlesnake. He swallowed nervously, then looked up. "Beggin' yer pardon, sir," he said in a thin, reedy voice, "but I don't shake hands." At Clayborne's look, he stepped back, raising his hands placatingly. "It's got nowt to do with yer color, sir, I swear it." Sweat was breaking on his brow. "But me fingers are me fortune, sir. If you take my meaning. I don't place them in anyone's hands. Sir."

Clayborne nodded. "Understood. I suppose a concert pianist wouldn't place his hands in a stranger's either."

Lamarche smiled gratefully. "Thank you for understandin', sir." His smile grew wider and more ingratiating. "Yer a credit to yer race."

Clayborne's smile vanished. "Perhaps you should refrain from any further commentary on that topic."

Lamarche bowed his head quickly. "Sir."

Clayborne took a moment to compose himself. "We need to enter a particular room at the end of a long hallway on the second story of a large house on Russian Hill. The entry must be obtained with maximum speed, as there are likely to be others in the house as well. Do you think you can accomplish that?"

"Any idea what sort of lock?" Lamarche asked. "Brand name? Style?"

Clayborne shook his head. "Sorry. We only got a brief glimpse. I suppose it was the standard lock you'd find inside a house."

"Beg pardon, sir, but that covers a lot of ground." Lamarche shrugged. "No matter. I can open your standard household lock so fast you think I'd brought the key with me. Anything more complicated might take a bit." He squared his shoulders and straightened his posture in sudden dignity. "But there ain't a lock made by the hand of man," he held up his own long-fingered hands, "that these hands can't open. I promise you that. However," he lowered his arms and regarded Clayborne gravely, "getting me to the lock is your lookout. The good Lord only made me clever in one thing."

Clayborne looked at Simonson. "You vouch for this man's skills?"

Simonson nodded. "I do. please do not ask me how I know."

"Wouldn't dream of it." He looked at Lamarche. "Your rates?"

"Usually based on the value of what's inside, sir. And the risk involved to me person."

Clayborne rubbed his chin. "What we're after is information. It may be worth nothing. Or its value may not be monetary. But I can assure you, your person will be safe."

Lamarche looked doubtful. "Truly?" He looked over at Simonson. "Is this fellow to be trusted?"

Simonson nodded. "If he says he and his partner will keep you safe, I believe him."

"Okay, then." He looked at Clayborne. "Ten dollars."

"Ten..." Clayborne hesitated. It was quite a sum.

"Do you need to consult with Mr. Cade?" Simonson said. The condescension in his voice pushed Clayborne to a decision. If necessary, they'd charge the client for the expense. "No. Five now, five upon completion of the task." He looked at Simonson. "All commissions to be between you and your client."

Simonson nodded smoothly. "Of course." He looked round the office. "Do you have the five now?"

Clayborne didn't know if they had that in the office drawer, and he didn't want to be embarrassed by looking into the desk and coming up short. "We'll arrange for it. Immediately. In the meantime, may we arrange for you to meet at the home of

Athena Givens tomorrow? Say around noon? And may I see you, Mr. Simonson, a bit later, say around two p.m.?"

Simonson nodded without expression. "We will be there. Understand, we are under no obligation until the first payment is made." He nodded to Lamarche, and the two men left without a further word.

Clayborne sat down heavily in the desk chair. He realized he'd just commissioned a criminal to break into their client's house at the client's expense. And he wasn't sure how to get it paid for.

"Shit," he muttered.

CHAPTER THIRTY-ONE

"So," Cade began, "how long have you been working for Miss Givens?"

"Since she got to San Francisco," the old groom said. "Two years ago."

"You were here before?"

"Oh, yeah." Mr. George grimaced. "I been here since '49."

"Ah. Came here for the gold."

"Yep. Thought I was gonna be a rich man. Eat off the best china and cut my meat with fine silverware." He shook his head ruefully. "I was a damn fool."

"Well, you weren't alone. Where'd you come from? Originally, I mean."

"Born in Indiana. But I spent my growin' up years in Liberia." He regarded Cade sourly. "You ever heard of it?"

Cade frowned. "Africa, right?"

George nodded. "White folks in Indiana thought it'd be a good idea to get the black folks out of America altogether. Ship 'em all back to the homeland." He snorted. "'Cept it weren't *our* homeland. There was already black folk livin' there that didn't take too kindly to all these Americans showin' up and tryin' to run things. And then there was the diseases. African fevers that people like my mama and daddy never run up against before." He sighed. "Mama died of fever when I was five. Daddy tried to make a go of it, but he died a couple years later. I got sent back to live with an aunt in Missouri."

"Not as a slave, though. You were still free."

"You had to carry a paper on you all the time sayin' you didn't belong to nobody, and if you didn't have that paper, you'd get chained up and thrown in jail till a bunch of white men got together and decide if you could be sold off. If'n you call that free, then I reckon so."

"I take your point. When did you come West?"

"Like I said, when the gold fever hit, I figgered I'd come to California and make my fortune." He sighed. "Didn't work out that way."

"Didn't find anything?"

"Oh, I found a claim. Real solid vein. But a white man staked the same claim, said he had it first. We even went to court over it. You can figger how that went."

Cade nodded. "Yeah."

"Anyway," George said, "I'd always been good with horses. Get along with them better than people, you want to know the truth."

"I know exactly what you mean," Cade said.

George smiled at him, the first genuine warmth Cade had seen from the man. "I reckon you do. Anyway, I could always find work."

"Let's talk about Miss Givens now. What's going on with all these séances and such?"

George frowned. "I don't involve myself in none of that white folks' business."

"You think any of it's real?"

"Don't know. Don't care."

The fragile rapport Cade had been building was rapidly evaporating. He decided to try another tack. "What about this Akbar? What do you know about him?"

George snorted. "I know he ain't no more an Ay-rab than I am." He held up a warning hand. "Don't mistake me. I got nothin' against the Injuns. Hell, I had an Injun wife for a time."

Cade blinked in surprise. "You did?"

George nodded, his eyes going far away. "Yeah," he said softly. "Pretty little Navajo girl. Sweet as pie." He shook the memory off and looked at Cade. "But I was bad to take a drink in those days. She got fed up and went back to her people." He sighed. "Took our son with her."

Cade looked at the stable. "So Jephthah isn't your son?"

"What? No. I just found that boy wandering in the street. Couldn't have been more than nine or ten. Half-starved and beat all to hell. Took him in." George scowled. "Remember what I said. You leave him be."

Cade left off that subject for the moment. "Was Akbar with Miss Givens when you were hired?"

George nodded. "She did all the talkin' at that point. He didn't start lordin' it over ever'one till later."

Cade nodded sympathetically. "I get how that could get up your nose a bit."

George snorted. "A bit, yeah." He leaned back and regarded Cade with an unreadable expression. "And you don't like him much either."

"No," Cade admitted, "but it ain't about what I like, or who. I'm just trying to get to the truth here."

George's eyes widened as if Cade had suddenly started speaking Ancient Greek. "Truth?" he said, then began to laugh. "Man wants to know the truth," he said, half under his breath, speaking as if only to himself. "In this place." He looked away as if Cade had already left. "Truth," he said finally, and shook his head.

Cade decided that subject had run its course. "What's the story with this fellow Clinton?"

George's face clouded over. "What about him?"

"I don't know. I'm just wondering why Miss Givens keeps that old drunk on. He's a surly son of a bitch."

George shook his head. "You don't even know."

Cade's ears perked up at that. "What does that mean? He's been an ass to the other staff here?"

George shook his head. "More white folks' business. I stay out of it."

"Can you at least tell me how long he's been here?"

George looked away. "Couple months. Maybe three."

"How'd he get the job? He have any kind of reference? Some connection?"

George shrugged. "Just showed up one day. Walked up to the front door, if you can believe that. Like he owned the damn place."

"Who hired him?"

George's attention seemed to be drawing farther and farther away. "Don't rightly know. One day he wasn't there, then he was."

Cade figured he'd mined that vein of inquiry about as deep as it was going to go, at least on that day. He stood up. "Thank you for your time, Mr. George," he said. He arched and stretched his back, putting his right knuckles into the base of his spine to work out the kinks. "Now I'll need to talk to your partner Jephthah."

George sprang to his feet. "Here now," he said, "I thought we agreed you was gonna leave that boy alone."

"I didn't agree not to talk to him, Mr. George. I promise you I don't mean him any harm."

George's face contorted in a snarl that startled Cade with its fierceness. "You ain't to bother that boy."

Cade held up his hands. "Easy, friend," he said. "No need to —" He was interrupted by the sound of screaming from the front lawn. It startled him to the point he'd unholstered his pistol before realizing he'd done it.

The voice came to him, muffled by distance, but unmistakably the voice of Athena Givens. "NO! NO!"

Cade glanced uncertainly at Mr. George, who was shaking his head. "More white folks' business," he said. His grin was as bitter as raw radishes. "You better go deal with it."

CHAPTER THIRTY-TWO

Cade hurried through the gardens, up the driveway to the porte cochere. A black police wagon was parked beneath the overhang, surrounded by three big bruisers in the uniform of the San Francisco Police. Cade spotted Tatanka being pushed down the steps, hands fastened behind his back with heavy iron cuffs. The man doing the pushing was all too familiar to Cade. He gritted his teeth and slid the Navy revolver into his shoulder holster. There was no percentage in getting into a shootout with the law, especially when this Captain Smith was running the show. He spotted Athena Givens, collapsed on the steps, weeping.

He stepped forward; hands raised as if he hadn't drawn. "What's going on here, Captain?" he said in as friendly a tone as he could manage.

Smith pushed Tatanka toward the Black Maria, handing him off to one of the big men surrounding it. He moved between the prisoner and Cade, squaring off while pulling back the hem of his jacket to show off the pistol he was carrying. "This is police business, Cade," he said. "Best step aside."

"Beggin' your pardon, Cap'n," Cade said, getting heartily

sick of keeping his voice calm and his expression ingratiating, "but exactly what is this fella bein' charged with?"

"I'll consider answering that question," Smith said, resting one hand loosely on the butt of his holstered revolver, "as soon as you explain to me exactly what connection you have with this matter."

Cade was losing his patience. "My connection, you officious little pissant," he began, but he was interrupted by Athena Givens, arising from her collapse on the front steps, the tip of her cane striking like a shot on the marble. A couple of the patrol officers stepped back as she rose, clad entirely in black, like some sort of eldritch apparition. Cade noted that one of the officers crossed himself. After a pause, Athena Givens spoke.

"Mr. Cade is in my employ," she announced in the same resounding voice she'd used at the suffragist's meeting. "He is authorized by me to deal with all matters of security involving me or my staff. Including," she fixed Smith with a withering glance, "matters involving Mr. Akbar Khan."

As Smith seemed about to speak, one of the officers by the police wagon raised his baton and advanced on Givens, "You keep your fucking mouth shut, you suffragist cunt."

Givens screamed and flinched away from the threat.

In a half second, Cade's gun had cleared its holster. "HOLD IT, you son of a bitch."

In a moment, every pistol on the scene was drawn, only one of them not pointed at Cade. Everyone stood frozen, as if waiting for the stroke that would spill them all over the edge into an orgy of bloodshed.

"Smith," Cade said, his voice tight with strain, "look at the front door." He cast a quick glance of his own at the ornately decorated front door, and the faces of the staff peering from behind the leaded glass.

"Lot of witnesses here, Cap'n Smith," Cade said. He didn't

take his aim off the officer who'd frozen, baton in the air. "Lot of people to testify your boys shot a man who was just trying to keep a woman from being beat. You ready to take that heat?"

Smith looked at the faces behind the glass. Then he sighed and rolled his shoulders. "Officer Cartwright," he said to the man holding the baton up near Athena Givens, "stand down."

Cartwright lowered the baton, his expression showing the same relief Cade felt.

Smith turned to Cade. "Mr. Akbar Khan, alias," he smirked, "for the Sioux known as Tatanka, is being taken into custody for fraud and for the attempted murder of Miss Athena Givens. We do have a valid warrant." He looked at Cade. "Sir, you've been quite fortunate so far in that when you've pulled your weapon, others have backed down and bloodshed has been averted. May I suggest there may come a time when that strategy will no longer avail you."

"Well, Cap'n Smith," Cade said, "I do hope when that time comes, you are there to experience the fulfillment of your prophecy firsthand."

Smith bowed his head slightly. "I look forward to it."

Before Cade could retort, he noticed someone walking up the driveway, approaching with slow, careful steps. Smith saw where he was looking and turned himself to see who was entering the scene.

"Mr. Clayborne," Cade called out. "We seem to have a situation here."

Clayborne stopped, his eyes moving over the tableau of armed and glowering officers and the sight of Tatanka in handcuffs. His voice was easy and calm as he answered. "Indeed, we do, Mr. Cade." He made no aggressive move, but he took up a position that put himself, Cade, and Smith at equal points on a triangle, so that Smith couldn't focus his attention on both of them at once.

He chose to turn toward Clayborne. "This is none of your business, boy," he said in a voice with more bravado than conviction. "Best move along."

"On the contrary," Clayborne said, his voice calm. "The security of this house and its inhabitants is very much a part of the business of my firm. I'm sure you know it. It's the one in which Mr. Cade and I are partners." He swept his coat back, not drawing his pistol, but clearing the way to draw.

"Indeed, we are," Cade said, enjoying the clear discomfort Smith was feeling in having to turn back and forth to see both of them.

Smith scowled. "You," he pointed at Clayborne, "go stand by him," he said, and swiveled his arm toward Cade.

Clayborne seemed to consider the order, then shook his head. "No, sir," he said, with that same maddening calm, "I don't think I will."

Smith's face reddened. "Are you refusing to obey—?"

"Cap'n Smith," Cade interrupted, "I don't think you brought enough men to arrest all of us. Especially considering the other members of the household."

"The other…?" Smith looked around.

Mr. George had appeared around the side of the house, a double-barreled shotgun held loosely down by his right leg. His assistant Jephthah stood a little way behind him, holding a rifle awkwardly, looking as if he'd rather be anywhere else than right there.

The police officers tensed, pistol barrels moving from one person to the next, the tension in the air building by the second.

Lord, Cade thought, *how in seven hells did I get here?*

Tatanka spoke up. He was looking down, but his voice was loud and clear. "Stop," he said. "I'll go." He looked up at Cade. "I don't want blood shed for me."

"Thank you kindly, Mr. Tatanka," Cade touched the brim

of his hat in salute. "I confess, I'm not eager for my own blood to be shed in any case. However, I do feel the need to assure the folks assembled here that the law is truly being upheld. So, Captain Smith, would you be so kind as to let me peruse that warrant you claim to have?"

Smith sneered. "What, you're a lawyer now?"

Cade shrugged. "Served as a deputy once or twice. I'm no great legal mind, but I flatter myself I know what a real warrant looks like."

Without another word, Smith took a folded piece of paper from an inside pocket, walked over to Cade, and handed it to him. Cade took it with his free hand and opened it. He looked it over and grimaced.

"Well," he said, "on its face, it looks like the real thing." He looked over at Tatanka, who'd spent the entire exchange standing as if he were made of stone. He holstered his weapon. "They're going to take you, *khola*," he said, using the Lakota for *friend*. "Stay strong. We'll come for you. I promise."

At those words, Athena Givens wailed "NO!" and lunged toward where Tanaka stood, head up, between two officers. "You can't take him! You CAN'T!"

Eleanor grabbed her around the shoulders and dragged her away, murmuring to her.

Cade went on. "Be strong," he said again. "Say nothing. We'll be working to get you out."

Tatanka didn't respond. He said nothing as they loaded him into the police wagon.

Cade spoke to Smith. "I sincerely hope, Captain, that I will find Mr. Tatanka in the same shape as we observed him here when we come to visit him soon. And by we, I mean myself and his lawyer."

Smith thrust out his chin. "That would depend on his behavior."

Cade smiled and shook his head. "Not entirely, Captain, not entirely. Just be aware that while the designated authorities may or may not hold you personally responsible for Mr. Tatanka's well-being, I intend to."

Clayborne spoke up. "*Quis custodiet ipsos custodes?*" At Cade's raised eyebrow, he translated. "Who watches the watchmen?"

"Ah," Cade said. "I guess that would be you and me, Mr. Clayborne."

Clayborne nodded. "It would."

Smith didn't answer. He turned away and gave terse orders to his officers, who piled into the wagons and set off, a couple of the officers glowering at Cade as they did.

When they'd cleared the gate, Cade took a deep breath. "That was a close one, Sam."

Clayborne took out his handkerchief and wiped the sweat from his face. "You have that right." He replaced the handkerchief in its pocket. "In the future, Levi, do you think you could give me some warning if I'm about to walk into a situation that's liable to get me killed?"

"I'll do what I can. But right now, we need to get a handle on this." He looked at the porch, where Givens's household staff was gathered, chattering in obvious agitation. "I'll go in and see if I can calm the lady of the house down."

Clayborne nodded. "She might be ready to give you some actual useful information now, instead of her usual mystical balderdash."

"Maybe. In the meantime, you got that translator lined up? And our, ah, lockbreaker?"

"Both." Clayborne grinned. "The translation will be provided by Mr. Simonson himself."

"Oh boy," Cade said without enthusiasm.

Clayborne went on. "And the picker of locks prefers the

term screwsman." At Cade's look, he chuckled. "Every day in this business is an education."

"That it is. And when do they get here?"

Clayborne looked uncomfortable. "Yes. Well. As soon as we can arrange payment."

"Okay. How much?"

Clayborne set his jaw defiantly. "Ten dollars."

"Ten..." Cade shook his head. "Jesus Christ, Sam, we ain't tryin' to bust into the White House."

Clayborne stiffened. "And you know what a screwsman is supposed to cost in San Francisco? Maybe you should have done the negotiating."

Cade raised a hand. "Okay, okay. What the hell, it ain't like we're spending our own money. I'll see if I can get an advance for expenses."

Clayborne relaxed. "Okay."

"Meanwhile," Cade said, "I need you to get a message to this lawyer, Jenkins. I'm thinking he's the man we need to try to spring Tatanka." He saw the look on Clayborne's face. "What?"

"Nothing," Clayborne said, then he shook his head. "It's just that you don't even like Tatanka much."

"No. But I like that bastard Smith even less." He thought about that for a moment, then laughed ruefully. "I'm picking sides based on who I dislike the least." He shook his head. "Once again, I find myself a stranger in a strange land, Mr. Clayborne."

"We all are." Clayborne looked down at his feet and sighed. "Well, I better get going. It's a long walk."

Cade frowned. "Walk?"

"Do you think I can hail a cab here, Levi?"

Cade grimaced. "Right." He turned and saw Mr. George headed back to the stables. "Mr. George!"

The old groom turned slowly, still holding the shotgun down by his side. "Suh?"

Cade gestured to Clayborne. "Do you think you could arrange transportation for my partner here? He needs to get downtown."

George regarded Clayborne sourly.

After a moment, Cade added, "Please?"

George nodded. "Come on, then," he said, and turned away.

"Well," Clayborne said, "that was a warm welcome."

"He's a prickly old bastard," Cade said. "You two might get on. Or you could walk."

Clayborne sighed. "Okay, then." He trudged after George.

Cade looked at the front door of the mansion. The staff who'd crowded around the glass doors had vanished. He sighed and rolled his shoulders, like a man preparing for a fight. *Well, back to work*, he thought.

CHAPTER THIRTY-THREE

T he first thing Cade encountered as he re-entered the Givens mansion was the sound of a woman wailing, crying out as if her heart was breaking. He put his head down and trudged up the stairs to the second floor. He was surprised when Eleanor met him at the top of the staircase.

"Mr. Cade," she said, "may I speak with you?" She cast her gaze back over her shoulder to the master quarters where the wailing was coming from. "It might shed some light on the situation."

Cade took off his hat and ran his hand through his hair. "Some light would be most welcome, Miss Eleanor." His eyes narrowed and his voice hardened. "Especially in regards to the actual relationship between Mr. Akbar, or let's just come out and say Mr. Tatanka, and Miss Givens."

"Yes," Eleanor said, then she looked away. "I can assure you," she said in a small, distant voice, "that the connection between Mr. Tatanka and Miss Givens is purely of a spiritual nature. There is no," she took a deep breath, "physical component to their relationship."

"So I've heard. But that," he looked down the hall toward

the sound of Athena Givens's wailing, "doesn't sound like someone who's just lost a spiritual connection."

Eleanor shook her head, and Cade couldn't tell if there was more sorrow or anger in the gesture. "You truly don't understand, do you?"

"No, Miss Eleanor, I do not," Cade said. "But I need to, if I'm going to keep Miss Givens safe. And right now, the best path I see to that understanding is to speak to Miss Givens." He took a step down the hallway.

Eleanor moved to block his path. "She isn't ready to talk to you now."

"That," Cade said, "is exactly the reason I need to speak with her now. When she's ready, she is all mysticism and moonbeams. Not meaning to be rude, Miss Eleanor, but I have had that sort of thing right up to my eyeballs, and I'm about done with it. So please move aside."

"And what if I don't?" the girl said. "You'll draw your pistol and shoot me?"

"No, ma'am," Cade said with gentle firmness. "But I will move you."

They stood regarding each other for a long moment, then Eleanor looked away. "In this place," she said, "you could do anything you want to a black girl, and there'd be nothing anyone would do about it."

Cade nodded. "Most likely, miss. But I'd like to avoid that kind of unpleasantness."

Her mouth twisted bitterly. "I'm sure you would, Mr. Cade." But she stepped aside.

Cade touched the brim of his hat. "Thank you, miss."

She didn't answer, just turned away and walked down the hall.

Cade sighed. He'd always despised officers who pulled rank to get their way rather than lead their men, and what he'd just done felt a lot like pulling rank. His tread was heavy as he walked down the hall. He put his hand on the door of Miss Givens's bedroom. The caterwauling had subsided to a low sobbing. He hesitated to turn the knob, then knocked heavily on the sturdy oak door.

The sobbing faded away for a moment, then a quavering voice called out, "Come in."

Cade entered to find Athena Givens stretched out, crossways and face down, on her four-post bed. Her head rested on her arms crossed beneath her, and she was whimpering as if her heart was broken.

Cade paused. He'd never known what to do with a crying woman, and this one was further gone than most. He cleared his throat. "Miss Givens."

She looked up at him, her face streaked with tears, her eyes red and swollen. "Oh, Mr. Cade," she said, "you must help Tatanka. You *must*."

Something about her delivery reminded him of the theatricality of her speech at the hall, and he immediately became wary. "Yes, ma'am. But if you recall, our original job is to protect you."

She sat up and dabbed at her eyes with a handkerchief. "Then your job has changed." The tears had left her voice, and hers was once more the commanding presence he'd seen onstage. "I am the one who employed you, and I am changing the terms of that employment. You must do whatever it takes to clear Tatanka's name."

Cade sighed. "Yes, ma'am. But..." He hesitated.

She frowned. "You are thinking that Tatanka is the one you might need to protect me from."

Cade considered for a moment how best to approach the subject, but she interrupted his thoughts. "I assure you, Mr. Cade, that is impossible. I urge you to put aside your prejudice against the red man, the bias that sees the Native as nothing more than a rapacious savage."

Cade shook his head. "It's not a matter of prejudice, ma'am, to think that someone who's as..." he stopped for a second, then plunged ahead, "...intimately involved with someone else might let their passions overtake them." He looked her in the eye. "That's not a matter of color. That's just human."

"Mr. Cade," she said, "you just don't understand."

Her condescending tone got his back up. For what felt like the hundredth time, he considered just getting up and walking away from this maddening woman and her crazy household. It was especially tempting in light of the offer he'd just been made. He fought the urge down. He wasn't quite ready to turn his back.

"Well, then, ma'am," he said with as much patience as he could muster, "maybe you could explain it to me. Starting from the beginning."

She looked at him for a moment, then she looked away, her eyes uncertain in a way he hadn't seen from her. Her voice was distant as she said, "The beginning." She looked back at Cade. "Do you really want to know about the beginning?"

The look in her eyes made him wonder, but he nodded. "Yes, ma'am. That's why I asked."

She nodded. "Very well, Mr. Cade." She took a deep breath. "I was born in Utica, New York."

Cade suppressed a groan. He hadn't meant for the woman to give out her whole life story. *But,* he thought ruefully, *you did say begin at the beginning.* He settled himself down to listen to what was looking like a long story.

CHAPTER THIRTY-FOUR

"My father...was not a good man. He was a drunkard, a bully, and a grifter. He spent most of his life trying to come up with some way to put one over on his fellow man." She sighed. "We spent much of my childhood moving from town to town, often one step ahead of the people he'd tried to cheat."

"Doesn't sound like much of a childhood for a young girl."

"Childhood?" Givens shook her head. "I never had what one could consider a childhood, Mr. Cade. My mother was...she was weak. In many ways, I had to assume the wifely role." She grimaced. "I had to be a woman before my time."

Cade's mind recoiled from asking the question that statement raised. She didn't seem to notice his discomfort, lost as she was in her own memories.

"When my...power began to manifest itself, my father didn't see it as a blessing. He only saw it as a way to make money."

Cade regained his voice. "How did the power begin?"

She didn't answer right away. She looked down for a moment, then back up. "I had a sister. She was born in the middle of winter, in a shack where we'd holed up outside of some god-awful town in Ohio. She died after three days. Along with my mother."

"I'm sorry," Cade said.

"Thank you." She looked him in the eye for the first time since beginning her story. "I carried that tiny body through the snow to a church for burial. The preacher told me that since my sister had never been baptized, never been accepted into the," her mouth twisted, "congregation of the saints, that she could not be buried in consecrated ground. That she was, in fact, at that moment, screaming in eternal agony in Hell." She leaned forward, her eyes burning. "A baby, Mr. Cade. A complete innocent."

Cade shook his head. His own father had tried his hand at preaching, but he'd never debated the tenets of infant baptism. "That sounds a mite harsh."

She laughed bitterly. "A mite, yes. I could never believe in a God who could condemn innocents to the fires of Hell for what was beyond their control."

"So, you came up with this idea for Spiritualism?"

She shook her head angrily, rising slightly from her chair. "I did not come up with anything, Mr. Cade. "This was revealed to me. And several other people at the same time, I might add. This was a new revelation that came to many at the same instant. Wouldn't that suggest to you some new disclosure from the divine?"

"Can't speak as to any revelations, ma'am. Or the divine. Let's talk about what you went through. Personally."

She settled back down. "Very well. As I sat by the side of the road near the church who had turned us away, wailing and sobbing out my sorrow, my sister appeared before me."

"Your sister. The one who'd just died. The baby."

Givens nodded. "Not in her form as an infant. In the form she would have worn had she achieved young womanhood."

Cade kept his face neutral. "Okay."

Givens smiled indulgently. "You have trouble believing. Trust me, Mr. Cade, so did I. But I tell you, I knew my sister." She clenched her fist and held it to her heart. "I knew that was my sister as much as I knew myself. And she told me of a place divorced from the ideas of Heaven and Hell, of a plane where the spirits of the dead dwelt in peace and harmony."

"And a place where they could talk to you and me. Or at least to you."

She settled back in her chair and smoothed her skirts. "What will it take to shake you from this skepticism, Mr. Cade? This reflexive mistrust?"

"Don't know, ma'am, but I'd observe that mistrust, as you put it, comes with the job you hired me for. So how does this, ah, vision relate to your relationship with Mr. Tatanka?"

"I soon discovered that there were others who'd experienced the same revelation I had. They taught me the value of obtaining a spirit guide."

"A spirit guide."

Her eyes were brighter now, almost burning with intensity, and she was leaning forward again. "Yes. A psychopomp. A guide and guardian in the spirit world. And many of those guides were Indians. Native men who had previously crossed over." She shook her head. "My father, of course, didn't understand. He just saw it as another game to make money." She looked at him defiantly. "But I still provided comfort to the people who came to us. Solace in their time of need."

There's always money in telling people what they want to hear, Cade thought, but he kept it to himself.

"As my power grew, I learned more and more ways to communicate with those on the other side. I learned to open the way for the spirits to communicate when their ethereal forms could not manifest. By manipulating physical objects on this plane. By tapping out messages."

"What, like a telegraph?"

She nodded, smiling. "Similar."

"So, the spirits know Morse code?"

The smile vanished. "Are you mocking me, Mr. Cade?"

"No, ma'am," he said quickly, inwardly cursing himself for the slip. "But if I'm going to start helping Mr. Tatanka, it's best I get started right away. So, all due respect, if we could just jump to the part where you two met."

She regarded him with narrowed eyes, then continued, her tone frostier than before. "It was in Salt Lake City. I was giving readings in a hotel downtown. People were beginning to flock to the sessions."

"How'd that sit with the Mormon elders?" Cade had passed through Salt Lake in his travels and had noted the iron hold the self-described Latter Day Saints exercised on the relatively new city.

She smiled tightly. "I think you can imagine." She sighed. "It's a shame. It seems to me the Mormons, whose faith is, after all, based on a new revelation from the other side of the Veil, would be more accepting of the premise that such a revelation could be ongoing. And, truth be told, there were some members of the Church who put forth the proposition that their prophet, Joseph Smith, may himself have been a spirit medium."

"I bet that went over well."

She shook her head. "I wasn't the one who put the idea in their heads. There was already a schism brewing in the church. I merely provided a scapegoat."

"You were horning in on their territory."

"Just so. One day, my father was lying drunk in his bed in the middle of the afternoon. I couldn't bear to listen to his snoring and blubbering, so I decided to go get myself something to eat. On my way to the market, I was waylaid by a group of men. In the street." She closed her eyes, remembering. "They surrounded me. Jeering and cursing. Calling me a heretic and... and a whore." She opened them and looked at Cade, levelly. "I have never been more frightened in my life. I was sure I was about to be killed. Or worse." The sober look left her face and she smiled. "That's when I saw Tatanka."

"He intervened?"

"Yes. The first thing I heard was his voice. Shouting something in his native tongue." She chuckled. "His name means *bull*, you know, and he did indeed sound like a bull roaring. He waded into that crowd of men, swinging a piece of firewood like a club. He scattered them like a flock of birds."

"Pretty brave."

She smiled sadly. "Raving drunk. But he saved my life." Her eyes went far away. "And when I saw him standing there in the street, I saw an aura like I had never seen before."

"A what?"

"All living things are surrounded by an aura, Mr. Cade. A sort of glow that shows the state of their inner self. Tatanka's aura was purest white. It was like watching the rising of a new sun."

"Right. What happened then?"

"At that time, I knew this was something that was destined to be." She grimaced. "First, I had to sober him up. And we had to get out of there. I sneaked him into my room up the back stairs and brought him coffee until he was more himself. Then we talked. We talked for hours." She frowned at the look on his face. "I swear to you, Mr. Cade, talk is all that passed between us. It is all that has ever passed between us."

Cade kept his face as expressionless as possible. "Yes, ma'am."

"By nightfall, I knew what needed to be done. I left Tatanka in my room while I went to the small lecture hall my father had procured and did my readings. I tell you, Mr. Cade, from that night, and every night since then, my powers have been at their peak. I feel as though the Veil through which I see the other side is as thin as gossamer." Her eyes took on a manic light. "I could almost walk through it." She blinked and her expression returned to normal. She looked at Cade. "But I didn't, and I don't. Not until my mission here on Earth is complete."

"What mission would that be, ma'am?"

"Why, to leave this world a better place. Fairer. More equal. And more in touch with the world on the other side." She reached out and put her hand on his. "A world where people no longer need to fear death. Is that not a world worth fighting for, Mr. Cade?"

"Yes, ma'am," he said. "It sounds like a wonderful place. But gettin' back to the world we have to deal with now."

She looked exasperated. "You are such a cynical man, Mr. Cade. Or so you would have people believe."

"Yes, ma'am. But back to Salt Lake. Where did you go from there?"

She sighed. "Very well. That night, my father, as usual, pocketed the money people had paid for the readings. By that time, our reputation had grown. Each reading brought a substantial sum. I knew he'd deposit the money in a lockbox he kept by his bed. What was left over after he came back from getting drunk again. All I had to do was wait."

"And when he came back?"

"I waited. Tatanka waited, too. With his knife in his hand."

"Wait a minute," Cade said. "Did you—?"

"We didn't kill him, Mr. Cade," she interrupted. "Because he didn't try to come into my room. He wasn't, as much. By then." She looked away. "I think he was tiring of me. I was getting too old."

Jesus, Cade thought. *No wonder she's crazy. A father like that...* He almost missed her next words.

"We waited for what seemed like hours. Not moving. Almost not daring to breathe. Until his snores began rattling the floorboards. We went into the room and took the lockbox. We took the horse and wagon from the stable, and we left. In the dead of night. I left my father behind, and my most fervent prayer is that I never see him again, in this world or the next."

"Didn't he follow you?"

She shrugged. "He may have tried. But he had no horse, no money, and besides, we went in a direction we didn't think he'd expect."

"And where was that?"

"Chicago."

CHAPTER THIRTY-FIVE

Kam was working in the small greenhouse attached to one side of the house, repotting geraniums. He was usually able to lose himself if the work, but the woman's visit earlier had unsettled him. From time to time, he glanced at the line of potted orchids along one wall. He shook his head. He had always assumed The White Orchid was just a story, a tale told to children and those in debt to the Green Dragon Tong to keep them in line. But now, he had actually seen her in the flesh. That flesh had, in fact, been pressed against him, and he flushed as he remembered the feel of her, the sight of those cold but beautiful eyes boring into his, that perfect and terrifying smile on her face. He had been as frightened as he had ever been in his life, but he had also been aroused. He shook his head. One of the worst things about this place was the lack of female companionship. Oh, there were prostitutes in abundance, and there had been times when he had been so lonely and desperate, he'd availed himself of one. But the ones he could afford were dead-eyed, limp creatures, most addicted to opium and with the aroma of death already faintly on them.

"Boy." A now-familiar voice said, making him jump. He turned.

The White Orchid was there again, standing a few feet away, smiling that chilly smile.

"I...I didn't hear you come in," he said, feeling stupid even as he said it.

"I know. And you never will. Unless I wish it." She came closer. "The police were here earlier. Why?"

He swallowed nervously. She must be watching the house. "They came for Tatanka. The Native man."

She frowned. "The big one? Why?"

"They think he is the one who tried to kill the lady of the house."

"Well? Was he?"

Kam shrugged. "How am I to know? I do know Miss Givens doesn't believe it."

"Hmm." She looked thoughtful. "They are together? You know how I mean."

Kam looked down. "I am only the gardener, miss."

"And Cade? The white devil with the gun? He is still here?"

"As far as I know, yes."

She nodded as if she'd made a decision. "You speak the white devil's language?"

He didn't like where this was going. "A little."

"Very well. I need you to go to him. Tell him a lady wishes to speak with him." She strode over to the potted orchids and casually plucked a white one from the pot. Kam suppressed a gasp. Those flowers were worth a week of his salary. She walked over and handed the flower to him. "Take this to him. He'll know what it means."

He took the blossom, his hands trembling. "Noble Lady," he said, "as I said, I am only the gardener. They won't let me in the house."

"Then give it to someone who'll give it to Cade," she snapped. "Come on, you donkey, move! Bring him to me here. In this place."

"Yes, Noble Lady," he said miserably.

"It was in Chicago," Givens said, "that I first met Mrs. Stanton. Elizabeth Cady Stanton. Are you familiar with the name?"

Cade had heard it before, but he couldn't recall exactly where. "Vaguely, ma'am. Maybe you could fill me in."

"Mrs. Stanton is one of the leading lights of the suffragist movement." Givens's face was almost worshipful. "She's the most wonderful speaker. Her lectures through the lyceum are among the most stirring I have ever heard. If you get a chance to hear her speak, don't pass it up."

Cade had never been partial to lectures of any kind; the very idea of sitting still for hours while someone talked at him made him itchy. "I'll keep it in mind. So it was her who got you into this whole votes for women movement?"

"Oh, it's more than just votes, Mr. Cade. Mrs. Stanton is calling for the reform of the absurd restrictions on women's attire. The reform of marriage, especially in regards to women's rights to own property. So many things. Anyway, when I was invited backstage, I was so overwhelmed, I could hardly speak."

Well, that's a wonder I'd have to see to believe, Cade thought.

Givens went on. "We spoke for hours, and there was so much sense in what she said. What we found ourselves most in agreement on, though, was that religion had been corrupted. That men had usurped the prerogatives of Jehovah himself to assign women a sphere of action and control their lives. It was at that moment, Mr. Cade, that I realized Spiritualism and suffragism were mutually compatible. That one could be wedded to the other."

"I get it, ma'am. But if we could get back to Mr. Tatanka."

She nodded. "Of course, of course. You must think me awfully flighty."

"You've had a shock, ma'am. I figure you've got a right to be a little discombobulated."

She smiled thinly. "You are becoming more diplomatic, Mr. Cade."

"I'm learning, ma'am. As I go."

"Yes. Well. During this period, Tatanka was developing his own powers, finding his own pathway through the Veil, as it were. But he was—is—becoming as good a medium as I. However," she frowned, "the prejudices of the small-minded have kept him from helping as many as he would like."

"People are scared of him, so they're not willing to pay for his help."

"Sadly, no."

"You're making more money than he is."

A frown line appeared between her eyes. "What are you saying?"

"Miss Givens," Cade said, then he hesitated. "Have you made out a will?"

The frown deepened. "I don't think I like where you're going with this."

"I have to follow the trail where it leads, ma'am. Can you tell me if Mr. Tatanka would receive anything from you if you were to, ah, pass through this Veil?"

She stiffened. "I have told you, Mr. Cade, that there is no way Tatanka would do me harm. No way in this world. The job I am paying you for is to clear his name. I suggest you get on with it."

"Yes, ma'am." Cade picked up his hat and started to leave.

As he reached the door, he turned. "Do I have one of those auras that you mentioned? Can you see it now?"

"Of course, Mr. Cade. Yours is a deep and vibrant red."

"And what, if I may ask, does that signify?"

She smiled. "Vitality. Strength. Passion." The smile faded. "Sometimes a proclivity for violence."

"Ah. Thank you ma'am. I'll let you know what I find out. Try to get some rest."

"Please do. And I will."

CHAPTER THIRTY-SIX

Outside in the hallway, Cade shook his head. Nothing Givens had told him made him sure that Tatanka wasn't the one who'd tried to kill her. The fact that she'd refused to answer whether or not the big Indian was in her will made it pretty clear to him that he was. And in Cade's experience, that kind of money, the kind of money it would take to live in a house like this, was as solid a motive for killing as you could find.

He thought about Givens's assessment of his aura: *Vitality. Strength. Passion.* He chuckled. Every fortune teller he'd ever met played the same game. Tell the mark something about themselves that they'd love to hear, and they'd wonder at how perceptive the medium was.

He heard footsteps around the corner of the hallway. Eleanor turned the corner and stopped suddenly, putting her hand to her mouth. "Oh," she said, "Mr. Cade."

He nodded "Miss Eleanor. Sorry to startle you."

She dropped her hand. "That's all right. I was actually looking for you. Something very strange is going on."

"Given recent events, miss, you'll have to be more specific."

"One of the gardeners, Kam, is at the back door, asking for you."

Cade frowned. "Me? What for?"

"He won't say. But he's holding a flower in his hand."

"What kind of flower?"

"It's an orchid. From the greenhouse."

A chill ran down Cade's spine. "An orchid? What color?"

She looked puzzled. "A white one."

"Shit," Cade muttered under his breath.

Her eyes widened. "Excuse me?"

"Sorry. Lead me to this gardener of yours."

"Follow me."

When they reached the stairs, Eleanor asked a question over her shoulder. "What's the significance? Of the flower?"

"Nothing you need worry about, miss. It's…kind of a symbol. Like a calling card."

"Of what?"

"Of someone you'd rather not meet."

She stopped at the foot of the stairs. "And that person is here?"

"Most likely."

She put her hands on her hips. "Is Miss Givens in danger?"

He shook his head. "I don't see any reason why she would be."

He started forward again, but she blocked his way. "Are you?" she said softly. "In danger, I mean."

"I don't think so. Last time we met, this person got me out of a pretty bad jam. They may be here to call in the debt."

"But you don't know for sure what that payment may be. Maybe you should wait for Mr. Clayborne to return."

"This person isn't likely to be patient, miss."

"Then I should get Lucius."

"Believe me, miss, it wouldn't make any difference. If this

personage wanted any of us dead, we'd be dead already. Please lead on."

Reluctantly, she turned. She led him through the dining room to the kitchen, where she opened the back door. "Kam," she called out.

A young Chinese man was there, dressed in the usual loose-fitting trousers and tunic. He was holding the white flower in his right hand, which he extended toward Cade. "You come, please."

Cade didn't take the offered flower. "She's here, then?"

The young man nodded. He looked distinctly unhappy.

"Don't worry," Cade told the young gardener. "We'll be fine." As the gardener turned to lead him down the path, he added under his breath, "So long as we do whatever she wants."

They found her along one of the paths through the gardens, sitting cross-legged on a bench in front of a thick hedge. She was dressed in the same loose-fitting outfit as Kam, but hers was a brilliant white. Her long black hair was bound with a simple silver clasp at the neck and flowed down her back. When she saw them coming, she rose gracefully and waited until Cade stopped and touched the brim of his hat.

"Ma'am. To what do we owe this honor?"

She looked quizzically at Kam, who was standing off to one side, head down. She barked a command at him. He answered sullenly. She nodded at Kam, then turned to Cade with a smile. As beautiful and enticing as that smile was, he didn't trust it. She said something in Chinese, looking into Cade's eyes.

Kam began to translate. "She says you have troubles. The..." he struggled for the words, "...the Native man."

"You're mighty well-informed, young lady. Have you been spying on me?"

Kam hesitated.

"Say it," Cade told him. "Just those words."

He did.

The White Orchid laughed and nodded, then spoke again, her eyes merry. Then she grew serious as she went on.

"She says of course. She believes she can help you with your difficulties."

"Thank her kindly, but she's done so much for me already, I couldn't impose more on her generosity."

Kam translated, and The White Orchid responded at length. He looked shocked at the words, but at a peremptory word from her, he went on.

"She says she understands that you do not wish to be indebted to Kwan Lee. Or to her. But she says..." Kam stopped and shook his head as if he couldn't believe what he was saying. "She says not to consider it a debt. She believes that you and Mr. Kwan could be...help to one another. Like..." he struggled for the words, "...like in war. Fighting on same side."

"Allies?" Cade said incredulously.

She picked up on that word and nodded.

Cade narrowed his eyes. "Is this Mr. Kwan's idea or yours?"

There was a brief exchange between her and Kam, and the young man said, "She asks would you meet with Kwan to discuss it. And," his brow furrowed, "the other thing you were thinking."

"You mean Marjorie?"

Kam looked puzzled at the unfamiliar word.

"No, don't translate that part," Cade said. "Tell her I'll meet with her boss. Some neutral ground. I don't want to get etherized again. It gives me a headache." At Kam's confused look, Cade said "Just tell her okay. I'll meet. Someplace safe."

He spoke, and she nodded.

"Safe," she said to Cade. "Promise." She spoke to Kam again.

He turned to Cade. "A carriage will come for you. You will be safe."

Cade nodded at Kam, then turned back to say goodbye. But The White Orchid was gone.

Cade shook his head. "Someday, I really want to learn how she does that."

CHAPTER THIRTY-SEVEN

"So," Kwan Fang said, "My brother is meeting with the white devil Cade at Mr. Zhi's."

"Yes, Great One," Fat Chung replied. "At noon tomorrow."

"You're sure about this."

Fat Chung nodded. "When we got there, I told the Pearl River whore I needed to use the privy. Instead, I snuck into the back and listened. She paid Zhi in gold to close the restaurant so they could meet alone."

Fang stroked his beard. "They don't want to meet at our house. Neutral ground." He looked at Fat Chung. "I don't suppose you overheard what they meant to discuss?" Without waiting for an answer, Fang waved his own question away. "It doesn't matter. What matters is that we can expose my brother as a collaborator with the white devils. That should bring any of the *boo how doy* who were sitting on the fence over to our side. My brother will be finished." He smacked a hand down on the table between them. Fat Chung jumped at the sudden report.

"This is the moment," Fang declared. "This is the

opportunity Fate has granted." He grinned at Fat Chung. "It would seem ungrateful to waste it, don't you agree?"

"Yes, sir," Fat Chung said. He swallowed nervously before adding, "Great One."

Fang nodded, acknowledging the honorific. "Take the men we can trust. Arm yourselves well. Kill The White Orchid and the white devil Cade."

Fat Chung nodded. "And your brother?"

"Take him alive if you can. Bring him to me. I will give him a choice of fates. I will offer to let him live out the rest of his life in exile. Back home. I owe him that much, at least." He smiled coldly. "He is family, after all."

"If he won't be taken alive, Great One?"

Fang shrugged. "Then he will have made his choice of deaths. That's more than most men get in this world."

"I don't know, Sam," Cade said. "I feel like I'm sticking my head in the lion's mouth here."

"More like the dragon's," Clayborne replied, deadpan.

"Not helping, Sam."

"Sorry."

To Cade's surprise, Clayborne had returned, not with an offer of an appointment with Lawyer Jenkins, but with the man himself, dressed to the nines in a fancy suit and bowler hat. He'd exited the carriage that brought him with the air of a man taking possession of a property, and from the way he'd stopped and regarded the house after stepping out, Cade wasn't sure he didn't mean to do just that as his fee. A young clerk with slicked back hair and a leather briefcase trailed in his wake. He was currently shut up with Athena Givens in the parlor, probably negotiating the fee of a lifetime. Cade and Clayborne were seated at the kitchen table, cooling their heels and drinking coffee grudgingly prepared by the fat French chef. However ungraciously the brew may have been prepared, the taste was excellent.

"Anyway," Clayborne said, "what's the harm in hearing the man out? We may be able to use his help. Maybe we can make a bargain." He smiled. "And maybe you'll get a nice Chinese meal out of it at this...what do you call it? Mr. Zhi's."

Cade shook his head. "I never was much of a horse trader, Sam. I don't much worry about them doin' me harm. I just don't want to get skinned in whatever deal Kwan offers."

"So don't agree to anything right away. Stroke your chin, look thoughtful, and say you'll need to think it over. Then come back and talk to the brains of this outfit."

Cade smiled. "That would be you, Mr. Clayborne?"

"Well, I don't like to brag, Mr. Cade."

Cade laughed out loud. "Oh, no, not you."

At that moment, Jenkins entered the kitchen. "Ah, there you are, gentlemen." He stopped and sniffed. "Is that coffee I smell?"

"Pot's over there on the stove," Cade said. "Cups in the cabinet above."

"Many thanks."

Cade and Clayborne looked at each other silently as Jenkins poured himself a cup. He took a seat at the kitchen table and inhaled deeply of the coffee before taking a drink. "Ahhh," he breathed. "Exquisite. Sumatran, unless I miss my guess."

"I wouldn't know," Cade said, "but are you gonna knock the cost of the coffee off the bill?"

Jenkins smiled sardonically at Cade. "You believe I'm taking advantage of Miss Givens, Mr. Cade?"

Cade looked him in the eye. "I believe she'd pay damn near anything to get that man out of jail."

"And that I'd take advantage of that." Jenkins said it without visible offense.

Cade didn't answer.

"I tell you what, Mr. Cade." Jenkins took another drink of the coffee. "Before I present my final bill for legal services to Miss Givens, I will run it by you. If you believe it's excessive, I'll discuss cutting it with you."

Cade looked down into his cup. "I don't know anything about what that kind of thing needs to cost here," he muttered.

"I know." Jenkins sighed and put his cup down. "I know you believe I'm just another shyster lawyer. But I do think an injustice is being done here. I also know, from experience, that it's going to take a great deal of time and effort to make it right. And I need your help, Mr. Cade."

Cade looked up. "Mine?"

Jenkins nodded. "And Mr. Clayborne's. My clerk is working on a motion for bail for Mr. Tatanka right now, which will be filed before the close of business today, and which I hope to have heard before Judge Farenholt tomorrow at two o'clock. Miss Givens will be there as a character witness for Mr. Tatanka. I'd like for you to be there as well to talk about what you've found in regard to this matter."

"Okay," Cade said. "But I don't know if what we've found so far is going to be much help."

Clayborne spoke up. "We're still investigating. And we'll keep you informed."

"I need to ask, Mr. Jenkins," Cade said, "what happens if we find out that Tatanka is actually the one who did it?"

Jenkins smiled and picked up his cup. "Then we will adjust our strategy accordingly."

"You'd defend a man you know is guilty?"

"Defense can take many forms, Mr. Cade." Jenkins put the cup back down and stood up. "But let's not get ahead of ourselves. Let's find out what there is to know." He bowed his head slightly and put his hat back on. "We have work to do, gentlemen. Let's get to it."

CHAPTER THIRTY-EIGHT

"So now we have the Indian," Smith said. "What do you want us to do with him?"

The banker looked up from the papers he'd been scanning on his desk, clearly annoyed that Smith had spoken before being spoken to. Smith didn't give a damn. He'd sat cooling his heels in the outer office for nearly a half hour before being brought into the office, where he continued to wait in the chair before the big desk while the banker pointedly ignored him. He was being ostentatiously put in his place, and he was getting sick of it.

"Do with him?" the banker said. "You squeeze him."

"Squeeze?"

The banker flung the papers in his hand down. "For information, man! Find out what he knows about this circus show they're running. Get him to admit it's all a fraud. A confidence game."

Smith shook his head. "He doesn't seem to want to talk."

The banker sighed. "Surely you have ways of persuading him."

"We do. But he's due in court tomorrow."

The banker frowned. "Tomorrow? For what?"

"Givens has hired a shyster to represent the Indian. A lawyer named Jenkins."

The banker looked as if he was about to spit. "That one."

"Yes, sir. And he's filing all sorts of legal mumbo jumbo. Got a hearing scheduled in front of Judge Farenholt tomorrow. And if the redskin comes in all banged up, there's liable to be questions."

"Damn it." The banker got up and went to the window. Smith felt a spiteful pleasure in seeing him nonplussed. The two men stood in silence until the banker turned from the window. "And Cade? You saw him at the Givens house?"

"Yes, sir."

"And what was he doing?"

Smith took a moment to figure out the best way to present what had happened at the arrest. "For a minute there, it looked as if he meant to interfere with our apprehension of the Indian. But he backed down."

"Did he now," the banker said thoughtfully. "Perhaps he is beginning to see the light."

Smith couldn't let that perception stand. "I don't know, sir. When we left, he seemed pretty dug into the Givens camp."

"Wavering, though," the banker said. "Just needs a little push to get him off the fence." He walked to his desk and picked up a small brass bell that sat on the edge of the broad desktop.

As soon as he rang the bell, a young clerk, dressed in an expensive-looking waistcoat and trousers cut in the latest style, bustled in. "Sir?"

"We're calling in the loans on the Hamrick Shipping Line," the banker said. "And the personal loans to the Hamrick family as well. You've prepared the paperwork as I instructed? It's ready?"

"Yes, sir."

The banker nodded with satisfaction. "Good man. Let's put the wheels in motion, then."

The clerk said nothing, just bowed his head and left the room quickly.

The banker turned to Smith. "If Mr. Cade thought I was bluffing earlier, what's about to happen to his whore, the," he smiled nastily as he pronounced the next words with heavy irony, "Widow Hamrick, will disabuse him of that notion. There is still time for him to come into the fold, but that window is closing rapidly."

"Yes, sir," Smith answered.

"First off," Cade said, "what exactly *is* a footman?"

Lucius slumped in one of the wooden chairs around the kitchen table, looking sullenly around him. He wouldn't meet Cade's eyes, and he refused to acknowledge Clayborne's presence at all. He shrugged. "Serve meals. Rides along in the carriage."

"An assistant to the butler, then?" Clayborne asked.

Lucius looked at Clayborne for the first time, then turned back to Cade. "Do I have to answer his questions, too?" He snorted. "Bad enough I got to talk to a former bluebelly."

"Ah," Cade said. "I believe I get it. You're from Missouri, I hear." He pronounced it *Mizooruh.*

"Yeah. What about it?"

"Well, young fella, I get the definite sense that you backed the wrong side there."

Missouri had been a border state during the war, torn apart by partisan warfare between pro-Union Jayhawkers and Confederate sympathizers known as Bushwhackers. Raids, looting, and massacres had rendered much of the state a bloody wasteland, and the Union Army's attempts to keep order had grown more heavy-handed until entire counties were emptied at the point of the bayonet and the farms within them burned to the ground. Even now, a gang of former Bushwhackers led by a pair of brothers named Frank and Jesse James were raising Hell in the state, robbing banks and murdering people they suspected of being former Jayhawkers.

For too many people, the war wasn't yet over.

Lucius set his jaw stubbornly. "Don't know what you're talkin' about."

"War's over for you, sonny," Cade said. "You best get used to that. And you're gonna answer our questions, 'less you want your skinny ass out on the street."

The young man's eyes narrowed. "You can't fire me. I don't work for you."

"I didn't say I was going to fire you," Cade said with deceptive mildness. "I said I was going to kick your ass into the street. So. You were supposed to be an assistant to Akbar?"

He shook his head. "Akbar's not the butler. There was another fellow. Name of Gideon."

"First name or last name?"

"Don't know. He was English. He said that Gideon was all anyone needed to know."

"What happened to him?"

"One day he was just gone. Miss Givens said he packed up and went home to England."

"Any reason?"

Lucius shrugged. "Guess he got homesick."

Cade thought that over for a minute before taking another tack. "Who started when?"

Lucius's eyes narrowed as he tried to recall. "From what I was told, Tatanka came here with her. I think Eleanor was hired next. Then Fabrice came. Fabrice hired Carine. Then

Eleanor found George and Jephthah. George was the driver originally."

"Originally? Clinton took George's place?"

Lucius nodded.

"How did Mr. George feel about that?" Clayborne asked.

"Relieved, I think. He never liked wearing the fancy clothes and driving out. He just likes to be in the stable with the horses."

Cade nodded. "When did Mr. Clinton join the staff?"

"About a month, month and a half ago." Lucius frowned. "Right before Gideon left."

Cade and Clayborne exchanged glances. "Was there some kind of bad blood between Gideon and Clinton?"

Lucius shook his head. "Nothing specific. Nothing you could put your finger on. But yeah, Gideon was kinda chilly toward Clinton. Not that he was all that friendly to anyone." He grimaced. "Kinda snooty, you want to know the truth. We all figured it was on account of him bein' English."

"Maybe he had a problem with Clinton bein' a drunk."

"Maybe. But he didn't say anything about it when he left. One day, he was just...gone."

"Why do you think he just packed up and went home? Without notice?"

Lucius shrugged. "He'd been talking about it. A lot."

"Huh." Cade thought about that for a moment. He took another tack. "You like working here, Lucius?"

The young man looked at him suspiciously. "It's all right. Why?"

"You're not mad you didn't get the butler job? That Akbar, or Tatanka, or whatever, seems to be doing that job instead?"

"I ain't sayin' I'm happy about it—hey, wait." He stood up, looking agitated. "You don't think I had anything to do with tryin' to kill Miss Givens!"

"Sit down, sonny," Cade said. "I'm just asking some questions here."

"You can take your questions and shove 'em up your ass," Lucius said, face red and fists clenched.

"I said *sit down*." Cade's voice was steady, but the look in his eyes made the young man step back. They stared at each other for a long moment, then Lucius sat back down.

"I didn't," he muttered. "I wouldn't."

"No," Cade said gently. "I don't think you did. I don't think you have it in you. That's a compliment, by the way." He stood up. "Okay. You can go."

Lucius stood up. "Really?"

"Yeah. Really. Get back to work. Go polish the silverware or something."

The young man looked suspicious for a moment, but he left the room.

CHAPTER THIRTY-NINE

"You really think he didn't have anything to do with it?" Clayborne asked.

"Nah," Cade said. "I don't think he's the kind that would stab a woman in the back."

Clayborne's mouth twisted sardonically. "He doesn't have that killing look you go on about."

"No," Cade said. "Laugh all you like. But I just don't see him as the one."

"Not to mention, he has an alibi," Clayborne said. "Remember, all the servants say they were in the kitchen during the séance."

"Yeah." Cade's shoulders slumped. "So they say. Which leaves us exactly nowhere. Well, we've still got guard duty to do."

Clayborne nodded. "Maybe you'd better take the first watch, and get to sleep early."

Cade nodded. "Makes sense."

His patrol of the grounds was uneventful, and when Clayborne took the watch at ten, Cade retired to one of the guest rooms set aside for him. The room was quiet, the bed one of the most comfortable he'd ever slept in, but sleep eluded him. The things he'd learned about Athena Givens and her household turned and tumbled in his mind. There was something not right about the whole story, the pieces fitting badly together like joints made by a drunken carpenter. When he turned his mind from those, he was wracked by worry about Marjorie and with guilt that it had been her loaning him and Sam the money to open their business that had caused her financial problems. *You can't shoot your way out of this one, Levi*, she'd said. She was right, and it made some small part of him wish he'd never come to this town. His life as a drifter had been hard, but at least he could figure it out. Finally, he drifted off into a fitful sleep.

The next morning, he awakened late to find that the clothes he'd hung up the night before had been freshly pressed. He went down to the kitchen to find Eleanor there.

"You missed breakfast, I'm afraid," she said with a smile, "but there's coffee, and a few sweet rolls left."

"Thanks," he said. "Point me at 'em."

She pointed to one of the chairs at the kitchen table where they'd been interviewing Lucius. "Sit. I'll get it for you."

He took a seat. "Thanks for pressing my clothes. They look right sharp."

She arched an eyebrow at him. "Oh, that wasn't me. That was Mr. Clayborne's doing." She handed him a cup of steaming coffee and a sweet roll on a plate.

"Sam?" he said.

"Couldn't let the firm be represented by a man in a suit that rumpled," Clayborne said as he came into the room.

Cade raised his mug to him. "Thanks."

"Don't mention it." He took another mug from Eleanor and took a seat. "Took me back to my days as a valet."

"I thought you were the driver."

"Driver, valet, whatever needed doing. It was a small staff."

"I guess. I take it things were quiet last night."

"As a country churchyard."

"Let's hope things stay that way."

Clayborne nodded. "We can hope."

The carriage Kwan sent for him arrived at 11:30 on the dot. But it wasn't The White Orchid awaiting him in the entrance hall. It was Mei, dressed in her usual sober gray skirt and immaculately clean white blouse. Cade smiled, genuinely glad to see her. "Good day, young lady."

She bowed her head gravely. "Mr. Cade."

"I suppose it's time for a meeting with Mr. Kwan?"

The girl glanced at Eleanor, who was staring at them, her eyes widening at the name. "Yes. We have a carriage waiting. If you would follow me."

"You want me to come with you?" Clayborne said from behind him.

Cade shook his head. "No. Stay here and look after the house. See if you can talk to Miss Givens about this Gideon fellow. Find out where he came from, and where he went."

"Okay. Be careful."

"I will." He nodded at Mei. "Lead on, miss." As he followed her out the door, he asked, "Where's your pal? The Orchid lady."

"She is waiting. At the meeting place."

The coach was a small brougham, its windows enclosed by curtains. The driver sitting up front on the open driver's seat was Chinese, a stout fellow who looked at him without expression. Cade stepped around Mei and beat her to the door, which he opened, then motioned her inside. "After you, miss."

He held out his hand to help her in. She glanced at the hand for a moment, blinking in surprise as if she didn't recognize it. Then she took it and allowed herself to be guided into the carriage. He followed and closed the door.

The interior was cramped, barely big enough for the two of them. Mei shifted away from Cade to sit pressed against the far door, clearly uncomfortable at being so close. He shifted his own body to put as much space between them as possible.

"I never got to thank you properly for the help you gave us. During that little set-to on the docks." When one of Marjorie's ships had been attacked by a gang of hoodlums intent on burning it to the waterline with Cade, Marjorie, and Marjorie's entire household aboard, Mei had led the flotilla of fishing boats that had taken them off the ship and rowed them to safety.

Mei frowned at what he figured was an unfamiliar expression. "You are welcome," she said. After a pause, she added, "It is what Mr. Kwan requested."

"I'll be sure to thank him as well." He made as if to raise the shade on the window next to him.

"Please," she said. "Mr. Kwan would like for you to leave the shade down. He wishes our meeting place to remain secret."

Cade let the shade drop. It made him uneasy, but he kept reminding himself that if the head of the Green Dragon Tong or his lethal bodyguard wanted him dead, they had plenty of less elaborate ways to make that happen. "Okay."

After that, they fell into silence.

Mei sat with her hands in her lap, occasionally stealing a glance at the white devil sitting next to her. She still didn't know quite what to make of him. Most of the white devils treated her, and all Chinese, like something not entirely human, when they bothered to notice them at all. But this one—even though he was rough and barbaric in his ways, he still at least attempted to show some manners. Lin, The White Orchid, had teased her, asking if she found the big white devil attractive. She looked at him from the corner of her eye and shuddered. No. He may have been kind, but he was too huge, too hairy. And while he seemed to bathe more often than the other white devils, in the close space of the carriage he still smelled somehow...wrong. Maybe it was the meat-heavy diet his people ate. Besides, he was too old for her, and if her information was correct, he already had a woman. Mei hoped to be married and have her own family someday, not to be any man's concubine. Certainly not a white devil's. She put her friend's teasing firmly out of her mind.

There was work to do.

CHAPTER FORTY

"They are on their way," One-Eyed Vang said. "Cade and the fishmonger's daughter. Fat Chung is driving them."

Fang nodded. "And my brother?"

"He and the Pearl River whore are in Zhi's restaurant. Waiting."

Fang smiled coldly. "I do hope Zhi is feeding them well. Are the men in position?"

"Yes, Great One. Two men with rifles on the rooftop of the restaurant and the building across the street. Two more are ready to move into the restaurant from the alley at the back. The plan is, when Cade arrives, the Pearl River whore will come out to greet him and bring him inside, after taking his weapons."

"Good. When she does that, have the riflemen and Fat Chung kill them both. Don't let her get a chance to use those damned swords of hers. The men in the back will take possession of my brother and bring him here. I'll offer him a choice. Exile or death."

Vang nodded. "What about the fishmonger's daughter?"

Fang waved a hand dismissively. "I don't care what happens

to her. If she lives, let her be the one to tell everyone The White Orchid is dead."

Vang bowed. "Yes, sir. It will be done."

Mr. Zhi's restaurant was a nondescript, flat-roofed wooden structure, sandwiched between a grocer's and a butcher shop in the labyrinth of streets that made up Chinatown. Mei had never eaten there, but it had a reputation for serving excellent cuisine in the Cantonese style. She wondered if they'd be fed. Her stomach was starting to growl. She put it out of her mind as the carriage slowed to a stop.

Cade looked at her. "What now, miss?"

She opened the carriage door. "Follow me."

The first thing Cade noticed as he stepped out of the carriage behind Mei was that the narrow street was empty and silent. That made him uneasy from the start. He'd been to Chinatown before, and the streets had always been packed with humanity. Chinatown was clearly where they were; the signs in the windows of the business showed that clearly. But it was as if a plague had struck. No one moved, nothing stirred. The buildings on the opposite sides of the street loomed like canyon walls.

"What's going on?" he whispered. "Where are all the people?"

Mei looked around, her face showing the same nervousness he was feeling. "I...I don't know. Maybe Mr. Kwan ordered the streets cleared."

"That'd be quite a trick in this place," Cade muttered.

His hand stole beneath his suit coat to rest on the butt of his pistol. He spotted The White Orchid in the doorway of the wooden building they'd pulled up in front of. She was dressed in a loose-fitting white shirt and equally loose white linen pants. The empty street didn't seem to bother her. Cade relaxed a little. The White Orchid began walking toward them, a welcoming smile on her face. Cade took note of the hilts of the cleaver-like swords he'd seen her use with devastating effect rising from behind her shoulders where the deadly blades were strapped to her back. Cade frowned. Was she expecting trouble? Mei began walking toward her. Cade followed, the fingers of his gun hand clenching and unclenching.

There was a sharp report. The White Orchid staggered back a step as if she'd been punched. She collapsed to the ground.

"LIN!" Mei screamed. She began to run toward the crumpled figure in the street as Cade instinctively drew the Navy revolver from its shoulder holster.

The sound had come from behind him, on the other side of the carriage. The first thing he saw when he turned in that direction was the fat driver standing up in the driver's seat, pointing a shotgun with a cut-down barrel at him. Without thinking, he fired upward, striking the man beneath the chin. The driver flopped backward onto the driver's seat, blood spraying into the air from where the bullet had blown out the top of his head. The shotgun flew from his hands, turning in the air like a juggler's club before landing in the street. Another shot rang out and a plume of dust spurted up at Cade's feet. He looked up and spotted a figure on the roof of the building across the way. He moved toward the carriage to put it between him and the gunman. Another shot rang out, this one smacking into the lacquered exterior of the carriage. *Crossfire*, Cade thought. *We're in a kill box.*

The horses were stamping and rearing, terrified by the noise and commotion. Then they broke and ran, the carriage swerving madly behind them, leaving Cade and his companions exposed in the middle of the street. He looked to where he thought the shot had come from and saw another man on the roof of the building The White Orchid had just come out of. His head whirled with confusion for a moment. Had she set them up? He quickly rejected that idea when he saw Mei crouched over the motionless body of her friend, sobbing and pleading in Chinese for her to get up.

He fired two quick shots up at the man on the roof of the restaurant, driving him back, then crouched to scoop up the shotgun and turned back to the man across the street. Walking backward quickly, he fired two more shots up at the head he saw poking above the roof. The head quickly withdrew, but it wouldn't be long before both of the gunmen would be back. Cade's quick backward walk turned into a backward jog, his eyes fixed on the rooflines, until he reached Mei. He only had one shot left before he had to reload, and that wasn't going to be enough against two riflemen. He cracked the shotgun open to confirm it was fully loaded, then put a hand on Mei's shoulder, his gaze traveling back and forth.

"Come on, sis," he said, "we've gotta get out of this goddamn street. Can you get her up?" He dared a glance down, and saw that The White Orchid was sitting up on her own. A steadily spreading blotch of red stained the left side of her white robe. Cade couched down. "Ma'am, can you walk?"

The White Orchid turned her gaze on him, and Cade felt an icy hand close around his heart.

A couple of years prior, Cade had worked on a ranch in Wyoming when a big mountain lion began taking prime cattle. The rancher had quickly organized a group of men from the ranch and the nearby town to go after the big cat. They'd trailed the animal for days with the help of an Arapaho tracker named Billy. Billy had taken them up over one rocky trail after another, until they'd spotted the cougar high on a rock ledge at the entrance to a narrow canyon. "That's where he lives," Billy had said. "Bottle him up there, then take him when he comes out to hunt." But one of the younger men from town, a tenderfoot named McCann, who Cade guessed was trying to make a name for himself, said, "Fuck that," raised his shiny new rifle, and fired.

At that range, it was pure chance that he hit anything, but the bullet took the beast in the abdomen, just in front of the left rear haunch. The cougar screamed in agony, a sound Cade would be grateful if he never heard again, then disappeared into the canyon. Billy had looked at McCann, then at the rest of him. "Sorry, fellows," he'd said, "you're on your own from now on." He'd turned and begun walking back to town, alone.

The group had slowly picked their way into the mouth of the canyon, the sweat running cold down their backs even as the sun climbed higher in the sky and turned the narrow, rocky defile into an oven. Finally, they'd turned a corner to come face to face with two hundred pounds of bewildered and pain-maddened cougar. Before they finally brought it down, the enraged cat had killed one man and crippled another. Unfortunately, neither of them had been McCann. The look in the cougar's eyes before it sprung had haunted Cade's dreams since.

That look was the same he saw now in the eyes of The White Orchid, a volcanic look of agony turned to molten rage. He'd seen her kill before, with the chilly dispassionate look of a marble statue on her beautiful face. This was different. This was the look of a Fury, a demon bent on bloody vengeance who'd burn down the world to get it.

As Cade stepped back, she rose to her feet, drawing the

swords on her back. They came out of their scabbards with a sinister hissing sound.

"Ah, ma'am?" Cade said. "We need to get to—"

She interrupted him with a scream that resounded off the fronts of the buildings and echoed in the deserted streets. It was a war-cry, full of enough menace and the promise of bloodshed to make an Apache decide to stay by his campfire. To Cade's astonishment, she charged straight at the door of the building across the street.

"What the hell?" he said, then he saw the dirt spray up at her feet where the gunman on top of the restaurant had begun firing at her.

Cade took a deep breath and handed Mei the shotgun he'd held trapped under one arm. "Hold this."

As she began to protest, he stepped out and aimed upward. He saw the rifleman standing up to get a better aim on The White Orchid, who'd reached the door of the building across the street. Before the rifleman could pull the trigger, Cade fired. The rifleman staggered, then fell forward, turning once in the air before landing in the street in front of the restaurant with a heavy thud. Cade ducked back under the overhang of the porch, opened the cylinder of the Navy revolver, and began fumbling for cartridges in his vest pocket. He was glad of the modifications made to the venerable weapon; the old cap-and-ball ammunition the gun had originally been chambered for made loading a slow and tedious process. But with Cade's pulse racing the way it was, even the act of sliding the metal bullets into the cylinder seemed to be taking forever. Finally, he snapped the gun shut.

Mei was holding the shotgun out to him. "Please. Take this."

"Keep it, sis," Cade said. "You may need to use it."

She looked aghast. "Me? I know nothing about guns." In her agitation, she didn't realize that she was holding the weapon pointed at him. He reached out with his free hand and gently moved the barrel away from him. "Point this end at the bad men," he said. "Only the bad men, understand? And when you do, pull those triggers. One or both. And mind the kick."

She shook her head. "No. No. I can't." Her eyes scanned the street and the building across from them. "Where is Lin? Where did she go?"

Cade figured that was The White Orchid's given name. He heard a bloodcurdling scream from the roof of the other building. A moment later, a round object came sailing over the parapet to land in the street. Cade squinted and saw that it was a man's head. A Chinese man, his long-braided queue still wrapped around his head in the style favored by the tong soldiers who were also known as highbinders.

"If I had to hazard a guess," Cade nodded toward the building, "I'd say she's on that roof yonder."

Mei's eyes were frantic. "We have to help her!"

"Looks like she's managing fine on her own." Cade took a deep breath. The White Orchid was doing exactly what he'd been trained to do in an ambush: attack into it. "What about Kwan? Is he actually here?"

Her eyes widened. "He is inside!"

She turned to run in, but he stopped her with a hand on her shoulder. "Easy, sis. We go chargin' in there, we don't know what's waiting for us." He stepped in front of her. "Watch my back. Don't let anyone get behind us."

She looked at the shotgun in her trembling hands. "I...I won't."

"Good girl. You're doin' fine." He eased the door open with one hand, his pistol raised in the other, and slipped inside.

The restaurant was one long and narrow room, a line of tables running down each side and another down the center, leaving two narrow aisles. There was a door at the far end, which Cade figured must open on the kitchen, and a heavy wooden door to the right. The place was totally empty and eerily silent.

"Mr. Kwan?" Cade called out softly. "It's Cade." He didn't know how much English Kwan could understand, but he figured he'd recognize the voice and the name. "I'm coming in." He advanced slowly down the right aisle, the gun moving from side to side with his gaze, his ears straining to pick up any sound. He heard nothing, saw no one. He reached the kitchen door and slowly eased it open with one foot.

The kitchen was as empty and silent as the rest of the place, the big iron stoves along the wall cold and dead. On a high table in front of Cade, a variety of ingredients were laid out, as if the chef was getting ready to prepare a meal. A small one, Cade figured. Maybe lunch for two. Cade recognized some of the vegetables, but a number of them were strange to him. A faint, pleasant smell of spices hung in the air. There was a cleaver lying on the table, on its side, as if the chef had just left it there. Cade stood there, staring at the abandoned preparations in bewilderment. He heard a sound from the outer dining room.

"Mr. Cade?" It was Mei. She'd probably gotten nervous outside by herself and come in looking for him.

He lowered the gun and started for the door. "It's okay, sis," he called out. "There's no one—"

At that moment, a pantry door to his right burst open and a man burst out, dressed in a black padded jacket and matching flowing trousers. His face was wrapped in a black cloth across his nose and mouth, his queue bound up around the top of his head. He was carrying a short-handled hatchet in one raised hand and a revolver in the other. Cade whirled on him and fired, striking the man in the center of his chest a moment before he fired his own pistol. The man staggered, his shot going wild and clanging off an iron pan hanging along the far wall, but he kept coming. Cade recalled that some of the *boo how doy* wore makeshift armor beneath their clothes to make them seem impervious to bullets. He aimed the second shot between the tong soldier's eyes and pulled the trigger. Blood and brains blew out the back of the man's head and he pitched forward onto the kitchen floor. He heard Mei scream from the dining room and stepped over the body of the *boo how doy,* trying to get to the door. His boot slid in the slowly expanding pool of blood and he stumbled, crashing through the door like a drunkard.

Mei was cowering back against one of the tables, the shotgun held loosely by her side. A big man in the same type of padded jacket as the one he'd just killed was advancing on her, his hatchet raised to split her skull. As Cade raised his pistol, a sobbing Mei brought the shotgun up and yanked the trigger, emptying both barrels into the man's midsection. The man staggered backward, then flopped on his back, clawing at his abdomen as if he was being eaten alive from inside before lying still. Mei collapsed as well, screaming hysterically.

Cade crossed the room to her, kneeling next to her. She'd tossed the now-empty shotgun away as if it was burning her hands. Cade put his free arm around her shoulder. "Easy, sis," he said soothingly. "It's okay. He's not gonna hurt you now."

She was babbling in Chinese, out of her mind with terror. Cade squeezed her tight, then let go and stood up. He walked over to where the *boo how doy* was lying on his back. He was still alive, breathing shallowly, but Cade could see the pattern of double-ought buckshot holes in the man's stomach and upper abdomen. He grimaced. Not just one belly wound, but several. Cade guessed this one wasn't wearing armor. He was going to regret that, and soon. Cade knelt down next to the man, who looked at him with narrowed, pain-filled eyes.

"Sonny," he said gently, "I don't think you're gonna make it."

The man wheezed out a few words in Chinese that Cade figured were probably some sort of curse, then turned his head away.

Cade reached out with his free hand and grabbed the man by his chin, turning him back to face the gun in Cade's other hand, which was pointed directly at his face. "Kwan," Cade demanded. "Where?"

The man gritted his teeth and said nothing.

"Mei," Cade called softly, not taking his eyes off the wounded soldier. The only answer was her sobbing. He raised his voice. "Sis. I need you."

Her sobs became short, shallow inhalations, then she spoke, her voice small. "I asked you not to call me that."

He grimaced. "Yeah. You did. Sorry. But I need you to translate."

He heard her stand up and shuffle over to stand beside him. He began to speak without looking at her. "Look here, fellow, you're done for. Your belly's shot full of holes. Right now, your guts are leakin' into your insides. I can smell it."

She'd started translating, but stammered to a halt at the last part.

"Say it," Cade ordered.

She picked up, hesitantly.

The man clenched his jaw tighter, but Cade felt a spasm of agony ripple through him and a small whimper escaped from behind his teeth.

"Feel that? That's just the beginning. When the infection really sets in, it's gonna get worse. A lot worse. You're going to rot from the inside, sonny. Slowly. I've seen men with wounds like that take days to die, screaming the whole time. I could leave you on this floor to die like that." He turned his head slightly to address Mei. "Am I goin' too fast, miss?"

"No," she said, her voice steadier. "You can go on."

He turned back. "Where was I? Oh, yeah. I can leave you here to die by inches, or," he raised the pistol, "I can send you on your way to whatever Heaven you folks have. All you've got to do is tell me. Where's Kwan?"

The man closed his eyes, a single tear running down his cheek. He whispered a single word.

"What's that, sonny? I didn't hear you."

He said it again, this time with a sob.

"Pantry," Mei said. "Mr. Kwan is in the pantry."

Cade patted the dying man on the cheek. "That's a good fellow." He stood up. "Come on," he said to Mei.

"Wait!' she protested. "You said you'd...you'd put him out of his misery."

Cade stared coldly down at the man on the floor. He pulled back the hammer of the Navy revolver with his thumb and pointed it at the center of the man's forehead. The *boo how doy* closed his eyes and took a deep breath. Cade held the gun on him, then dropped it to his side. "I can't do it," he muttered. "I can't shoot a man lyin' helpless on the goddamn floor."

The dying man opened his eyes. He saw Cade lower the gun and began cursing him in a low, hoarse voice.

"Don't bother to translate," Cade told Mei. "I get the gist. Tell him we'll try to fetch a doctor. As soon as we can."

In a shaky voice, Mei spoke to the man.

He turned his invective on her, until his back arched in another spasm of agony and a low, keening whine came from his throat.

She spoke more quickly, tears running down her face. Cade thought she might be apologizing for shooting him.

"I wouldn't waste too much time on feeling sorry for this son of a bitch," he told her. "He was gettin' ready to chop you up with a damn hatchet after all." He looked down. "Besides, I think he passed out." He picked the hatchet off the floor and took the long knife he saw stuck in a scabbard on his waist. "Come on."

They found Kwan in a pantry off the kitchen, bound hand and foot and glaring furiously over a gag stuck into his mouth and held in place by a filthy rag.

Cade holstered his weapon and pulled the gag from Kwan's mouth, then used the knife from his boot to cut the tong leader's bonds. When he held out a hand to help him to his feet, Kwan looked at the offered hand for a moment as if deciding whether his dignity would allow him to take it. He sighed and let Cade raise him up.

Kwan spoke quickly to Mei, his voice shaking slightly.

She answered, her head bowed as if not daring to look Kwan in the eye.

Kwan turned and addressed Cade.

"He wants to know where Lin,. the one you know as The White Orchid, is."

"Don't know, sir," Cade replied. "Last I saw, she was cuttin' the head off the bastard who shot her."

At the translation, Kwan looked as if he'd been punched in the gut. He turned to Mei, a torrent of words pouring out. Mei tried to answer, looking as if she were about to burst out crying again. Kwan's voice grew more impatient as he demanded information.

"Easy there," Cade said, adding, "Sir," at the last second.

Kwan turned to him, his eyes furious. He may not have understood the words, but he clearly didn't like Cade's tone.

Cade met his eyes. "She's shook up. She just shot one of the men who were in on this business. Whatever the hell it is." He looked at Mei. "Tell him what you just did. It's okay."

In a wavering voice, she spoke to him. She looked like she was on the verge of collapsing.

Kwan's expression softened. He reached out and grasped

the young girl's shoulder gently, speaking to her in a low, earnest voice, more soothing than the peremptory tone he'd used earlier. Whatever he was saying, it seemed to steady her. She answered him in a calmer voice, and they had a brief exchange. She glanced at Cade a few times, so he assumed that part of the colloquy involved him.

Finally, Kwan turned to him and spoke. He looked as if the words hurt him to say.

"Mr. Kwan Lee wishes to thank you for the help you have given him today," she said. "He is in your debt. Very much." When she finished, Kwan gave him a brief, curt nod. Cade figured that was as close to a bow that the stiff-necked old bastard could manage to a white man.

"Tell Mr. Kwan it was an unexpected honor."

She spoke, and Kwan raised an eyebrow at her words. He turned to Cade and spoke. "Unexpected?"

Cade nodded with a slight smile.

Kwan shook his head. "Unexpected." He began to chuckle, then to laugh out loud. "Unexpected."

Cade began to laugh with him. It wasn't really that good a joke, but Cade had felt this before. In the aftermath of a battle where life and death had been a matter of chance and inches, almost anything could set men laughing, more from the sheer relief at being alive than anything else.

They were still sharing the laugh when the door to the kitchen slammed open. Cade drew his pistol, moving Mei out of his line of fire with his free hand. Kwan whirled, a defiant snarl on his face.

The White Orchid entered the kitchen, her back as straight as if someone had strapped a steel post to her spine. Her formerly white robe was all crimson across the belly now. Cade couldn't tell how much was from her blood. There were streaks of blood across her perfect face, and a long hank of her black hair hung down in front of her shoulder, soaked in so much gore that it was plastered to her front. She walked carefully, like a woman on a tightrope, her eyes straight ahead. She was carrying something in her right hand. Several somethings in fact, round objects dangling from what looked like black ropes. Cade saw with a sick feeling that she was holding severed heads by their long black queues. There were four of them, and Cade saw that one of them was the man he'd left dying in the outer room. *Well,* he thought, *at least that's taken care of.*

They stood silently as The White Orchid approached. Her eyes, which had seemed fixed on nothing, locked onto Kwan's. She walked up to him and dropped the heads at his feet. They made a sickening squelch as they landed, like dropped pumpkins. She wavered slightly, like a drunkard. She said something to Kwan, then bowed deeply. She didn't straighten up from the bow, but pitched forward toward the floor.

Cade went to one knee and grabbed her with his free arm. Mei leaped to her other side and together they guided her to an awkward sprawl on the floor in the pool of the blood still leaking from the severed heads.

"Well, hell," Cade said. "This ain't good."

CHAPTER FORTY-ONE

"I thought Mr. Cade was going to be joining us today." Jenkins stood by the railing of the bar in the small and stuffy courtroom.

Marjorie looked around. "I don't see him." She frowned. "It's not like him to be late." She turned to Athena Givens, who was seated beside her, staring straight ahead as if she was willing herself to be somewhere else. "Don't worry, Athena," she said soothingly, "he'll be here."

Athena's voice came in a whisper. "It doesn't matter. Nothing does."

Marjorie gave her friend's hand an affectionate squeeze. "Don't be like that, dear. Everything's going to be fine. Mr. Jenkins is an excellent lawyer." She smiled at him.

He smiled back. "I am, actually." His face turned serious as he looked at Athena. "Are you all right, madam?"

She didn't answer, just continued that blank stare.

"Of course. She's fine." Marjorie leaned over and whispered in Athena's ear. "Chin up, Athena. People are watching."

It was true. The courtroom was packed with a variety of rough-looking characters: men whose faces hadn't seen a razor in a while, tired-looking women in thick make-up who Marjorie assumed were prostitutes, a huddle of raggedly dressed Mexicans whispering to each other in their own language, and a pair of Chinese who sat without expression, their hands in their laps. Many of the people were looking curiously at the two well-dressed women seated in the front row. One who seemed to be taking a particular interest was a skinny man with greasy hair, a cheap suit, and a notebook he kept scribbling in.

"I also believe someone from the newspapers is here," Marjorie whispered.

At those words, Athena stiffened. She looked around at the courtroom as if seeing it for the first time. She took a deep breath and turned to Jenkins. "I'm fine, Mr. Jenkins."

"Good," the lawyer said. "Because you're going to be our star witness." He looked around again. "I do wish Mr. Cade was here." He addressed the last words to Marjorie, as if Cade's absence was her fault.

She stared back at him frostily. "If Mr. Cade is not present, I'm sure there is some pressing matter keeping him." *And that's what worries me,* she thought to herself. She'd been apprehensive ever since Cade had told her he was going to speak to the Chinese tong leader Kwan on her behalf. Cade was many things, she thought, but the last thing the man she loved was, was a diplomat.

Her thoughts were interrupted by the sound of a door opening behind the imposing bench at the front of the courtroom and the entrance of a large, red-faced man in a faded black robe.

"ALL RISE," the bailiff called out, and there was a rustle as the people stood. She heard Jenkins mutter a soft obscenity under his breath as the bailiff went on: "Oyez, oyez, this Police Court for the City and County of San Francisco is now open for the dispatch of business. The Honorable J. Stanley Wilkinson presiding."

Wilkinson? Marjorie thought. She leaned forward. "I thought the judge's name was Farenholt." But Jenkins was already moving away, taking up his position at the counsel table.

The judge took his seat and picked up the papers lying on the bench. He took a moment to look through them, his lips moving slightly as he read. He looked up at Jenkins, blinking myopically. "Mr. Jenkins?" he said in a high, reedy voice.

"Here, Your Honor," Jenkins said.

Wilkinson squinted, as if he was trying to make out Jenkins's face. "You are here in the matter of the People versus," he looked down at the papers again, "Tatanka, alias..." he struggled with the next word, "...Akbar?"

"That's correct, Your Honor." Jenkins cleared his throat. "I hope Judge Farenholt hasn't been taken ill."

Wilkinson scowled. "Ill? Why would you think that?"

"It was our understanding that Judge Farenholt would be presiding today."

"Well, Mr. Jenkins, I'm sorry to disappoint you, but Judge Farenholt personally asked for me to fill in for him today. He had another engagement."

"I understand, Your Honor," Jenkins said, although it was clear he didn't.

"Bring in the prisoner," Wilkinson said.

"Are you okay, Mr. Lamarche?"

The lockpicker—or screwsman, as Clayborne recalled he preferred to be known— was sweating and looking around the foyers nervously. He'd showed up at the appointed time, collected his payment, but he still seemed as skittish as a cat at a dog convention. "Beggin' yer pardon, sir," he said in a low whisper, "but I'm not accustomed to workin' in the daytime, if ye take my meanin'."

"I understand," Clayborne said. "But this is the best time. The lady of the house is at court. Clinton drove her, and Lucius went for extra security. The kitchen staff's busy at their duties, and I checked to make sure that Eleanor's out back hanging laundry. It's all clear, but you need to move quickly."

Lamarche swallowed nervously, but nodded.

Clayborne led him up the steps and down the hallway to the sealed room. "This is the place."

Lamarche bent down and peered at the lock. "Ahhh," he crooned after few moments. "I know you, me beauty."

"You can open it, then?"

Lamarche snorted, his earlier nervousness evaporated. "Child's play." He pulled a slim leather case from his coat pocket. "I almost feel bad about chargin' you as much as I did." He grinned. "Almost."

Clayborne didn't smile back. "Best get to work, then."

"Yes, sir." Lamarche withdrew a pair of thin metal objects from the case and set to work. In a few seconds, the lock clicked. Lamarche stood up, beaming proudly, and turned the doorknob. The door swung open, and Lamarche stepped back. "Open sesame. Done and done."

Clayborne entered. The room was dim, heavy curtains drawn tightly against the sunlight. He heard footsteps and turned to see Lamarche backing quickly away. "Hey," he called out.

The screwsman gave him a cheery wave. "Seein' as how my work here is done, sir, I'll just be takin' my leave. Pleasure workin' with you, sir, and if you need any further services, don't hesitate to contact me through Mr. Simonson."

"Wait," Clayborne said, but the screwsman turned and

bolted for the stairs as if the police were already on his heels. Clayborne sighed. He hoped he wasn't going to find any other items requiring Lamarche's skills, such as safes or lockboxes. But that would probably have cost extra. He turned back to the room. In the shadows, strange silhouettes loomed, unfamiliar outlines that didn't look like furniture. He moved carefully to the window and pulled the curtains aside, then turned to examine the room. What he saw made him gape in amazement.

CHAPTER FORTY-TWO

"We need to get her up off this floor," Cade said. He nodded toward the table in the center of the room. "Clear that table off, sis."

"Is...is she dead?" Mei's lower lip was quivering, and her eyes were already filling with tears.

"She's still breathing," Cade said, "but she didn't do herself any favors by going after those bastards with that wound in her belly. We need to get her to a doctor. Or get one here. Come on, get moving and get that stuff off the table."

He didn't wait to see if she complied. He undid the straps on the scabbards holding the twin swords to The White Orchid's back, got his arms under her slim frame, and lifted, using his legs to take the strain. The young woman, slender as she was, was dead weight in his arms, and he grunted as he got unsteadily to his feet. Mei had brushed all of the ingredients off the table into a nearby trash can, clearing the way for Cade to lay the unconscious woman on the prep table. She was breathing shallowly, her face pale. Her white shirt was soggy with blood, stuck to her skin. He could see the ragged hole low on her left side where the bullet had struck.

Gently, he began to lift the shirt. He felt Mei's hand clamp down on his wrist.

"What are you doing?" she demanded, her voice cracking.

"Easy, miss," he said. Her fingers were digging into Cade's arm to the point of pain. He pried them away carefully. "I need to see how bad it is." He raised the edge of the shirt and sucked in his breath. The wound was bright red and ragged at the edges. Blood pulsed slowly from it.

As he examined the unconscious woman, Kwan was speaking to Mei in a low, urgent voice. A look of shock crossed her face, and she answered him in a questioning tone. He answered sharply and gestured to the back door.

Mei addressed Cade. "He says the owner of the restaurant, Wong Zhi, and the other workers are locked in a shed out back."

"Best go let 'em out, then. And hope one of 'em's a doctor."

She nodded and scurried out.

Cade turned to Kwan. "Now that it's just you and me, maybe you can admit that you speak better English that you let on."

Kwan looked at him stolidly, then smiled. "Some."

Cade shook his head. "So why...never mind. You understand *bandage*?"

Kwan nodded. "I find."

"Thanks." He turned back and looked at the wound more closely, then sniffed lightly. He didn't smell anything but the coppery tang of blood. Maybe her guts hadn't been perforated like the poor bastard whose severed head now lay a few feet away.

Kwan was back, bringing a handful of clean napkins. At least they looked clean. They'd have to do until the real thing came along. The White Orchid couldn't stand to lose much more blood. Working quickly, he fashioned a makeshift bandage from the napkins by knotting them together.

As he worked, the back door open and Mei re-entered, followed by a half-dozen Chinese. They were led by a middle-aged man who Cade assumed was the owner, Mr. Zhi. The man stopped, aghast. He let out a wail which Cade didn't need Mei to translate. It clearly was along the lines of, "My KITCHEN!"

Kwan straightened up and addressed the man in a voice that cracked like a whip. Zhi immediately began bowing and muttering what must have been an apology. Kwan pointed at a young man cowering behind Zhi and barked an order. The man looked at Zhi, who nodded. The man left out the back door. Kwan continued to issue orders and soon had the whole kitchen staff off on various errands.

Cade shook his head in admiration. He'd seen few men with that ability to command. George Armstrong Custer, the glory-seeking bastard Cade had once served under, had had it. When he had that look in his eyes, that light about him, his men would follow him into Hell. Problem was, the damn fool had led them there a little too often for Cade's liking. He'd always had the feeling that Custer was going to get a lot of people killed someday, and he hoped that Kwan wouldn't be doing it today.

When he was done organizing his new unit, Kwan turned to Cade. "You stay?" He nodded at The White Orchid, still passed out on the table, and at Mei. "Need your help. Keep them safe."

The question startled Cade. He'd expected to be ordered, but Kwan was asking, and making it about protecting the women. Which, Cade realized with a shake of his head, was exactly the right tack to take. Kwan had read him like a book. At that moment, he knew which side he had to pick.

"Well, sir," he said, "I guess I'll stick. Seein' as how I don't even know my way home, anyway." He took out his pocket watch and grimaced. Looked like he wasn't going to make it to court.

CHAPTER FORTY-THREE

A pair of officers, one on either side, brought Tatanka into the courtroom, shuffling in a pair of heavy iron leg shackles. His hands were bound before him with an equally weighty set of manacles. He was dressed in a gray prison uniform that was too small and made him look even bigger than he already was. Without his turban and Arab garb, his long black hair hung lank and greasy around his face. He looked every inch the savage red Indian that haunted the nightmares of the white men and women of the West.

Marjorie heard Athena draw in her breath, then mutter a very unladylike oath. She put a hand on her friend's arm to steady her.

"Your motion, Mr. Jenkins," the judge said in a bored voice.

Jenkins bowed his head slightly. "Thank you, Your Honor. Mr. Tantanka's employer is here, Miss Athena Givens. She—"

"The suffragist?!" the judge interrupted, pronouncing the last word with clear disgust.

Jenkins clenched his jaw. "Miss Givens may hold some unpopular opinions, Your Honor, but—"

Wilkinson snorted. "She should count herself lucky she's

not the one in the dock. Spreading seditious nonsense." He leaned forward. "If this is your idea of a character witness, Mr. Jenkins, then I don't think you have much of a chance here."

"She is not a character witness, Your Honor." Jenkins was clearly struggling to hold on to his temper.

Some of the toughs in the gallery were elbowing one another and grinning. The man with the notebook was jotting away furiously. Marjorie was feeling sick to her stomach. Some sort of fix was in that she didn't understand.

Jenkins went on. "Miss Givens is the victim of the crime of which Mr. Tatanka is accused. She is here to seek dismissal of said charges, on the grounds that she herself does not believe him guilty. She is, in fact, willing to testify that—"

"That's very interesting," another voice spoke up from the prosecutor's table. A man stood up, someone who looked familiar to Marjorie.

"Your Honor," Jenkins protested the interruption, "if I may be permitted to finish—"

"We'll hear from Captain Smith," the judge said.

Smith. That was the name. She'd met him, and she didn't trust him.

Smith was speaking again. "What's interesting, Your Honor, is that Mr. Tatanka, alias Akbar the Arab, has made a full confession to the attempted murder of Athena Givens." He turned to regard the gallery. "He's even said he will attempt to do the same if he is released."

A ripple of conversation ran through the crowd, quickly silenced by the pounding of the judge's gavel.

"Order!" Wilkinson bawled. "Order in this court!"

Athena Givens, however, was not one to be cowed by the mere bang of a little wooden hammer. She rose to her feet, shaking off Marjorie's warning hand on her arm.

"This confession is fakery!" she declared in the same voice

she used in declaiming from the podium at one of her rallies. "Procured by trickery, or..." she paused significantly, "...physical torture."

The crowd was nearly beside itself with joy. This was the best entertainment anyone could remember being seen in the police court for days, maybe even weeks.

Another flurry of sharp raps from the judge's gavel shoved the hubbub back down to a low rumble. The judge turned to Smith. "What of this accusation, Captain Smith? Has the prisoner been subjected to trickery or physical duress?"

Smith shook his head. "Not at all, Your Honor. In fact, he was most eager to," he couldn't repress a smirk, "unburden his conscience."

"LIES!" Athena was nearly sobbing now. She stretched out her hands toward Tatanka, standing in the dock. "Tell them. Please. Tell them."

Tantanka stared straight ahead, not acknowledging her presence.

"Madam," the judge said in a freezing voice, "if you do not restrain yourself, I will have you removed from this courtroom. In shackles, if necessary." The way he licked his thin lips suggested that he was devoutly hoping for that necessity. He turned to Jenkins. "If there is nothing else, Counselor, I suggest we progress to my ruling."

"Yes, Your Honor," Jenkins said, his shoulders slumped.

"Bail is denied. The prisoner will be bound over for trial." The judge banged his gavel. "Next case."

CHAPTER FORTY-FOUR

At first, Clayborne couldn't take in what he was looking at. It was a strange apparatus, consisting of what looked like a wooden desk, curved in a broad half-moon around a padded and comfortable-looking chair in the middle. Sitting on the desk was a panel of levers and handles protruding from a walnut cabinet. A series of metal pipes rose from behind the desk, each one flaring into a trumpet-like device pointed at the chair which sat before it. Clayborne drew nearer. Each set of levers and handles seemed to correspond to one of the trumpets pointed at the chair, and each one had a label on it: PARLOR. GUEST BEDROOM. SÉANCE ROOM. The last label seemed to have the most trumpets and levers assigned to it.

Suddenly, Clayborne realized what he was looking at. This was the backstage of a theater, and here, directly above the séance room, were the controls for the theater's effects. He reached over and pulled one of the levers, hard. A muffled report, like a distant gunshot, resounded from what sounded like the room below. He pulled another lever. Another sharp rap from below. He pulled one lever after another and was rewarded by a series of thumps and bangs from the room below. He saw a trapdoor in the floor and walked over to it. There was a pile of linen lying next to the trapdoor. He picked up a piece and saw that it was a long white gown with what looked like a hood attached. In the dim light, it gave off a strange luminescence.

Clayborne felt his anger boiling up inside him, the anger he'd kept carefully banked for so long. The apparitions he'd seen, the manifestations he'd believed and feared...it had all been a trick. Theater. The ghost of his mother who had confronted him, terrified him, shamed him, had all been a sham, a bit of manipulation engineered by Athena Givens to try to get Clayborne on her side. Cade had been right, and the realization made Clayborne even angrier.

He stalked out of the room, leaving the door open behind him. As he reached the end of the corridor, he met Eleanor coming up the steps, holding a stack of laundry in her arms and humming happily to herself. The humming died when she saw his face.

"Sam," she said, "what's the matter?"

He wanted to strike her. He wanted to throw her down the stairs. Instead, he gritted his teeth and said, "I opened the secret room. The one where..." He closed his eyes and tried not to shout. "The one where Miss Givens puts on her little shows." He opened his eyes and looked at her. "Tell me, Eleanor. And please. For once, tell the truth. Were you part of that? That deception?"

She sighed, the look she gave him one of pity. "Let me put these away," she said, "and we'll talk."

Clayborne felt his heart crack in his chest.

CHAPTER FORTY-FIVE

Within the hour, the kitchen had begun to fill with Chinese. Most of the new arrivals were the same type of evil-looking types Cade had come to associate with the *boo how doy*: scarred, ill-favored men of varying ages, but all of whose very walks gave off an air of menace. They all bowed to Kwan as they came in and gathered in a knot around him, talking in low, subdued voices.

"What's going on with that pow-wow over there, miss?" Cade whispered to Mei.

She frowned in confusion. "What is pow-wow?"

"Sorry. That little circle of fellows gathered around Kwan."

She hesitated. "They are Kwan Lee's men. The ones who came when he sent for them." She paused, and he could see she looked worried. "Not as many as he had hoped, I think."

It was hard to tell, the way they were milling around, but he figured the number at about a dozen. "Maybe you can tell me what the hell—sorry, what's going on here."

Another pause. She was clearly wrestling with how much to tell Cade. He was still the outsider here. Finally, with a sigh, she made her decision. "Kwan Lee's brother Fang is trying to take over leadership of the tong." She cast her glance at The White Orchid stretched out on the table. He could see her lower lip trembling. It struck him again that, for all her self-possession, she was still just a kid. A kid whose best friend might be dying.

Cade nodded grimly. "And he thought taking your pal there out of the picture would grease the wheels." She looked confused again, and he added, "Make it easier for him to take over."

She nodded.

"What I don't get is where I come in."

She looked as perplexed as he felt. "I do not know either." She shrugged. "Perhaps you were just in the way."

"Maybe. But it felt a mite more personal than that."

Mei just shook her head. She looked so vulnerable that Cade wanted to put an arm around her again, but something held him back. He glanced over at the meeting still going on at the far end of the room. Kwan was seated in a tall stool, his soldiers gathered around him. The kitchen staff moved gingerly around the small knot of men, trying to clean up the mess in the kitchen, but not daring to look at Kwan or the *boo how doy*.

He noticed one of the ruffians looking at him and gesturing, a scowl on his ugly face as he spoke in a low voice. "I don't think that guy likes me very much."

Mei nodded. "That one wants to know what a white—" She stopped, embarrassed.

"White devil," Cade finished before she could. "It's okay. I know what kwy low means."

"*Gwai loh*," she corrected his pronunciation without thinking.

"That, too." He shook his head as an idea came to him. "Maybe that was why Fang made his move now. Catch Kwan dealing with the white devils, and the rest of the gang might have a problem with it. Maybe he figured they'd think it's time for new management."

Her brow furrowed. "Perhaps."

"So, the sooner I get out of here—" Cade began.

He was interrupted by a commotion at the back door. Cade reached for his pistol. But it was only an old man, dressed in a long silk robe and carrying a satchel over one shoulder. He had long, flowing white hair and a truly impressive mustache that drooped at the corners of his mouth. A ripple of awed conversation ran through the room.

"Who's this gentleman?" Cade whispered.

Her voice was hushed. "It is Dr. Yan Ming. He is a very famous physician."

"Good," Cade said. "Looks like you folks have things pretty well in hand. You think you can find me a ride out of here?"

She shook her head. "Mr. Kwan wants you to stay. He has said this to his men."

"Why? I'm part of the reason Fang sprung this ambush when he did." He nodded toward the glowering *boo how doy* across the room. "And I'm not helping Mr. Kwan's argument with the ones who are sticking with him."

"I confess, I do not understand him wanting this either. But it is what he wants." She looked the little squad of gangsters over and shrugged. "Perhaps you are one of the people he trusts."

"Oh, joyful day," Cade muttered.

The doctor was standing by the table, not touching his patient, but surveying her gravely, stroking his long mustaches. Finally, he bent and gently parted the robe. He frowned slightly and raised his head. He spoke sharply.

"He wants to know," Mei said, "who put this bandage on."

Every eye turned to Cade, who sighed. "That would be me, sir."

The doctor raised one bushy eyebrow and spoke again, at greater length.

"He says the bandage is too tight," Mei translated. "The proper flow of the body's energy is cut off. He says it is fortunate that he was called here when he was."

Cade fought his annoyance down. "Tell him he's right. We're lucky to have him."

Mei translated, which only made the doctor scowl. He eyed Cade suspiciously, as if trying to decide if he was being mocked. The look Cade gave him back was all wide-eyed innocence. The doctor grunted, then added something that made the gangsters across the room laugh.

"Do I want to know what he said?" Cade asked.

"He said at least you have manners."

"At least? Do I want to hear the rest?"

"I do not think so."

"Thanks."

The doctor had taken a stoppered glass bottle out of the satchel on the floor. He poured something onto his fingers and rubbed them together. He waved the fingers under the unconscious woman's nose.

The effect was immediate, and judging from the doctor's reaction, unexpected. The White Orchid suddenly sat up, her face twisted in a rictus of agony that made her look even more like a trapped animal. One hand shot out and grasped the venerable doctor by the throat. The people who were gathered round, both the staff of the restaurant and the gathered tong soldiers, all recoiled from the rage in her eyes. She hissed a furious stream of Chinese at the doctor.

The old man froze, his hand raised in the air, his eyes wide. He answered his patient in a quavering voice.

The White Orchid wasn't having it. She shook the doctor's throat like a terrier on a rat and raged at him in Chinese.

Cade raised his hands in what he hoped would be recognized as a placating gesture and started toward the table, but Mei moved faster. She rushed to the side of The White Orchid, speaking quickly in a low, soothing tone.

She turned and didn't seem to recognize Mei at first. Then she broke out into a smile. She reached out the hand that wasn't locked around the doctor's throat and touched Mei's cheek, then turned her head and looked at Cade. He saw her jaw clench as the pain she'd been trying to hold at bay broke through again. She let go of her death grip on the doctor, dropped her head back onto the table, breathing deeply, and motioned to Cade.

He moved to her side as well. "Hang tough, sister. I hear this doc they brought in is the top of the line. Best in the business. He's gonna fix you right up."

Mei didn't get a chance to translate. The White Orchid addressed Cade in a torrent of Chinese. Mei answered in what sounded like an interrogative tone, and got a quick answer. Mei turned to Cade. "The White Orchid asks that you stay, and that you help Mr. Kwan to safety. She asks this for the debt that you owe her. For what happened on the ship."

Cade sighed. Well, that settled it. He should have figured this was coming. The White Orchid, with Mei's assistance, had pulled him and his people literally out of the fire, and he'd always known that debt would need to be repaid. Now, in the back room of this nondescript Chinese restaurant, the marker was getting called in. "Tell Miss Lin I understand the debt, and I'll do my best." He looked around the room. "Let 'em know."

After a brief translation by Mei, a murmur of conversation went around the room.

Cade looked at Kwan. "Sir," he said, then hesitated. He looked at Mei. "I'll ask you as a personal favor, young lady. Translate this exactly as I say it. I don't want any misunderstandings. We clear?"

Mei looked worried, no doubt wondering what the crazy *gwai loh* would say next, but she nodded.

"Sir," Cade began again, "I told you before, I wasn't going to be your assassin. My gun wasn't going to be at your beck and..." he looked at Mei and amended his idiom, "...at your command, to kill anyone you pointed me at." He nodded at The White Orchid lying on the table. "But I owe this lady a life. Several lives, actually. My own, and," he paused and took a deep breath, "the lives of people dear to me. She's asked me to repay that debt to her by guarding your life," he nodded his head to Kwan, "the same way she does." He looked around the room and raised his voice slightly. "I know you people don't have any reason to trust me. I'm just a," he glanced over at Mei and grinned, "white devil. But I pay my debts. You can ask anyone."

When he was done, the *boo how doy* looked at Kwan, who nodded gravely. They looked around at each other, then back at Cade. Finally, the one who'd previously had the objections to Cade's presence spoke up. "You fight for us?"

Cade nodded at Kwan. "I fight for him. How about you? Can Mr. Kwan trust you?"

Mei didn't translate.

Cade nodded at her. "Go ahead and say it."

Mei rattled off a string of Chinese, her head down. The *boo how doy* who'd addressed Cade looked at him, eyes narrowed, and answered in a low, furious voice.

"He says," Mei said, her voice shaking, "that he should kill you for questioning his loyalty."

"Fine," Cade said, "he's welcome to try, as long as he agrees not to do it today. We've got a lot to do."

Mei translated.

The man stared at him. Cade stared back. The man nodded and said something to Mei, finishing with a tight smile.

"He says okay," Mei said. "He will kill you later."

Cade smiled back. "Deal. What's your name, anyway?"

A brief exchange, then Mei said, "He says you can call him Mingquan. It means..." she paused, searching for the words, "... mean dog."

Cade nodded. "Pleased to meet you, Mr. Dog." He looked around. "Now somebody round up those rifles those bastards were trying to kill us with. And if anyone can lay their hands on more guns, that'd be good. I'd prefer long guns, but any shooting iron you can get will be a help. And as much ammunition as we can pile on."

Mei was translating as fast as she could, and when she was finished, they looked stonily at him, then at Kwan, who just nodded. Only then did the men disperse.

Cade turned to Kwan. "I need to speak with you, sir. In private."

CHAPTER FORTY-SIX

"Mr. Jenkins," Marjorie said, "do you mind telling us exactly what just happened in there?"

Jenkins shook his head, his brow furrowed. "I'm not sure."

They were in a hallway outside the courtroom. The place was crowded, but with people milling about or headed one place or another. No one paid them much notice, although a few did glance at Athena Givens. She was sitting on a scarred and badly scuffed bench against the wall, staring into space with the air of one who'd just witnessed a horrific accident.

"I'm sorry, sir, but that's not good enough. You assured us that this was all arranged. You even had the judge picked out."

"I know," Jenkins muttered. "I thought it was. I thought I did."

A short young man in an expensive-looking suit and bowler hat hurried up and took Jenkins by the arm. The lawyer bent down to listen as the young man whispered something urgently in his ear. Marjorie couldn't hear the exact words, but she saw the look of shock on Jenkins's face.

He straightened up, a determined look on his face. "We need to go."

"What?" Marjorie demanded. "What's happened?"

Jenkins looked around as if searching for eavesdroppers, then lowered his voice. "Mr. Lee Kwan, the leader of the Green Dragon Tong, and," he paused, "the benefactor who had arranged much of what I had planned was ambushed in Chinatown today. It's not known if he survived."

Marjorie felt a shock run through her. She put her hand to her mouth. "Mr. Cade was to be meeting with Mr. Kwan today."

Jenkins nodded. "Yes." He looked at Athena, who was now slumped on the bench, head leaning back against the wall, her eyes staring at the ceiling. "Can you get her up? We need to go."

Marjorie went to her friend's side and put her arm around her. "Athena. Dear. We need to go. We may not be safe here."

Givens seemed to rouse herself as if from a sound sleep. "Not safe? How?"

Marjorie pulled her to her feet. "We need to get you home." *And find out what's happened to Levi*, she thought. *There's no way he can be dead. I'd feel it if he was. Wouldn't I?*

Clayborne was seated in the big leather chair before the control desk when Eleanor returned. With grim satisfaction, he'd tracked her progress through the house by listening to her movements through the cunningly devised sound pipes that apparently ran throughout the mansion. He'd considered shouting at her through the system, berating her in the type of spirit voice that Givens and whatever cohorts she'd employed used, but he felt too weary to do it.

When she appeared in the doorway to the secret room, she

was carrying a bottle of whiskey in one hand and a pair of glasses in the other. "I thought maybe you could use a drink," she said softly.

He didn't answer. She walked over to where he sat and put the glasses on the desk. She poured two fingers of the rich amber whiskey into each glass and slid one over to him. He looked at it, but didn't pick it up. She perched herself on the edge of the desk and took a sip.

She looked around the room, taking in the complex apparatus that filled it as if seeing it for the first time. "It really is a marvelous machine," she said.

Clayborne reached out and seized his own glass. He drank the whole glass in one savage gulp, then slammed the glass back down onto the desk.

She looked at him sadly. "You're angry, I know."

He shook his head. "Angry doesn't begin to cover it, Miss Eleanor."

She inclined her head coquettishly. "So, we're back to formality again?"

"Do not try flirtation with me again, miss," he said between gritted teeth. "Do not."

She sighed. "What do you expect me to say, Samuel?"

"Maybe you can explain to me what you're doing, wrapped up in..." he gestured at the apparatus surrounding them, "...all of this?"

She arched an eyebrow as if she couldn't quite believe the question. "What I'm doing, Sam, is trying my best to survive. To make my way in this world."

"By defrauding people? By playing on their...?" He stopped, unable to go on.

She leaned forward and put her hand on his. "I'm sorry about the...visitation you experienced."

He laughed bitterly. "Is that what you called it? I'm sure the two of you had a good laugh at my expense."

"No." She shook her head emphatically. "I begged her not to do it. I told her it wasn't necessary."

"And why did our Miss Givens think it was?"

Eleanor sighed. "She said that if we showed you just enough, that you'd want to stay and find out more."

"And how did she know? About my parents, I mean. About how I'd abandoned them to their fate."

"She didn't know that specifically. And if you'll remember, there weren't any specifics in what you saw or heard. How she knew that you'd left a parent, or parents, behind..." Eleanor shrugged. "I don't know how she figures out some of the things she does about people. Maybe she truly is gifted in some way. But she told me you looked like a man who was looking for a family because he'd lost his own."

"Or maybe," Clayborne said grimly, "her good friend Marjorie told her about the poor black boy they took in because his family had been murdered, and he'd run away."

Eleanor nodded. "That could be."

He clenched his fists. "I could have sworn I recognized my mother's voice. I could have *sworn* it."

"You were hearing what you wanted to hear. That's her power. Knowing what that is."

Clayborne grimaced. "Givens hooked me but good. She played me like a fish on a line."

"It's what she does, Sam."

"And you helped."

She raised her head defiantly, in the way he'd found so attractive before. "Yes. I do. I do what I have to. Just like her. Just like you, Sam. We're all just trying to get by in this city. In this world. Which, if you haven't noticed, crushes people under its heel without a thought." She paused and her voice grew softer. "Especially people like us."

"You don't have to defraud people, to...to use people to survive, Eleanor."

"Don't I?" Her jaw clenched in a hard line, then she took a deep breath and her expression softened. "We give people hope, Sam." She gestured at the apparatus. "Sure, this is all smoke and mirrors and stage magic. It's a show. But that show lets people believe their departed loved ones are in a better place, a happier one than this." She rose to her feet. "All the preachers do is tell them the people they love will be screaming in agony for all eternity if they didn't say the right words at the right time or if they had water sprinkled on their little heads as babies instead of what *they* regard as a proper baptism, being half drowned in a muddy pond. If that's fraud, Samuel Clayborne, I'll own up to it." Her voice had risen to a near shout and there was fire in her eyes as she delivered those last words. She looked down at him as if daring him to answer.

"I see you've learned some of the arts of oratory from your mistress," Clayborne said in a dry voice. "Had I not seen her in action, I might even believe you were sincere. That this all isn't just for money."

She threw herself down into a nearby chair. "Money, Mr. Clayborne," she said in a normal voice, "is something I am very sincere about. Money is safety, Mr. Clayborne. Money is protection. You know it, and I know it. Someday, God willing, people like you and I will have the protection of the law. That's one of the things Miss Givens is striving for in her other work."

"For women, at least."

"For everyone, Sam. But until that day comes, I'm trusting in the power of cash."

That was the one statement Clayborne could believe. "It doesn't seem, though," he observed, "that money has exactly kept Miss Givens safe. Someone did try to murder her, after all." A thought occurred to him. "Unless that was more flimflammery as well."

"No," she said, her face somber. "That was very real. The doctor confirmed it. And I saw the blood."

"Which brings us back to the reason Mr. Cade and I are here in the first place. Who is it that tried to do Miss Givens in? Do you know?" *And was it you?* he thought to himself.

"I don't know," she said. "Truly. But once again, it all comes down to money. I'd look first for the person who stands to make the most from her death."

Clayborne drummed his fingers on the table as he thought. "Do you know if she has a will? And if so, where she keeps it?"

Before she could answer, there was the sound of a door slamming downstairs, then a raised hubbub of conversation that they could hear through the speaking tubes.

Eleanor leapt to her feet, wide-eyed. "They're home." She turned to Clayborne. "Say nothing about this. Please." He must have looked dubious, because she threw herself to one knee in front of him, her head down in supplication. "I'm begging. Please. It would get me thrown out. I have nowhere to go. Please." She looked up at him, her eyes filled with panic, like a trapped animal's. "Please."

Clayborne put out a hand and she took it. He raised her to her feet. "For the moment, I'll keep quiet. But I do have to tell my partner."

"Thank you," she said fervently, then planted a quick kiss on his cheek before dashing out.

He followed, locking the door behind him as he left. He rubbed the cheek where she'd kissed him. He was sure he was being manipulated again, but for the moment, he'd live with it.

CHAPTER FORTY-SEVEN

Cade led Kwan to the darkened dining room. Mei followed. One of the kitchen staff was on his hands and knees, scrubbing hard at the bloodstains on the floor. He looked up briefly, then quickly back down, as if he'd seen something he shouldn't. Cade cursed under his breath. "Any place we can speak privately?"

Kwan raised a hand and pointed to a door across the room. The door was made of oak, with heavy padding secured by brass nails. He spoke briefly.

"He says, 'Private dining room,'" Mei translated.

"Good." He looked at her. "You okay?"

She nodded. "I am well, Mr. Cade. I hope you can help us."

"You and me both." He led them to the door. "Stand back," he said, redrawing his weapon. "Given how this day is going, I'm gonna be careful about closed doors."

Neither of them responded. Cade yanked the door open.

A beautifully carved teakwood table dominated the room, surrounded by luxuriously padded chairs. Someone had already lit the gas lights that illuminated the cozy space.

"I guess this is where we were supposed to meet?" Cade

asked, turning to Kwan, who nodded. Cade stepped aside and gestured to the head of the table. "After you, sir. I guess we won't be getting lunch."

No one smiled. Kwan sat down and folded his hands on the table, looking at Cade without expression.

Cade took a deep breath. "Sir," he said, looking the older man in the eye, "if I'm going to help you, I need to know what's going on. I know a little about your problem with your brother. I also need to know how many men we can depend on. And how many you think may have joined this revolt your brother's started."

Kwan looked away, still expressionless. When he spoke, it was clear he was barely holding on to his temper. Whether or not that was from the betrayal of his brother or from the impudence of the man questioning him, Cade didn't know, and he couldn't afford to care. They couldn't very well stay here, and wherever they were going, it was a safe bet they were going to have to fight their way there. He needed to know the forces he had and the forces he was facing.

Kwan spoke at length, with several pauses in which he seemed to be gathering his thoughts, or possibly considering how much to tell the outsider. Only when he was done, did Mei begin.

"He says the men who are here are loyal to him. They are not as many as he'd hoped. The senior man of his soldiers, the one you know as Mean Dog, says that many of the *boo how doy* are waiting to see how things occur."

"They want to know who's going to come out on top, so they can say they backed the winner all along."

Mei spoke to Kwan in Chinese. He nodded grimly.

"Okay, then. We're just going to have to get a good lick in early on. We're back on our heels a little, but if we can show we're game, your brother may pull in his horns."

He looked at Mei, who was blinking in confusion, and grimaced. "Sorry." He turned to Kwan. "We've been hit hard. We need to hit back harder, to show we can."

That brought another nod from Kwan. He stood and spoke for a few moments.

"There is a place nearby," Mei said. She hesitated. "A place where there is much gold belonging to Mr. Kwan. If we have that place, the *boo how doy* will follow the gold."

"Well, then," Cade said, "seems to me that's our next objective."

Mei spoke. Kwan replied in a low, hard voice. "He asks if he can truly trust you. You are not even Chinese."

Cade nodded. "No, sir, I'm not. But like I told your men out there, I pay my just debts." He paused. "And if you have trouble believing that, well, there's another debt to pay. Some sons of bitches working for your brother just tried to kill me. Let's just say I object to that. And I need to make that objection clear, so everyone knows how things are."

When she finished translating, Kwan actually smiled. He spoke a few words to Mei.

"Mr. Kwan says he has not previously met any white men who understand honor. Who understand face." Mei paused. "He says perhaps you have Chinese ancestors."

Cade smiled back. "Not that I know of, sir. But I'll take that as a compliment."

Kwan's smile vanished, and he was once again all business. "Come now," he said in English.

Back in the kitchen, Cade was amazed to see The White Orchid sitting up on the table. She was bent over slightly, her back exposed, her robe clutched over her breasts. The doctor was standing behind her, holding something that looked like a long, thin needle in his hand. As Cade watched in horror, he began thrusting the needle gently into a space just beside her spine, halfway up her back.

"Hey!" Cade started forward. "What the hell?"

He was restrained by Mei's hand on his arm. "Don't interfere," she whispered. "This is Chinese medicine. It will ease her pain."

Cade stared at her. "Sticking a needle in someone eases pain? I ain't buying it."

He tried to shake Mei's hand off, but she held fast. "Please," she said. "Dr. Yan Ming is very famous. Very learned."

The doctor looked up from his work, an annoyed expression on his lined face. He called out to Mei in a high, querulous voice. She answered him soothingly. He said something else, then laughed.

The White Orchid hissed something impatiently at him. He snapped something back at her before going back to his work. He plucked another long needle from his bag and began twisting it into the woman's spine. He made an offhand comment that seemed to be directed to Mei, then laughed again.

"What was that?" Cade asked.

Mei hesitated.

"Go on, tell me."

She sighed. "Dr. Yang Ming says for you not to worry. The Chinese were practicing medicine while you white devils were wearing animal skins and living in mud huts." She swallowed nervously. "Please do not be insulted."

"I don't have time for that, miss." As he watched, The White Orchid sat up straighter, took a deep breath, and nodded. With a swift motion, the Chinese doctor pulled the needles out. Cade turned his eyes away as The White Orchid rewrapped her robe around her and fastened the sash. She slid off the table, only a slight wince showing that she was suffering any discomfort at all.

Cade shook his head. "I'll be damned."

"Pardon?" Mei said.

"Nothing." He bowed slightly to The White Orchid. "Glad to see you up and around." His voice grew serious. "You sure you're okay?"

She looked at him intently, as if trying to gauge his sincerity. Then she smiled, that beautiful, brilliant smile that, even in this circumstance, left him a little dazzled, as if he was staring into a bright light.

"Oh-kay, Cade," she said.

"All right, then." He turned to Kwan. "Where exactly are we going, sir?"

Kwan didn't wait for the translation. "The Golden Mountain," he said.

CHAPTER FORTY-EIGHT

"How?" Kwan Fang raged. "How are they still alive?!"

One-Eyed Vang kept his gaze down. "I do not know, Great One. The first shots missed. After that, the white devil Cade and the Pearl River whore began killing our men."

"How many?" Fang asked.

The question you should have asked first, One-Eyed Vang thought. "Fat Chung. Lei Bo. Heng Fei." He paused. "And Vang Peng."

"Bastards." Fang spat.

He didn't acknowledge the loss of One-Eyed Vang's brother. *Kwan Lee would have at least made mention of my family's loss,* Vang thought. He was beginning to wonder if he'd picked the right side. He'd hoped for faster advancement under Kwan Fang than his brother had allowed, but the odds of that seemed to be diminishing rapidly.

Fang gathered his composure. "How many *boo how doy* have come to our banner?"

One-Eyed Vang grimaced. "Seventeen. That we can depend on."

Fang rounded on him. "You lie!"

Vang bowed. He thought again of Kwan Lee. The older man had always taken bad news stoically, then he'd gone back to calculating. He hadn't needed to be placated.

"That is not to say, Great One," he said unctuously, "that the balance has flocked to your brother. They are waiting to see which way the wind blows." He hesitated before going on. "There is a rumor that The White Orchid received a fatal wound, to the head, but she still lives and breathes. Some are saying she is immortal."

Vang had expected another explosion of temper. He was relieved to see Fang smiling, then unsettled at the quality of the smile as it grew wider. "Immortal, they say?" He chuckled. "We will see how immortal she is when she and her white devil meet the Steel Dragon."

One-Eyed Vang felt a chill. "The Steel Dragon, sir?"

"Come with me." Fang turned and swept out of the room like the king he aspired to be. Vang followed in his wake, baffled.

"They will make for the Golden Mountain," Fang said as he led Vang down the narrow hallways of the sprawling structure the Lee family called home. From outside, the place looked like a warehouse. Inside was a labyrinth of passageways leading to rooms decorated in a fashion luxurious enough to make the emperor himself envious. Down they went from the upper levels to the lower, until they reached a plain wooden door on the lowest level. Fang produced a key from the folds of his robe and flourished it impressively. "Did I not say that I would bring the Green Dragon Tong into the modern age? That we would keep such old ways as were useful, but take the best this new age has to offer?"

Vang couldn't remember those exact words, but he bowed. "You did, Great One."

"Then come see," Fang said, fitting the key in the lock and

turning it, "the Steel Dragon. Dragon of the modern age." He stepped through the door, Vang following.

The room was large, the smell of hay still lingering in the air marking it as a former stable. But there was none of the unmistakable earthy smell of horse in the place. The overriding scents here were of machine oil and grease. Vang stopped and blinked his sole eye at what he saw in the cavernous space.

The lower part was familiar. It was just a wooden wagon, larger than most, configured to be drawn by two horses. But the object that rested in the wagon bed had Vang shaking his head in puzzlement.

It was some kind of machine, that he could tell. There was a metal apparatus like a tripod projecting up from the wagon bed. It held up a strange collection of tubes, all pointed in the same direction. There was a metal crank projecting from the side that seemed designed to turn a set of gears.

"The Steel Dragon," Fang said with satisfaction.

One-Eyed Vang approached the wagon, stepping as slowly as if he were approaching an actual dragon in slumber. As he drew nearer, he saw boxes piled in the wagon bed. On each one, in ragged black letters, was stenciled US ARMY. Suddenly, things became clear to One-Eyed Vang. This was some kind of rifle, but with a myriad of barrels.

"A repeating gun," Fang said. "Capable of firing two hundred bullets in a minute." He laughed, the sound making One-Eyed Vang's bowels clench. "Invented by a white devil named Gatling." Fang leaped nimbly onto the wagon and stroked the black barrels of the weapon as if caressing a favored pet. "This cost me a pretty penny," he said. "And the white devils would quake in their beds if they knew we had one of these."

What they'd more likely do, Vang thought, *is bring a hundred of these devil machines against us, kill us all, and burn Chinatown to the ground.* But he kept the thought to himself.

Kwan Fang laid his cheek against the uppermost barrel of the gun and caressed it. "When the Steel Dragon speaks," he said, "we will see just how immortal this White Orchid will prove to be. Her and her white devil." He straightened up. "Summon the *boo how doy.* And spread the word that those who do not join us will suffer the consequences."

"Yes, Great One," One-Eyed Vang murmured. *Maybe,* he thought, *this plan will work after all.*

CHAPTER FORTY-NINE

layborne met Marjorie Hamrick coming up the stairs. "Samuel," she asked in a shaky voice, "have you heard from Levi?"

Clayborne shook his head. "No, ma'am. Is there something wrong?"

As she removed her gloves, Clayborne could see that her hands were shaking. "Do you know if he got to his meeting with Mr. Kwan?"

"I assume so, ma'am. He left with the Chinese girl we met before. And their driver. What's wrong, ma'am?"

"We have news that Mr. Kwan was attacked. Some sort of tong business."

"Attacked?" Clayborne said. "Where? How?"

"We don't know, Sam. I don't even know where he was going. Just some place in Chinatown."

Clayborne's jaw tightened. "I bet I know who can give us directions."

"Wong Zhi's?" Kam said, his eyes suspicious. "Sure. Everyone knows Wong Zhi's." He grimaced. "Although not many can afford it."

"That's the place where my partner was supposed to meet with Mr. Kwan," Clayborne said.

The young man whistled. "Serious business."

"Yeah. But word is, someone ambushed them. We don't know if Mr. Kwan, or my partner, is dead or alive."

Kam shook his head. "Best to not get between the tongs when they're fighting. Even for white—" He stopped, embarrassed, before starting again. "Even if not Chinese."

"Your concern is noted," Clayborne said dryly. "Now can you tell me how to get there?"

"Us," Marjorie said. She'd been standing behind Clayborn as he quizzed the young gardener.

Clayborne turned. "Beg pardon, ma'am?"

"I said *us*, Mr. Clayborne," Marjorie said firmly. "I intend on going with you."

Clayborne turned to her. "Ma'am," he said in a patient voice that indicated that said patience would not be abundant, "I can't let you do that."

She arched an eyebrow. "Let me, Mr. Clayborne? Last I remember, I do not work for you. Nor are you in my employ." She smiled to soften the words. "Not any longer, at least."

"It's too dangerous," Clayborne protested, but he'd seen that look in his former employer's eyes before.

"Pfft," she said lightly. "My father taught me to shoot, and I can ride as well as any man." Her voice grew chilly. "And the man I love, a man who saved my life, may be in danger. It'll never be said that Marjorie Hamrick failed to repay a debt, whatever those fat bankers in their offices say."

Clayborne sighed. There was no stopping her when she was like this. He turned to the gardener. "Give us the directions."

The path to the Golden Mountain was an inconspicuous alleyway off a side street on the edge of Chinatown, near the corner of Dupont and Pacific Streets. Kwan Fang steered the wagon into the mouth of the alley, pulling the horses to a stop.

A dozen *boo how doy*, dressed in their loose trousers and padded jackets, stood in a double line on the other end of the alley. Some held pistols loosely by their sides, others dangled their favored weapons: hatchets, longer axes, a few swords. They sneered defiantly at the man on the wagon, accompanied as he was by a mere two attendants riding behind him, one on either side of something shrouded in a white tarpaulin that rose from the wagon bed.

Fang jumped down from the driver's seat, smiling broadly. "Brothers!" he called out. "I'm glad to see you here." His smile faded, and he looked sorrowful. "I do wish there were more of you here, to hear what I have to say."

The man in the center of the double line of tong soldiers stepped forward. "We are the guardians of the Golden Mountain. We have sworn our lives to Kwan Lee." His lip curled in contempt. "We have heard what you did. There is nothing we want to hear from you, traitor. Oath breaker." He spat on the ground.

Fang took no apparent notice of the insult. "I understand your vows, brothers. I was there when you swore them. And you recall, you swore not to my brother, but to the Kwan family."

There was no answer. The line of tong soldiers continued to glower.

"Well," Fang said, "it is with a heavy heart that I tell you this. My brother is dead." He paused. "Betrayed and murdered by the whore from the Pearl River. Leaving me as the sole leader of the Kwan family, and of the Green Dragon Tong."

A few of the *boo how doy*, all of them in the second rank, exchanged doubtful glances.

The leader, on the other hand, didn't change expression. "Where is your proof? Have you seen the body?"

"Proof?" Fang never lost his ingratiating smile. "Here is your proof." He raised his left hand. At the signal, the men in the back of the wagon pulled the tarpaulin aside, revealing the machine crouched in the wagon bed. As the *boo how doy* blinked in baffled surprise, Fang's men took up positions, one behind the machine, the other on the side to feed it.

The Steel Dragon roared.

When it was done, a pile of torn and bloody corpses littered the ground. Sprays of blood festooned the walls behind where the guards once stood. Nothing stood between Fang and the Golden Mountain. Or so he thought.

CHAPTER FIFTY

Eleanor stood in the shelter of the porte cochere, watching Clayborne and the Hamrick woman moving off down the driveway. Each of them was mounted on one of the horses from the stable. Marjorie Hamrick rode a gray gelding, carrying Lucius's Sharps rifle in a holster by the saddle. Clayborne was mounted on the black mare named Midnight.

Eleanor sighed. It was a fool's errand for them to go looking for Cade, who was most likely dead in whatever ambush that had done for Lee Kwan. The odds were better than even that Clayborne and the Hamrick woman would end up dead as well if they went blundering around Chinatown in the midst of a tong war. *Maybe that would be for the best,* she thought. Oh, she liked Clayborne well enough, and there was no denying he was a handsome young man. Both Cade and Marjorie Hamrick had been decent to her. But Clayborne had discovered the house's secret, and that imperiled the life that Eleanor had clung to for her safety for so long. She'd been in a state of constant anxiety since the attempt on Miss Givens's life, wondering who it was in the household who could have dreamed of such a thing. If Athena Givens were to die, what would become of the rest of them? She shook her head and squared her shoulders. That danger, she judged, was past. Tatanka, who she'd never fully trusted, was in jail, and he'd confessed to the assault. Eleanor needed to just ride this storm out, and everything would be back to normal. It had to be. The alternative was unthinkable. In the meantime, her mistress was in distress, and keeping things on an even keel meant doing her duty. She went back inside and mounted the stairs to the second floor. As she approached Miss Givens's suite, she heard voices raised in anger, a man's and a woman's. She stopped, blinking in confusion. The woman's voice was unquestionably Athena Givens, the other impossible. It sounded for all the world like the voice of Clinton, the carriage driver. But instead of the accustomed drunken slur of the slovenly coachman, this voice was sharp and cruel. She couldn't make out the exact words through the heavy wooden doors, but the tone filled her first with dread, then with a desperate resolve to protect her benefactor.

She stepped to the door and rapped sharply. "Miss Givens!" she called out. "Are you all right?"

The voices fell silent.

Eleanor knocked again, more firmly. "Miss Givens!"

There was a sound of shuffling feet behind the door, then it swung open. Athena Givens stood there, dressed in a silk dressing gown. Her eyes were red-rimmed, but she wasn't crying at the moment. "I'm fine, Eleanor," she said, her voice trembling.

"I don't think so, ma'am," Eleanor said. "Can I get you a cup of tea? Perhaps something else?" She looked over Givens's shoulder to see Clinton standing there, his face red and furious. "Mr. Clinton," Eleanor said. "Such a surprise to see you here." She smiled with a poisonous sweetness. "I believe Miss Givens has experienced enough upset for one day. Would you not agree?"

Clinton looked at her as if he'd like nothing better than to have his hands around her neck. She met his eyes, shivering deep inside herself, but she'd be damned if she was going to let him cow her. His gaze broke first. He strode to the door, and Givens stepped aside. After a second, Eleanor did the same, and Clinton walked past, almost, but not quite, shouldering Eleanor aside. He stopped in the hallway and looked back at Givens. "Remember what I said."

Givens looked sick. She turned away and stumbled toward the inner chamber where her bed lay.

Eleanor turned to the coachman. "That will be all for now, Mr. Clinton."

He glared at her, with that look that nearly turned her insides to water. Then he smiled nastily. "We'll talk again, Miss Eleanor. I look forward to it." He turned and strode away.

Kwan Fang stood before the massive door of the vault, fuming. He'd spun the wheels of the combination lock a half dozen times in the sequence he knew as well as he knew his own name, but the door to the Golden Mountain refused to budge.

"It seems your brother has changed the combination, Great One," One-Eyed Vang murmured.

Fang turned and backhanded the man so hard he almost knocked him to the ground. "You think I can't tell that, you ass?!" He turned back toward the door of the great vault, glaring at it as if the fury of his gaze could melt its way through inches of tempered steel.

The vault was set into the wall in the basement of an unmarked and unremarkable building at the end of the long alley. The building itself was owned by one of Kwan Lee's companies, and left unoccupied except for a couple of guards who rotated in and out on a regular schedule. If the people working in the shops and factories or sleeping in the boarding houses in the area found that strange, they kept their questions to themselves.

Vang straightened up, wiping the blood from his split lip with the back of his hand. "Apologies, Great One," he murmured. "Perhaps another way can be found into the vault? From above or below?"

Fang shook his head, gnawing at his lower lip. "My brother had this vault built by one of the same companies that makes them for the white devils' great banks. We could break through with fire and dynamite. Eventually." He looked back at the soldiers milling about in the yard. "I don't know if we have that long. When the word gets out that my brother and the Pearl River whore still live..." He trailed off, his brow furrowed as he tried to plan. Finally, his face took on an expression of stony resolve. He turned to Vang. "We need to tell the men first. But tell them to take my brother alive. And an extra share for the man who makes him give up the combination to the Golden Mountain."

Vang was aghast. "You mean to torture your own brother?" That was practically begging for bad fortune to visit the house of Kwan.

Fang shook his head, his face grim. "I will not shed a drop of his blood. But I will not ask questions of the man who brings me the combination." He saw the look on Vang's face and smiled bitterly. "The money in that vault is the only thing keeping us alive, my friend. It is the key to the loyalty of the tong's soldiers."

At least those who remain, Vang thought, thinking of the men whose devotion to Kwan Lee had led them to be slaughtered at the door to the vault. He wondered if the best men of the tong forces hadn't been killed in this war already, before the doors to the Golden Mountain. But, he thought, the die was already cast. There was no turning back for him now. If

Fang's faction didn't win this war, there would likely be no mercy for the likes of him. He shuddered at the thought of falling into the hands of The White Orchid. The things she had done to enemies of the tong, when she was given the time to devise punishment, were related among the *boo how doy* in late-night whispers. The only way to survive was through the Golden Mountain.

CHAPTER FIFTY-ONE

"So what the hell is this Golden Mountain, anyway?" Cade asked Mei.

They were bumping along the narrow streets of Chinatown in an open wagon, with one of Kwan's loyal men driving. Cade had objected at first. "We need to keep you under cover, sir," he'd said. "There's most likely still some bastards out there ready to take a shot at you." He'd hefted the rifle he'd been provided in one hand and pulled his coat open to reveal the Navy revolver with the other. "I'll cover you as best I can. But, all due respect, riding around with your ass hanging out like you're proposing is crazy."

Mei had translated. Cade was getting better at following Chinese, and he smiled a little as he saw Mei hesitating over the idiom of "ass hanging out." When she was finished, Kwan looked at him and nodded, before saying one word, looking Cade straight in the eye. "Face."

Cade had sighed. He couldn't say he didn't understand. Kwan needed to show the people of Chinatown that not only was he still alive, he was a man still in command. He knew there were other tongs out there. If they sensed weakness on the part of the Green Dragon, they'd fall on them like wolves on a broken-backed deer.

So now Cade was crouched in the back of an open wagon, his head on a swivel, looking from street corner to balcony to alleyway for crouched and lurking assassins, surrounded by people he didn't know who didn't understand his language and who'd cheerfully be cutting his throat if he hadn't been under the protection of the man who stood upright beside the driver. Kwan's face was stony, his arms folded across his chest. Cade still wasn't completely sure where they were going or why, so he'd asked Mei the question.

She turned to Kwan and spoke as if asking permission. He just nodded, not looking around.

"The Golden Mountain is the treasury of the Green Dragon Tong," Mei said. "It is in a secret place."

The White Orchid was sitting cross-legged in the back of the wagon, her eyes closed, her swords resting across her lap. She was breathing slowly and deeply, as if asleep, but at Mei's words, she opened her eyes and spoke to Mei. There was a brief conversation in Chinese, then Mei spoke to Cade again.

"In China, when they speak of America, they call it the Golden Mountain. They hear of great wealth to be found here." She grimaced. "But most Chinese do not find it to be like that."

Cade nodded. "They ain't alone." He glanced at Kwan. "So he sets himself up as the king of the mountain."

Mei didn't answer for a moment. Then she nodded. "But he is not the only one who wants to be king."

Cade chewed that over for a bit. "Yeah," he said finally. "He's not."

They moved on. Cade noticed that the previously deserted streets were beginning to fill up again, the hustle and bustle of Chinatown beginning to restore itself. He also noticed that the wagon was beginning to attract its own set of followers, men dressed in familiar padded linen jackets and loose trousers. More and more of them as they assembled were carrying weapons: a few pistols, but more hand weapons like clubs, short handled axes, even a couple of long, wicked-looking pikes. They walked along beside and behind the wagon, not explicitly acknowledging it or the man they were following, but clearly a force assembling behind a leader. The *boo how doy* were massing. The battle lines were being drawn.

Cade stole a glance at Kwan. He stood in the front of the wagon, arms still folded across his chest. At last, he spoke briefly to the driver, and the wagon pulled up to a stop. The assembled soldiers stopped on either side of the road. The spectators on the sidewalks paused and stepped back. Cade stood, scanning the crowd. It would only take one traitor with a gun and the ambition to get on the good side of the new top dog to bring Kwan down.

Kwan looked his troops over, as if evaluating them, then gave a slight nod. Cade saw the men straighten almost imperceptibly, just from that glance. Maybe this was going to work, but it was going to take more than one man's charisma to do it. He sat back down, but he still held the rifle.

Kwan began to speak to his men.

Cade looked at Mei, who was gazing raptly at the tong leader. "Can you translate?" he whispered.

She shook her head, as if coming out of a dream. "Of course." She took a breath and began to speak. "My children," she whispered to Cade, "have we not always shared? Do you not prosper as the Green Dragon prospers? Have I ever been stingy in my..." she stumbled for a word, "...shares to you?"

The men looked around. No one seemed willing or able to express any grievance, but they weren't exactly cheering either.

Kwan shrugged, as if unconcerned by their lack of enthusiasm. "Who can explain to me this revolt? Who is unhappy with their lot, and why," his face took on the look of an aggrieved parent, "do your brothers not feel they could come and talk to me? Have I not always been as a father to you in this strange place?"

The battle-toughened thugs of the Green Dragon Tong actually looked down and shuffled their feet shamefacedly. Finally, one mustered the courage to speak up. "What about her?" He nodded at the figure of The White Orchid, still sitting silently in the back of the wagon. "Why do we have to be under her thumb?"

The White Orchid, who'd seemed to be napping during the exchange, suddenly opened her eyes. She stood up and faced the young man who'd spoken, but with a bright smile on her face.

"Younger Brother," she said gently, "do I take the food from your plate?" Her smile widened. "Look at me. Do I live like a mandarin or," her face twisted with disgust, "some fat merchant? Do I enrich myself at your expense? Do I tell you how to live? What have I ever asked but to fight for our father and to kill our enemies?"

The tong soldiers around the wagon looked at each other. A mutter of conversation ran through the crowd.

"How's it looking?" Cade whispered to Mei.

She cocked her head to one side, listening. "I can't make it all out," she murmured back.

Cade noticed a few of the men engaged in debate were glancing at him. "Looks like I may be a topic of conversation as well."

Mei nodded. "That I can hear."

One of the *boo how doy* spoke up from the crowd, his voice strident. He was gesturing at Cade.

Mei started to translate. Cade stopped her with a raised

hand. "I get his meaning, sis," he said. "You ready to speak for me?"

She nodded.

Cade stood up. The crowd fell silent, the tong soldiers scowling at him, the rest of the crowd staring as if Cade was a circus exhibit.

Cade decided to keep it simple. "Some of you are wondering what a *gwai loh* is doing here." He used the Chinese term, even pronouncing it mostly correctly this time. Some of the men looked at each other in amazement. "Mr. Kwan," he gestured at the man standing beside the driver, "has always played straight with me. I owe him a debt for my life." He paused to let Mei catch up. "His brother, who I never met, by the way, just tried to kill Mr. Kwan. He also tried to kill me." Cade held up his rifle. "I mean to make him answer for that."

That was something the ruffians gathered around the wagon could understand. There was another ripple of conversation among them, then a few nods and a general refocusing of attention on the figure of Mr. Kwan. He began speaking to the crowd again.

Cade leaned over and spoke to Mei in a low, urgent voice. "Okay, sis. Thanks for your help. But things are about to get really hairy—I mean, really dangerous. Best thing for you to do is hop off this wagon, head back to your family business, and hunker down till this war is over."

"Hunker..." Mei shook her head in irritation over yet another idiom, but she'd gotten the gist. "No." She looked over at The White Orchid, who was once again sitting bolt upright, back braced against the back of the wagon, breathing slowly and deeply, her eyes focused on nothing. "I am not leaving my friend."

Cade gritted his teeth. "We're heading into a gunfight, sis. It's gonna get ugly. I don't know if I can protect you."

She gazed at him, her eyes bleak. "Do you forget? I just fired two barrels of a shotgun into a man's belly. I know what it's like to take a life."

"Yeah," Cade said. "I was just hoping you wouldn't get used to it."

She put her small hand on top of his rough one. "Thank you, Mr. Cade. You are a kind man. But things are as they are."

"Yeah. They are," he said. He sighed. "Goddamn it."

CHAPTER FIFTY-TWO

Cade could tell they were approaching their objective by the way the loyalist tong soldiers grew quiet, their faces growing taut with strain. The White Orchid stood up straight in the back of the wagon and stretched her back, only a slight grimace indicating that she was in any discomfort at all. *Whatever this Chinese needle medicine is,* Cade thought to himself, *I need to get some of it.* Cade noticed that the old men and the few women were dropping away from the area of the wagon and the streets were beginning to thin out again. He felt a tightness across his temples, the feeling he always got before going into battle. He checked that his rifle was fully loaded, patted the butt of the Navy revolver through his coat, and checked his belt for the ammunition he knew was there. His mind knew that everything was in its appointed place, but he needed to have something to do with his hands. The wagon pulled to a stop, and Cade turned from his unnecessary fidgeting to look around.

They'd come to an intersection, where the major thoroughfare crossed a smaller street. The entrance to the cross street was blocked by a line of scowling Chinese, armed similarly to the men who'd joined the wagon, with knives, small axes, and short pikes. The contingent by the wagon fell out into a straight line, facing the men across from them. Each of the two lines stood glowering at the other, neither one afraid to make the first move, but neither wanting to do it.

Kwan stood up. Cade wanted to reach out and yank the man back down out of harm's way, in case someone in the crowd across from them had a pistol and a hankering to make himself a rising star, but he paused at the idea of laying his hands on the leader of the Green Dragon Tong. He contented himself with raising his rifle to his eye and scanning the opposing force for anyone taking aim. So far, nothing.

When Kwan started talking, Mei began to whisper a translation in a hoarse voice, but Cade silenced her with a raised hand. "Save it, sis," he whispered back, "I know the gist by now."

Mei fell silent as Kwan continued to speak. As she did, the opposing tong soldiers did something extraordinary. They dropped their eyes, and when they looked up, their faces seemed filled with shame. A couple threw down their weapons, then knelt in the sandy soil of the cross street, bowing their heads to the ground as if begging for forgiveness. The rest began to step backward, down the street they'd been blocking.

The *boo how doy* in Kwan's service began jeering, calling out insults in Chinese. They started forward, advancing in what Cade judged to be reasonable order, their weapons raised. The men before them fell back, almost falling over each other in their eagerness to retreat.

Alarm bells immediately went off in Cade's head. "Wait," he called out.

Kwan Lee seemed to have the same sense that something was off here. He shouted an order to his men, demanding that they stop and get back into line. The White Orchid was on her feet as well, screaming at the now-charging *boo how doy* to get back in ranks. All of the orders, warnings, and imprecations fell on deaf ears. Kwan's loyalists had their blood up, and they were ready to charge into Hell for their leader.

Which was exactly what they did.

As Kwan's soldiers disappeared around into the side street, the Steel Dragon roared again.

———

"The problem," Marjorie said to Clayborne as they rode abreast through the streets of Chinatown, "is finding where Mr. Cade has gone."

"We have an idea of where the restaurant where the meeting with Kwan was supposed to take place," Clayborne replied. "So we'd best start there." He didn't mention his fear that Cade might already be dead.

Suddenly, in the distance, he heard the sound of rifle fire, a sound he'd heard before, but with a curious rhythmic pounding. "Or," he observed wryly, "we can simply follow the sound of the guns, with the assurance that the field of battle is where Mr. Cade is most likely to be."

"Mr. Clayborne," Marjorie Hamrick said with a grim smile, "your reasoning is, as always, impeccable." Without further comment, she spurred her horse in the direction of the sound. All Clayborne could do was follow.

CHAPTER FIFTY-THREE

With no idea what else to do, Eleanor busied herself with sweeping and dusting. She was engaged in cleaning the mantlepiece in the unused and darkened ballroom when she heard the front doorbell ring. The sound nearly made her groan out loud. *Dear Jesus*, she thought, *what now?* She put down her feather duster and went to the door.

At first when she opened it, she thought no one was there. She squinted curiously into the courtyard, then the sound of ostentatious throat-clearing made her look down. What she saw made her blink in surprise.

The man on the front steps was no more than four feet tall, but he was dressed in an exquisitely cut silk suit that fit his diminutive frame perfectly. He held an expensive-looking bowler hat in one hand and a business card in the other. "Good day, miss," the little man said in a high voice with a trace of British accent. He held out the card. "My name is Simonson. I am here for my appointment with..." he hesitated, "...Mr. Clayborne. Or possibly Mr. Cade. Either will do, I suppose."

She looked at the card. *R. Simonson*, it read. *Haberdasher and Specialized Services.*

"I'm sorry, sir," she said. "I'm afraid Mr. Clayborne and Mr. Cade were called away on urgent business."

Simonson looked disgruntled. "Hmph. Well. I would like for you to let them know that my original retainer is non-refundable." He turned as if to leave.

"Wait, sir," Eleanor called to him. "Perhaps you can still be of assistance."

He turned back, looked her up and down. "I?"

She nodded. "Yes, sir." She looked at the card. "May I be so bold as to ask if the reason you are here pertains to the haberdashery, or," she looked him in the eye, "the specialized services mentioned here?"

He scowled. "I don't see how that's the business of a servant."

She fell to her knees and added a quaver to her voice as she held out her hands beseechingly. "Please, sir. Everyone's gone and I don't know what to do. I'd hoped you were here to help."

This time it was Simonson's turn to blink in surprise. "I am here to provide translation," he said. "Nothing more."

"Translation?" Her mind raced. There was only one foreign language spoken in the house as far as she knew, since Tatanka never conversed in his native tongue. And French translation could only mean talking to the cook's assistant Carine. If this was someone Clayborne wanted to talk with, this was someone Eleanor wanted to talk with first. Knowledge was, after all, power, and knowledge acquired first was even more powerful.

Since she was on her knees, she was looking him in the eyes. "Would that be French translation, sir?"

He nodded. "It would."

She didn't rise. "If you would come inside, sir, I believe we can accommodate you."

His scowling face relaxed, but he was still frowning, puzzled. She gave him her best wide-eyed, helpless stare. He cleared his throat. "Very well. We'll see what can be done."

She bowed her head and kissed his hand. "Oh, thank you. Thank you, sir. I've been so afraid." She stood and led him into the house, smiling as she turned away. Big or small, men were so easy to manipulate.

CHAPTER FIFTY-FOUR

C ade recognized the steady hammering of the Gatling gun as soon as he heard it. "Fuck," he whispered. "Fuck. Fuck." He turned to Kwan. "Call them back," he yelled. "Get them out of there."

Kwan stood in the wagon, head inclined slightly, listening with the air of a man hearing music he didn't comprehend. He spoke to Mei in a querulous voice.

Before she could translate, Cade spoke up. "It's a Gatling gun." He struggled to express himself. "It's something they can't fight with axes and pistols. For God's sake, *get them out of there.*"

Mei began to translate, but before she'd truly begun, the living evidence of what Cade had said began to stumble back out of the killing box they'd been drawn into. Some of Kwan Lee's loyal *boo how doy staggered* into view, dragging wounded comrades with them. Kwan looked stricken. He turned to Cade and spoke angrily.

"He says," Mei translated, her voice shaking, "what devilment is this?"

"Fang's gotten his hands on a Gatling gun," Cade said wearily. "It...how do I describe it...it turns one rifleman into many." He took a deep breath to try to explain. "It's a machine that allows one man to fire many rifles at once." He shook his head. "I don't know how to fight it."

The tong soldiers had fallen back to the wagon. Cade knew a broken unit when he saw it, and this company was so beaten up, they couldn't assault a chicken coop. Men gathered around where wounded and dying comrades lay, groaning and whimpering. Mei was trying to translate, but the *boo how doy* were muttering and cowering in what was on the verge of becoming a routed mob.

Cade took a deep breath. He spotted the tong soldier who'd called himself Mean Dog. "Hey!" he barked out. "May Kwa!'"

The man turned, scowling. No doubt he was offended by Cade's mispronunciation, but there was no time for that. "Sergeant. Report."

The man scowled, shifting the hatchet he held from one hand to the other. "Miss Mei," Cade said, "can you help me out here?"

She frowned. "I do not understand this word *sergeant*."

Cade grimaced, trying to come up with an explanation. "Soldier who commands a small group of other soldiers. Soldier with great experience, and great respect, but not a general."

Mei nodded. She turned and addressed the tong soldier.

The man looked baffled for a moment, then he looked at Cade and seemed to stand a little straighter. He rattled off a long string of Chinese.

Mei listened, then turned to Cade as the man ran down. "He says the traitors have some sort of machine from the white..." She hesitated.

"The white devils," Cade said impatiently. "Just assume I'm not going to take offense, okay? But can he tell me where the gun is?"

There was a quick exchange, then Mei nodded. "He says it is on a wagon. At the end of the alley."

"Okay. Now ask Mr. Kwan to tell me about the layout. Where this Golden Mountain is, exactly."

Mei spoke to Kwan, who looked at Cade for a moment, as if weighing him up, then answered.

"It is what you call a safe. Like in a bank. But very large."

"A vault."

She nodded. "Mr. Kwan had it built specially. It is in the basement of the building that is at the end of the alley that goes off that side street."

"Fang has that Gatling parked in front of the vault." He thought for a moment, then jumped down onto the packed earth of the street. Kwan was still standing in the front of the wagon, and Cade motioned to him to come down. The tong leader frowned, clearly nettled at the idea of taking orders, but he climbed down off the wagon and stood by Cade, who went down on one knee on the street. "Come here, please, miss," he said. Mei came to stand beside him.

"Here," Cade said, drawing a long letter U with his finger in the dirt. He tapped the bottom of the U. "This is where the gun is." He looked up at where Mean Dog was leaning over, watching with interest. "Right?"

The man nodded.

"So," Cade said, tracing the arms of the U with a finger, "what's all along here?"

Kwan shrugged and spoke to Mei.

"Storage space," she translated. "Some workshops. Some lodging for Chinese workers." She paused to listen to Kwan. "He wants to know why you ask."

"Fang thinks he's got himself in an invulnerable position," Cade said. "But all he's really done is bottle himself up. He probably expected to be into the vault and gone by now. Maybe Mr. Kwan can explain why he's not."

Mei asked, and Kwan answered with a tight smile. "He says he changes the combination often. Only he knows it."

Cade nodded. "Smart. So, we have a standoff." He looked at Kwan. "At some point, I expect we're going to get a proposal to make a deal. You open to that, sir?"

Kwan shook his head and spoke to Mei. "He says that if Fang surrenders without conditions, he will consider letting him keep his head. Otherwise, there will be no agreement."

Cade sighed. "I figured that would be his answer." He looked at Mei. "Face, right?"

She nodded. "Face."

Cade shook his head. "Okay. We can't go at that Gatling straight on. We're going to have to flank it."

Mei frowned. "Flank?"

"Come at it from the side," Cade said. "Or try to get around behind it."

The White Orchid had joined the circle by this time, looking down at the picture Cade was drawing in the dirt.

He looked up at her. "You getting this?" he asked.

She didn't answer, just continued to look down without expression.

Cade stood up and dusted the dirt from his fingertips on his jeans. "You okay?" It wouldn't be the first time he'd seen a wounded soldier collapse after seeming to be back in the fight.

Before she could answer, Cade was distracted by a commotion in the street. The few *boo how doy* that weren't sitting or milling around looking shattered fell into a loose circle around the wagon, pistols and axes at the ready. Cade was astounded to see Clayborne and Marjorie ride into view.

The nervous tong soldiers looked ready to jump at them, but Cade called out, "Hold up! These are friends!"

Mei translated frantically, and the *boo how doy* settled down a little, even as they continued to stare and fondle their weapons, scowling at the interlopers.

Cade stepped out, putting himself between the crowd of Chinese gangsters and the two who'd arrived. "Just what in the blue blazes are you two doing here?"

Clayborne looked down at him from his mount, smiling sardonically. "I was concerned as to the welfare of my partner, and thus of our mutual business enterprise."

"Thanks for your concern," Cade answered. He looked at where Marjorie sat on her own mount, her hair loosened and wild from her fast ride, and tumbling over her shoulders. She looked so beautiful it hurt. "Honey lamb," he called to her, "this is a dangerous place. You need to go back home."

She looked at him with cool amusement. "I do not believe I will, Mr. Cade. After all, I have my own investment to protect, wouldn't you agree?"

Cade gritted his teeth and looked at Clayborne. "Why in God's name did you let her come, Sam?"

Clayborne looked puzzled. "You have, I believe, met Mrs. Hamrick?"

"What? Sam, you know damn well I have."

"And how, then, do you believe I, or any man in this world, have the power to stop her?"

Cade sighed. "Fair point." He looked over at Marjorie. "Can I get you at least to stay back, out of range of that damned Gatling gun?"

"Oh, is that what that noise was?" she said. "Well, Mr. Cade, I may be many things, but I am not stupid. So, I don't think that will be a problem."

"Wonderful."

"What's all the hubbub about, Levi?" Clayborne asked.

Cade pointed. "Kwan's cashbox is in the basement of a

building at the end of the alley where that Gatling is stationed. His brother's trying to get into it, but he hasn't got the combination."

Clayborne nodded. "Standoff. And how you propose to break it?"

"I'm going to go around. Try to flank the bastard. I need you to keep their attention to their front."

Clayborne chuckled. "Once a cavalryman, always a cavalryman."

"You got it." Cade looked around the circle of puzzled Chinese faces. "Friends," he said, gesturing toward Clayborne and Marjorie. As Mei translated, he noticed that The White Orchid was gone. "Hey, sis," he called to Mei, "where's your pal?"

Mei looked around, then turned to Cade, a stricken expression on her face. "I do not know."

Cade gritted his teeth. He was working up a plan in his mind, but if Kwan's assassin was out there doing God knows what, any plan was subject to being disrupted. "Okay." He took a deep breath and looked around at the crowd of tong soldiers gathered around the wagon, looking for the tools and weapons he needed. "You," he pointed at a man holding a long-handled ax, "and you," pointing at another tong soldier hefting a shorter-handled hatchet, "Come with me."

The two men scowled at the peremptory tone as Mei translated, but a word from Kwan had them bowing their heads and falling in behind Cade, who nodded his thanks.

"Sam," he called out. "You and the other fellows keep that bastard bottled up in the alleyway. If he comes out and wants to parley, keep him talking. But don't let him or his people out of there."

Clayborne nodded. "But what if he tries using that Gatling to fight his way out?"

"We'll deal with that if it happens. It'll be tricky to move that damn thing and fire it at the same time. And I don't think Fang'll come off that pile of gold he's standing in front of without a fight."

"Understood."

Cade and his two new helpers headed up the street.

Clayborne looked down from his horse at Mei and touched the brim of his hat in greeting. "Good day, Miss Mei. Might I ask your assistance?"

She smiled. "I would be pleased to help, Mr. Clayborne."

"What I need is for four or five riflemen, or pistoleers if no riflemen can be found, to ride with me across the mouth of that alley and take up a position to fire on the people holding the end of it. There'll be a brief moment of danger when we break cover, but I believe we'll be able to secure good firing positions after that. We don't mean to expose ourselves to unnecessary danger, but to keep those people at the end of the alley occupied. Can you explain that?"

"I believe I can." She rattled off a long string of Chinese. Some of the *boo how doy* looked interested, but others looked down, unwilling to meet her eyes. Her voice sharpened, causing a few of the tong soldiers to look up, their faces angry. Mei's voice grew sweeter, more placating. In the end, five of the *boo how doy* crossed over to stand beside Clayborne. Four of them carried an assortment of rifles; the fifth carried a long-barreled pistol that might have come from the last century.

Clayborne nodded. "Thank you, ma'am." He nodded to where Marjorie sat astride her horse. "Now, if you could persuade the same number to take positions on the near corner to provide similar galling fire?"

Mei hesitated a moment, then spoke at length to the remaining tong soldiers. This time there were no takers. It took a few minutes for it to register that none of the Chinese were going to follow her.

Marjorie scowled. "Very well, then," she said stiffly. "I will do it myself."

"Ma'am," Clayborne protested.

Marjorie ignored him. With a toss of her hair, she spurred her horse to a trot toward the cross street and the alley beyond it. It took a moment for Clayborne to react, but he soon got his own mount moving, calling out "*Boo how doy,* to me!"

Mei shouted her translation, and in moments, the tong soldiers obeyed, falling into line behind Midnight.

The small column took a moment to match Marjorie's speed, but they were nearly together when they reached the cross street. Clayborne raised his hand to stop them as they gathered. He looked down and grimaced. Several bodies lay around the mouth of the alley, torn and bloody. His tiny command seemed entirely insufficient to the task ahead. *Well,* he thought, *here goes nothing.* He dropped his hand and pointed forward. *Follow me.* He spurred the black mare into a gallop as the Gatling gun opened up. She took off like a shot, accelerating so quickly Clayborne had to clutch the reins to keep from being dismounted. The bullets whined and hissed around them as he charged across the narrow mouth of the killing box, followed by the five tong soldiers who darted across the narrow space, unscathed by the fire focused on their leader. On the near side of the alley, Marjorie Hamrick took up her lone position and cocked her rifle. She turned and fired around the corner. Immediately, the Gatling gun turned in her direction, splinters flying from the corner of the building. Marjorie ducked back into cover, sliding down the wall into a seated position, her face a mask of determination. The Gatling pounded its rhythmic beat, and more splinters flew.

CHAPTER FIFTY-FIVE

Eleanor had left Simonson with a cup of tea in the parlor while she fetched Carine. She found the girl alone in the kitchen, peeling potatoes for the evening meal. She didn't appear displeased from being taken away from the task.

When she saw the diminutive figure sitting in the leather chair, her blue eyes widened and she giggled behind her hand. *"Mais il est si petit,"* she said. *"Comme une poupee."*

Eleanor didn't know much French, but she knew *petit* was most likely a reference to Simonson's height. She stole a glance at him. He was frowning sternly at Carine, but more like a schoolmaster than a man offended.

"Est-ce là les manières que votre mère vous a apprises, mam'selle?"

The smile left the girl's lips and her face fell. She looked ashamed. *"Je m'excuse monsieur. J'ai été impoli."*

He nodded. *"Vous êtes pardonné."* He gestured to the couch. *"Asseyez-vous s'il vous plaît."*

The girl took a seat. Eleanor sat beside her.

Simonson frowned again at that. "Neither Mr. Cade nor Mr. Clayborne will be in attendance?"

She shook her head. "As I said, sir, they were called away. But I know what they wanted to ask. I believe I could stand in."

He shook his head, looking dubious. "This is most irregular."

"Please, sir." She gave him her brightest smile. "I know your time is valuable. I would hate for you to have wasted your trip."

"Hmph." He still looked disgruntled, but waved a hand dismissively. "Ask your questions, then."

Eleanor turned to the young blonde and spoke in a gentle voice. "Carine. Can you tell us where you were on the night Miss Givens was attacked?"

Simonson hesitated, then spoke to the girl in French.

Carine's eyes widened, then, to Eleanor's astonishment, she burst into tears.

Marjorie sat in the dirt with her back against the building. She'd been through storms at sea aboard her father's ships and a marriage to a cruel husband who'd made an attempt on her life, but she couldn't remember ever being as afraid as she felt right then. A dead body lay a mere foot away, one of the Chinese who'd fallen in the first ambush by the Gatling gun. With a shiver of revulsion, she saw that flies were beginning to gather in the mess of blood and brains that were what was left of the side of his head. She closed her eyes and steeled herself to pop back out and let off a few shots at the terrifying weapon that crouched at the end of the alleyway. The sound of quick footsteps and the impact of a body landing in the dirt beside her made her eyes fly open. Cade was crouched in the dirt beside her.

"You okay?"

She smiled at him. "Never better, Mr. Cade. But it seems to

me there was a plan we're supposed to be carrying out that involved you going up the street to flank that gun."

"That plan didn't involve you facing *that*." He nodded down the alley. "You said you weren't going to do anything stupid."

She reached out and stroked his cheek. "I'm fine, Levi. Sam and I will handle this end. But you need to hold up yours." At his look, she leaned forward and kissed him, hard. She broke the kiss and smiled. "Come on, Mr. Cade, you have work to do."

The Gatling was pounding again, tearing at the buildings on the other side of the alley. The gunners had changed their aim from the edges of the structures, hammering at the interiors, as if they meant to bring down the buildings that blocked their aim. Cade could hear screaming from inside. There were people in there who were going to be killed for no greater reason than being in the way of this war if Cade didn't do whatever it took to stop it.

"Okay," he said, and gave Marjorie another quick kiss. "I'll be back."

She nodded. "I know."

"So, once again, will you please get back to the wagon? Sam and his crew have the place bottled up. All you're going to do at this point is give me something else to worry about."

She sighed, then nodded. "Okay. But you better come back to me."

"That's the plan, ma'am." He rolled away and sprang to his feet, bolting for the wagon and the line of tong soldiers around it. When he got there, he saw that Mei had turned on the *boo how doy* remaining around the wagon. He couldn't tell exactly what she was saying, but it wasn't anything resembling praise. From her tone of voice and the expression on her face, she was giving them a tongue-lashing for the ages, pointing at the place where Marjorie was still holding one end of the alley and lacerating the *boo how doy* with a stream of invective. The hardened tong soldiers recoiled in astonishment at the sudden righteous anger of the young girl who'd been so mousy before.

One of them growled something deep in his throat and looked as though he was about to start for her, but at a sharp word from Kwan, he stopped. They looked up at their leader uncertainly, then at a nod from the one who called himself Mingquan, they began to advance toward the side street.

Cade spotted the two he'd picked out earlier. "Come on, boys," he said. "Let's get to it."

The two didn't look at Cade, but at Mei, who gestured imperiously and barked a command at them in Chinese. The men fell in on either side of Cade.

Cade turned to Mei. "Little sis, you may not know what a sergeant is. But I can tell you, you'd make a damn good one."

She shook her head. "All I wanted to do was protect my family. And my friends."

"Yeah. That's how people like us get into fixes like this." He turned to the two *boo how doy* who stood there with axe and hatchet. "Let's go."

CHAPTER FIFTY-SIX

Marjorie got slowly to her feet, still careful to keep the edge of the building between herself and the weapon that crouched at the end of the alley. She brushed the dust from her skirt with one hand and took a deep breath. Levi was right. She wasn't doing any good there by taking random pot shots at the crew of the Gatling. As far as she could tell, none of her shots had had any effect. She resolved to keep in better practice with the rifle. Her father had trained her to ride and shoot on land, as well as handle and steer a sailing ship. These days, only the former set of skills seemed likely to remain relevant, and she'd let them atrophy. Those were the thoughts in her mind as she started back toward the wagon where the head of the Green Dragon Tong and his loyalists awaited the outcome of Cade's mission.

A frantic tapping sound made her pause and turn around. One of the buildings at the corner of the alleyway had a set of windows facing the main thoroughfare on either side of the wooden door. She could see faces through the window, terrified faces of Chinese women and a couple of children. One of the women tapped again on the inside of the window, her face a mask of terror. Marjorie immediately realized that these people were among those at risk when the Gatling gun turned its terrible firestorm on the buildings lining the alley. She needed to get them out of there. Slinging the rifle on her back, Marjorie ran quickly to the door. Before she could reach for the knob, it swung wide. There didn't seem to be anyone on the other side. She moved just inside the darkened space. No one was there. She frowned, then the realization hit her. *Trap.* She fumbled for her slung rifle, but a pair of pistols, each wielded by a grinning Chinese, froze her in her tracks.

Eleanor turned to Simonson as she put a protective arm around the trembling shoulders of the sobbing kitchen girl. "What the devil did you say to her?"

Simonson's eyes were wide with shock. "Nothing! I mean, I translated your question. Just as you asked! Nothing more!"

Carine had her face buried in Eleanor's shoulder. She was shaking like someone in the throes of a fever and babbling a stream of French. "What's she saying?" Eleanor demanded.

Simonson's head was inclined slightly as she tried to take in the words. "Hard to tell," he muttered. "She's speaking so fast, and crying at the same time. But she's clearly terrified. She's saying she didn't mean for anything bad to happen. She didn't do anything wrong. And she keeps talking about someone named Clinton."

Eleanor felt her blood run cold. "What about Mr. Clinton?"

"You know the name, then?"

She nodded. "He's the coachman."

"Whatever he is, this poor girl is terrified of him."

"But why?" Eleanor pulled the weeping girl's face from her shoulder and looked into her eyes. "It's going to be all right,

Carine. You're not in any trouble. But you must tell me what happened. What about Mr. Clinton?"

She heard Simonson translating, but his voice was closer. She turned and saw him standing at her elbow, holding out a silk handkerchief. He handed it to Carine.

The girl stopped sobbing long enough to take it. "*Merci,*" she said in a quavering voice, then vigorously blew her nose.

Simonson grimaced. "Japanese silk," he muttered. Carine tried to hand it back, but he stepped away. "Best keep it."

"Now, Carine," Eleanor said, a bit more sternly. "Tell us what you know."

"Too goddamn much," a voice growled from the doorway.

They turned. Carine gave a short scream.

Clinton was standing in the door to the parlor, holding a shotgun pointed at them. "You should have kept your mouth shut, you little bitch," he said to Carine.

CHAPTER FIFTY-SEVEN

They advanced up the deserted street, Cade looking for the place where they could go in through the front of one of the buildings that backed up on the alley and flank that Gatling gun. He didn't know exactly how far the alley went, but if he came in too far ahead of the gun, he and his two companions would be easy meat for the multi-barreled rifle. If he came in behind, he didn't know what he'd find. Possibly he'd be blocked by the walls of the massive secret vault hidden in the wooden buildings. He got some guidance from the sporadic sound of the gun firing at the people at the mouth of the alley, but he gritted his teeth at the thought that every one of those bullets could be directed at someone he loved. He'd commanded men in battle, and he'd cared for them as well as any sergeant could care for men he knew from the beginning he might have to send to their deaths. But Sam and Marjorie hadn't known from the beginning that they were signing up for a war.

Finally, he stopped before the doorway of a nondescript wooden building that he estimated would bring them to a place just abreast of the Gatling. There were no windows in the front, as would be expected from an average store, just a simple wooden door in the center of a blank wall, under a narrow porch that ran the width of the building. There was a crudely lettered sign on the wall by the door, but it was in Chinese. He turned to his two companions. "Any idea what the hell this is?" They just looked at him blankly, but then the shorter of the two, the one carrying the long-handled axe, glanced at the door and muttered something. Then the two of them, almost as one, reached up and took hold of the long, braided queues they wore dangling down their backs. They wrapped the queues around their foreheads and tucked them in in a complicated fashion that led to the braids being tucked up. *Highbinders*, Cade thought. The term described the way the tong men bound up their long hair before going into battle so that an enemy couldn't grab it. "Well," Cade said, "I guess that's what passes for fair warning." He walked up the short stairway to the blank door and hesitated before rearing back and kicking it, hard. It didn't budge. Cade swore under his breath and aimed another, harder kick. The door shivered in its frame, but didn't give. Cade was getting ready to deliver a third kick when the door suddenly swung open.

An old Chinese woman stood there, scowling at him from a face that looked like a dried apple. She was dressed in a shapeless gray dress that hung from her thin body like the clothes of a scarecrow. She stepped out onto the porch, extended a long, bony finger at him, and blasted him with a string of Chinese invective.

He may not have been able to comprehend the exact wording, but the intent was pretty clear. He touched the brim of his hat and spoke in what he hoped would be recognized as a conciliatory tone. "Beggin' your pardon, ma'am," he began, only to be cut off by another torrent of furious Chinese.

One of the *boo how doy* with him, the one with the hatchet, stepped up and brandished it, answering with his own string of words that only seemed to anger the old woman more. The other man stepped in, shouting at the old woman, who only put her hands on her hips and shouted back.

"HEY!" Cade bellowed over the din. When that did nothing to calm the waters, he swore under his breath and fired his rifle into the ceiling of the porch. That shut everyone up. The old woman and the two men stared at him, goggle-eyed.

"Sorry to cut this argument short," he said, then pointed at the door of the building. "But we're in a kind of a rush. So, we're going through," he pointed the rifle at the door, which was slightly ajar, "that place right there. Understand?"

Without waiting for a response, he shouldered the old woman aside and walked into the building. After a moment, the two tong soldiers followed, then the old woman, muttering what Cade figured was probably some sort of curse. Just inside the door, he stopped to get his bearings.

The long, narrow room was hot and stuffy and dimly lit by a single lantern at the far end. The heavy, earthy smell of tobacco filled the air. All of the floor space was taken up by a triple row of long tables that ran the length of the room. Chinese men sat on stools at the tables. Piles of shredded tobacco were heaped in front of them, and many of the men held leaves of the same substance between their fingers. The cigar rollers looked up at Cade, nervous expressions on their faces. Dimly, through the wall at the back of the room, he could hear part of the reason as the Gatling continued to hammer away. It sounded as though Cade had picked the right spot. He shook his head in wonder. In the middle of a war zone, the Chinese bosses kept their people working.

"Come on." He gestured to the two soldiers, and made his way between the tables to the wide door at the back of the room.

They followed, the old woman trailing in their wake, her complaints ramping up again.

A blanket hung across the doorway was the only divider between the factory floor and whatever lay beyond. Cade hesitated, then drew the blanket aside. The old woman was shouting again now, and the hatchet man turned and backhanded her to the floor.

"HEY!" Cade yelled at him, "take it easy!"

The man just looked at him resentfully. The old woman, on the floor, did the same.

Cade shook his head and entered the back room. He saw immediately the reason for the old woman's consternation.

The narrow space at the back of the building was apparently her private quarters, with a narrow iron bedstead and a basin on a rickety-looking wooden nightstand. A large gray cat sat in the center of the bed, eyeing him suspiciously before standing up, stretching with elaborate calm, and jumping down to the floor where it began cleaning itself.

Cade turned back to the old woman. "Don't worry, granny," he said, "we're not going to bother your kitty."

He was beginning to get the lay of the land here. This was one of the tiny cigar factories that dotted Chinatown, and she was the boss. He moved to the back of the room, passing the cat, which mewed at him in annoyance before stalking off, tail held high. He could hear voices shouting commands on the other side of the wall, but there didn't seem to be any access to the back of the building from the tiny alcove. Cade bit his lip in thought. He'd brought the ax man and the hatchet man with him in case they needed to break through a wall, but this close to their enemy, the racket would alert them someone was coming, and they'd be picked off as they attempted to come through the hole.

He heard the Gatling firing again, and the frustration made him want to scream. He had no idea what was happening to his friends, and no way to find out without exposing his own position. He knew the two *boo how doy* were looking at him, waiting for him to tell them what to do, but he didn't have any idea what that might be. It was then that he noticed the cat again, strutting past, tail still waiving its disapproval at the continued intrusion on its domain. It walked stiffly to the other side of the room, glared at Cade, then slipped behind a plywood partition he hadn't noticed before. He looked over at where the old woman was standing, arms folded across her chest, looking at Cade with a venom that rivaled the cat's.

"Hey, granny," he said, gesturing at the partition, "what's back there?"

She stared at him uncomprehendingly, with no slackening of her hostility.

Cade walked over to where the cat had gone. It was a narrow space, and he had to turn sideways to get his bulk through it, but on the other side was a tiny, cramped area, like a closet. It was so dark Cade could barely make out anything, so he fumbled a match out of his coat and struck it. As it flared into life, Cade spotted a large hole in the floor. He advanced on it slowly, the guttering match in one hand casting a jittery light. There was a wrought iron spiral staircase in the hole, leading down. He leaned over and looked into the darkness, but darkness was all he saw.

The match went out, leaving Cade blind. When he lit another, he saw the two *boo how doy* had crowded in behind him. One of them was holding an unlit lantern, probably taken from the dormitory in the front room. Both were looking at the hole in the floor apprehensively, as if it might be a doorway to Hell. Cade didn't really blame them, but he didn't see much alternative to pressing on. Maybe there was a doorway to the cellar in the next building over, the place where he was told Kwan's vault was tucked away. If not, maybe they could cut one without attracting too much attention.

"Well, boys," he said, "looks like down we go."

He looked at the man with the lantern. He'd come to think of the two tong soldiers as Ax Man and Hatchet Man, since he had no other way of naming them besides their chosen weapons. It was Ax Man who was holding the unlit lantern, looking as if he'd rather be anywhere else than where they were. Cade knew the feeling. He gave Ax Man a sympathetic nod and pulled out the last of his matches. He pointed at the unlit match and then to the lantern, gesturing the man to come closer. Ax Man hesitated. Cade gritted his teeth in frustration.

Before he could speak again, Hatchet Man spoke up. He spoke to Ax Man in a singsong tone that even Cade, unaccustomed as he was to Chinese, could recognize as mockery. Ax Man's face tightened with anger, but he stepped forward and held out the lantern.

"Thanks," Cade said. He leaned against the wall, sparked the match on the heel of his boot, and lit the lantern. After taking a deep breath, he looked at the two men. "Okay." He wrapped a hand around the hand of the Ax Man where it held the lantern and squeezed hard. "You." He pointed in the man's face, then gestured with his thumb to the space behind. "Follow me." He pointed upward. "Raise the light high."

Cade was relieved to see that Ax Man was no dummy; he nodded and took up his position behind Cade. Hatchet Man, however, didn't inspire the same confidence. He was looking at the hole in the floor and the stairway leading down as if nothing on Earth could compel him to go down there. Cade sighed. Best he could count on for this one was as a rear guard. He patted Hatchet Man on the shoulder and pointed at the floor next to the stairway.

"Stay here," he said. "Don't let anyone get in behind. Okay?"

Hatchet Man may not have understood English, but he

knew that Cade's gesture would let him stay back from the worst danger. He nodded gratefully, bowing slightly to Cade.

Cade descended the steps slowly, carefully, testing each tread of the winding staircase before putting his weight on it, praying under his breath for it not to squeak. None of them did; he could only hear Ax Man behind him from his soft breathing. *If I can get to the bottom without that bastard splitting my skull,* he thought, *I guess I'll be able to trust him.* He held his rifle at the ready, pointed out past the circle of light from the lantern of the man behind him.

The spiral stairs ended in a cellar with a packed dirt floor. The dim lantern light flickered off the rough wood walls. The place had a musty odor, the smell of mold and mildew coming from a pile of worn mattresses against one wall. A few crates with their wooden lids pried off were scattered around the low-ceilinged room. It was the door across from the staircase, however, that held Cade's attention. Yellow light shone from beneath the doorway. If the vault was where he'd been told, they'd flanked its defenders.

Cade took a deep breath, turned to Ax Man, and held out the rifle. The man looked confused as he took it, but comprehension dawned on his face when Cade drew the Navy revolver from his shoulder holster. "Guess it's just you and me, friend," he said.

Ax Man peered at him for a second, as if sizing him up, then set down his hand weapon and took the rifle. He checked the weapon over with the air of one who knew his way around a firearm, then looked at Cade and nodded. He seemed confident enough.

Cade cat-footed his way to the connecting door. He pointed at Ax Man with his free hand, then put it on the blackened and pitted brass doorknob. He pantomimed yanking the door open. He pointed at his own chest, then through the door jabbing his finger rapidly. *You open the door, quick. Then I go through. You follow.* He raised an eyebrow. *Understand?*

The *boo how doy* nodded, looking almost eager.

Cade took up a position at one side of the door. The Chinese man cocked his rifle and put his hand on the doorknob. Cade pulled the hammer back on the Navy revolver and took a dep breath. Then he nodded.

Light flooded into the cellar as the door swung open. Cade went in crouched, the pistol held out in front of him, then crab-walked to one side to let the *boo how doy* move up on his right. The man entered, rifle at the ready, the barrel moving from side to side, looking for targets.

There was only one person in the room, a man in a long formal silk robe who stood before a large steel door set into the wall of the basement room. He had his hands tucked into the folds of the robe, and he was regarding the metal door with the look of someone contemplating a complex and difficult painting.

"Hands up," Cade said. "Let me see 'em. Now."

The *boo how doy* beside him shouted something in his own language.

The man before the vault seemed unperturbed by the commotion. He turned slowly, pulling his hands from inside of the robe. Cade's finger tightened on the trigger, then relaxed ever so slightly as he saw the man was empty-handed and unarmed. Cade instantly saw the resemblance to Mr. Kwan, but the younger brother's face was leaner, sharper, with a more pointed nose that gave him a foxy look.

His bright eyes focused on Cade's. "You are Cade?" He spoke in heavily accented English, but as calmly as if Cade had come to his house for tea, and it rattled him for a moment. The man smiled at his discomfiture. "I am Kwan Fang," he said.

Cade kept his voice level and his weapon trained on the

man before the vault. "Pleased to make your acquaintance. I think your brother would like a word with you."

Fang stroked his chin, as if contemplating the offer. "No. I think...no."

"You don't have much choice. Sir."

Fang frowned at him, as if contemplating what to do with an insolent servant, then spoke in a soft voice to the *boo how doy* standing to one side, guarding Cade's flank with the rifle. Cade didn't know the words, but he figured a bribe was being offered.

"Don't buy it, friend," he muttered, as much to himself as to the tong soldier, who he knew couldn't understand a word. "He'll fuck you, pal. You know it. I know it."

Ax Man may not have understood the words, but he got the meaning, and he seemed to agree that Kwan Fang was not to be trusted. He growled something, deep in his throat, and gestured with the rifle.

Fang shrugged, seemingly unperturbed, with the same enigmatic smile on his face. He raised his hands above his head in a sign of defeat that still managed to make Cade feel distinctly uneasy. He didn't know how much English Fang understood, but he suspected it was more than the bastard let on.

He gestured upward. "You get those men on that Gatling gun to stand down."

Fang looked up. His brow furrowed for a moment as if he was perplexed. Then comprehension seemed to dawn on him. He looked back at Cade. "We go up?"

Cade's anxiety was multiplying by the second, but he gestured with the pistol toward the nearby stairs. "Yeah. You first."

Still smiling that disturbing smile, Fang mounted the stairs.

Cade followed behind, his pistol trained on the center of Fang's back. Ax Man brought up the rear. Cade felt a shiver up his back at the idea of the tong soldier behind him with a gun, but he let it go. The man had proved his loyalty so far.

The stairs rose up into another barren room. There was a door across from the stairwell. Fang crossed to the door and pulled it open.

Sunlight spilled into the room from the alleyway. Cade was momentarily dazzled by the light, and his finger tightened on the trigger, expecting some trickery from Fang. But the man turned, raising his hands above his head, and backed out of the door. Cade followed, Ax Man to his right and slightly behind.

They emerged in the shadow of a covered porch that ran the width of the alleyway. A wagon was parked just in front of the porch, a pair of Chinese men standing on either side of the deadly machine that stood in the wagon bed, their attention focused on the mouth of the alley. Another man stood next to the wagon. He turned to see who was coming out of the door, and Cade could see the look of surprise on his face as the three of them—Fang, Cade, and Ax Man—walked out. Cade saw the man by the wagon had only one eye, the other covered by a black cloth. He realized with a start that this was one of the highbinders who had come aboard Marjorie's burning ship to rescue them. Cade touched the brim of his hat and nodded in recognition.

The one-eyed man nodded back, but there was no friendliness in his eye. He said something to Fang, his voice rising interrogatively at the end of the sentence.

Fang answered in a confident tone, even as he kept his hands up. He called to the men on the gun, but they didn't move away.

Cade raised the pistol to point at the center of Fang's head. "Tell them to stand down."

Fang's smile widened. "I do not believe I will, Mr. Cade."

He spoke with only the merest trace of accent. He nodded. "Look."

Cade looked down toward the mouth of the alley. What he saw made his heart freeze in his chest.

A pair of *boo how doy* had rounded the corner, each one holding a pistol to the head of the figure slumped and stumbling between them.

Marjorie.

CHAPTER FIFTY-EIGHT

"Well," Simonson said, "I believe my services here are no longer needed." He slid off the chair and straightened his waistcoat. "I'll just be—"

Clinton turned on him with the shotgun. "Sit the hell down, shorty."

Eleanor glanced at him from the corner of her eye. Simonson's face was a blank mask, but she could sense the seething rage behind it. She'd hidden her own behind just such a façade often enough.

"Now," Clinton said, "I need to know what she told you." He glowered at Carine.

The girl cowered back against the couch cushions, still whimpering.

Despite her own fear, the sight of the young girl being terrorized got Eleanor's back up. "Leave her alone, you damned bully!"

Clinton stared dumbly at her for a moment, clearly stunned at the idea of any defiance from a black servant. He crossed the room in three great strides and backhanded Eleanor to her knees. "Shut the fuck up, you black bitch," he snarled.

The pain was stunning, debilitating, and Eleanor's world went gray and fuzzy for a moment. When she looked up, she saw Athena Givens standing in the doorway to the parlor. The brief moment of hope she felt was snuffed out quickly when her mistress turned to Clinton and asked in an eerily calm voice, "What seems to be the problem, Daddy?"

From the other edge of the alley, Clayborne saw the trio come from around the corner of the building, two of the tong soldiers flanking a person between them. The gait seemed strangely familiar and figure was clearly female, but the bodies of the *boo how doy* blocked his view. It was only when they reached the center of the alley that he recognized the tumble of red hair and realized that the person being shoved to the center of the alley was his former employer. "Son of a bitch," he muttered. He turned to the Chinese tong soldiers he'd brought with him, wondering how he was going to explain what was going on, and realized it didn't matter. They were running off, down the side street, not even looking back.

"Goddamn it." He turned back, raised his rifle, and took aim. What he saw made him grit his teeth in frustration. He could hit one of the men flanking Mrs. Hamrick, but that risked the other one shooting her in the head. And then there was the menace of that goddamn Gatling gun that she was facing head-on. He looked behind him at the only one who'd stuck with him —the black mare Midnight. He smiled wryly. "Any ideas, girl?"

The mare pawed at the ground, ducked her head, and snorted.

Clayborne chuckled. "You seem a damn sight more game than I feel."

The horse whinnied.

"Mr. Cade," Fang said, "perhaps we can agree on one thing. That the tables have turned."

"You son of a bitch," Cade snarled. "Let her go, or so help me God, I'll kill you where you stand."

"If you do," Fang said, "my men will use that gun to chop the woman into a pile of bloody meat. I can tell she means something to you." He lowered his hands and said something in Chinese.

Cade looked over to his left. Ax Man now had his rifle pointed at Cade's head.

"Drop the pistol," Fang said.

Cade didn't see any choice. He lowered the Navy revolver, then let it fall to the wooden floor of the porch.

Fang barked an order, and the one-eyed man scuttled over to pick up the weapon, scampering back and pointing it at Cade in an awkward grip. Fanng nodded with satisfaction. "Now," he said to Cade, "go out there and join your woman."

"Look," Cade said desperately, "this isn't going to work. Your brother's never going to bargain with the two of us."

Fang shook his head. "This is not negotiation. This is to show what happens to *gwai loh* who meddle in our business." He smiled coldly. "No, Mr. Cade, this is not bargaining. This is an execution." The smile vanished. "Now get out there."

One-Eyed Vang listened to Fang's words with horror. Warfare inside the tongs, and even between them, was something that mostly passed beneath the notice of the white authorities. But now Fang was not only acquiring the weapons of the white devils, he was proposing to murder them with the same weapons in the belief that that would warn them off from interfering in Chinese business. He knew the exact opposite was true. The survival of the Chinese population of California had been hanging by the thinnest of threads for decades. Fang's plan risked bringing down the full wrath of white America on them. There would be no mercy for the people. Kwan Fang was flirting with extermination. Vang realized with a sick feeling in his stomach that he had thrown in his lot with a madman.

CHAPTER FIFTY-NINE

"Daddy," Eleanor said. "Now it all makes sense." She got slowly to her feet and wiped her mouth with the back of her hand. It came away bloody. She looked over at the man she'd only known as Clinton, the drunken coachman. "Now I know why Miss Givens hired you in the first place. And why she puts up win your drunken antics. You're the father she left behind."

"Eleanor," Athena Givens began.

"What I don't understand," Eleanor went on, looking back at her, "is what hold he has on you that you not only take him in, you provide him with a false identity, and," she shook her head, "you forgive him, even after he stabbed you in the back." Realization dawned on her. "Or did he?"

Cade felt like he was wearing lead boots as he walked across the packed dirt of the alleyway toward where Marjorie slumped between the grinning Chinese tong soldiers.

She raised her head at his approach and a low moan of despair escaped her throat as she saw he was unarmed.

When he reached them, he looked the one nearest him in the eye. "Take your fucking hands off her, boy," he said in a low, flat voice, "or so help me sweet Jesus, I will make sure you die first with my goddamn teeth in your throat."

The man scowled. He clearly had no idea of Cade's actual words, but there was no mistaking the menace in any language. He hesitated, then muttered something in Chinese and stepped away from Marjorie. His compatriot on the other side of her did the same.

He rushed to her side just in time to keep her from falling to the packed earth of the alleyway. "I got you, honey lamb," he murmured.

"Levi." Her voice was a low whisper. Her eyes were fixed on the terrible killing machine at the end of the alley. "I don't want to die. Not like this."

"I don't want that either, Marjorie. Not like this, or any other way."

"I want to watch my daughter grow up."

"Me, too." He raised his voice. "Mr. Clayborne!"

The reply came from the mouth of the alley. "Yes, Mr. Cade?"

Cade glanced backward. "I assume you can see our need for assistance."

"I do, sir. But I fear I do not have a clear shot at the gentlemen working that weapon." There was a brief pause. "I do believe, however, I can offer spiritual encouragement."

"Spiritual..." Cade gritted his teeth. "Goddamn it, Sam."

Clayborne's voice rang out like a preacher's. "I will lift up my eyes to the hills," he intoned. "From whence comes my help."

"I don't need a goddamn—" Cade began, but Clayborne cut him off, his voice rising.

"*Lift up your eyes*, Mr. Cade."

The voice was compelling enough that Cade looked up. He saw a figure moving across the roof of the building at the end of the alley. It was a woman dressed in white, her garments streaked with crimson. She was scuttling across the shingled roof like a spider. Cade could see the hilts of the swords strapped on her back.

"Is that...?" Marjorie whispered.

"Yeah." Cade shook his head. "If we get out of here, I'm never getting out of debt to this goddamn crazy woman."

Clinton swung his gun to bear on Eleanor. "You think you're pretty damned clever, don't you, bitch?"

Eleanor shook her head. "It was all for show. All fakery. But how? I could swear I saw your blood. And the doctor you had me call..." She stopped. "He wasn't a doctor at all, was he?"

Givens looked down, unable to answer.

"I can figure how the illusion was done," Eleanor said. "You're a mistress of that, aren't you? You and your father. You've trafficked in illusion since your childhood. But that doesn't answer why. Why this charade? And why blame Tatanka for an attack that never really happened?"

"Money," Simonson spoke up from his perch on the chair. All eyes turned to him. He had a sour expression on his face. "Whenever you ask the question why in this town, the answer is always money. She's been raking in cash since word of the attack got out." He looked as if he wanted to spit. "Everyone loves a martyr."

"But why sacrifice Tatanka for the illusion?" Eleanor

persisted. Her voice softened as she addressed her employer. "He loves you, you know. He'd lay down his life for you."

Givens continued to stare at the floor. "Tatanka was never part of the plan," she murmured. "That was Captain Smith's doing. Seeking to get at me."

Clinton spoke up. "But it's not like it matters. One more Indian, dead or in prison." He shrugged. "Who cares?"

Eleanor looked over at Givens. She thought she saw a single tear fall to the floor from her bowed head. "Just like Mr. Gideon," she said. "He saw through you, didn't he, Mr. Clinton?"

Clinton sneered. "And that's one less nosy bastard to deal with."

"Did you murder him, too? Or did you just frighten him off?"

As they'd been speaking, Eleanor had been sidling toward the fireplace on the side of the room nearest the door. There was a set of fire tools in a rack by the mantel, including a poker with a spike and hook on its business end. She glanced over at Carine, who was curled up on the couch, staring straight ahead. There'd be no help there. The poor child was literally scared out of her wits. A look at Simonson provided a little more hope.

The little man was regarding her shrewdly. His eyes flickered to the fireplace tools in their stand, then back to hers, and he gave an almost imperceptible nod.

As he did, Clinton swung his pistol back to bear on Eleanor. "I told you to stand still, bitch," he snarled.

CHAPTER SIXTY

Clayborne peered down the alleyway, counting the forces confronting them. Two tong soldiers on the Gatling, the man who stood beside the wagon who was clearly the one in charge, the pair of gunmen who'd brought Mrs. Hamrick to the killing ground taking up positions on either side of the gun, and the one-eyed man skulking in the background. Another man with a rifle, who Clayborne could have sworn he'd seen heading off with Cade, took up a position off to the right. He grimaced. He'd seen The White Orchid wreak havoc, even when greatly outnumbered, but that had been against a disorganized rabble of hoodlums. He didn't feel sure that she could take on seven of these killers alone. And the lives of his friends were in the balance.

Samuel Clayborne took a deep breath. The weight of guilt he'd always felt for deserting his family to a horrific fate had never felt heavier on his shoulders. There was only one way to shrug it off.

He looked at Midnight, who was stirring restlessly, but who hadn't left his side like the others. "Well, girl," he murmured, "I don't have any right to ask you to fight this battle with me. But

I'm asking it anyway." He used the reins to draw her close, then put one foot in the stirrup and swung aboard. The horse tossed her head, then settled. He patted her on the neck. "Good girl." He took the reins between his teeth and checked the rifle. Loaded and cocked. He took a deep breath. "Okay, then."

"When she moves," Cade whispered to Marjorie, "get behind me. Then run like hell back where Kwan and his people are."

"What are you going to do?" she murmured back.

"Try and draw fire. Till she does what she does."

"What if they kill you?"

"Then they kill me and not you."

"Levi..."

"Goddamn it, woman, do as I say," he said harshly.

"Okay," she answered, her voice cool. "But when this is over, we are going to have a discussion about your tone."

"Looking forward to it."

He saw Kwan Fang raise his hand, as if preparing to give the signal to fire. The White Orchid had reached the edge of the roof.

"Now!"

One-Eyed Vang heard Fang murmur some witticism to the gunners on the Steel Dragon that had them chuckling. He trembled at the thought of what he was about to do. As Fang raised his arm dramatically, Vang raised the pistol they'd taken from the white devil and took aim.

He never had time to pull the trigger.

As Fang's arm began to drop, a figure dressed in white fell

from the eaves of the porch above, landing at the back of the wagon. The man on the right side of the gun, the one working the crank that fired the multiple barrels, barely had time to look up before his head was rolling free from his shoulders, blood exploding from the stump of his neck. The rifleman on the right side of the wagon leaped aside, shouting in disgust as the head of the Gatling gunner landed at his feet and the spray of gore from the falling body spattered him from head to foot. The White Orchid wasted no time in turning and slashing at the man feeding the weapon on its left side. This time, the blade sunk deeply into the man's guts. He barely had time to scream before the second blade, wielded in The White Orchid's other hand, plunged deep into his chest and pierced his heart.

Vang scuttled backward, mewling in terror at the sight of the carnage before him. He saw the riflemen on either side of the wagon stepping back and taking aim. *Good,* he thought hysterically, *whatever happens, we need to be rid of this demon.*

As Cade saw The White Orchid drop from the roof into the wagon, he pushed Marjorie behind him and charged forward. Unarmed as he was, if he could draw fire from her and let her get away, he'd die content.

He was startled to hear a cry of "HI-YAH!" and the thudding of hoofbeats to his left. He glanced over to see Clayborne, astride the black mare Midnight, the reins held in his teeth, firing the rifle he held in both hands. Cade put his own head down and screamed at the top of his lungs, pounding straight down the alley, waiting for the shot that would end his life. He'd long suspected he wasn't destined to die in bed, but he never expected he'd get shot down in a Chinatown alley, unarmed.

It didn't look, however, as if it was going to happen that way either. He raised his eyes as he reached the end of the alley and saw the rifleman there falling backward, his rifle dropping from his hands as the back of his head seemed to explode from Clayborne's rifle shot. Cade stopped, panting, then saw Ax Man taking aim at someone. It was either Clayborne or The White Orchid, but it wasn't Cade, so he snarled, deep in his throat, and charged again. He hit Ax Man around the waist, wrapped his arms around him, and bore him to the ground.

One-Eyed Vang watched with horror as everything went catastrophically wrong for the rebellion he'd backed. Fang was screaming at the men on the wagon, even as The White Orchid was reducing them to so much cooling flesh. The black white devil was charging down the alley on horseback, firing, and Vang was suddenly covered in the blood of Chang Sing, a man he'd drunk wine and broken bread with, now falling to the ground, half his head blown away. The black man reached the end of the alley, drew the horse up, and pointed his rifle at Vang. He shouted something in the white devil's tongue. Vang didn't know the exact words, but he could hear the intent. But instead of dropping the big pistol he held, he turned it on Fang, smiling ingratiatingly at the man on the horse. The contemptuous curl on the black white devil's lip matched the look of disgust on Fang's visage. Vang didn't care. This was his chance of getting out of this debacle alive.

When The White Orchid leaped down from the wagon, her blades flashing faster than Vang's eyes could follow at the back of Fang's neck, Vang realized with a sick feeling in his guts that his improvised plan might not work.

CHAPTER SIXTY-ONE

"What I don't understand," Simonson said, nodding at Carine, "is what part this poor child has to play in this sordid little plan? Why terrorize her?"

Clinton turned the gun back on him. "I thought I told you to shut up, shrimp."

Simonson looked pained. "Please. You're obviously prepared to kill all of us. At least grant me the dignity of dying for something I actually know." He turned to Carine and spoke gently. "*Que c'est-il passé, petit? Pourquoi cet homme tu effraie-t-il autant?*"

The girl didn't seem to hear him at first. Then she spoke in a whisper, her blue eyes brimming with tears. Simonson listened, a grave expression on his face, then nodded.

He turned to Eleanor. "She saw him in the passage outside of the séance room the night of the attack. Waiting, no doubt, with a prop knife and a pot of stage blood. She didn't know what was happening, but after the," he cleared his throat, "attack, she put two and two together. So now," he looked at Eleanor, "he has to kill all of us. Everyone who knows about this plot. You, me, this poor girl here."

He raised an eyebrow. "And how, I wonder, will you explain those deaths? Will you blame them on your poor mad daughter?" He turned to Athena Givens. "Will she need to die, too?"

Cade had knocked Ax Man to the ground, but the tong soldier had stubbornly held onto his rifle. With Cade on top of him, however, he couldn't bring the long gun to bear. It didn't stop him from trying. He flailed and struggled, bucking like a bronco. Cade raised up, straddling the man, and hit him in the face as hard as he could. He put all his fear and rage behind the blow, and behind the next one as well. He punched as if he meant to drive his fist into the ground behind the man's head, and didn't stop until the man lay limp and unresisting beneath him, his face bloody and misshapen. He paused, gasping for breath, then staggered to his feet. He'd lost his hat in the struggle, and he stood stupidly for a moment, his gaze moving back and forth between the hat upended on the ground and the rifle that lay mere inches away from the hand of the man he'd just beaten unconscious. It took him a moment to decide to pick up the rifle first, then the hat. He looked around, then moved to the other side of the wagon.

Kwan Fang was on his knees, his hands in the air. The White Orchid stood behind him, one of her swords held in a two-handed grip at his neck. The Chinese man Cade had seen pick up his pistol earlier was, to Cade's surprise, holding the pistol pointed at Fang's head.

"Well, sir," Cade said in a hoarse voice, "it seems you have suffered something of a reversal of fortune."

"Yes," Fang said dryly. He took a deep breath. "I would like to talk to my brother."

"I'll just bet you would." Cade looked at The White Orchid, and was worried at what he saw. The woman's usually alabaster skin had taken on a shade of gray, and her dark brown eyes seemed cloudy and unfocused. Her robes were caked with blood, some fresh crimson, more that had dried to crusted black. "You okay, sis?" he said.

The White Orchid smiled at him. "Oh-kay, Cade." The blood he could see on her teeth made him think otherwise. She was bleeding inside. *She needs some more of that Chinese doctoring,* Cade thought. *We need to end this shit, and fast.*

Cade pointed the rifle at the one-eyed Chinese man holding the Navy revolver on Fang. He raised the rifle and pointed it at the man's head. "First things first. Give me my goddamn pistol back, you son of a bitch."

CHAPTER SIXTY-TWO

"Great Sir," Mei said desperately. She could hear the shots and screams from the alleyway. She felt a sickness in her heart, thinking of what might be happening to her friends. "The battle is joined. People are fighting. For you, sir. Will you not help them?"

Kwan Lee sat in the front seat of the wagon, his head cocked like a curious dog's, listening to the battle with a detachment that made Mei want to scream. Finally, he turned to the *boo how doy* moving restlessly around the wagon. "Go," he barked, "help your brothers."

The men looked at each other, then at Kwan, then they began moving in a desultory fashion, not with any degree of eagerness.

Kwan growled something deep in his throat, clearly displeased at their reluctance. He stood up in the wagon. Before he could speak, a group appeared at the intersection. Mei's heart thudded in her chest as she made them out.

The black man Clayborne was the first person she recognized, but only because he was mounted and moving behind the main group. Then she saw that leading the way were Kwan Fang and the soldier Mei had met and knew only as One-Eyed Vang. The two were walking with slow, deliberate steps, hands raised. Mei craned her neck to try to see better. She spotted a familiar hat and knew that Cade was behind Fang. Next to him, obscured by the figure of Vang, Mei caught sight of a white robe, and her heart thudded in her chest. As they drew nearer, Mei saw that it was indeed her friend Lin, but The White Orchid was clearly in terrible shape. Her skin was a ghastly hue, and her usually graceful stride had turned into a clumsy shamble. Her white robes were a mosaic of red, white, and bloodstains drying to black.

"Great One," she choked out, her voice cracking with emotion.

"I see," Kwan said gently. "Be silent now."

As the group drew closer to the wagon, the group of *boo how doy* parted, then drew around them in a circle. Mei could see that the group also included Cade's woman, the redhead she'd met at her house. She, too, looked badly shaken, but when she spotted Mei in the crowd, she straightened a bit and nodded politely. Mei bowed back. She wondered if she'd ever get over being surprised at a white devil with manners. Even a woman.

When Kwan spoke from his perch on the wagon, it was The White Orchid he addressed. "Daughter," he said, "what have you brought to me?"

She stepped forward, tottering on unsteady feet, then fell to her knees and put her forehead on the ground. She staggered as she rose, but drew herself up to her full height. "Father," she said in a dry croak. "I have brought you the traitor Kwan Fang. And Vang Lun. He betrayed you, but," she sneered, and the expression revealed the blood on her lips and teeth, "he turned his coat again at the last moment."

Kwan Lee nodded, his face still impassive. "You have done well, Daughter." He looked down at Vang. "Is this true?"

Vang fell to his knees and knocked his head against the ground so hard Mei thought he meant to bash his own brains out. "I beg forgiveness, Father," he blubbered. "I was led astray. I swear I will be loyal to you from now on. From now until the heavens fall."

Kwan looked down at him, face as stern as a carved patriarch on a cathedral, but his voice was sorrowful as he spoke. "You have given much in my service, Vang Lun. Even lost an eye in battle for me. But after this, how can I ever trust you again?"

Vang didn't try to answer, just bowed his head to the ground again.

The tong soldiers moved in closer, awaiting the order to strike. Finally, Kwan Lee sighed. "For your former service," he said, "and because you came to your senses, I will grant you your life." His face grew stern. "But you are dismissed. You are no longer a member of the Green Dragon Tong. Now go."

The man looked up, tears streaming down his face. "Great One," he whimpered, "where shall I go? How shall I live?"

Kwan's eyes narrowed. "Would you prefer I end you now?"

Vang bowed to the ground again. "No, Great One. Truly. I thank you for the gift of my worthless life. But may I not—"

"No." Kwan's voice cracked like a whip. "Now go. Before I change my mind."

One-Eyed Vang stood, wiping tears from his eyes and snot from his nose with the sleeve of his jacket. He turned to leave, and the crowd parted to let him out.

As he began to slink away, Kwan stopped him. "One more thing."

The man stopped and looked back at his former leader, his shoulders slumped, cringing like a beaten dog.

"If you think you can take your knowledge and your meager skills to another tong, you worthless traitor," Kwan said, "I will consider this deal forfeit. And I assure you, in that event, your death will be something whispered about for decades."

Vang didn't answer. He ducked his head and scurried off.

Kwan turned his gaze to regard his brother.

Unlike his former conspirator, Fang didn't slink or grovel. He stood with his head high and his chin raised.

"So, *brother*," Kwan said, and his calm voice was gone. Now it dripped with pure venom. "What are we to do with one who conspired against his own family?"

"Family?" Fang sneered. "You speak to me of family? You, who took the scum of a Guangzhou gutter and elevated her above your own kin? You, who consorts with," he looked behind him at Cade, then turned and spat on the ground, "the *gwai loh*, who would sell us all as slaves if they could? The ones who wouldn't just rather see us all dead, I mean."

Kwan shook his head. "We are here. Now. We have to live in this place. We can use the money we make to—"

Fang's voice rose to a shout. "They will never allow it!"

"And for that belief," Kwan said, "you would kill your own brother?"

Fang shook his head. "I meant to offer you a choice. You could go back to China. Have a prosperous and calm life. I would have allowed it."

"Allowed..." Kwan's face flushed with outrage, then he calmed himself. He smiled coldly. "Very well. I will offer you the same choice. Death. Or exile."

Fang smiled. "Thank you, brother. Of course, it is an easy choice. I will choose exile."

The tension that had been gathering in the group of *boo how doy* began to dissipate. Fang was popular among the soldiers of the Green Dragon Tong, even the ones who hadn't joined his rebellion, and there was a palpable sense of relief that no one was going to have to execute him.

That relief was shattered when The White Orchid stepped forward. Her voice was low, but as hard as steel as she spoke one word.

"No."

CHAPTER SIXTY-THREE

"What do you mean?" Athena Givens said. "Kill...me?"

Eleanor saw Simonson give a slight shrug, as calm as if he were discussing the possibility of afternoon thunderstorms or the predictions for the next horse race. "It seems as if your father's only hope, Miss Givens, is to eliminate every witness to his schemes. But that many missing or dead persons would need to be accounted for."

He turned to the former coachman. "Tell me, Mr. Clinton, how do you intend to explain these deaths to the other servants? Or the families of the missing?" He nodded again at Carine. "Surely this young lady has family who'd notice her loss. Or do you mean to kill everyone, burn the place to the ground, and blame," he shrugged, "I don't know, the Chinese? That seems to be quite *en vogue* these days."

Clinton rounded on him, raising the pistol. "You need to be quiet now."

Eleanor took the opportunity to edge closer to the fireplace and its assortment of potential weapons.

Simonson raised his hands in a placating gesture, high above his head. "In mere moments, I'm sure, you'll silence me for good. But for the moment, I'd like to ask your daughter here a question." Without waiting for permission, he smiled at Athena Givens. "Have you changed your will yet, Miss Givens? In favor of your driver here?"

Mei watched with a sick feeling as her friend stood before the head of the Green Dragon Tong and scolded him as if he was a schoolboy.

"Are you simple?" she demanded. There were no honorifics and none of the respect she'd always shown her employer. "This man meant to kill you and take everything you had. He sent assassins to murder all of us. You cannot let him live."

Kwan looked stunned for a moment, but he quickly composed himself. "Be silent, woman!"

"I will *not*," she snapped back. She swayed for a moment, then straightened herself by sheer force of will. "He will stab you in the back at the first opportunity. Were you hit in the head when his men tied you in that closet? Have you lost your wits?"

Fang looked at her with a sly smile before turning back toward Kwan as if to say something. He never got the chance. Swords flashed, and in a half second, Fang's body was toppling to the ground, spouting blood at the neck.

Mei screamed. Some of the tong soldiers gathered around cried out in in shock, but they recovered quickly. Seconds later, they all had weapons drawn.

"LIN!" Mei screamed and leaped forward. She went to her knees before The White Orchid, clasping her around the legs.

Lin tottered for a moment, then regained her balance. Mei felt a gentle hand stroking her hair, then Lin spoke in a hoarse, exhausted voice, nothing like the whiplash tones she'd just used on Kwan. "Step away, Younger Sister. I'm ready to take what I have coming to me." She laughed softly. "Perhaps what I've always had coming to me."

Mei shook her head. "No." Without relinquishing her grip, she turned and looked up at Kwan. "Please, Great One. She has done so much for you. She has nearly died in your service." Her voice caught in her throat. "She may yet." As if in confirmation, she felt a shiver run through her friend's body. She saw movement out of the corner of her eye and turned her head. She cried out as she saw a *boo how doy* standing a few feet away with a rifle pointed at her head.

"Get up!" the man ordered roughly in Chinese. "Get away."

Another movement from the other side, and she turned to see Cade standing beside her, his pistol pointed at the rifleman's head. "Boy," he told the man in a low, deadly voice, "you want to be pointing that goddamn rifle somewhere else."

The man's eyes narrowed, and he suddenly moved so the rifle was pointing at Cade's head. He was grinning.

Cade regarded him calmly. "Better. But you might want to consider your next move real carefully." He gestured with his chin to look behind him.

Mei looked over and saw the black white devil Clayborne and Cade's woman pointing their own rifles at the man menacing Cade. His grin faded.

"Enough!" Kwan barked.

Cade looked at him. "Agreed. Sir." He looked at Mei. "Can you get up, sis? I hate to ask you right now, but I need you to translate."

Mei stood up, knees shaking so badly she thought she might collapse to the street again. She looked down at Fang's body, lying in a rapidly spreading pool of blood, and felt sick to her stomach. She took up a position on one side of her friend Lin, putting an arm around her shoulder. Cade did the same on the other side.

"Yes," Mei said in a shaky voice, "I will translate."

"Good girl." Cade looked up at Kwan. "Sir. May I have a word?"

Kwan looked down at him stonily and spoke a single word.

Cade took it as permission. He took a deep breath. "This young lady here," he nodded at The White Orchid, who barely seemed aware of his presence, "has done some pretty remarkable things in your service. Took a bullet today in your service, as it happens. She's got the benefit of some of that Chinese needle medicine, but I'm thinking all the blood she's lost might have affected her thinking."

Kwan scowled as Mei translated. "What do you mean?"

"I'm saying that maybe when she did..." he nodded to Fang's dead body on the ground, "...that, she might not have been completely in her right mind."

As Mei translated, she felt Lin stiffen. "What?" she said in Chinese.

"Shhh," Mei responded.

"You can't hold someone responsible for what they did when off their head. That's not just. And everyone says you're a just man."

Kwan scowled and spoke.

"He says he does not require you to flatter him," Mei said.

Cade bowed his head slightly. "Then I'll speak plain." He looked again at Fang's body, then back to Kwan. "Whether she was in her right mind or not, she wasn't wrong. That man may have been your brother, but he meant to kill you. If not today, then as soon as he could."

Kwan's scowl deepened. "She disobey," he said in English.

Cade nodded. "That she did. No doubt. I've been a soldier,

sir, and no one knows better than me that disobeying an order is gonna have consequences."

Kwan smiled grimly and spoke again in Chinese.

"You speak as a man who has disobeyed orders," Mei translated.

"Yes, sir. Lost my stripes," he glanced at Mei, "sorry, my rank more than once for it. But I never did it without good reason." He smiled. "Once I even saved my Captain's ass—I mean, his life by doing it."

Kwan listened to the translation, then nodded. He didn't speak for a long moment before looking back down at Cade and answering.

Mei hesitated before providing the translation. "You agree, though, that there must be consequences?"

Goddamn it, Cade thought. *What have I talked that girl into?* All he could do was nod.

"Very well." He addressed The White Orchid. "You are dismissed from my service. Make your own way from here."

Mei sobbed something that sounded like a plea, but The White Orchid straightened from where she slumped between Mei and Cade. She clasped her hands before her and bowed from the waist, so deeply that Cade feared she would topple over. When she straightened up, both Mei's and Cade's hands had fallen from her shoulders. She spoke to Kwan, then took Mei's hand and kissed it, her eyes closed, before letting the hand fall. She looked over at Cade and smiled sadly.

"We need to get you to a doctor, girl," Cade said, his voice choked with emotion. "Stick by us. We'll get you out of here."

The White Orchid leaned toward him. Cade almost flinched, but he relaxed when all she did was kiss him on the cheek. She looked back at Marjorie standing behind him and said something in Chinese. She ended with an aside to Mei.

"She says," Mei began, then stopped, her voice failing her.

The White Orchid spoke gently. Mei took a deep, shuddering breath and turned to Marjorie. "She says this is a good man." She laughed, a little hysterically. "For a white devil. You should hold on to him."

Cade didn't turn around to see Marjorie's reaction, but he could hear the emotion in her voice as she responded. "Thank your friend for her wise counsel." She looked at Cade. "I mean to."

After the translation, The White Orchid nodded. She turned and saw a wall of hostile *boo how doy* blocking her path. Raising her chin defiantly, she said a single word that parted the crowd like Moses parting the Red Sea. She walked out between them, not looking either to the right or the left. People were beginning to come out of the buildings lining the street, sensing that the worst of the battle was over. All of them stood silently and watched her go. She walked up to a corner, turned it, and was gone.

Mei was sobbing, on the verge of collapse. Marjorie rushed to the girl and put an arm around her shoulders. She looked up at Kwan, who was staring pensively at the place where The White Orchid had vanished. "What in the world is wrong with you?!" she demanded.

Kwan didn't answer, or acknowledge Marjorie's presence.

It was Cade who provided an answer. "I know what the problem is." He grimaced. "Face."

Marjorie turned to him. "What does that mean?"

Cade sighed. "Miss Mei there can probably explain better. But this thing they call face is a big deal to the Chinese. It means reputation. Respect."

"Well, Levi," Marjorie said, "those aren't just Chinese concepts."

"I guess. But for someone like Kwan, it's everything. It's survival." He turned to Mei. "Right, sis?"

The young woman only nodded. She looked as if she'd been stunned by a blow to the head. "She defied Mr. Kwan."

"And," Clayborne added dryly, "she did chop his brother's head off." He nodded at where a pair of *boo how doy* were picking up the body by arms and legs while another gathered up the head.

"Yeah," Cade said. "The son of a bitch had it coming. Even Kwan knew that. But he couldn't take being called out like that." Cade fought back the urge to spit on the ground in disgust. "In this case, face is just stupid fucking pride." He noticed that Kwan had stepped down from his perch on the wagon. He was surrounded by Chinese, all of whom seemed to be congratulating him on his victory. He shook his head. "Let's go home. Anyone bring me a horse?"

Marjorie and Clayborne looked at each other. Clayborne was still mounted on Midnight. "Sorry," Clayborne said. "We only brought the two."

"And I'm not sure where...ah, there she is." A Chinese man was leading a gray mare back to the group. Marjorie turned to Cade and smiled. "I suppose you could ride behind me."

"Um..." Cade said.

Before there was any further discussion, he saw that Kwan had raised his voice to call over to them. Mei hurried over. Her eyes were red from crying, but her voice was steady. "Mr. Kwan requests your presence." She paused. Cade was inclined to tell the man to go to Hell, but then Mei went on. "He wishes you to see what you have fought to keep for him. He wishes you to view the Golden Mountain."

CHAPTER SIXTY-FOUR

ivens smiled at Simonson, a glint of triumph in her eyes. "As it happens, Mr. Simonson, I have not yet done so. If your theory is that my father intends to kill me to try and inherit my money, then..." She looked back at Clinton with a fond smile that froze on her face as she saw her father's look of shock.

"You...you said..." His face darkened with blood as shock turned to anger. "You promised me. You said you were going to talk to the lawyer."

The blood drained from Givens's face. "I was going to, Daddy," she said, her voice suddenly drained of its confidence. It was the pleading tone of a little girl, caught in some failure for which she knew there would be terrible retribution. "But...but... the thing with Tatanka came up and..." A note of panic came into her voice as she saw her father's face darkening from anger to rage. "Please, Daddy. I'll do it right away. I just forgot. Please."

Eleanor was stunned at the sudden transformation in the woman she'd looked up to for so long. It was as if years of confidence and accomplishment had been sheared away in an instant and she was once again a terrified, abused child begging not to be hurt.

She stole a look at Simonson and was almost as startled at the expression she saw on the little man's face. His hands were still raised as if in surrender, but his eyes were narrowed and he spoke from behind teeth clenched with rage. "So, Mr. Clinton," he said, "it seems your plans are all gone sideways." His arms abruptly snapped down as if he was shaking water from the ends of his fingers. Eleanor saw the glint of silver blades appearing in each hand. "Our revels now are ended," he said.

Eleanor didn't hesitate. She moved to the stand where the fireplace tools were stored and snatched up the poker. As she turned, raising it above her head in both hands, she saw Clinton pointing the gun at Simonson.

Carine screamed from her place on the couch. But instead of firing, the coachman suddenly shrieked in pain and began clawing at his face with his free hand. Eleanor could see the glint of a knife that seemed to have magically appeared and lodged itself in one eye. He didn't drop the gun, however, so Eleanor charged, bringing the iron poker down on the top of Clinton's head as hard as she could. The spike on the end of the implement drove deep into the top of the man's skull, and he screamed again. He tried to turn toward her, the gun still in his hand, but another blade sprouted from the side of his neck. Incredibly, he still refused to fall. Sobbing with horror, Eleanor pulled the poker free of the man's skull with a sickening slurping sound. His hand was shaking, but he was still trying to turn and bring it to bear on her, so she raised the poker high and drove it down again, into the center of his forehead. That finally dropped him. The pistol fell from his hand as he slumped to the floor with a crash.

"DADDY!" Givens screamed, and dropped to her knees beside his limp body, tears streaming down her face. She turned him onto his back and howled like an animal as she saw the blades protruding from his eye and neck and the spiked poker still lodged in his brain.

Eleanor slumped to the floor beside the body, staring in shock at what she'd done. Some impulse made her pull the spiked poker from Clinton's forehead and lay the implement carefully, almost reverently, alongside the body.

"Daddy, please," Givens was babbling, "please wake up. Please. I'll be good, I'll be ever so good, I promise, just please wake up."

Jesus Christ, Eleanor thought, suddenly overcome with exhaustion, *will you please shut up?*

Kwan and his entourage led the way, walking in a knot of Chinese. Some were *boo how doy* with their queues still wrapped high around their heads in readiness for combat, some apparently were mere hangers-on. But they surrounded Kwan, who was marching with the confident stride of a general walking across the field of victory. Like such a general, he ignored the efforts being made to gather the bodies they passed. Cade, Marjorie, and Clayborne followed. Cade was on foot, with Marjorie leading the gray mare and Clayborne still mounted.

Cade looked around and spotted Mei, trailing behind, her head down, trudging like a woman walking through deep snow. He drew up short. "Hey," he called softly. Marjorie and Clayborne halted with him, waiting for Mei to catch up. Cade put his arm around Mei's shoulder. Marjorie stepped up and did the same from the other side, holding the gray mare's reins with her free hand. "She'll be okay, sis," Cade murmured. "She's tough as leather."

Mei didn't answer. She kept walking with her head bowed.

Cade looked over at Marjorie. She looked back, her expression as helpless as Cade felt.

Soon enough, they reached the end of the alley. A pair of highbinders were dragging the wagon with the Gatling gun away, straining at the wagon tongue like draft horses. The bodies had already cleared, and some Chinese women were cleaning the bloodstains from the end of the alleyway.

Kwan stood at the door leading to the interior of the building, a pair of his tong soldiers flanking him. He looked so sleek and self-satisfied that Cade wanted to strike him. Kwan called out something to them.

Mei raised her head. "He wants us to come with him." Her voice sounded dead. "Below."

"All of us?"

Mei spoke to Kwan, her voice rising interrogatively at the end.

Kwan answered with a shrug and a few words in Chinese.

Mei turned to Cade. "He doesn't care if the black..." She paused. "If the black man comes."

Cade looked up at Clayborne. Before he could speak, Clayborne said, "It's fine, Mr. Cade. I'll stay her and watch the horses. And," he glanced significantly at the milling *boo how doy*, "make sure none of these fellows gets up to any mischief."

Cade nodded. He turned back to Mei. "You going to be okay?"

Mei looked back at him, her eyes bleak. "I do not think I will. But I will do what I am here to do."

"Okay, then." He turned to Kwan. "Lead on."

CHAPTER SIXTY-FIVE

Eleanor didn't know how long she sat on the floor, paralyzed by shock and fear. She could still hear Givens, sobbing like the broken child she'd reverted to. She turned her head, mutely watching as Simonson walked over and stood beside the body.

He studied the corpse gravely before turning to the weeping woman. "Miss Givens," he said. Eleanor noticed through her mental fog that the little man's voice had lost its usual supercilious tone. When Givens didn't answer, he spoke up again. "Miss Givens!"

She looked up at him, her eyes red and tears on her face. "Is he really dead?"

"Yes, he is. And whatever hold he had on you, madam, is forever broken." He went to one knee and looked at her intently. "You are free. Truly free."

"Free." She said it was if it was a word from a foreign tongue. Then she shook her head in what looked like disbelief. "Free," she whispered.

Simonson stood up. "Yes." His voice was once again all

business as he looked at Eleanor, but it was not unkind. "Now. We all have some difficult decisions to make."

They stood before the door of the great vault, its combination lock in the center the size of a dinner plate. The same pair of *boo how doy* that had flanked Kwan above ground had accompanied him below, along with Cade, Marjorie, and Mei.

Kwan spoke.

"He asks," Mei said, "that you all turn your backs. So as not to see the combination."

Cade saw that the tong soldiers with Kwan had already complied. "Fair enough."

He, Marjorie and Mei turned to look at the far wall a scant few feet away. He could hear the gentle hiss of metal moving smoothly on metal, then a soft click, then another, more solid one.

"Can we turn around now?" he asked.

"Yes," Mei answered.

Cade turned. The massive door had swung open on hinges so well-lubricated as to make the opening as soft as a whisper. Kwan had stepped inside and lit a lantern, so Cade could see beyond him at what lay within the vault. "Holy shit," he said softly.

He stepped into the vault behind Kwan and looked around. To his right and his left were barrels, like the casks beer or wine or crackers would be transported in. But there was no alcohol or food in these. The tops were open, and shining from the opening of every barrel was the glint of gold or silver coins. The gold predominated, and as Cade stepped over to one of the barrels, he could see that it was filled to the brim. He picked one of the coins up and studied it. On one side was an engraving of an odd-looking man with a bald head and impressive chin whiskers. Cade flipped the coin over. The other side bore the image of a double-headed bird, possibly an eagle, with a head looking off to either side.

"That's an Austrian florin," Marjorie breathed, coming up beside him to examine the coin that gleamed in the lantern light as only gold could. She stepped over to another barrel and plucked another coin from the hoard. "These are from Spain." She went to the next barrel and stirred the mass of gold coin inside it with her hands. "American twenty-dollar pieces." She looked up and shook her head in wonder. "Levi, there's probably more gold here than in any bank in California. Maybe in the entire country."

"The Golden Mountain," Cade said softly. No wonder Fang had been willing to kill his brother for control of it. He looked at Kwan. "Okay, sir, you made your point. You're the biggest swinging dick..." He saw the confusion on Mei's face and sighed as he once again adjusted his idiom. "You've got the cash to do whatever you want. Where do we go from here?"

Kwan bowed his head slightly and spoke.

"He says," Mei translated, "that we go anywhere you wish to go. Mr. Kwan is happy to provide...what is the word..."

"Capital," Marjorie said.

Mei shook her head. "I do not know this word."

"I'm thinking you will soon," Cade said.

Marjorie nodded. "Tell Mr. Kwan I would be happy to discuss future financial arrangements with him. On," she smiled at Kwan, "a mutually agreeable basis that all parties can live with."

Well, Cade thought to himself, *there's another decision made.*

"Decisions," Eleanor said. "Yes." She shook her head vigorously to clear the cobwebs away and looked around the room. Carine had fled the room when no one was noticing. She finally looked at the body. "What do we do about...this?"

Simonson addressed Givens again. "Madam. You need to look away. Move to the other side of the room, please."

She blinked in confusion, but did as he asked.

Simonson reached over Clinton's body and deftly plucked the throwing knives from his eye socket and the side of his throat. With quick efficiency, he wiped them clean with the handkerchief he'd used earlier and slipped them into his pockets. He looked down at the body and spoke in a vicious voice, so low only Eleanor could hear. "This is what you get for calling me shorty, you cocksucker." She noticed that the ostentatious British accent had mysteriously vanished. He turned back to the room, his face calm. "Now," he said, the accent restored, "our problem is this."

"Our problem?" Eleanor said.

Simonson nodded. "While I did not ask for or expect to be embroiled in whatever brouhaha is going on in this household, I find that I am now in that position." He looked at Eleanor. "You, young lady, while brave in the defense of your mistress, are of African complexion. I," he grimaced, "even though a man of considerable means, am regarded as a freak. While there is no doubt in my mind that we have acted in self-defense and," he nodded at Givens, "the defense of others, I doubt that either of us will receive a sympathetic hearing from the authorities."

Eleanor cast a worried glance at Givens, who was now sitting on the couch, rubbing her hands together as if trying to warm them. Her eyes looked far away. "I concur, Mr. Simonson. What do you suggest?"

Simonson smiled grimly. "As I am sure you have been made

aware, I can connect people with certain services in this city. Including," he cleared his throat, "disposal of waste."

"You mean, you can make..." Eleanor glanced at Clinton's body, "...this go away?"

Simonson nodded, then sighed. "It may require an unexpected expenditure on my part, and," he looked at Givens, "cooperation from all concerned."

Eleanor looked over as well. Athena Givens seemed to snap out of her reverie as she noticed their attention. She straightened her posture and the light seemed to come back into her eyes. She snorted. "Bosh. I see no need for such subterfuge."

Eleanor blinked in surprise. "Ma'am?"

Simonson looked equally stunned. "Beg pardon?"

Athena Givens rose form the couch to her full height. Her eyes flashing with the same fire Eleanor had seen when her mistress was addressing a suffragist or Spiritualist gathering. "All we need, my friends, is the truth." She nodded with withering contempt at the body of her father on the floor. "This miscreant, this *assassin*," she hissed the last word, "insinuated himself into my household with the intent to murder me, most likely for my suffragist work. Having failed to do so at a séance, he tried again today, in my own drawing room. Fortunately, I was able to defend myself." She walked over and picked up the poker. "With this."

"The truth," Simonson murmured.

Givens nodded at him. "Yes."

The little man smiled sardonically. "A truth which preserves your bona fides both as a medium and as a suffragist firebrand."

Givens smiled back, but her smile was serene and outwardly untroubled. "Truth is truth."

"Of course. And what about the servants? Particularly the

girl Carine, who might have, ah, a different perspective on the truth?"

Givens's jaw set firmly. "I will deal with the servants."

"Indeed." Simonson bowed. "Since truth does not require my presence, I shall take my leave." He nodded at Eleanor. "Miss."

She rose and smoothed her skirts. "I will see you to the door, Mr. Simonson."

"And would you be so kind, sir," Givens said, "as to convey a message to my attorney, Mr. Jenkins? That it is imperative I see him at once?"

"Yes, madam." The corner of Simonson's mouth quirked. "As it happens, I am familiar with Mr. Jenkins, and I commend your choice to seek legal counsel sooner than later." Eleanor had drawn closer to him as he turned to leave, close enough to hear him mutter under his breath, "You're going to need all the help you can get to pull this game off."

She followed him out toward the front door. Neither spoke until they reached the porte cochere outside, and when they did, it was Eleanor who spoke first as she handed him the hat and walking cane she'd retrieved for him from the rack by the door. "Is there any chance this will work?"

Simonson laughed, a harsh bark with little humor behind it. "She has the money to make it work. That matters. And she has some connections, although there are many in the city who'd love to see her brought low." He shook his head. "For my own part, I'm not overjoyed about trusting my fate to the vagaries of a madwoman."

Eleanor looked back at the front door. "I'm not sure she's mad."

He followed her gaze. "Perhaps not anymore. But..." He shook his head. "Whatever that man did to her, it broke her. I don't know if she can put the pieces back together again on her own."

"Maybe with help."

He regarded her gravely. "Maybe. You would be perhaps the best person to provide that, I think."

She smiled. "May I say something, Mr. Simonson?"

"Of course."

"From my first meeting with you, I must say..." She hesitated. "I didn't expect you to be kind."

He bowed slightly. "Thank you, miss. That is not a word used often to describe me, I confess. Let's just say I know what it's like to be different." His face twisted. "To be despised."

"I'm truly sorry," she said quietly.

He just nodded, placed the hat back on his head, and started to walk toward the gate, then turned back. "Miss Eleanor."

She'd started back in, but turned back at his call. "Yes, sir? Do you need me to call you a cab?"

"No. Thank you kindly. I will hail one. Or walk." He hesitated. "I know this is an awkward time to be asking. But when all of this has blown over, would you mind if I called on you?"

She blinked. "Called? On me?"

He nodded.

"Like...like a lady?"

"Exactly like."

She smiled. "I would like that very much."

He smiled back. "Very good. I will be in touch."

The little man was whistling as he strode off down the drive.

The question of who would ride where was solved when Kwan offered his coach to deliver them back to the Givens mansion. Cade and Marjorie would ride inside, while Clayborne offered to trail behind on Midnight, with the grey mare in tow.

"Truth be told, Mr. Cade," Clayborne said, patting the horse's neck, "I find that this lady and I are developing an affinity."

Cade nodded. "She's a rare one." He turned to Mei, who was standing nearby. *The poor kid looks like she's about to collapse,* he thought. "You did good today, little lady," he called out. "You did your family proud. Hope Mr. Kwan appreciates all you do for him."

She gave him a tired smile. "I am sure." Then she gave a slight bow. "Be well, Mr. Cade."

"And you, miss."

Inside the carriage, Cade and Marjorie sat side by side. They were silent at first, each lost in thought, until Cade noticed that Marjorie was trembling. "Come here, sweetheart," he murmured, and she gratefully slid closer. He put his arm around her shoulder and she sagged against him, her face buried in his shoulder.

"God, Levi," she said in a small voice, "I've never been so afraid in my life."

"Me too," he whispered back. "I didn't think we were getting out of that."

"But we did. Thanks to her." There was no need to be more specific.

Cade nodded. "Second time she's done that."

"We need to try to find her. We need to help her."

Cade shook his head. "I've got no idea how to go about that, honey lamb. And I don't know if she'd take our help if we could find her. Proud as Lucifer himself, that one is."

"She has reason to be." She thought for a moment. "What about the other girl? Mei? Maybe she could help."

"Maybe." Cade hesitated. "Marjorie," he said at last, "there's something I need to tell you."

She pulled away slightly and gave him a quizzical look. "What?"

He took a deep breath. "This banker, one of the big wheels around here, I had a meeting with him. Before I met with Kwan."

She frowned. "A meeting? Why?"

"Actually, he called on me. He wanted to make me an offer."

She sat back, listening, taking Cade's hand. "What sort of offer?"

"An offer to lend you money. To bail your business out without you having to go in with the Chinese."

Her eyes narrowed. "And he approached you why, exactly? Considering it was my business he was proposing funding."

"There were some conditions."

She nodded, her face expressionless. The look worried him. "Naturally. And those were?"

"I'd have to cut all ties with Athena Givens. With the Chinese. With..." He paused. "With Sam."

"I see." She was still regarding him with that worryingly blank look. "I suspect there was an offer made to you as well."

He nodded. "A job, working security at this new hotel he's building. More money than I've ever seen in my life. A luxury suite."

"The high life."

He shrugged. "I guess."

She leaned forward and looked at him intently. "And what was your intention regarding this offer, Mr. Cade?"

The sudden formality startled him. "What?"

"Were you on your way to Chinatown today to reject Mr. Kwan's offer? On my behalf?"

He shook his head. "I don't know. I wanted to hear his offer, I guess."

"And, I hope, you were going to bring both offers to me, in their entirety?"

He blinked. "Yeah. I guess."

She smiled then. "Good." She laughed ruefully. "If you intend to sell your soul on my behalf, Levi—and don't think I don't appreciate the sentiment—I'd like to at least be consulted in the matter."

"Sell my..." He stopped.

She took his hand again. "Levi, when Sam heard you were in trouble, he didn't hesitate. He saddled the nearest horse he could find and rode to help you. He even tried to keep me from coming. If you'd turned your back on a friend like that, even for my sake, well," her face grew serious, "then you would not be the man I thought you were. You wouldn't be the man I love."

He smiled at that. "I guess you're right."

She patted his hand. "Of course I'm right. And, Levi?"

He took her hand and squeezed. "Yes, honey lamb?"

She squeezed his hand back, then whispered in his ear, "If I ever find that you're making decisions about my business without consulting me first, I promise I will turn you out into the street, however good in bed you might be." She leaned back, clearly amused at the shock on his face, then she grew serious again. "I want us to be partners in life, Levi. But the shipping company is mine."

He nodded. "Got it." After a brief pause, he spoke again. "About the other thing you just said..."

She smiled wickedly. "About you being good in bed?"

"That, too. But about being partners. In life."

She arched an eyebrow. "Yes?"

"Did, ah, you just ask me to marry you?"

She looked startled for a moment, then chuckled, her eyes widened mischievously. "Well, now, Mr. Cade. That would hardly be proper, would it?"

He played along. "I reckon not. You didn't offer me a ring, for one thing."

"Ah," she said. "A traditionalist."

"In some ways." The carriage was slowing, and Cade looked out the window.

They'd arrived at the Givens mansion, but something was wrong. There was a gathering of people in the driveway. Cade spotted Athena Givens, the servant girl Eleanor, and Lucius the footman. They were all engaged in what looked like an intense conversation with the lawyer Walter B. Jenkins.

"What the hell's he doing here?" Cade said.

As the carriage pulled to a stop, Cade got out. He glanced back to see Clayborne riding up behind. As Clayborne dismounted and walked up to stand beside Cade, holding the two horses' reins, Jenkins advanced on them, his face a mask of fury. "And just where the hell have you two been?!"

Cade and Clayborne looked at each other. "We got into a little fuss down in Chinatown. What's going on here?"

Jenkins drew himself up to his full height and glared at the contemptuously. "What's happened is, while you two were gallivanting around Chinatown, Miss Givens has been the victim of another attempt on her life."

"What?" Cade exclaimed.

"Who?" Clayborne joined in.

"The would-be assassin was Clinton. The coachman. Insinuated into the household by nefarious forces we can only guess at. And you two, who were supposed to protect her, were off doing God knows what, while this great lady," he gestured back toward where Athena Givens was standing, as expressionless as a stone sculpture, "was forced to defend her own person."

The words and the tone were getting Cade's back up. "Now listen here, sonny—" he began.

Jenkins startled him into silence by leaning forward and whispering urgently, "Play along. I promise you, all will be revealed later."

Cade's mouth snapped shut as he looked over and saw Captain Smith exiting the house, followed by a uniformed constable. He looked distinctly unhappy, which had Cade feeling a little better.

The policeman and his escort approached Jenkins. He gave Cade the barest of glances before addressing the lawyer. "So, if I have this straight, this fellow Clinton, for no reason at all, attacked Miss Givens and her Negro servant in broad daylight, with a pistol. At which point, Miss Givens beat the man to death with a fireplace poker. And the man never got a shot off." He glanced over at Cade and Clayborne. "While her bodyguards were mysteriously absent."

"Your story is correct in most of the particulars, Captain. Except we are still investigating how and why this mysterious man with no apparent past managed to find his way into this household. And as for the bodyguards," Jenkins cast a narrow-eyed glance at Cade and Clayborne, "their mysterious absence is something we will be looking very carefully into. For instance, a meeting Mr. Cade here recently had with a well-known figure in this city, a man of known hostility to the suffragist movement." He turned a sardonic eye on Smith. "Would the newspapers be interested in whether a prominent member of San Francisco's elite plotted to bribe Miss Givens's bodyguards to facilitate her murder?"

"Hey now," Cade protested.

"Wait a minute," Smith joined in.

Jenkins shrugged. "All of these are questions I'm sure the public would be thirsty to find the answers to. If questions need to be asked." He sighed. "As it is, all I request is that my client be allowed to rest now. She's had a very trying day." He turned to Cade. "As for you gentlemen," he said with a curl to his lip, "you are dismissed from service."

Cade looked over to where Athena Givens stood in the drive, flanked by servants, He thought of calling out to her, then shrugged before turning to Clayborne. "We might as well go home, partner."

Clayborne slid down from the saddle with a heavy sigh. He wrapped an arm over the neck of the black mare. "It's been nice, girl," he murmured. "I hope I'll see you again."

CHAPTER SIXTY-SEVEN

Two weeks later found Cade and Clayborne in their accustomed places, with Cade propped up in his desk chair reading the daily *Alta California* and Clayborne scribbling away in his notebook. Cade looked over to regard his partner's efforts for a moment, then returned to his perusal of the newspaper.

Clayborne raised his eyes from his notebook. "Mr. Cade."

Cade looked up from his newspaper with elaborate casualness. "Yes, Mr. Clayborne?"

"I believe you'd shown an interest in what I was writing before."

Cade nodded. "And I believe you'd indicated it was none of my damned business."

Clayborne smiled. "If I was unnecessarily abrupt, I apologize. It was on account of the work not being ready for anyone's eyes but my own."

Cade's brow furrowed. "The work?"

In answer, Clayborne slid the book over the desk. Cade picked it up and looked at the front page. His brow furrowed in concentration as he studied the handwriting. "*Two Gun Slim, A*

Novel of The West." Cade looked up in amazement. "I'll be damned. You're writing a dime novel."

Clayborne stared back at him defiantly. "And why not?"

Cade shook his head and chuckled. "No reason I can think of, Mr. Clayborne. None at all."

"I've met with the publisher of the *Pacific Appeal*. One of the newspapers owned by blacks here in the city. He believes that we can make a go of publishing my work."

Cade nodded. "As you say, why the hell not? It's just that..." He paused.

"Just what?"

Cade shrugged. "I'm just curious as to where these literary aspirations came from."

"Oh, that's easy. From reading page after page from one barely literate writer after another and thinking, *Christ Almighty, I could do better than this fool.*"

Cade laughed. "Fair enough. Well, I wish you success as a man of letters." He grimaced. "Maybe it'll pay better than this business."

The chimes on the front door rang. Cade was startled to see the maid Eleanor enter, and even more startled to see the tailor Simonson enter behind her. Eleanor had a parasol over her shoulder, which she proceeded to fold as Simonson looked around the office with the air of a man freshly landed on a foreign shore and trying to decide whether to get back on the boat.

"Miss Eleanor," Clayborne said. "Mr. Simonson," he said with less warmth.

"To what do we owe the pleasure?" Cade said.

Eleanor smiled. "We're here on assignment from Miss Givens. To deliver your payment for services rendered." She reached into the purse that dangled over one shoulder and drew out an envelope. She laid it gently on the desk.

"I don't understand," Cade said. "I thought we were fired."

Eleanor smiled. "Miss Givens has reconsidered. Your services were instrumental in flushing out the assassin Clinton, as well as helping secure the freedom of Mr. Tatanka." She grimaced. "Even though she was forced to deal with the villain herself."

"Yeah. Well," Cade said. "I fear she's been blackguarding this firm's reputation since. We'll be lucky to get a job guarding a pigsty after this."

Simonson spoke up. "Actually, she's said nothing of the sort. And nothing as to this matter, including your own participation in same, is likely to attract public notice. The local papers seem to have lost interest."

"Must have cost a pretty penny to buy them off this kind of scandal," Clayborne said.

Simonson shrugged. "I have no idea. But I have had several conversations with Mr. Jenkins." He smiled ingratiatingly. "Who sends his regards by the way, as well as any regrets for any misunderstandings regarding recent events."

"Uh-huh," Cade said.

Simonson ignored the tone. "Between the two of us, we believe we can provide you with sufficient business to not only keep this concern afloat, but make it prosper."

"And all we have to do," Clayborne said, "is not inquire too much about what really happened at the Givens house."

Eleanor hadn't lost her smile, but it turned a little chilly. "That particular assignment is concluded, Mr. Clayborne." She nodded at the envelope she'd laid on the desk. "If that is not sufficient, please contact Miss Givens though her attorney, Mr. Jenkins."

"That'll be the goddamn day," Cade muttered, but Clayborne spoke over him. "Thank you, Miss Eleanor. Mr. Simonson."

As they turned to leave, Cade called out. "One more thing, Mr. Simonson."

Simonson turned. "Yes?"

Cade took a deep breath. "I might soon be in the market for a ring."

Simonson raised an eyebrow. "An engagement ring, perhaps?"

Cade just nodded.

Simonson smiled. It was the most genuine smile Cade had seen on the little man's face. "My congratulations. Stop by my establishment. I'll be sure to have several items for your perusal."

"Thanks." As they left, Cade turned to his partner. "You're okay with this?"

Clayborne shrugged. "I'm a bit miffed that Eleanor has decided to take up with the little tailor, but I've learned to be philosophical about—"

"To hell with that! Doesn't it bother you that we're being lied to about what happened at the Givens place?"

"Maybe you should pick up that envelope and see what's in it."

Reluctantly, Cade reached over the desk and lifted the envelope Eleanor had laid there. He hefted it, then looked inside and sighed. "There's about twice as much here as we'd originally agreed on. We're being bought off." He looked up at Clayborne, who looked as if he were about to speak, and held up a warning hand. "Sam," he said through gritted teeth, "aside from Marjorie, you are the best friend I have in this world, but if you say, 'Welcome to San Francisco,' again, I swear to God, I will knock you down."

"Okay, I won't say it. But I will ask you this: are you sure some injustice is being done here? That an innocent is being abused? That someone helpless is being oppressed?"

Cade had to shake his head. "No."

"Then we should let this go."

Cade thought for a moment, then nodded. "Okay. But I don't have to like it."

"No, you don't." He counted out several gold coins. "Now, if you'll excuse me, I think I'm going to go make an offer on a horse."

EPILOGUE

The day had been cool and foggy, but the fast pace of sales at the fish market had Mei wiping the sweat from her eyes with a silk cloth as she tended to business. Her grandfather had begun the morning working by her side, but as the sun rose higher, his energy had begun to flag and Mei had gently suggested he go inside and rest. The stock of seafood was growing sparse and the crowd thinning when Mei noticed the young man standing back, not approaching to buy anything, watching her. She frowned, but then another customer had demanded her attention and she forgot about him for the moment. Finally, the crowd died down and Mei began the process of cleaning the bins. As if on cue, a dozen or more cats emerged from the nearby alleys, mewing imperiously for scraps. She smiled and tore off bits from the few remaining leftovers, tossing them here and there to spread them out among the prowling felines. She looked up from her work to see that the young man was still there, looking at her intently.

"May I help you, sir?" she said, with barely a hint of politeness. She decided on closer inspection that he was a handsome young man, but that didn't excuse him looking her over like a filet on the ice of the fish market.

He drew nearer, smiling shyly, and she saw that he held a plain wooden box in his hands. "My name is Chiang Kam."

She gave the slightest of bows. "Pleased to meet you, Chiang Kam. I am Mei." She deliberately omitted her family name. After all, she didn't know this fellow, and while he had a very nice smile, life had taught her caution.

He bowed back, more deeply. "I've seen that you work very hard."

"Yes. I do what is necessary to help my family."

He nodded. "I know what that is like. I do what I need to do to take care of my father."

Mei stepped back and folded her arms across her chest. "What do you want, Chiang Kam?"

He held out the box. "I was told to give you this."

She frowned. What sort of trickery was this? Then she looked it over. It was just a plain wooden box. She stepped forward and took it. It was light, as if there was nothing inside. She opened the lid and looked down. What was inside the box made her head spin in astonishment. Nestled on a velvet cloth was a freshly cut flower.

A white orchid.

Mei looked up, her eyes wide. "Who told you to give this to me?"

He met her gaze, his eyes somber. "You know."

"She's alive," Mei whispered.

"Oh, very much so," Kam said.

"And how was she? Did she seem well?"

Kam nodded. "Well enough that I thought I needed to do what she said."

Mei wanted to throw her arms around the young man and hug him for the news, but her sense of propriety won out. She looked at Kam. "Why did she choose you to deliver this message?"

Kam smiled. He really did have a kind smile, Mei thought. "I think she wanted us to meet." He shrugged. "And when she wants something done..."

"It's best to do it." Mei laughed quietly. "You'd better come inside to meet my family. I'll have grandmother make us all some tea."

THE END

ALSO BY J.D. RHOADES

LD Cade Series

The Killing Look

The Jack Keller Thrillers

The Devil's Right Hand

Good Day in Hell

Safe and Sound

Devils and Dust

Hellhound on my Trail

Won't Back Down

The Tony Wolf Series

Breaking Cover

Broken Shield

Fortunate Son

ABOUT THE AUTHOR

Born and raised in North Carolina, J.D. Rhoades has worked as a radio news reporter, club DJ, television cameraman, ad salesman, waiter, attorney, and newspaper columnist. His weekly column in North Carolina's *The Pilot* was twice named best column of the year in its division. He is the author of five novels in his acclaimed Jack Keller series: *The Devil's Right Hand, Good Day in Hell, Safe and Sound, Devil and Dust, Hellhound On My Trail* as well as *Ice Chest, Breaking Cover,* and *Broken Shield.* He lives, writes, and practices law in Carthage, NC.

A NOTE FROM THE PUBLISHER

Thank you for reading this book. If you enjoyed it please do consider leaving a review on Amazon to help others find it too.

We hate typos. All of our books have been rigorously edited and proofread, but sometimes mistakes do slip through. If you have spotted a typo, please do let us know and we can get it amended within hours.

info@bloodhoundbooks.com

www.ingramcontent.com/pod-product-compliance
Lightning Source LLC
Chambersburg PA
CBHW030526190726
48283CB00006B/1784